William Hepworth Dixon

Personal History of Lord Bacon

From Unpublished Papers

William Hepworth Dixon

Personal History of Lord Bacon
From Unpublished Papers

ISBN/EAN: 9783337326234

Printed in Europe, USA, Canada, Australia, Japan

Cover: Foto ©Raphael Reischuk / pixelio.de

More available books at **www.hansebooks.com**

PERSONAL

HISTORY OF LORD BACON.

FROM UNPUBLISHED PAPERS.

By WILLIAM HEPWORTH DIXON
OF THE INNER TEMPLE.

BOSTON:
TICKNOR AND FIELDS.
M DCCC LXI.

AUTHOR'S EDITION.

University Press, Cambridge :
Stereotyped and Printed by Welch, Bigelow, & Co.

NOTE FROM THE AUTHOR.

I FEEL happy and proud that an arrangement with Messrs. Ticknor and Fields to reprint The Personal History of Lord Bacon gives me the opportunity of pleading before the American public for the good fame of one who, dear as he is to the Old World, has an especial claim on the sympathies of the New.

W. HEPWORTH DIXON.

CONTENTS.

CHAPTER I.

THE BIOGRAPHERS.

CHAPTER II.

EARLY YEARS.

CHAPTER III.

THE EARL OF ESSEX.

a *

CHAPTER IV.

TREASON OF SIR JOHN SMYTH.

CHAPTER V.

THE IRISH PLOT.

CHAPTER VI.

THE STREET FIGHT.

CHAPTER VII.

THE NEW REIGN.

CHAPTER VIII.

SOLICITOR-GENERAL.

CHAPTER IX.

St. John and Peacham.

CHAPTER X.

Race with Coke.

CHAPTER XI.

Lord Chancellor.

CHAPTER XII.

Fees.

b

CHAPTER XIV.

AFTER SENTENCE.

APPENDICES.

FRANCIS BACON.

CHAPTER I.

THE BIOGRAPHERS.

1. A FINE wit has told the world that all men and
women, all youths and girls, are true poets, save only
those who write in verse. In such a saying, as in all
good wit, there lies a core of truth. Men who have kept
the poetry of their lives unshaped by art stand face to
face with nature, seeing the blue sky, the bursting leaf,
the hush of noon, the rising and setting sun, the green
glade, the flowing sea, as these things are ; not as they
appear in books, cut off into lengths of lines, tricked into
antithetical phrase, rounded and closed by rhyme. No
false rule of art impels a man who sees and feels, but who
does not mean to write or paint, to squint at a group of
elms, to peer through his hand at moonlight shimmering
on a lake, or at sunset on the tops of a range of hills ;
for such a man has no thought of how tree, lake, and alp
may be described in verse of five or six feet, or of the
lines in which this or that old painter would have framed

I. 2.   them. He comes fresh to nature, and has an intimate
——   and poetical relation to her.

2. As with nature, so with man. That figure, decked
by Pope, —

The wisest, brightest, meanest of mankind, —

over which fools have grinned and rogues have rubbed
their palms for more than a hundred years, has never yet
been recognized by honest hearts. Men who trust the
face of nature, not the point of satire, turn from this
daub as from a false note in song, or from a painted living face. The young and pure reject satire, and they
do well to reject it; for satire is the disease of art. The
young and pure will not believe a thing true because it is
made to look false. Taught by heaven, and not by rules,
they judge of character in the mass. Nature abhors
antitheses; loving the soft approach of dawn, the slow
sprouting of the seed, and moving by a delicate gradation
through her round of calm and storm, of growth and life.
Her forks never flash from a blue vault, nor do her waves
cease to crest when the wind which whipped them lulls.
Gradation is her law. If she may make a god or devil,
she will not put the two in one. That is the task of art;
but of art in its lowest stage of depravity and decline.

3. Can you be good and evil, wise and mean? Gazing
on the girl-like face in Hilyard's miniature, conning the
deep lore of the Essays, toying with the mirth of the

Apothegms, lingering on the tale of a gay and pure, a
busy and loving life, — how can they who judge by wholes
and not by parts admit that one so eminently wise and
good was also a false friend, a venal judge, a dishonest
man ?

4. Yet this comedy of errors has run its course from
Alexander Pope to John Lord Campbell. Strange to say,
the grave writers have gone nearly as far astray from fact
as those bright Parthians who, in choosing their shafts,
look rather to the feather than the flight. With them
Bacon is, in turn, abject, venal, proud, profuse, — ungrateful for the gifts of Essex, mercenary in his love for Alice
Barnham, callous to the groans of Peacham, servile in
the House of Commons, corrupt on the judicial bench !

5. The lie against nature in the name of Francis Bacon broke into high literary force with Pope. Before his
day the scandal had only oozed in the slime of Welden,
Chamberlain, and D'Ewes. Pope picked it, as he might
have picked a rough old flint, from the mud ; fanged it,
poisoned it, set it on his shaft : —

Meanest of mankind !

What if it be a lie ? May not a lie kill ?

It was not the only scum which in Pope's day frothed
to the head. What man then believed in nobleness, even
in intellect, unless that intellect were of the lowest type,
or served the basest cause ? The sole end of wit was

I. 5. defamatiou, the sole end of poetry vice. Of pure genius
there was little, of high virtue less. All glorious characters, all serious things, if not gone wholly from the minds
of men, lingered in their memories only to be reviled.
When Bacon became the meanest of mankind, Raleigh
was assailed, and Shakespeare driven from the stage.
Rowe was tainting our national drama, St. John undoing
our political philosophy, Hume training his mind through
doubts of God for the task of painting the most manly
passage of arms in all history as our greatest blunder and
our darkest shame. How should Francis Bacon have
escaped his share in this moral wreck ?

6. No man of rank in letters had yet soiled his fame;
for the foes who had lived in his own age, who had danced
with him in the Gray's Inn masques, or had bowed to
him as he rode down to the House, — even those who,
like Sir Robert Cecil and Sir Edward Coke, had most to
fear from his gladiatorial strength, and in the madness
of that fear pursued him with taunts and hate, — had
never dreamt of denying that his virtues and his courage
stood fairly in line with his vast abilities of tongue and
pen. They had called him blind when they could not
see, as he could, all the faces of an object. They had
denied to his gratitude the strong vitality of his intellectual power. They had spoken of his vanity, of his pre-
sumption, of his dandyism, of his unsound learning and
unsafe law; but the malice of these rivals had never
strayed so far as to accuse him, to the ears of men who

heard him in the House of Commons and met him at I. 6.
the tavern or the play, of a radical meanness of heart.
Coke had called him a fool. Cecil had fancied him a
dupe. But neither his rancorous rival at the bar, nor his
sordid cousin at Whitehall, had ever thought him a rascal. That was the invention of a later time.

The age that took Voltaire to be its guide, found out
that Bacon had been a rogue.

7. Since then he has been the prey of painters and
pasquins; his offences deepening, darkening, as men have
moved yet farther and farther from the springs of truth.
Hume is comparatively fair to him. Hallam is less fair;
though he will not, even for the sake of Pope, call Bacon
the meanest of mankind. Lingard paints him with a
more unctuous hate. Macaulay, in turn, is fierce and
gay: his sketch of Rembrandt power: his lights too high,
his smears too black: noon on the brow, dusk at the
heart. Nature never yet made such a man as Macaulay paints.

8. But of all the sins against Francis Bacon, that of
Lord Campbell is the last and worst. I wish to speak
with respect of so bold and great a man as our present
Lord Chancellor. He is one who has swept up the slope
of fame by native power of heart and brain; in the
proud course of his life, from the Temple to the Peerage, from the Reporters' Gallery to the Woolsack, I ad-
mire the track of a man of genius, — brave, circumspect,

I. 8. tenacious, strong; one not to be put down, not to be set
—— aside; an example to men of letters and men of law.
But the more highly I rank Lord Campbell's genius, the
more I feel drawn to regret his haste. In such a case as
the trial of Bacon's fame he was bound to take pains; to
sift every lie to its root; to stay his condemning pen' till
he had satisfied his mind that in passing sentence of
infamy he was right, beyond risk of appeal. A statesman and a law-reformer himself, he ought to have felt
more sympathy for the just fame of a statesman and law-
reformer than he has shown.) Not that Lord Campbell
finds fault with Bacon where he speaks by his own lights.
Indeed, there he is just. He has no words too warm for
Bacon's reforms as a lawyer, for his plans as a minister,
for his rules as a chancellor. When Lord Campbell
knows his subject at first hand, his praise of his hero
rings out clear and loud. But there is much in the life
of Bacon which he does not know. He has not given
himself time to sift and winnow. Like an easy magistrate on the bench, he has taken the pleas for facts.
That is his fault, and in such a man it is a very grave
fault.

9. (What Hallam left dark and Campbell foul should
be cleansed as soon as may be from dust and stain. It is
our due. One man only set aside, our interest in Bacon's fame is greater than in that of any Englishman
who ever lived. We cannot hide his light, we cannot
cast him out. For good, if it be good, for evil, if it

must be evil, his brain has passed into our brain, his soul   I. 9.
into our souls. We are part of him; he is part of us;
inseparable as the salt and sea. The life he lived has
become our law. If it be true that the Father of Modern Science was a rogue and cheat, it is also most true
that we have taken a rogue and cheat to be our god.

10. In front of all detail of fact, a general question
must be put.

Bacon seemed born to power. His kinsmen filled the
highest posts. The sovereign liked him; for he had the
bloom of cheek, the flame of wit, the weight of sense,
which the great Queen sought in men who stood about
her throne. His powers were ever ready, ever equal.
Masters of eloquence and epigram praised him as one of
them, or one above them, in their peculiar arts. Jonson
tells us he commanded when he spoke, and had his
judges pleased or angry at his will. Raleigh tells us he
combined the most rare of gifts; for while Cecil could
talk and not write, Howard write and not talk, he alone
could both talk and write. Nor were these gifts all flash
and foam. If no one at the court could match his tongue
of fire, so no one in the House of Commons could breast
him in the race of work. He put the dunce to flight,
the drudge to shame. If he soared high above rivals in
his more passionate play of speech, he never met a rival
in the dull, dry task of ordinary toil. Raleigh, Hyde,
and Cecil had small chance against him in debate; in
committee Yelverton and Coke had none.

Why was he left behind?

I. 11.   11. Other men got on. Coke became Attorney-General,
——   Fleming Solicitor-General. Raleigh received his knighthood, Cecil his knighthood. He alone won no spur, no
place. Time passed. Devereux became a Privy Councillor. Cobham got the Cinq Ports, Raleigh the patent
of Virginia. Years again raced on. A new king came
in, and still no change. Cecil became an Earl, Howard
an Earl. What kept the greatest of them down? It
was certainly not that he was hard like Popham, or crazed
like Devereux, or gnarled like Coke. A soft voice, a
laughing lip, a melting heart, made him hosts of friends.
No child, no woman, could resist the spell of his sweet
speech, of his tender smile, of his grace without study,
his frankness without guile. Yet where he failed, men
the most sullen and morose got on.

   12. Why did he not win his way to place? He sought
it: never man with more passionate haste; for his big
brain beat with a victorious consciousness of parts: he
hungered, as for food, to rule and bless mankind. This
question must be met. While men of far lower birth
and claims got posts and honors, solicitorships, judge-
ships, embassies, portfolios, how came this strong man
to pass the age of forty-six without gaining power or
place?

   Can it have been because he was servile and corrupt?

   13. Rank and pay, the grace of kings, the smiles of

ministers, were in Bacon's days, as in other days before
and since, the wages of men who knew how to sink their
views, to spend their years, to pledge their thought, their
love, their faith, for a yard of ribbon or a loaf of bread.
If Bacon were a man prostituting glorious gifts and strong
convictions for a beck or nod, a pension or a place, why
did he not rise? why not grow rich? If he were a rogue,
he must have sold his virtue for less than Popham, his
intelligence for less than Coke. How, then, could he be
wise?

Wisest and meanest, — there is the rub! But turn the
case round. How if his virtues, not his vices, kept him
down so long? How if his honesty, tolerance, magna-
nimity, not his heartlessness, his servility, and his corruption, caused his fall?

14. Look at the broad facts of the man's life first.
Small facts may be true, broad facts must be true. One
day in a man's course is hard to judge; a year less hard;
a whole life not at all hard. It is the same in nature.
Watch for one night the track of a planet. Can you say
if it move to the right or left? You are not sure. It
seems to go back. It seems to go on. Watch it for a
month, and you find that its path is forward. Is the star
in fault? Not in the least. It is your own base that
moves. Look at any chasm, peak, or scar on the earth's
face: you see the earth jagged, crude, motionless. Take
in the whole orb at once: you find it smooth, round,
beautiful, and swift. In Bacon's own words, a wise man

1*

"will not judge the whole play by one act." Still less by one scene, one speech, one word, will he judge.

In taking Bacon's course as a whole what do we find ? A man born to high rank, who seeks incessantly for place, who is above all men and by universal testimony fit for power; yet one who passes the age of forty-six before he gets a start; one who, after serving the Crown for more than fourteen years in the highest offices of the most lucrative branch of the public administration, dies a poorer man than he was born.)

15. Bacon was fifty-two when he became Attorney-General; fifty-seven when he became Lord Chancellor. For one who had been Elizabeth's young Lord Keeper at ten, who had been a bencher of Gray's Inn at twenty-six, Lent Reader at twenty-eight, this rise in his profession came late in life; later than it came to barristers who could boast of neither his personal force nor his father's official rank.

Coke was Attorney-General at forty-two. Egerton was Lord Keeper at forty-six; Bromley Lord Chancellor at forty-seven; Hatton at forty-eight.

It was much the same at Court as at the Bar. Youth was at the prow and beauty at the helm. At twenty-two Sydney went ambassador to Vienna; at thirty he went governor to Flushing. At twenty-six Essex was a Privy-Councillor ; at twenty-nine Commander-in-chief. At thirty-two Raleigh received his powers to plant Virginia.

16. Again : if Francis Bacon rose later in life than
Egerton or Coke, even after he had risen to the loftiest
summit of the Bar he won for himself none of the sweets
of office. Alone among the great lawyers of his time
he died poor. Hatton left a prince's wealth. Egerton
founded the noble House of Ellesmere, Montagu that
of Manchester. Coke was one of the richest men in
England. Popham bequeathed to his children Littlecote
and Wellington. Bennet, Hobart, Fleming, each left a
great estate. How explain this rule and this exception?

Surely they are not explained by the theory that
Bacon's servility held him down, while Coke's servility
sent him up; that Bacon's corruption kept him poor,
while Popham's corruption made him rich !

17. To judge a man's life in mass may not be the way
to please a Cecil or a Coke; the libidinous statesman
who made love to Lady Derby, who sold his country for
Spanish gold, who gave power to his infamous mistress
Lady Suffolk to vend her smiles; or the acrid lawyer
who gibed at Raleigh, who married a jilt for her money,
who gave his daughter for a place. Nor is it the way
to please those painters and lampooners who prefer dash
to truth; for a man so judged is not to be hit on paper
in a mere smudge of black and white, by dubbing him
wise and mean, sage and cheat, Solomon and Scapin,
all in one.

18. The lie, it may be hoped, is about to pass away.

I. 18. An editor worthy of Bacon has risen to purge his fame.
—   Such labors as those undertaken by Mr. Spedding demand a life, and he has not scrupled to devote the best
years of an active and learned manhood to the preliminary toil.   Lord Bacon's Literary, Legal, and Philosophical Works are already before the world in seven of Mr.
Spedding's princely volumes, printed and noted with the
most skilful and loving care.   Three or four volumes
of Occasional and Personal Works are still to come, for
which we may have to wait as many years.   Meanwhile,
the appearance of this new edition has drawn men's
thoughts to the character of Bacon as painted by his
foes ; and the instinct, strong as virtue, to reject the
spume of satire and falsehood, has sprung at the voice
of Mr. Spedding into lusty life.   To aid in some small
part in this good work of obtaining from men of letters
and science a reconsideration of the evidence on which
true judgment will have to run, the new facts, the new
letters, the new documentary illustrations comprised in
this Review of the Personal History of Lord Bacon are
given to the world.

CHAPTER II.

EARLY YEARS.

1. Sweet to the eye and to the heart is the face of Francis Bacon as a child. Born among the courtly glories of York House, nursed on the green slopes and in the leafy woods of Gorhambury; now playing with the daisies and forget-me-nots, now with the mace and seals; one day culling posies with the gardener or coursing after the pigeons (which he liked, particularly in a pie), the next day paying his pretty wee compliments to the Queen; he grows up into his teens a grave yet sunny boy; on this side of his mind in love with nature, on that side in love with art. Every tale told of this plaything of the court wins on the imagination: whether he hunts the echo in St. James's Park, or eyes the juggler and detects his trick, or lisps wise saws to the Queen and becomes her young Lord Keeper of ten. Frail in health, as the sons of old men mostly are, his father's gout and stone, of which he will feel the twinge and fire to his dying day, only chain him to his garden

II. 1.

1561.
Jan. 22.

1. Sir Amias Paulett's Despatches in the Cott. MSS., Calig. E. vii. 3, 8, 16, 31, 57; Lady Bacon to Anthony Bacon, Lambeth MSS. 651, fol. 54; Bacon to Lady Paulett, Lambeth MSS. 649, fol. 214.

II. 1. or his desk. When thirteen years of age he goes to
read books under Whitgift at Cambridge ; when sixteen
to read men under Paulett in France. If he is young,
he is still .more sage. A native grace of soul keeps off
from him the rust of the cloister no less than the stain
of the world. As Cambridge fails to dry him into
Broughton, Paris and Poictiers fail to melt him into
Montjoy. The perils he escapes are grave ; the three
1577. years spent under Whitgift's hard, cold eye being no
less full of intellectual snares than are the three years
spent in the voluptuous court of Henri Trois, among
the dames and courtiers of France, of moral snares.
In the train of Sir Amias Paulett, he rides at seventeen with that throng of nobles who attend the King
and the Queen-Mother down to Blois, to Tours, to
Poictiers ; mixes with the fair women on whose bright
eyes the Queen relies for her success, even more than on
her regiments and fleets ; glides in and through the hostile camps, observes the Catholic and Huguenot intrigues,
and sees the great men of either court make love and
war. But Lady Paulett, kind to him as a mother, watches
over his steps with care and love,—a kindness he remembers and repays to the good lady, and to her kin, in later
years. For him the d'Agelles sing their songs, the Tos-
seuses twine their curls in vain.

2. No one lapse is known to have blurred the beauty
of his youth. No rush of mad young blood ever drives

2. Sylva Sylvarum, x. 946, 986.

him into brawls. To men of less temper and generosity than his own — to Devereux and Montjoy, to Percy and Vere, to Sackville and Bruce — he leaves the glory of Calais sands and Marylebone Park. If he be weak on the score of dress and pomp; if he dote like a young girl on flowers, on scents, on gay colors, on the trappings of a horse, the ins and outs of a garden, the furniture of a room; he neither drinks nor games, nor runs wild and loose in love. Armed with the most winning ways, the most glozing lip at court, he hurts no husband's peace, he drags no woman's name into the mire. He seeks no victories like those of Essex; he burns no shame like Raleigh into the cheek of one he loves. No Lady Rich, as in Sydney's immortal line, has cause

> To blush when *he* is named.

When the passions fan out in most men, poetry flowers out in him. Old when a child, he seems to grow younger as he grows in years. Yet with all his wisdom he is not too wise to be a dreamer of dreams; for while busy with his books in Paris he gives ear to a ghostly intimation of his father's death. All his pores lie open to external nature. Birds and flowers delight his eye; his pulse beats quick at the sight of a fine horse, a ship in full sail, a soft sweep of country; everything holy, innocent, and gay acts on his spirits like wine on a strong man's blood. Joyous, helpful, swift to do good, slow to think evil, he leaves on every one who meets him a sense of friendliness, of peace and power. The serenity of his spirit keeps his intellect

II. 2.   bright, his affections warm ; and just as he had left the
—   halls of Trinity with his mind unwarped, so he now, when
          duty calls him from France, quits the galleries of the
          Louvre and St. Cloud with his morals pure.

1579.   3. At the age of eighteen he fronts the world.   The
          staff of his house being broken, as the dream had told
          him, he hies home from France to Lady Bacon's side.
          The Lord Keeper had not been rich, and his lands have
          passed to his son by a former wife.   Ann Lady Bacon is
          left a young widow with two sons, Anthony and Francis,
          a meek, brave heart, and a slender fortune ; a little family
          of three persons, who make up in love for each other all
          that they lack in pelf.   Lady Ann, the Olympia Morata
          of Elizabeth's court, is one of five sisters, daughters of that
          fine old scholar who drugged King Edward with Latin
          ·verse, Sir Anthony Cook of Giddy Hall in Essex ; all the
          five pious and learned as so many Muses, but unlike the
          Muses all made happy wives ; Mildred by Lord Burghley,
          Ann by the late Lord Keeper, Katharine by Sir Henry
          Killigrew, Elizabeth first by Sir Thomas Hoby and next by
          John Lord Russell, Margaret, the youngest sister of the
          five, by Sir Ralph Rowlet.   So that Francis claims through
          his mother close cousinry with Sir Robert Cecil, with Eliz-
          abeth and Anne Russell, with the witty and licentious race
          of Killigrews, and with the future statesman and diploma-

          3. Lord Bacon to Burghley, Lansdowne MSS., xliii. 48; Lady Bacon to An-
          thony Bacon, Lambeth MSS. 648, 649, 650. The portrait of Lady Bacon by
          Nathaniel is at Gorhambury.

tist Sir Edward Hoby. Lady Ann is deep in Greek and II. 3.
in divinity; her translation of Jewell's "Apology" is
praised by the best critics, and has been printed for pub- 1579.
lic use by orders from the Archbishop of Canterbury; yet
the good mother is not more at home with Plato and
Gregory than among her herbs, her game, her stewpans,
and her vats of ale. Nathaniel Bacon, with hearty humor
and a play upon her name and habits, has made a portrait
of her dressed as a cook and standing in a litter of dead
game. She is very pious: in the words of her son "a
Saint of God." Not quite a Puritan herself, she feels a
soft and womanish sympathy for men who live the gospel
they proclaim; brings up her sons in charity with all
Protestant creeds; hears the preachers with profit; and,
without any air of patronage and protection towards
them, speaks to her great kinsman, the Lord Treasurer,
the word which spoken in season is quick to save. A
bright, keen, motherly lady; apt, as good women are, to
give advice. To her, her famous children are always two
little boys, who need to be corrected, physicked, and fed:
when they are forty years old, and filled with all knowledge of men and books, she not only sends them game
from her own larder and strong beer from her own casks,
having no great faith in other people's work, but lectures
them on what they shall eat and drink, when they shall
purge or let blood, how far they may ride or walk or drive
in a coach, when they may safely eat supper, and at what
hour in the morning they shall rise from bed.

II. 4.　　4. Lady Ann lives at Gorhambury. Anthony is abroad,
———　now in France, now in Italy, now in Navarre, conning
1579.　the languages and manners, the politics and events, of
these famous lands. Francis falls to his terms at Gray's
Inn, seeks the help of his great kinsman Burghley, and
finds a seat in the House of Commons for himself at the
age of twenty-three.

1580.　　A letter, now to be put in type, will show that he has
July 11.　fixed his tent at Gray's Inn as early as the summer of
1580, a few months after his nineteenth year. This note
is curious as the earliest known piece of writing from his
hand, and as a sample of his boyish style. Macaulay
dwells on the change from his early to his later manner;
the statuesque severity of that of his youth compared
against the glow, the imagery, the wit, the license, and
the color of that of his later time. At twenty Mino, at
forty he had grown into Raffaelle. How grave, how cold
this message to Mr. Wylie!

BACON TO MR. WYLIE.

From Gray's Inn, 11 of July, 1580.

MR. WYLIE, —

This very afternoon, giving date to these letters of
mine, I received yours by the hands of Mr. Wimbanke,
and to the which I thought convenient not only to make
answer, but also therein to make speed, lest, upon supposition that the two letters enclosed were, according to their

---

4. Gray's Inn Reg., cited in Craik's Bacon, i. 12; Bacon to Wylie, July 11,
1580, in Lambeth MSS. 647, fol. 14.

directions, delivered, you should commit any error, either
in withholding your letters so much the longer when peradventure they mought be looked for, or in not withholding to make mention of these former letters in any other
of a latter despatch. The considerations that moved me
to stay the letters from receipt, whether they be in respect
that I take this course to be needless or insufficient or
likely to lead to more inconvenience otherwise than to
do good, as it is meant in some such, they are that they
prevail with my simple discretion, which you have put in
trust in ordering the matter to persuade me to do as I
have done.

My trust and desire likewise is that you will report (?)
and satisfy yourself upon that which seemeth good to me
herein, being most privy to the circumstances of the matter, and tendering my brother's orders as I ought, and
not being misaffected to you neither, by those at whom
you glance, while I know whom you mean. I know likewise that you mean amiss; for I am able, upon knowledge, to acquit them from being toward [in ?] this matter. For mine own part, truly, Mr. Wylie, I never took
it that your joining in company and travel with my
brother proceeded not only of good will in you, but also
of his motion, and that your mind was always rather by
desert than pretence of friendship to earn thanks than
to win them. Neither would I say this much to you,
if I would shrink to say it in any place where the contrary was inferred: and in that I rectified my brother of
this matter being delivered unto me for truth. I had

II. 4.
———
1580.
July.

this consideration that among friends more advertisements are profitable than true. My request to you is, that you will continue and proceed in your good mind towards my brother's well-doing; and although he himself can best both judge and consider of it, yet I dare say withall that his friends will not be unthankful to misconstrue it, but ready to acknowledge it upon his liking. And as for this matter, as you take no knowledge at all of it, I will undertake it upon my knowledge that it shall be the better choice. Thus betake I you to the Lord.

Your very friend,
Fr. Bacon.

1585.
Nov. 23.

Though he enters the House of Commons, he finds no public work. Not that Burghley pets and lures him only to chain him fast; the great Protestant minister is a man too high and noble for such a part, nor can Englishmen afford to soil his fame. Bacon, at least, never dreams that his uncle plays him false. That he does not push him with all his might is true: but this may be, not because he dreads in him a rival to his son, as is often said, so much as because, being old and timid, fearful of adventure and speculation, of risking those measures of Religion and State in which his name is forever bound up, he dreads the daring and original genius of his nephew, apt, he may think, in his flush of youth and intellectual strength to dash at success, to fly at the nearest road, to bridle and ride the popular storm.

5. Rawley, Mallet, Montagu, and Lord Campbell have each in turn slurred the ten or twelve years in which Bacon grew from a boy of nineteen into a man of thirty or thirty-one, though in drama and instruction these years hold rank among the noblest of his life. The writers set him high on the stage for the first time in 1592, when he is thirty-one. "In the parliaments which met in 1586 and 1588," says Lord Campbell, "he had been returned to the House of Commons; but he does not seem to have made himself prominent by taking any decided part for or against the Crown."

What is the truth? In 1592 he is returned to parliament for Middlesex, the most wealthy, liberal, independent shire in England, — the West Riding of the time and of long succeeding times. He is young, poor, out of place. He is even out of favor, since his uncle has turned from the young reformer his powerful face. Having neither rood of land nor hope of inheritance within the shire, the squires and freeholders of Middlesex choose him. Why, and how? Did penniless genius ever start in life by winning the first constituency in the realm? Burke had to woo the electors of Wendover before he dreamt of Bristol. Pitt began with Appleby, and only at his height of power won the University of Cambridge. Brougham had suffered defeat at Liverpool, and had been glad to sit for Knaresborough, ere he tried to conquer the West Riding. So with Bacon. Service and success, of which the writers have never heard, lifted

II. 5.
——
1585.
Nov.

5. Willis, Notitia Parliamentaria, iii. 101, 113, 121; D'Ewes, 337.

him to the height of Middlesex. When he rose at Brentford in 1592, he spoke to freeholders who knew his name and voice, not only as one of the most youthful, but as one of the most daring and effective members of a former House.

Bacon had, indeed, served in Parliament prior even to the sessions of 1586 and 1588. He entered the House of Commons in 1585, when he was only twenty-four. He then sat for Melcombe. In the Parliament of 1586 he sat for Taunton, and in that of 1588 for Liverpool.

6. These three sessions not stirring! The author of Tom Jones has a passage on the advantage of a writer knowing his subject; the great humorist should have told us of the ease and comfort which a writer finds in *not* knowing his subject. Will not his soul be more at peace? No truth will curb the freedom of his judgment — no fact interrupt the flow of his style. See how Hallam hesitates and halts! He knows too much. Only your blind horse will leap into the chasm, or wait his death-gore from a horn of the bull.

A month at books on any subject will not weight one much. A diplomatist used to say that when he had been four weeks in London he felt able to write a book on English life; when he had been a year, he had doubts if he yet understood the whole of his theme; when he had been ten years, he gave up the book in despair.

Not stirring! Why, the three sessions in which Bacon

6. D'Ewes, 332, 439; Townshend, i. 29.

II. 6.
—
1585.
Nov.

served his parliamentary apprenticeship, though slipped as void and waste by his biographers, abound in scenes of high and tragic conflict,—scenes in which he played an active and conspicuous part, and which colored and shaped for him the course of his political life. These three sessions had to save the liberties of England, the faith of nearly half of Europe. They crushed the Jesuits, they founded the Defence Association, they sent out Raleigh to plant new States, they laid Mary on the bier at Fotheringay, they broke and punished the Romanist conspiracies, they shattered and dispersed the Invincible Armada!

7. Nor were these early Parliaments less bright in composition than brave in deed. On swearing the oaths as member for Melcombe, Bacon takes his seat on the same benches with the chief lights of law and government,—with Hatton and Bromley, Egerton and Walsingham,—as well as near those younger glories of the Court, the poets and warriors to whom secretaries of state are but as clerks, with Sir Philip Sydney, Sir Walter Raleigh, Sir Francis Drake, Sir Charles Blount, and hosts of others scarcely less renowned than these in love and war.

Yet from the ranks of this group he leaps like fire into fame. Burke's spring was not so high, Pitt's popularity was not so wide. At twenty-five he has won the ear of that fastidious House. Wit so radiant, thought so

7. Not. Parl., iii. 99, 107; Bacon's Essays, No. 3.

fresh, and lore so prompt, had not before, and have never since, been heard within those famous walls. Yet his hold on the men of his generation is due less to an intellectual than to a moral cause. They trust him, for he represents what is best in each. The slave of Whitgift, the dupe of Brown, can each give ear to a churchman who seeks reform of the church, a lawyer eager to amend the law, a friend of the Crown who pleads against feudal privileges and unpopular powers. When a colleague proposes some change in the church which would destroy it, he replies to him: "Sir, the subject we talk of is the eye of England; if there be a speck or two in the eye, we endeavor to take them off; he would be a strange oculist who would pull out the eye." Of no sect, he represents in Parliament the patriotic spirit of all the sects. Not himself a Puritan, he pleads with Hastings for reform; not a Roman Catholic, he lifts his voice against persecution for concerns of faith; not a courtier, he votes with Cecil for supplies. In one word, he is English. To sustain the Queen in her great strife with Spain, to guard the Church from abuse and from destruction, are as much his objects as to break the bonds of science and lead inquiry back from clouds to earth. When he strikes at corruptions in the State, when he resists the usurpations of the Peers, when he saps the privileges of the Crown, he speaks in the name of English progress and English strength. He fights for reform of the law, for increase of tillage, for union with the Scots, for plantations in Ulster, for discovery and defence in Virginia, for free Parliaments and for ample grants, because he sees that increase, union, freedom, and a rich executive are each and all essential to the growth and grandeur of the realm.

8. How he appears in outward grace and aspect among these courtly and martial contemporaries, the miniature by Hilyard helps us to conceive. Slight in build, rosy and round in flesh, dight in a sumptuous suit; the head well-set, erect, and framed in a thick starched fence of frill; a bloom of study and of travel on the fat, girlish face, which looks far younger than his years; the hat and feather tossed aside from the broad, white brow, over which crisps and curls a mane of dark, soft hair; an English nose, firm, open, straight; mouth delicate and small, — a lady's or a jester's mouth, — a thousand pranks and humors, quibbles, whims, and laughters lurking in its twinkling, tremulous lines: — such is Francis Bacon at the age of twenty-four.

9. No session ever met under darker skies than that of 1586. Babington's conspiracy has just exploded; fleets are arming in Cadiz bay; money and men are ready in Rome, in Naples, in · Leghorn, for a crusade against the heretics; Parsons is hounding on the Pope, Sixtus hounding on Philip; in the Tagus, at the Groyne,

8. Hilyard's miniature is in the possession of Adair Hawkins, Esq., of Great Marlborough Street.

9. Dom. Papers of Queen Eliz., ccxxii.; Andreæ Philopatri ad Elizabethæ Reginæ Angliæ edictum responsio; Toulmin's History of Taunton, 365.

II. 9.

1586.
Oct. 29.
in the cities of Brabant and Flanders, armaments wait
but a word to cross over into Kent, to seat Mary Queen
of Scots on the throne, to reduce England to a fief of the
Church. England flushes with heroic pride. London,
Dover, Portsmouth swarm with soldiers; drums are roll-
ing in every hamlet, yeomen mustering in the market-
places of every shire. But no part of England burns
with more fervent heat than the western counties,
nor in these counties than the town of Taunton.
Taunton is the seat of trade and manufacture, — a
Manchester of a milder clime; next to Bristol the richest town between the Severn and the Scilly Isles; next
to London the most patriotic town between the Irish
Sea and Dover Straits. In the day when everything dear
to man appears to be at stake, this populous and enter-
prising town sends Bacon to Westminster to speak in its
name and give its vote.

10. The writs having gone out while the ruffians who
prated of friendship and sentiment are on trial for their
crimes, the passionate patriotism of the land storms up,
too strong for Burghley to breast, too strong for Elizabeth
herself to ride. When the Peers and Commoners meet,
a cry goes up to the throne that Mary shall be brought
to trial, and, on proof of her guilt, shall be put to death.
In this stern prayer the burgess for Taunton, tolerant as
he is of mere opinion, joins. The Crown dares not
refuse. Menaced on every side, England can give no

10. State Trials, i. 1127 – 1162; D'Ewes, 393.

answer to the threats of invasion save an open trial and
solemn execution of the Queen of Scots.

11. What to do with Mary had been a dismal question
for honest men since the day when she had first sought
refuge in Carlisle from her licentious barons and her faithless son. In her room at Chartley, guarded by the old
moat, shut in with her women and her priests, she had
scared the Protestant imagination more than either the
Kaiser in Vienna or the Pope in Rome. Her position
was, indeed, most strange: to-day a prisoner, to-morrow
she might become a queen. She had no need to make a
party, to risk her head, in order to win her game. She
had only to live: certain, as fall will follow spring, of
rising one day from her bed of durance to find the necks
of her enemies beneath her feet. An accident, a crime,
might give her, any hour, the crown. A stumbling jen-
net, an unwholesome meal, a prick of Babington's knife,
a snap of Salisbury's dagg, might take away the life
which alone stood between her and the English crown.

Put on trial, her complicity proved, her cousin would
still have spared her life. But the Burghleys, Davisons,
and Pauletts were in no position to treat this profligate
woman with the leonine clemency of the Queen. To
Elizabeth she was, indeed, a danger and a snare; but to
the Protestant gentleman who loved his religion and his

11. Dom. Papers of Eliz., cxciv.; D'Ewes, 393–410; Davison to Walsingham, Oct. 10, 1586, in the State Paper Office; Burghley to Davison, Nov. 24,
1586, S. P. O.

II. 11.
—
1586.
Oct. 29. country, her removal or succession was a question of life or death.   She could neither break Elizabeth on the wheel nor roast her at the stake; for, unless a Spanish force should succeed in seating her on the throne, her day of evil could not come until the Queen was safe from the revenge of King and Pope.   But what prelate on the bench, what councillor at the board, what magistrate in his shire, would feel his head safe on his spine should the trumpets bray the accession of Mary to the English throne? They had seen another Mary. Old men recalled the day when Latimer perished.   Half the citizens of London could tell how Rogers had gone to heaven in the Smithfield fires. All England shook with news of the more recent massacres of Paris, — massacres solemnly approved and commemorated in Rome as services to God. Men firm in their own faith, loyal to their own Queen, pretended no pity for a woman who to Helen's loveliness of person.added more than Helen's dissoluteness of mind. They saw in Mary a wife who had married three husbands and was eager to marry more.   They saw in her the murderess of Darnley, the destroyer of the Kirk. They saw in her a pretender to the English crown, in whose name Sixtus had resumed the kingdom, and Philip was preparing to lay it waste. Was such a woman to live and become their Queen?

Had Mary refrained from plots, content to bide her time, the peril of such a future would have been hard to meet; but when her complicity in Babington's treason was proved in court, then Davison urged, and the House

of Commons demanded by petition, that for the security
of life, liberty, and true religion in time to come, the
prisoner of Fotheringay should suffer the just sentence
of the law.

II. 11.
——
1586.
Oct. 29.

12. The Queen holds out. A grand committee, of
which Bacon is a member, goes into the presence, and
the lords spiritual and temporal, the knight and squire,
the lawyer and goldsmith, kneeling together at her feet,
demand that the national will shall be done, — that the
Protestant faith shall be saved. She will not hear them.
When the deed is done that makes England free, —
done by Davison's command if not by the Queen's, —
she casts the courageous minister from power; nor will
she to her dying day consent to see his face or hear his
name. There ought to be no doubt of the sincerity of
her grief.

Nov. 12.

1587.
Feb. 8.

13. The letters which have been printed in more recent times, suggesting that Elizabeth, while affecting to
withhold her consent to Mary's death, instigated Paulett to commit a private murder, are odious and clumsy
literary forgeries. These letters have been adopted by
Lingard, and have half imposed on the cautious Hallam. Yet the originals are nowhere to be found, the
name of the pretended discoverer of them is unknown,

12. Nicholas, Life of Davison, 1823; D'Ewes, 394–400; Camden, Ann. 1586.
13. Comp. Hallam, Hist. of Eng., i. 159 *n.*; Lingard, viii. 282; with a Note in
Charles Knight's Hist. of Eng., iii. 205.

II. 13. and they have never been seen by and competent or
—— reputable man! The circumstances of their publica-
1587. tion suggest forgery for a political end, while the style
Feb. 8. and statement of the letters prove them to be inventions of a later time. The alleged discovery of these
papers, so damaging to the English Church and so fatal
to the Protestant Queen, was made by partisans of the
Papist Pretender in the hottest days of the Jacobite feud.
The dates, the names, the facts adduced, establish the
comparatively recent fraud.

The Queen, slow to shed blood, meant to save Mary
from the block ; but her people and her parliament, free
from her woman's weakness and her ties of blood, required that high political justice should be done. Mary
was the first and worst of all their foes ; the princes
of Spain and Italy were her soldiers, the Babingtons
and Salisburys of London her assassins. England could
only meet the league of Kaiser, Pope, and King by
snatching away their flag. Mary gone, the invaders
were without a cause, the conspirators without a cry.
Who shall say what might have chanced had Mary been
alive, when the Duke of Medina Sidonia rode off the
Lizard, to excite a rising in the western shires, or even
to divide the loyalty and check the courage of the English fleet.

14. Bacon's fame as a patriot, as an orator, is in these

14. Phillippes to Davison, Oct. 5, 1586, S. P. O. In citing those State Papers
from which a main portion of the following narrative will be derived, I must

transactions formed and fixed. To know him is to be
happy; to have been at school with him, distinguished.
William Phillippes, wanting a place under Davison for
his son, thinks it enough to remind the great minister
that his boy had been trained with the young member
for Taunton.   •

II. 14.
—
1587.
Feb. 8.

15. Years hurry past. The Armada comes and goes.
While the watch-fires are yet burning on the cliffs, the
wrecks of a hundred keels yet tossing in the foam from
Devon to Caithness, Parliament meets. Bacon now sits
for Liverpool. Danger is past; the Queen has been to
thank God at St. Paul's, and a merry Christmas has
been kept in hall and cottage, many a spar washed up
from the wrecks of the Spanish fleet crackling in the
festive fires.

1589.
Feb. 4.

In this new session Bacon serves on the most important committees, speaks on the most important bills:
now standing for the privileges of the House of Commons, now assaulting the Royal purveyors, now denounc-
ing the forestallers, regrators, and engrossers. The
great debates of this year occur on subsidies and grants.

express my obligations to Sir John Romilly, Master of the Rolls, for the facili-
ties which, during many years, he has given to my researches among the public
documents of which he has the legal charge. My thanks are no less due to
Lord Stanley and Sir Edward Bulwer Lytton, for the courtesy with which,
when Secretaries of State, they listened to my proposals for certain changes in
the State Paper Office favorable to historical students, and for the promptitude
with which they consented to remove restrictions that had made any general
and critical study of the State Papers next to impossible.

15. Not. Parl., iii. 121; D'Ewes, 430–439; Statutes of the Realm, 31 Eliz.
c. 15.

II. 15.
———
1589.
Feb. 4.

Hatton proposes two subsidies and four fifteenths and tenths; to which Bacon, whose soul is in the patriotic tug, agrees: he moves, however, to insert in the bill a clause explaining that these grants are extraordinary and exceptional, meant for the war, and only for the war. To this the Queen objects, as fettering her future acts: enough for the squires to pronounce their Yea or Nay. The squires stand firm. Many men support what one man dares. After much debate, the Crown proposes to lay the bill, with Bacon's amendments to it, before the Learned Counsel; to which the House of Commons, insisting first that the author of the amendments shall be present at the sittings of that learned board, consents. Under his soft, persuasive tact, the interests of the sovereign are reconciled with the interests of her people, and the bill is passed to the satisfaction of Queen and Commons. Power and fame now seem to be in his grasp. Elizabeth sends for him to the palace; the electors of Middlesex cast their eyes upon him; and, when parliament meets again, he will represent the wealth and courage of that great constituency. From the session of 1589 dates his firm ascendency in the House of Commons.

16. Lady Bacon and her sons are poor. Anthony, the loving and beloved, with whom Francis had been bred

16. Wotten's Baronetage, edited by Johnson and Timber, i. 8; Patent Rolls, 16 Eliz., par. 6, mem. 3; Lady Bacon to Anthony Bacon, Lamb. MSS. 648, 106, 650, 75, 651, 54; Lady Bacon to her brothers Francis and Anthony Bacon, Lamb. MSS. 648, fol. 10.

at Cambridge and in France, has now come home. II. 16.
His health, bad at the best, has broken in the south ;
so he lies for a long time in bed or on a couch at his 1591.
brother's rooms in Gray's Inn Square. The two young
fellows have little money and expensive ways. Anthony,
as the elder brother, owns a seat at Redburn, in Hert-
fordshire, with a few farms lying round it. Gorhambury, too, will be his when Lady Bacon dies. But the
rents fall far below his needs, not to speak of the needs
of his brother, who is now prominent at court, a leader
in the House of Commons, and a candidate for the
glory of representing in parliament the metropolitan
shire. Their half-brother Sir Nicholas, who inherits Redgrave and the broad Suffolk acres left by the Lord
Keeper, a man with penurious habits and a swarm of
children, deems his own nine sons and three daughters
burden enough, without having to pinch for the off-
spring of Lady Ann. When he marries a daughter they
may get an invitation to Redgrave ; but his brotherly
hospitalities end with the feast. Nathaniel may paint
their portraits and present them with game on canvas,
but the artist can do nothing to fill their mouths.
Edward has a lease from the Crown of Twickenham
Park, a delightful place on the river, of which Francis
makes a home. Lady Ann starves herself at Gorhambury that she may send to Gray's Inn ale from her
cellar, pigeons from her dovecote, fowls from her farm-
yard ; gifts which she seasons with a good deal of
motherly love and not a little of her best motherly ad-

II. 16.　vice.　The young men take the love and leave the ad-
—　　vice, as young men will.　Like Buckhurst, Herbert,
1591.　and the race of gay cavaliers, while waiting for better
days and brighter fortunes, they relieve their wants by
help of the Lombards and Jews.

17. Francis looks for an opening to mend their means.
1592.　A rich alderman dies, leaving his son a ward.　The
Feb. 18.　guardianship of a Queen's ward is often a profitable toil,
and the care of Hayward's son is in Burghley's gift.
Francis urges Lady Ann to apply to her sister's husband for this lucrative trust.

BACON TO LADY BACON.

From my Lodgings, Feb. 18, 1591–2.

MADAM, —

Alderman Hayward is deceased this night.　His eldest son is fallen ward.　My Lord Treasurer doth not
for the most part hastily dispose of wards.　It were
worth the obtaining, if it were but in respect of the
widow, who is a gentlewoman much recommended.
Your ladyship hath never had any ward.　If, my Lady,
it were too early for my brother to be gone with a suit
to my Lord before he had seen his Lordship, and, for
me, if I at this time procure (?) my Lord to be my
friend with the Queen, it may please your ladyship to
move my Lord, and to promise to be thankful to any

17. Lambeth MSS. 648, fol. 5, 106, 110.

other my Lord oweth pleasure unto. There should be no time lost therein. And so I most humbly take my leave.

II. 17.

—

1592.
Feb. 16.

Your Ladyship's most obedient son,

FR. BACON.

My Lord (Lord Burghley) is a leal friend to him with the Queen; a little slow, as his nature is, but honest, sage, and sure. While waiting for a post, and only that of Attorney-General or Solicitor-General will serve his turn, the young barrister fags at his books; framing in his mind a magnificent scheme for reducing and codifying the whole body of English law, as well as shaping his more colossal plans for re-constituting the whole round of the sciences. Like the ways of all deep dreamers, his habits are odd, and vex Lady Ann's affectionate and methodical heart. The boy sits up late of nights, drinks his ale-posset to make him sleep, starts out of bed ere it is light, or may be, as the whimsy takes him, lolls and dreams till noon, musing, says the good lady, with loving pity, on — she knows not what! Her own round of duty lies in saying her morning and evening prayers, in hearing nine or ten sermons in the week, in caring for her kitchen and hen-roost, in physicking herself, her maids, and her tenants, in making the rascals who would cheat her pay their rent, and in loving and counselling her two careless boys. Dear, admirable soul! How human and how humorous, too, the picture of this good mother,

II. 17.
—
1592.
May 24.

warm in her affections, scolding for us our broad-browed
awful Verulam!

LADY BACON TO ANTHONY BACON.

Gorhambury, 24th May, 1592.

Grace and health. That you increase in amending I
am glad. God continue it every way. When you cease
of your prescribed diet, you had need I think to be very
wary both of your sudden change of quantity and of season of your feeding, specially suppers late or full; procure
rest in convenient time, it helpeth much to digestion. I
verily think your brother's weak stomach to digest hath
been much caused and confirmed by untimely going to
bed, and then musing, I know not what, when he should
sleep, and then, in consequence, by late rising and long
lying in bed, whereby his men are made slothful and himself continually sickly. But my sons haste not to hearken
to their mother's good counsel in time to prevent. The
Lord our heavenly Father heal and bless you both, as His
sons in Christ Jesus!

I promise you, touching your coach, if it be so to your
contentation, it was not wisdom to have it seen and known
at the Court. You shall be so much pressed to lend, and
your man for gain so ready to agree, that the discom-
modity thereof will be as much as the commodity. I
would your health had been such as you needed not to
have provided a coach but for a wife; but the will of God
be done. You were best to excuse you by me, that I

have desired the use of it, because, as I feel it too true, II. 17.
my going is almost spent, and must be fain to be bold
with you. It is like Robert Bailey and his sons have
been to seek some commodity of you; the father hath
been but an ill tenant to the wood, and a wayward payer,
and hath forfeited his bond, which I intend not to let slip;
his son a dissolute young man, and both of them crafty.
Likewise young Carpenter may sue to be your man. Be
not hasty; you shall find such young men proud and bold,
and of no service, but charge and discredit. Be advised.
Overshoot not yourself undiscreetly. I tell you, plain folk
in appearance will quickly cumber one here, and they will
all seek to abuse your want of experience by so long absence. Be not hasty, but understand well first your own
state. There was never less kindness in tenants commonly than now. Farewell in Christ.

Let not your men see my letters. I write to you, and
not to them.

Your mother,

A. BACON.

This coach which the two brothers, both of them sick,
both racked with gout and ague, have set up, weighs
heavily on her spirits. Again and again she returns
to the charge. "I like not your lending it to any
lord or lady. It was not well it was so soon seen
at court. Tell your brother, I counsel you to send it
no more. What had my Lady Shrewsbury to borrow
your coach?"

18. If the post of orator of the House of Commons is no easy one to win, it is one more difficult to hold. Wit, sense, readiness, repartee, power, patience, mastery of men and books, are parts of the round of faculties and acquirements for one who is to seize the direction and sway the votes of an English House of Commons. At thirty-two, when Bacon, in the session of 1593, takes his seat for Middlesex, he finds on the benches right and left of him men the most renowned in English story. Coke is Speaker; Cecil leads for the Crown; Raleigh and Vere sit nigh him; Fulk Greville, the friend of Sydney, John Fortescue, Lawrence Hyde, Henry Yelverton, Edward Dyer, Henry Montagu, rival speakers and lawyers, are but six of a conspicuous crowd. The war continues, and events look grave. Battalions crowd Dunkerque and Calais; the flag of Leon and Castile flaps within sight of Dover-pier; London stands under arms; troops hurry for Flanders, Dublin, and Kinsale; the Sussex founderies cast guns; and fort on fort rises along the coast from Margate to Penzance. Yet the war without is not more harassing than the disease within. London gasps with plague. No lute or tabor sounds from the tavern-porch; no play draws dames and gallants to the Globe; no pageant crowds the Thames with citizens and 'prentice boys. An order from the Lord Mayor puts down all games, — the bear-bait at

18. Not. Parl., iii. 131; Council Reg., Jan. 28, July 19, 1593; Mem. of Men for Ireland, April 6, 1593, S. P. O.; Elizabeth to Godolphin, May 9, 1593, S. P. O.; Mem. by Burghley, May 9, 22, 31, 1593, S. P. O.; List of Parishes in London infested with Plague, Lamb. MSS. 648, fol. 152.

Paris Garden, the sports of the inn-yards, the song and
jollity of the ale-clubs. Yet, in the midst of woe and
death, the recruiting-sergeant beats to arms. Henri the
Fourth, who has mounted the throne of France, pressed
by the victorious Spaniards, calls for help, and levies are
being raised for him in London and in places usually
exempt from such a tax.

II. 18.

1593.
Feb.

While yielding the Queen's government support on her
money-bills, the feeders of the war, Bacon forces on the
topic of reform, and defeats an extraordinary attempt at
dictation by the ministers of the Crown.

19. The House has not sat a week — not yet proved its
returns — before he hints at his scheme for amending and
condensing the whole body of English law. The House
starts up. The tide might have come in from the Thames.
Reform the code! Bacon tells a House full of Queen's
counsel, Queen's sergeants, and utter barristers, that laws
are made to guard the rights of the people, not to feed
the lawyers. The laws should be read by all, known to
all. Put them into shape, inform them with philosophy,
reduce them in bulk, give them into every man's hand.
So runs his speech. A noble thought, — a need of every
nation under the sun, — a task to be wrought at by him
through a long life, — to be then left to successors, who,
after revolutions and restorations, commissions and re-

Feb. 26.

19. Townshend's Historical Collection, 60; Bacon's Works, vii. 313; Les Aphorismes du Droit, traduits du Latin de Messire François Bacon, Grand Chancelier d'Angleterre, par J. Baudoin, 1646.

II. 19.
———
1593.
Feb

ports, have it still in hand — undone! The plan, of which this fragment of a speech is the root, developed in his Maxims of the Law, and proposed as part of his great reform in the De Augmentis, has had more success abroad than it has found at home. It was universally read, and most of all in France. It was translated by Baudoin, and inscribed to Segrier, Chancellor of France. In that country it has blossomed and come to fruit. But a French revolution alone had power to achieve this vast design against established things ; and the Code Napoléon is even now, in 1860, the sole embodiment of Bacon's thought.

March.

20. Ten days later he gives a check to the Government, which brings down upon his head those censures of Burghley and Puckering which are said to have represented in fact, if not in word, the personal anger of the Queen. The story of this speech has been so told as to rob Bacon of all credit for his daring, the ministers of all reason for their wrath.

Lord Campbell writes, that he votes for the grants proposed by the Crown, but pleads for time in which the people shall be called to pay them ; that Burghley and Puckering bully and threaten him ; that he bows to this storm of indignation a penitential face. Lord Campbell pictures the young barrister as whining under the lash, kissing the rod that smites him, pledging the tears in his eyes that he will never in that way offend her Majesty again !

20. Campbell's Lives of the Lord Chancellors, art. " Bacon " iii. 15.

21. The offence lies deeper than Lord Campbell dreams : an offence of two parts ; one of which parts has wholly escaped his sight.

The Government seeks from the House of Commons a very .extraordinary grant of money. It is usual to ask for half a subsidy a year. Half a subsidy is ten per cent, — two shillings in the pound a year. Burghley proposes to demand from the burgesses a double rate : one whole subsidy a year ; four shillings in the pound. So high a tax will not, he knows, be voted by the House, with all its eagerness for war, unless the whole authority of the Crown and Government can be brought to bear. He forms his plans. Drafting such a bill as he hopes may pass, he sends word to Mr. Speaker Coke that he must beat down, in the Queen's name, all such noisy members as shall presume to prate of things in Church and State. No idle threat, as Bromley and Wentworth find ; ere many days are gone Wentworth has talked himself into the Tower, Bromley into the Fleet.

Burghley now asks the House to confer with the Peers on a grant for the Queen's service ; and a committee goes up ; among them, in frill and feather, gown or sword, Vere, Raleigh, Greville, Hastings, Cecil, Bacon, and Coke. They hear the Lord Treasurer's words ; and the next day Cecil reports, in their name, to the Com-

---

21. Inhibitions delivered to Coke from the Queen, Feb. 28, 1593, S. P. O.; Message from Coke to the House of Commons, Feb. 28, 1593, S. P. O.; Confession of Laton, Feb. 1593, S. P. O.

mons, that the Peers have decided for them what they shall give, and at what times: three subsidies in three years,—four shillings in the pound each year. For them to hear is to obey.

Knight and squire gaze at each other. Four shillings in the pound a year! And the Commons robbed of even the credit of their own gifts! Such a speech is resented as a slur on their patriotism, a curb on their debates.

22. Who rises to warn the minister? Is it the fiery Raleigh, the martial Vere? Where sits the noisy Hastings, the sagacious Greville, the turbulent Coke? Not one of these flames up. Soldiers who have pushed through Parma's lines, advocates bronzed in cheek, and Puritans steeled in the fire of controversy, stare and wait. No marvel either. Not one of these men, in a plain, good cause, would have shrunk from a threat of Little Ease, or Beauchamp Tower. The difficulty is, to defend their right of making grants and subsidies without seeming to oppose a war on which the country has set its soul, and without showing to the hosts of home and foreign enemies a broken front. To the bill itself the capital objection is only one of form. Cecil counts on the heat for battle; and to fight for the power of free taxation, against the passionate haste of the people for clash of pikes and roar of guns, needs courage of a lofty and peculiar kind. Coke may fear

22. D'Ewes, 468–83.

to offend the Queen, Raleigh to embolden the King of
Spain, Hastings to vex the musters and the fleet. Bacon starts up.

A few clear words declare that he does not mean to
touch the grant. No man will grudge the funds to fit
out ships and man the guns. But there he stops. To
give is the prerogative of the people, — to dictate what
they shall give is not the duty of the House of Peers.
In framing this bill the Government, he says, has gone
beyond its powers; and he counsels the Commons, in defence, to decline any further conferences with the Lords
on a money-bill. From his vest he takes an Answer to
the Lords, which he proposes shall be read, and if approved, sent up. This Answer is referred to a committee
of fifty-one. The committee cannot agree; and return
their commission to the House. Hot debates ensue.
Burghley hides himself behind the Queen; but even her
august and sacred name appears to have lost its force.
Broad lines are drawn; and the members fall into either
camp. The courtiers stand with Cecil for continuing the
conferences on the money-bill; the reformers with Bacon
for resisting this encroachment on the constitutional laws.

Coke puts the question from the chair, — for a conference; yea, or nay? A hundred and twenty-eight gentlemen cry Yea. Two hundred and seventeen gentlemen
cry Nay.

23. A raid of Parma's pikes through Kent would

23. Bacon to Burghley and to Puckering, Montagu, xii. 275, Notes E. E.

II. 23.
———
1593.
March.

have startled Burghley less than such a vote. It is the first great check he has ever known ; it stops the whole machinery of legislation ; it covers himself, his measures, and his friends with public shame. He scolds his nephew ; he sets the Lord Keeper on to scold him. ˉ These functionaries threaten him with the Queen's ire ; but Bacon defends what the Knight for Middlesex has said and done. If words not used by him are put upon him, he will deny them ; if his words are misunderstood, he will explain them ; but to the sense of his speech he must hold fast. How can he unsay the truth ? This is his apology and defence. If her Highness, as they urge, is angry with him, he shall grieve ; if she commands him into silence, he must obey ; but in thwarting this invasion of popular rights by the House of Peers, he has done no more than his duty to his Queen, his country, and his God.

24. Though the progress of the bill is stopped, all sides agree that the fleet must be manned, — the musters armed. Raleigh starts a compromise. Flushed with his glorious voyage, red with spoil from the Santa Clára and the Madre de Dios, the adventurer burns to be again at sea, chasing the Spanish ships, or forcing the rivers of Guiana. Every day given to debate he grudges as lost to victory and revenge. To him, delay is disaster ; talk is treason. Vote the supplies, — send out the fleet, — dash at Cadiz or Malaga, — sweep the plantations, — snap

24. Townshend, 67 ; D'Ewes, 488.

up galleon and carrack, — death to the yellow flag! cries
that impetuous soul. The members warm to his voice.
Resolve, he says to confer with the Lords on the perils of
the realm. Say no more about grants. Listen to what
the Government may have to tell about the Papal bull
and the Spanish fleet. When you have saved the point
of form, vote the money-bill as you list. Well spoken,
Raleigh! Not a tongue cries Nay.

25. Set free by this device to discuss their money-bill
the Commons fall to work. Cecil stands to the old plan
of three subsidies, to be paid in three years. Bacon,
neither cowed nor penitent, rises once more to oppose
the court; not on the amount, which he approves, but
on the time, which is, indeed, the essential point. He
asks for six years in place of three; in other words, for
two shillings in the pound a year, in place of four.
Even for the joy of smiting Spain, he cannot drain the
sources of industry, seize the craftsman's tools, the farm-
er's cider-press and milk-pans. Raleigh storms upon
him. Will he starve the war? Cecil smiles and cajoles.
But Bacon, who has won the ear even of this warlike
auditory, insists that time shall be given, and that the
grants shall be described as exceptional and extraordinary. In the end, against the warmth of Raleigh and
the wiles of Cecil, he compels the Government to meet
his proposal half-way, to extend the period proposed

II. 24.

1593.
March.

April.

25. Lords' Jour., ii. 184; D'Ewes, 493; Townshend, 72; Statutes, 85 Eliz.,
c. 13.

II. 25. for the raising of these taxes a year (in other words,
—— to take three shillings in the pound each year in
1593. place of four), and to insert a clause in the bill de-
April. claring that the money is given solely for the war
against Spain.

CHAPTER III.

THE EARL OF ESSEX.

1. SIX months after this brush with the Government
Bacon is a candidate for place. The Rolls are vacant,
and the rise of Egerton must leave the post of Attorney
void. Coke claims to succeed. Some at the bar and on
the bench would prefer Bacon's rise to Coke's : each has
his troop of friends ; and thus, at an early stage, begins
that rivalry between these famous men which is to run
through every phase of their careers, and only end with
their lives. Coke gains his move, as is only just. Bacon's
claim to the place left void by Coke, that of the Solicitor-
General, is much more strong. Born at the bar and
nursed on law, he has served to his profession an apprenticeship of fourteen years. If Philosophy has been his
Rachel, Law has been his Leah. A bencher and Reader
of his Inn, he enjoys a good reputation in chambers
and in the courts. The best judges at the bar approve
his rise. Burghley and Cecil cautiously promote his suit,
and Egerton presses it with a noble friendship on all who
have power to help or harm. Yet in the end Thomas
Fleming gets the post, a man only known to the world for

III. 1.

—

1593.
Sept.

1. Chron. Jurid., 177; Lane's Reports, 22.

III. 1.

1593.
Sept.

having stood in Bacon's way, and to the profession for his singular and disastrous ruling in the case of Bates.

Bacon owes this loss of place to Robert Devereux, Earl of Essex: out of which cruel disappointment to him springs the charge of ingratitude to a patron,—treason to a friend.

A plain history of events will show that the connection of Bacon with Essex was one of politics and business; that it brought no advantages to Bacon, and imposed on him no obligations; that it ceased by the Earl's own acts; that personally and politically Essex separated himself from Bacon, not Bacon from Essex; that Bacon, in his efforts to save Essex while he believed him a true man, went the extremest lengths of chivalry; and that, in acting against him when he proved himself a rebel and a traitor, he did no more than discharge his necessary duty to his country and his Queen.

2. One of the nearest friends of Queen Elizabeth had been Catherine Carey, afterwards Lady Knollys, her cousin in the first degree of the Boleyn blood. They had been sisters' children, and had loved each other with more than sisters' love. Catherine had died young in years, and had been buried by her sovereign in Westminster Abbey with regal pomp. Essex was Catherine Carey's grandson; in everything but the name he was a grandson to the childless Queen. This tie of blood the slanderers of

2. Craik's Romance of the Peerage, I. 5; Council Reg., April 13, 1589, April 14, 1591, June 21, 1592.

III. 2.

1593.
Sept.

her fame forget to state.   Yet Essex and the two Careys were her only male relations on her mother's side, as James of Scotland was her sole surviving kinsman of the royal race.   He had been born into her lap and into her heart.   She loved him, too, for his father's sake ; Walter, Earl of Essex, having been a leal friend to her in those young days when friends were few and cold.   As she seared into age, it pleased her eye to see the sons of her first stanch peers around her throne.   She had made Hunsdon chamberlain ; she meant to make Cecil Secretary of State.   She had loved Sydney for his father's virtues ; she endured Essex in remembrance of his father's fate.   She had indeed much to bear with and forgive. More profuse than generous, more rash than brave, he tried her affection by his petulance and brawls ; but she clung to the orphan boy with that clannish pride which she had always felt for her mother's kin.   She loaded him with favors.   His jerks and whims, so galling to the council and the court, amused the Queen as signs of the Boleyn blood.   Her mother had them ; his mother has them.   That she ever loved him more than a lady of sixty years may love her cousin's grandchild is a monstrous lie.   No woman can believe it: no man but a monk could have dreamt it.

3. Yet this lie against chastity and womanhood has

3. Elizabethæ Angliæ reginæ, hæresim Calvinianam propugnantis, in catholicos sui regni edictum, quod in alios quoque reipublicæ christianæ principes contumelias continet indignissimas. Promulgatum Londini 29 Nov. 1591. Cum responsione ad singula capita: qua non tantum sævitia et impietas tam iniqui

been repeated from generation to generation for two hundred and sixty years. It oozed from the pen of Father
Parsons. It darkens the page of Lingard. Like most of
the scandals against her, — her jealousy of the wives of
Leicester, of Raleigh, of Essex even, — it came from those
wifeless monks, men of the confessional and the boudoir,
who had spent their nights in gloating with Sanchez
through the material mysteries of love, and in warping
the tenderness and faith of woman into the filthy philosophy of their own " Disputationes de Sancto Matrimonii
Sacramento." Against such calumniators the Queen
might appeal, like Marie Antoinette, to every woman's
heart. Jealous of Lettice Knollys, of Bessie Throckmorton, of Frances Sydney! Elizabeth was indeed vexed with
them; but had she not cause? Had not each of these
courtiers married, not only without her knowledge as
their Queen, but without honesty or honor? In secret,
under circumstances of shame and guilt, Leicester had
wedded her cousin's daughter Lettice. Would the head
of any house be pleased with such a trick? Raleigh had
brought to shame a lady of her court, young, lovely,
brave as ever bloomed on a hero's hearth; yet the daughter of a disloyal house, of one who had plotted against
the Queen's crown and life. Could any prince in the
world approve of such an act? Essex himself, a member
of her race, a descendant of Edward the Third, had married, in secret and against her will, a woman of inferior

edicti, sed mendacia quoque et fraudes ac imposturæ deteguntur et confutantur.
Per D. Andream Philopatrum. 1592.

birth, without beauty, youth, or fortune, a widow, who took him on her way from the arms of a first husband into those of a third. What kinswoman would have smiled on such a match?

Love for Essex warmer than that of an aged gentlewoman for a young and dashing kinsman would have been in her sin against nature not less than sin against nature's God. The letters of Catherine's grandson to the Queen, if bright with poetry, playfulness, and compliment, are, in tone and substance, dutiful and chaste. In the Queen's letters to him there is not a line she might not have written to a grandson of her own.

4. She girt him with the fondness and with the fear of a mother. She never sent him from her side without a pang; for she knew that he would knock his head against stone walls, that he would hurry brave men to a foolish end. Proud and high though his temper was, he could neither lead others to victory like Raleigh, nor defend his own face from harm like Montjoy. If he sailed for Cadiz with Nottingham and Raleigh to slack his fire, the Queen's work might be done, and he himself shine the bravest of the brave. If he went to Rouen alone, he scared the sleep from her pillow, and wrung the blood from her heart, by his reckless waste of her veteran troops. She petted him as a boy hopelessly brave, heroically frail; but she deemed him such a fool, though a charming one, that anything he raved for must be wrong. If he fumed and fretted, put

4. Lives and Letters of the Devereux Earls of Essex, 2 vols., 1853, vii.-xiv.

III. 4. his head on her footstool, rushed into the country, pout-
———   ed, and sulked, and raged, like a great spoiled child, she
1593.   would not yield to his caprice.   Forever asking some-
Sept.   thing that he should not have, he would be Master of the
         Horse ; he would have the Cinq Ports ; he would com-
         mand fleets and camps.

5. In an evil day for Bacon this petulant noble swears
he shall succeed to Coke.   Essex and Bacon have been
drawn together, less by the magnetism of character,
though the Earl has a thousand showy and alluring
ways, than by their common wants.   Bacon is poor and
works for bread.   His brother Anthony is poor and lame.
In the rooms at Gray's Inn they lie sick together, racked
with pain and pestered by duns.   Lady Ann does her
best : sending them hogsheads of March beer, with plenty of good advice and scraps of Greek ; but the most she
can do is little, and neither Greek nor good advice will
discharge their weekly bills.

A letter from Francis to Lady Bacon gives a glimpse
into these troubles, — the sickness, the fraternal love, the
worrying debts.

FRANCIS BACON TO LADY BACON.

From Gray's Inn, April 16, 1593.

My duty most humbly remembered.   I assure myself
that your ladyship, as a wise and kind mother to us both,

5. Lambeth MSS. 649, fol. 67, 100.

will neither find it strange nor unwise that, tendering
first my brother's health, which I know by mine own
experience to depend not a little upon a free mind, and
then his credit, I presume to put your ladyship in remembrance of your motherly offer to him the same day you
departed, which was that to help him out of debt you
would be content to bestow your whole interest in markes
upon him.   The which unless it would please your ladyship to accomplish out of hand, I have just cause to fear
that my brother will be put to a very shrewde plunge,
either to forfeit his reversion to Harwin (?) or else to
undersell it very much; for the avoiding of both which
great inconveniences I see no other remedy than your
ladyship surrender in time, the formal drafte whereof I
refer to my brother himself, whom I have not any way
as yet made acquainted with this my motion, neither
mean to do till I hear from you.   The ground whereof
being only a brotherly care and affection, I hope your
ladyship will think and accept of it accordingly: beseeching you to believe that being so near and dear part
of me as he is, that cannot but be a grief unto me to
see a mind that hath given so sufficient proof of wit (?)
in having brought forth many good thoughts for the
general to be overburdened and cumbered with a care
of clearing his particular estate.   Touching myself, my
diet, I thank God, hitherto hath wrought good effect,
and am advised to continue this whole month, not meddling with any purgative physic more than I must needs,
which will be but a trifle during my whole diet; and
so I most humbly take my leave.   F. B.

III. 6.
——
1593.
Sept.
6. No young fellow of Gray's Inn, waiting for the tide to flow, is sharper set for funds than the young knight for Middlesex or his elder brother. Anthony tries to raise his rents, and some of the men about him — godless rogues, as Lady Bacon says — propose that he shall let his farms to the highest bidders. Goodman Grinnell, who has the land at Barly, pays less than he ought: let him go out and a better man come in. But Goodman Grinnell speeds with his long face to Lady Ann. "What!" cries the good lady to her son; "turn out the Grinnells! Why, the Grinnells have lived at Barly these hundred and twenty years!" So the brothers have to look elsewhere. Bonds are coming due. A famous money-lender lives in the city, Spencer by name, rich as a Jew and close as a miser; him they go to, cap in hand, and with honeyed words. The miser is a good miser and allows his bond to lie. Francis writes to him from his brother Edward's house at Twickenham Park, to which he has removed from Gray's Inn for the benefit of country air.

FRANCIS BACON TO MR. SPENCER.

Twickenham Park, Sept. 19, 1593.

GOOD MR. SPENCER, —

Having understood by my man your kind offer to send my brother and me our old bond, we both accept the same with hearty thanks, and pray you to cause a new

6. Lambeth MSS. 649, fol. 109.

to be made for half a year more, which I will both sign
and seal before one Booth, a scrivener, here at Isleworth,
and deliver it him to your use, which you know will be
as good in law as though you were here present. True
it is that I cannot promise that my brother should be
here at that time to join with me, by reason of his daily
attendance in court, by occasion whereof I am to be
your sole debtor in the new bond. As for the mesne
profits thereof, you will receive them presently. I have
given charge to my man to deliver it. And so with my
right hearty commendations from my brother and myself, with like thanks for your good-will and kindness
towards us, which we always shall be ready to acknowledge when and wherein we may, I commit you to the
protection of the Almighty.

Your assured loving friend,

Fr. Bacon.

III. 6.
——
1593.
Sept.

One likes to know that this good miser rose to be
an alderman of London, and lived to see his daughter
married to a peer. One dares not say, however, that
one would like to have been Lord Compton, the husband of her choice, and heir of the miser's enormous
hoard.

7. Bacon lies sick the whole summer of 1593, as a
note to his old friend Lady Paulett shows. Her ladyship, who had been so kind to him in his younger days

7. Lambeth MSS. 649, fol. 214.

III. 7. in France, is now a widow; his good friend Sir Amias
———   sleeping the great sleep under a splendid tomb in the
1593.   chancel of St. Martin's Church. Bacon is proud and
Sept.
         glad to do the widow service.

FRANCIS BACON TO LADY PAULETT.

Twickenham Park, Sept. 23, 1593.

MADAM, —

Being not able myself, by reason of my long languish-
ing infirmity, to render unto your ladyship by a personal visitation the respect I owe unto your ladyship, I
would not fail to acquit some part of my debt by sending this bearer, my servant, expressly to know how your
ladyship doth, which I beseech God may be no worse
than I wish and have just cause to wish, considering
your ladyship's ancient and especial kindness towards
me.   Which if I have not hitherto acknowledged it hath
been only for want of fit occasions, but no way of dutiful affection, as I hope in time, with God's help, I shall
be able to verify by good effects towards the young gentleman Mr. Blount, your nephew, or any other that
appertains unto your ladyship. This is, good madam,
much less than you deserve and yet all I can offer,
which, notwithstanding, I hope you will accept, not that
it is aught worth of itself, but in respect of the unfeigned good-will from whence it proceedeth. And so,
with my humble and right hearty commendations unto
your good ladyship, I beseech God to bless you with

increase of comfort in mind and body, and admit you
to his holy protection.

Your ladyship's assured and ready in all kind affection to do you service,

FR. BACON.

8. Essex has need of strength such as these penniless men of genius have to spare. Francis Bacon has won all nature for his province. Anthony is a man of many parts; gay, supple, secret; fond of society and of affairs, of good wines and bright eyes; at home in cloister and in court; easy in morals, tolerant in creed; hail fellow with the vagabond and the noble, the King's mistress, the professional conspirator, the free lance, and the travelling monk. The two brothers enter into the Earl's service; Francis as his lawyer and man of political business, Anthony as his secretary; hoping, as many wise men hope, to make him the court leader of that great patriotic band of which Raleigh, Drake, and Vere are the fighting chiefs; the one part for which he is gifted beyond all other men. Under their eyes he so far gains in gravity and sense that the Queen swears him of her Privy Council, and even trusts to his care much of her correspondence abroad. Day and night their tongues and pens are busy in this work. Anthony writes the Earl's letters, instructs his spies, drafts for him despatches to the agents in foreign lands. Francis shapes for him a plan of conduct at the court, and writes for

8. Lambeth MSS. 649; Devereux, i. 277; Sydney Papers, i. 360.

3 *

III. 8.   him a treatise of advice which should have been the
—   rule and would have been the salvation of his life.
1593.
Sept.   For all these labors the workmen must be paid.

Oct. 8.   9. Duns weigh on the two brothers. Here are two
notes to Lady Ann, both from Francis, full of the same
sad romance of love and debt. One runs : —

Francis Bacon to Lady Bacon.

From the Court, Oct. 3, 1593.

Madam, —

I received this afternoon at the Court your letter,
after I had sent back your horse and written to you
this morning. And for my brother's kindness it is accustomed; he never having yet refused his security for
me, as I, on the other side, never made any difficulty
to do the like by him, according to our several occasions. And therefore, if it be not to his own disfur-
nishing, which I reckon all one with mine own want, I
shall receive good ease by that hundred pounds; specially your ladyship of your goodness being content it
shall be repaid of Mr. Boldroe's debt, which it pleased
you to bestow upon me. And my desire is, it shall
be paid to Knight at Gray's Inn, who shall receive
order from me to pay two fifths [?] (which I wish had
been two hundred) where I owe, and where it presseth
me most. Sir John Fortescue is not yet in Court;

9. Lambeth MSS. 649, fol. 298, 274.

both to him and otherwise I will be mindful of Mr. Downing's cause and liberty with the first opportunity. Mr. Neville, my cousin, though I be further distant than I expected, yet I shall have an apt occasion to remember. To my cousin Kemp I am sending. But that would rest between your ladyship and myself, as you said. Thus I commend your ladyship to God's good providence.

III. 9.
—
1593.
Oct. 8.

Your Ladyship's most obedient,

FR. BACON.

FRANCIS BACON TO LADY BACON.

Nov. 2.

Twickenham Park, Nov. 2, 1593.

MADAM, —

I most humbly thank your ladyship for your letter and sending your man Bashawe to visit me, who purposeth with God's help so soon as possibly I can to do my duty to your ladyship, but the soonest I doubt will be to-morrow or next Monday come sennight. My brother, I think, will go to Saint Albans sooner, with my Lord Keeper, who hath kindly offered him room in his obscure lodgings there, as he hath already resigned unto him the use of his chamber in the Court. God forbid that your ladyship should trouble yourself with any extraordinary care in respect of our presence, which if we thought should be the least cause of your discontentment, we would rather absent ourselves than occasion any way your ladyship disquietness. As for Sotheram, I have been and shall be

III. 9.
—
1593.
Nov. 2.
always ready to hear dutifully your ladyship's motherly admonitions touching him or any other man or matter, and to respect them as I ought. And so, with remembrance of my humble duties, I beseech God to bless and preserve your ladyship.

F. B.

March. Essex is poor. Dress, dinners, horses, courtesans exhaust his coffers. If he cannot pay in coin he will pay in place. His servant Francis Bacon shall be the Queen's Solicitor. Essex swears it.

10. Until he swears it all goes well. Burghley supports his nephew. Egerton and Fortescue urge his suit with admiring friendship on the Queen. Cecil is warm in his behalf; not alone begging in his own name, but stirring up friends and making a party at the Court. Every one at the bar, save only Coke, admits his claim to place.

Essex spoils all. At first the Queen is gracious; extols his eloquence and his wit, while doubting if he be deep in law. It only needs that his nomination shall be made in the proper way; because it is the best, not because this or that lord of her Court may wish it made. This does not please the Earl. Pledged to make Bacon's fortune, he will not stoop to see his debts paid by another hand. The work must be his own: "Upon me," he says, "must lie the labor of his establishment; upon me the disgrace will light of his refusal."

10. Lambeth MSS. 649, fol. 37, 60, 197; 650, fol. 109.

The Queen gets angry at this selfish pride. When he III. 10.
talks of Bacon she shuts her ears; but night and day
he hammers at the name; doing his full of mischief; 1594.
fretting and sulking till he drives her mad. Never were Mar. 24.
good intentions worse bestowed. A brief note from the
Earl to Bacon brings the impatient Queen and her impor-
tunate suitor on the scene: —

The Earl of Essex to Francis Bacon.

24 March, 1594.

SIR, —

The Queen did yesternight fly the gift, and I do wish,
if it be no impediment to the cause you do handle to-
morrow, you did attend again this afternoon. I will be
at the Court in the evening, and go with Mr. Vice-Chamberlain, so as, if you fail before we come, yet afterwards I
doubt not but he or I shall bring you together. This I
write in haste because I would have no opportunity omit-
ted in this point of access. I wish to you as to myself,
and rest

Your most affectionate friend,

ESSEX.

The Queen will not see him. She will not have her
freedom of selection curbed.

11. Bacon is surprised and hurt. His hopes for the May 1.

11. Lambeth MSS. 650, fol. 125.

III. 11.
———
1594.
May 1.
moment dashed, he perceives no chance of succeeding even at a better time, unless the Queen can be induced to leave the Solicitorship for the present void. To this end he applies to his cousin Cecil. Here is his note : —

FRANCIS BACON TO SIR ROBERT CECIL.

Gray's Inn, May 1, 1594.

MY MOST HONORABLE GOOD COUSIN, —

Your honor in your wisdom doth well perceive that my access at this time is grown desperate in regard of the hard termes that as well the Earl of Essex as Mr. Vice-Chamberlain, who were to have been the means thereof, stand in with her in acceding to their occasions. And therefore I am now only to fall upon that point of delaying and preserving the matter entire till a better constellation, which, as it is not hard, as I conceive, considering the proving business and the instant Progress, &c., so I commend in special to your honor's care, who in sort assured me thereof, and upon [whom] now in my lord of Essex' absence I have only to rely. And if it be needful, I humbly pray you to move my Lord your father to lay his sure hand to the same delay. And so I wish you all increase of honor.

Your poor kinsman in faithful prayers and duty,
FRANCIS BACON.

Cecil, who knows that the Earl, and none but the

Earl, stands in the way of his cousin's rise, writes back, III. 11.
on the same sheet of paper, in the left corner, these ——
words: — 1594.
May 1.

Sir Robert Cecil to Francis Bacon.

Cousin, —

I do think nothing cuts the throat more of your
present access than the Earl's being somewhat troubled
at this time. For the delaying, I think it not hard ;
neither shall there want my best endeavors to make it
easy, of which I hope you shall not need to doubt.
By the judgment which I gather of divers circumstances
confirming my opinion, I protest I suffer with you in
mind that you are thus yet gravelled ; but time will
founder all your competitors and set you on your feet,
or else I have little understanding.

12. For the first time in his life Bacon is now a
stranger at the court. Lady Ann lies sick at Gorhambury ; so sick, that the " good Christian and Saint of
God," as her son affectionately calls her, makes up her
soul for death. Two of her household have been
snatched away from her side by plague or fever. She
is down with ague. Bacon wrestles with her resigna-
tion, praying her to use all helps and comforts that
are good for her health, to the end that she may be
spared to her children and her friends, and to that

12. Lambeth MSS. 649, fol. 232; 650, fol. 140.

church of God which has so much need of her.. Here is the letter from which these particulars are drawn : —

FRANCIS BACON TO LADY BACON.

June 9, 1594.

My humble duty remembered, I was sorry to understand by Goodman Sotheram that your ladyship did find any weakness, which I hope was but caused by the season and weather, which waxeth more hot and faint. I was not sorry, I assure your ladyship, that you came not up, in regard that the stirring at this time of year, and the place where you should lie not being very open nor fresh, might rather hurt your ladyship than otherwise. And for anything to be passed to Mr. Trot, such is his kindness, as he demandeth it not ; and therefore, as I am to thank your ladyship for your willingness, so it shall not be needful but upon such an occasion as may be without your trouble, which the rather may be because I purpose, God willing, to come down, and it be but for a day, to visit your ladyship, and to do my duty to you. In the mean time I pray your health, as you have done the part of a good Christian and Saint of God in the comfortable preparing for your duty. So nevertheless, I pray, deny not your body the due, nor your children and friends, and the church of God, which hath use of you, but that you enter not into further conceit than is cause ; and withal use all comforts and helps that are good for

your health and strength. In truth I have heard III. 12.
Sir Thomas Scudamore often complain, after his quar-
tain had ceased, that he found such a heaviness and
swelling under his ribs that he thought he was buried
under earth all from the waist; and therefore that
accident no bad incident. Thus I commend your ladyship to God's good preservation from grief.

1594.
June 9.

Your ladyship's most obedient son,

FR. BACON.

It may be I shall have occasion, because nothing is
yet done in the choice of a Solicitor, to visit the Court
this vacation, which I have not now done this month's
time, in which respect, because having sent to and fro
spoyleth it, I would be glad of that light bed of stripes
which your ladyship hath, if you have not otherwise
disposed it.

13. The Saint of God is spared to her sons for a Aug. 20.
little while. When Francis makes her a visit he finds
her weak with pain, her memory failing like her health,
but her tongue and pen as swift to advise as ever. Anthony's easy nature, his indulgence of his men, his
love of finery and show and pleasure, wring the poor
lady's heart. She wants to see him marry and amend
his ways; but she sings of a wife in vain to this gay
companion of the young Earl of Essex, Rutland, and
Southampton. She would not mind stripping her house

13. Lambeth MSS. 650, fol. 168, 171, 223.

E

of everything for him, her pictures, her carpets, and her chairs, if her eldest born would only marry a sober and religious girl. But all pretty faces are to him the same. When Francis rides away from Gorhambury, she sends after him a string of pigeons and a world of pious and tender exhortations for the good of body and soul.

LADY BACON TO FRANCIS BACON.

20th Aug., 1594.

I was so full of back-pain when you came hither, that my memory was very slippery. I forgot to mention of rents. If you have not, I have not, received Frank's last half-year of Midsummer, the first half so long unpaid. You will mar your tenants if you suffer them. Mr. Brocquet is suffered by your brother to cosen me and beguile me without check. I fear you came too late to London for your horse: ever regard them. I desire Mr. Trot to hearken to some honest man, and cook too as he may. If you can hear of a convenient place I shall be willing if it so please God; for Lawson will draw your brother wherever he chooses, as I really fear, and that with false semblance. God give you both good health and hearts to serve him truly, and bless you always with his favor. I send you pigeons taken this day, and let blood. Look well about you and yours too. I hear that Robert Knight is but sickly. I am sorry for it. I do not write to my Lord-Treasurer,

because you like to stay. Let this letter be unseen. III. 13.
Look very well to your health; sup not, nor sit up late. —
Surely I think your drinking to bedwards hindereth 1594.
your and your brother's digestion very much. I never Aug. 20.
knew any but sickly that used it, besides being ill for
heads and eyes. Observe well, yet in time. Farewell
in Christ. • A. BACON.

At court affairs look gray. Elizabeth will not have
a name forced on her for selfish ends. She hears bad
news enough to worry the stoutest heart: now a stir
among the Irish rebels, now a threat of a descent from
Spain. Francis writes to Anthony:—

FRANCIS BACON TO ANTHONY BACON. Aug 26.

Gray's Inn, Aug. 26, 1594.

BROTHER,—

My cousin Cook is some four days home, and appointeth towards Italy that day sennight. I pray take
care for the money to be paid over within four or five
days. The sum you remember is 150*l.* I hear nothing
from the Court in mine own business. There hath
been a defeat of some force in Ireland by Macguire
which troubleth the Queen, being unaccustomed to such
news; and thereupon the opportunity is alleged to be
lost to move her. But there is an answer by the coming in of the Earl of Tyrone as was expected.

I steal to Twickenham, purposing to return this night,

III. 13. else I had visited you as I came from the town.   Thus
———   in haste I leave you to God's preservation.
1594.
Aug. 26.   Your entire loving brother,

FR. BACON.

Anthony is not now at Gray's Inn Square, having
taken a house in Bishopsgate-street, a fashionable part
of the city, near the famous Bull Inn, where plays are
performed before cits and gentlemen, very much to the
delight of Essex and his jovial crew, but very much,
as Lady Ann conceives, to the peril of her son's soul.
The good mother cannot put old heads on young necks,
say what she will.   "I am sorry," she writes to her
easy elder-born, "your brother and you charge yourselves with superfluous horses; the wise will laugh at
you; being but trouble to you both; besides your debts,
long journeys, and private persons.   Earls be earls."
There is the rub.   Lady Ann knows, and does not love,
these madcap earls.

By help of Cecil, and the Vice-Chamberlain, Fulke
Greville, Bacon succeeds so far as to get the nomination of Solicitor put off.   For more than a year the
situation undergoes no change.

14. The Queen is full of care; the tug and tempest

14. J. Cecil to Sir R. Cecil, Mar. 1594, S. P. O.; Examination of Capt. Edward Yorke, Aug. 12, 1594, S. P. O.; Declaration of Henry Yonge, Aug. 12,
1594, S. P. O.; Confession of Richard Williams, Aug. 27, 1594, S. P. O.; Cata-
logue of Rebels and Fugitives receiving Pensions from Spain, Sept. 1594, S. P.
O.; Council Reg., Oct. 29, 1594.

of her reign being close at hand. The league of Pope
and King, baffled by the swift scene at Fotheringay, broken by the loss of the Invincible Armada and the victories of Henri Quatre, has again been formed. Plans for seizing Guernsey and Jersey, arming the Ulster insurgents, throwing troops into Wales, and rousing a London mob, have been warmly debated in Madrid. Medina Cœli commands a mighty force at Cadiz. Philip at Madrid, Cardinal Archduke Albrecht at Brussels, are counting, pensioning, directing the English exiles, men amongst whom Wright and Winter, Stanley and Tresham, enjoy conspicuous favor. Father Parsons, Father Creswell, and Father Holt, the most bigoted and brazen of the English Jesuits, busy themselves among the needy and fanatical desperadoes of foreign courts and camps, everywhere vilifying the land which has cast them out, and whetting against their Queen the assassin's knife. Nor do they toil in vain. Two military ruffians, Captain Richard Williams and Captain Edward Yorke, offering to become the Clements — the Ravaillacs — of a more atrocious crime, have crossed the sea, and when taken, knife in hand, and flung into the Tower, confess that they have come into England commissioned by their spiritual and military chiefs for murder. They implicate by name Sir William Stanley and Father Holt.

15. Bacon is sick of heart; looks wan and thin, as

15. Lambeth MSS. 651, fol. 144. Patent Rolls 38 Eliz. par. vi. 25.

III. 15.
—
1595.
June 3.

all the world takes note. The heady Earl has proved to him a fatal friend. Lady Ann pours on her son her counsels and consolations.

LADY BACON TO ANTHONY BACON.

June 3, 1595.

I am sorry your brother with inward secret grief hindereth his health. Everybody saith he looketh thin and pale. Let him look to God and confer with him in godly exercise of hearing and reading, and continue to be noted to take care. I had rather ye both, with God's blessed favor, had very good healths, and were well out of debt, than any office. Yet though the earl showed great affection, he marred all with violent courses.

I pray God increase His fear in his heart and a hatred of sin ; indeed, halting before the Lord and backsliding are very pernicious. I am heartily sorry to hear how he [the Earl of Essex] sweareth and gameth unreasonably. God cannot like it.

I pray show your brother this letter, but to no creature else. Remember me and yourself.

Your mother,

A. B.

If the Queen hangs back, and if Burghley hesitates, it is not from dislike or distrust to Bacon ; but simply because so grave a nomination as a successor to Coke

ought not to be made as a bounty or a submission to
the Earl. The more they feel that such a post can
never be filled in such a way, the more they strive to
let the world see that the advocate, not the candidate
is in fault.

At the express suggestion of Burghley and Fortescue,
the Queen appoints Bacon one of her Counsel Learned
in the Law, and confers on him, at a nominal rent, a
good estate. This grant comprises sixty acres, more
or less of wood, in the forest of Zelwood in the county of Somerset, known as the Pitts; which Bacon receives from the Crown on a rent of seven pounds
ten shillings a year, payable at the feasts of St. Michael the Archangel, and of the Annunciation of the
Virgin.

16. If Elizabeth pauses in her choice of a Solicitor-
General, her servants see that Bacon's hopes are for the
moment dead. Lady Ann hears this bad news at Gorhambury, and writes to console her son.

LADY BACON TO ANTHONY BACON.

Aug. 7, 1595.

If Her Majesty have resolved upon the negative for
your brother, as I hear, truly, save for the brust a little,
I am glad of it. God in His time hath better in store I

16. Lambeth MSS. 651, fol. 211.

III. 16.
———
1595.
Aug. 7.

trust. For considering his kind of health and what cumber pertains to that office, it is best for him I hope. Let us all pray the Lord we make us to profit by His fatherly correction; doubtless it is His hand, and all for the best, and love to His children that will seek Him first, and depend upon His goodness. Godly and wisely love ye, like brethren, whatsoever happen, and be of good courage in the Lord, with good hope.

A. B.

And how does Bacon bear this prospect of defeat? Merrily, it seems. There is a glimpse of him in his mother's notes to Anthony: "With a humble heart before God, let your brother be of good cheer. Alas!- what excess of bucks at Gray's Inn! And to feast it on the Sabbath! God forgive and have mercy upon England!"

Sept.

17. A fleet has gone from Plymouth under Drake. A fleet more terrible to the Don is arming under Raleigh. Drake is a marauder, Raleigh a statesman. If he can burn Nombre di Dios and spoil the carracks of Margarita, Drake will be at peace. Raleigh, fresh from his romantic voyage to the Amazon, flushed with the hope of conquest and discovery, is bent on founding States.

Bacon, who sees in Raleigh, not alone the nimble wit,

17. Elizabeth to Raleigh, Nov., 1595, S. P. O.; Notes of the Supplemental part of the Entertainment given at York House, Nov. 17, 1595, S. P. O.

III. 17.

1595.
Sept.

the proud courtier, the dashing seaman, but the leader of vast horizon, of philosophic thought, would like to keep Essex on easy terms with him; the two men holding, as far as might be, a common course in politics and in war. Their loves and hates are the same. Each longs for war; a war of books and laws against Rome, a war of pikes and culverins against Spain. Each in his own person represents the youth and genius of the time: Essex that of the nobles, Raleigh of the gentry. Each of the two seems to Bacon needful to the other and to the common cause: the Queen's kinsman to uphold it against timid counsels at court, the founder of Virginia to maintain it against Philip's admirals on the Spanish Main. A frank and loyal union of these two men would have given England the free use of all her arms; in the long run it would have saved them both from the block. With tongue and pen Bacon labors to make peace between them. He seeks to push the new expedition. In spite of Raleigh's pride, which often mars his work, he repeats to Essex that Raleigh will be his stanchest and safest friend.

Essex is preparing to receive the Queen at York House in the Strand with a grand entertainment and a sumptuous masque given in her honor; for which Bacon is composing characters and words. The play being given in Essex's name, here are the means for a striking and conspicuous compliment to Raleigh. Bacon frames a scene of the masque in happy allusion to the Amazon and to Raleigh's voyage.

4

III. 18.

—

1595.

Nov.

18. Essex has not the grace to let it stand. The glory of Raleigh breaks his rest, for he himself aspires to be all that Raleigh is, — renowned in war even more than in letters and in courts. He strikes his. pen through Bacon's lines, which drop from the acted scene and from the printed masque. A contemporary copy of this suppressed part remains in the State Paper Office ; a proof how much, five years before the Earl rushes into high treason, Bacon leans to the side of her Majesty's Captain of the Guard.

The opportunity thrown away by Essex, Burghley, and Cecil hug to their hearts. They give, not only their countenance to Raleigh, but their money to the Guiana voyage ; Burghley contributing five hundred pounds, Cecil a new ship, the hull of which alone costs him no less than eight hundred pounds.

Nov. 5.

19. The Earl's want of tact and temper is more hurtful to his friends than to his foes. He does Raleigh no great harm ; he causes Bacon the most grievous loss. Give me this place of the Solicitor, — he drums and drums at the Queen's ear. She thinks her law officers should be chosen by herself, and for their good parts, not to please the fancy or make good the pledges of a carpet knight. She will not do a right thing for a bad reason or in a wrong way. Her courts are

18. Entertainment given to the Queen at York House, Nov. 17, 1595; Sydney Papers, i. 377.

19. Warrant Book, Nov. 5, 1595.

crowded with able men. She is old enough to choose
a servant for herself. As Essex grows hot, she cools:
when he storms upon her and will not be denied, she
turns from the spoiled boy, her nomination made. Bacon must wait; Fleming shall be her man.

III. 19.

1595.
Nov.

20. Lord Campbell says, as writers have said from the
days of Bushel, that the Earl atoned to Bacon for his
failure by a gift of Twickenham Park. It happens, however, that Twickenham Park was not, and never had
been, the Earl's to give. That lovely seat, which blooms
by the Thames, close under Richmond Bridge, fronting
the old palace, and some of the elms of which stand,
venerable and green, in the days of Victoria, had be-
longed to the Bacons for many years. In 1574, while
Essex was a boy at Chartley, Twickenham Park, together
with More Mead and Ferry Mead, the adjoining lands,
had been granted by the Queen to Edward Bacon on
lease. The lease is enrolled, and may be examined in
the Record Office. Francis lived in the house, as his
letters prove, long before his patent of Solicitor passed
the Seal. It had all the points of a good country-house;
a green landscape, wood and water, pure air, a dry soil,
vicinity to the court and to the town. From his windows he could peer into the Queen's alleys; in an hour
he could trot up to Whitehall or Gray's Inn. Every
plant that thrives, every flower that blows, in the south
of England, loves the Twickenham soil. There were

20. Rolls, Mar. 3, 16 Eliz., Record Office.

cedars in the great park, swans on the river, singing-birds in the copse; every sight to engage the eye, every sound to please the ear.

He loved the house, and lived in it when he could steal away from Gray's Inn. It was his house of letters and philosophy, as the lodging in Gray's Inn Square was his house of politics and law. In fact, when the Earl ferried over from Richmond Palace, he leaped from his barge on to Bacon's lawn.

21. Unable to pay his debt by a public office, Essex feels that he ought to pay it in money or in money's worth. The lawyer has done his work, must be told his fee. But the Earl has no funds. His debts, his amours, his camp of servants eat him up. He will pay in a patch of land. To this Bacon objects: not that he need scruple at taking wages; not that the mode of payment is unusual; not that the price is beyond his claim. Four years have been spent in the Earl's service. To pay in land is the fashion of a time when gold is scarce and soil is cheap. Nor is the patch too large; at most it may be worth 1,200*l*. or 1,500*l*. After Bacon's improvements and the rise of rents, he sells it to Reynold Nicholas for 1,800*l*. It is less than the third of a year's income from the Solicitor-General's place. Bacon's doubts have a deeper source. Knowing the Earl's fiery

---

21. Sir Francis Bacon, his Apologie in certain imputations concerning the late Earl of Essex, written to his very good Lord the Earl of Devonshire, 1604, 13, 16.

temper, and sharing in some degree his mother's fears, he shrinks from incurring feudal obligations to one so vain and weak. Hurt by his hesitation, Essex pouts and sulks; being, as he truly says, the sole cause of this loss of place, he will die of vexation if he be not allowed in some small measure to repair it. Bacon submits. Yet even in taking the strip of ground, he betrays the uneasy sentiment lurking in his heart. "My Lord," he says, "I see I must be your homager and hold land of your gift; but do you know the manner of doing homage in law? Always it is with saving of his faith to the King."

III. 21.

1595.
Nov.

22. What says the Queen? Writers who laud the generosity of a man to whom Bacon owed loss of character and loss of place, denounce the stinginess of a woman to whose noble and unfailing friendship he owed almost everything which he possessed on earth. These scribes are hard to please: they treat Bacon as a rogue whom it is the duty of honest men to scourge; yet decry the Queen for laying on the lash. What would they have? If Bacon were the rascal they have made him, surely the Queen would have done well in starving his powers of mischief! Their reasoning is faulty as their facts. Inquiry at the Rolls Office would have shown them that, even while she was naming Fleming for her Solicitor-General, Elizabeth was Francis Bacon's most warm and munificent friend.

22. Montagu, xvi. part i. 27.

III. 22.

1595.
Nov.

She long ago gave him a reversion of the Registry of the Star Chamber; a post, when he should get it, worth 1,600*l.* a year. As he could no more spare his jest than Tully, he said it was like having another man's land near his house: it improved his prospect, but did not fill his barn. With woful lack of humor, Rawley mistook this truly Baconian laughter for a groan; and the poor chaplain's petulant wail misled Montagu into dreaming, contrary to all the evidence of Rolls and grants, that Elizabeth put the yoke on Bacon's neck. This blunder of Rawley drove Montagu to the drollest shifts. Knowing how Bacon cherished her fame in his heart of hearts, how was the biographer to reconcile this fable of her stinginess to him with the fact of his undying gratitude to her? He hit on the queerest explanation. Does a father who loves his son spare the rod? Are not pangs and stripes good for the soul? Yes, the great Queen must have understood the great man; in mercy to the world, she crossed him at the bar and starved him at the court! Macaulay rent and tossed this amazing theory; but neither he nor Lord Campbell ever paused to ask if it were true that Elizabeth left him to starve.

23. The reversion of the Star Chamber, the grant of Zelwood Forest, the post of her Counsel learned in the Law, are but a foretaste of her love. Edward Bacon's lease of Twickenham Park has just expired; that lovely home by the water-edge will be his no more. The house

23. Rot. 36 Eliz., pars vi. 20, Record Office.

has an importance beyond the beauty of its site ; a merit III. 23.
rarer than the green mead, the leafy wood, the rushing
stream, the whitening swans ; it stands all day in the
sovereign's sight.   To live in such a place is to be a daily
guest in her Majesty's mind.   The house is good, the
park spacious ; within the pales are eighty-seven acres of
lawn and pasture, lake and orchard ; beyond the pales
five or six acres of mead and field.   It is a home for a
prince.

Fourteen years ago the park had been leased to Milo
Dodding for thirty years, commencing from the expira-
tion of Edward Bacon's term ; but on passing to Fleming
the patent of his place, the gracious Queen makes over to
Francis Bacon a reversion of this lease.   On the fifth
of November Fleming gets his commission as Solicitor-
General ; on the seventeenth of November, the day of
his masque at York House, of his proposed compliment
to the Guiana voyage, Bacon's grant of the reversion of
Twickenham Park passes under the Privy Seal.

1595.
Nov. 17.

CHAPTER IV.

TREASON OF SIR JOHN SMYTH.

IV. 1.
———
1596.
May.

1. THE Queen not only endows Bacon with lands, and with the reversion of lands and offices, but employs him in her legal and political affairs; often in business which would seem to belong exclusively to the department of Fleming or of Coke. As her Counsel learned in the Law, he is engaged in the prosecution of William Randal. He is consulted in the more momentous charge against Sir John Smyth, who stands accused of no less a crime than that of an attempt, under circumstances of peculiar guilt, to provoke a military mutiny and insurrection against the Queen.

2. In the spring of 1596 an expedition, meant to anticipate the Roman league, has been arming in the Thames. Its destination is unknown, though the few suspect that a blow will fall on the most prosperous and beautiful of Spanish ports. Raleigh is still at home; Keymish having gone with his fleet of ships to the

---

1. Egerton, Fleming, and Bacon to the Council, May 3, 1596, S. P. O.; Lucas to the Council, June 23, 1596, S. P. O.
2. Lambeth MSS. 657, fol. 29, 30.

mouths of the Amazon. Vere and Effingham are drilling
troops. Essex — martial, if not military — is pouting
for command. Anthony and Francis Bacon busy themselves in collecting news for the Queen from foreign
spies and foreign Gazettes. While the Earl of Essex
lies at Plymouth, waiting for Raleigh and the rear-
guard of his fleet to come round, Francis writes to his
brother : —

IV. 2.
—
1596.
May 15.

FRANCIS BACON TO ANTHONY BACON.

May 15, 1596.

MY VERY GOOD BROTHER, —

I have remembered your salutation to Sir John
Fortescue, and delivered him the Gazette, desiring
him to reserve it to read in his barge. He acknowl-
edgeth it to be of another sort than the common. I
delivered him account so much of E. Hawkins's letter
as contained advertisements copied out; which is the
reason I return the letter to you now; the Gazette being
gone with him to the court.

The next words consecutive I have not acquainted
him with, nor any of them. The body is for more apt
time. So, in haste, I wish you comfort as I write.

Your entire loving brother,

FR. BACON.

Fourteen days later, the fleet now riding in Plymouth
Sound, he writes again. Anthony, tiring of the Earl's

unprofitable service, wishes to be sent abroad as agent or ambassador, — a post for which he is eminently fit. To his suit for such a place Francis refers: —

FRANCIS BACON TO ANTHONY BACON.

From the Court, May 81st, 1596.

GOOD BROTHER, —

Yesternight Sir John Fortescue told me you had not many hours before imparted to the Queen your advertisement, and the Gazettes likewise, which the Queen desired Mr. H. Stanhope to read all over unto her; and her Majesty commandeth they be not made vulgar. The advertisement her Majesty made estimation of, as concurring with the other advertisements, and belike concurring also with her opinion of the affairs. So he willed me to return to you the Queen's speeches. Other particulars of any speech from her Majesty of yourself he did not repeat to me. For my Lord of Essex and the Lord-Treasurer, he said he was ready and disposed to do his best. But I seemed to make it only a love-suit, and passed presently from it, the rather because it was late in the night, and I was to deal with him on some better occasion after another manner, as you shall hereafter understand from me. I do find in the speech of some ladies, and the very fairest of this court, some additions of reputation as methinks to be both; and I doubt not but God hath an operation (?) in it that will not suffer good endeavors to perish. The Queen

saluted me to-day as she went to supper. I had long
speech with Sir Robert Cecil this morning, who seemed
apt to discourse with me. Yet of your hest not a
word (?) This I write to you in haste, *aliud ex alio.*
I pray you, in the course of acquainting my Lord, say
where presseth, at first by me, after from yourself, I
am more and more bound to him. Thus, wishing you
good health, I commend you to God's happiness.

Your entire loving brother,

Fr. Bacon.

IV. 2.
——
1596.
May 31.

3. Against the Queen's sounder sense, Essex gets command of the land forces told off for a dash at Cadiz. On
the eve of sailing, conscious that, though he may have
meant the best, he has done for Bacon the worst that
man could do, he writes in kindly but superfluous words
to recommend him to the care of his oldest and sagest
friend. Thus, in generous helplessness, he writes to
Egerton : —

Essex to Lord Keeper Egerton.

May 27, 1596.

My very good Lord, —
I do understand by my good friend Mr. F. B. how
much he is bound to your Lordship for your favor. I do
send your Lordship my best thanks, and do protest unto
you there is no gentleman in England of whose good for-

3. Lambeth MSS. 657, 90.

IV. 3.   tune I have been more desirous. I do still retain the
——   same mind ; but, because my intercession hath rather
1596.   hurt him than done him good, I dare not move the
May.   Queen for him. To your Lordship I earnestly commend
the care I have of his advancement ; for his parts were
never destined to a private and (if I may so speak) an
idle life. That life I call idle that is not spent in public
business ; for otherwise he will ever give himself worthy
tasks. Your Lordship, in performing what I desire, will
oblige us both, and within very short time see such fruit
of your own work as will please you well. So, commending your Lordship to God's best protection, I rest,
at your Lordship's commandment,

ESSEX.

June.   4. At length they are gone ; Effingham, Raleigh, Vere,
Montjoy, all the great fighting men, on board ; leaving
England for the moment bare of fleets or troops. Twelve
days have worn since the ships weighed anchor in Plymouth Sound, and not one word of news has come to
shore. They may be hundreds of fathoms deep in the
Bay of Biscay, or lie crushed and strewn under Lisbon
rock. Should they have perished as the Invincible Armada perished ! It is known that the Twelve Apostles,
gigantic Andalusian war-ships, float in Cadiz bay ; that a
fleet of transports rides at the Groyne ; that a Spanish

---

4. Gilbert to Raleigh, Mar. 16, 1596, S. P. O.; Gorges to Burghley, April 12,
1596, S. P. O.; Proclamation by the Earl of Essex, April 14, 1596, S. P. O.;
Queen Elizabeth to Cobham, June 7, 1596, S. P. O.; Council Reg., June 1 to
August 7, 1596.

army of horse and foot crouches behind the heights of San Sebastian and the walls of Bilboa; that a body of victorious troops, flushed with the assault of Calais, occupies the dunes which look on Dover cliffs. It is felt that a storm, a repulse, even a dead calm, may give the signal for a swarm of Pandours and Walloons to burst into Kent.

Some, in this day of dark suspense, dispute the policy of having sent the fleet on such a cruise, — many blame the ambition which pulls the weaver from his loom, the hind from his plough. Every one has to submit to loss of money or loss of time. The trainbands garrison the city and protect the Court. Lord Cobham holds the Cinque Ports. Sir Thomas Lucas puts the men of Colchester under drill. The bombardiers of Dover, Plymouth, and Milford Haven stand to their guns. Musters for defence gather even in the midland and northern shires; where, at a call from the Privy Council, yeomen snatch down their bills and pikes, often rusty and out of date, bills which had been swung in Bosworth field, bows which had been drawn at Agincourt. On every village green, and under every market-cross, drums beat and tabors sound the local force to arms.

5. Now is the time for friends of Rome to strike. Where there is much to bear, a man of weak under-

5. Elizabeth's Letters Patent to raise troops in Kent, Sussex, Middlesex, and Surrey, for relief of Calais, April 1596, S. P. O.; Smyth to Cecil, Mar. 14, 1600, S. P. O.; Discourse of the Providence necessary to be had for the setting up of the Catholic Faith, Aug. 1600, S. P. O.

standing will infer that, despite ambition and pride of race, there must be fires of discontent ready to flare out. When discontent is armed, it may be led to abuse its strength; so at least reasons the rich country gentleman, Sir John Smyth.

Smyth is a Roman Catholic, owner of Baddow and Coggeshall, in Essex; a friend of the great Scymour family; an ally of Catherine de' Medici; a correspondent of the foreign Jesuits and priests. His life has been one long plot. In the war now booming, all his love lies beyond the sea. The doctrine taught by Parsons and Bellarmino, that a good Roman Catholic must fight and pray for his Church, even against his native sovereign and his native land, is an active portion of his creed. Others may wish to maim the government, may pray for storms to whelm or cannon to crush the English fleet; Smyth alone is fool enough to risk his neck by active measures in support of the allies of his Church. The fighting men gone, he beholds the Queen, the lords of her Council, all the peers of her realm, at the mercy, as he thinks, of an armed, uncertain mob. A march on London, a fight under the windows of Whitehall, may cause the fleets to hie back to Plymouth, or the Spaniards to cross the Straits.

Cries are never wanting to a traitor. There is the old, old feud of poor against rich; the old, old aversion of local troops to serve the Crown in its foreign wars. Unhappily both these feuds are now malignant: that between rich and poor being imbittered by the recent conversion of a vast extent of plough-land into pasture, by the destruction of a great number of cottages and holdings, and by the increase of sheep-walks and of parks for the preservation of red and fallow deer; that between the local troops and the Crown, by reports that the musters have been forced to go on board the fleet, and that soldiers raised in the metropolitan shires have been sent by the Government into France.

The decay of tillage, the increase of sheep and deer, are for the yeoman class, and for the country of which they are the thew and sinew, dark events. The yeomen kick against the goad; for, not being skilled in science, they cannot see that they are driven from their farms by the operations of a natural law. If they have ever heard that, as wool pays better than rent, their landlords prefer sheep to men, the news has not reconciled them to the conversion of their old farms into sheep-walks or deer-parks. Smyth, as a country gentleman, sees this sore, and fancies he may turn the discontent against the Queen.

6. Like his neighbors, Smyth hands down from his walls the rusty arms, calling in Frost of Colchester to edge his swords and string his bows. Thomas Seymour, one of those weak descendants of Mary Brandon whose blood is too red for their sovereign's comfort, or their own, joins him in his freak. With an army of two

6. Examination of John Lucas and others, June 12, 1596, S. P. O.; Examination of Frost, June 22, 1596, S. P. O.; Smyth to Mannocke, June 13, 1596, S. P. O.

IV. 6.
———
1596.
June 12.

mounted followers, Smyth and Seymour ride into the field at Colchester in which Sir Thomas Lucas, fiercely loyal, drills his troop. Reining their steeds in front of the yeoman line, Sir John cries, " Who will go with me ? There are traitors round the Queen who grind the poor into bondmen ; who send them out of the realm ; who break the laws ; who weaken the country, who ruin the yeomen. These traitors have killed nine thousand foot in their foreign wars, and they will send you out of England to be slain."

" Shall we go with you, Sir John ? " asks a trooper.

" You shall go with a better man than me, — than Sir Thomas Lucas," shouts Smyth. " Here is a noble man of the blood royal, brother to Lord Beauchamp ; he shall be your captain. I myself shall be his assistant. Down with Burghley ! Who goes with me, hold up his hand."

Not one. No hand, no cry is raised. Treason that stops is lost ; and whoever is not with the traitor is against him. Meshed in a fearful crime, the four horsemen prick from the field, part in the slob, and hide themselves from pursuit in the sands of the sea-shore. Smyth seeks a boat for France ; but the summer morning dawns on him staggering, faint and hopeless on the coast ; when, crazed with fear, he skulks home to Baddow, where he vainly hopes to hide his face from the local magistrates, now hurrying on his track.

June 19.   7. Sent up to London, lodged in the Tower, Smyth

7. Smyth to the Council, June 19, 1596, S. P. O.; Council to Coke, Fleming,

confesses his crime. Coke and Fleming receive orders
from the Privy Council to call in Bacon and Waad, a
clerk of the Council, and then to take the evidence, look
up the law, and, if they find the offence treason, prepare
articles of indictment against Smyth. These four commissioners meet, find the acts at Colchester treason, and
report that the offence is punishable by a special statute.

Bacon, not content, like the Attorney-General and
Solicitor-General, with setting the law in motion to hang
this wretched man, asks himself how a country knight,
not wholly crazed, could ever have dreamt that, on a cry
of "Down with sheep and deer," honest men could be
roused to mutiny against their Queen. To a philosophic
mind the reason of a thing is often of larger interest
than the thing itself. Is there discontent among the yeomen? If so, is there cause? He makes a wide and
sweeping study of this question of Pasturage versus Tillage, of Deer versus Men, which convinces him of the
cruelty and peril of depopulating hamlets for the benefit
of a few great lords. This study will produce when Parliament meets again a memorable debate and an extraordinary change of law.

8. While Coke and Bacon wind out of Smyth's confessions the threads of his interrupted treason, comes in,

Waad, and Bacon, June 27, 1596, S. P. O.; Smyth's Examination, June 28,
1596, S. P. O.; Abstract of Evidence against Sir John Smyth, July 1596, S.
P. O.

8. Carey to Cecil, July 16, 1596, S. P. O.; Report from Cadiz, July 16, 19,
21, 1596, S. P. O.; Report of the Spoil taken at Cadiz, Aug. 11, 1596, S. P. O.

IV. 8.
———
1596.
July 16. wave on wave, the news of such a victory as only twice or thrice in a thousand years has stirred our English phlegm. It comes in first by a Dutch skipper, who puts three men on the Devonshire coast. The tale they tell is beyond belief: the city of Cadiz taken, an armada sunk, Porto Santa Maria wrapt in flame, the Duke of Medina Cœli driven from his lines, the road from San Lucar to Seville blocked up with the fugitive population of a great province hurrying for their lives. Some nine days pass when a Scotch boat drops into Dartmouth with the same news. A few hours later still the van of the victorious fleet rides into Plymouth Sound, laden with such spoil, such heaps of plate, gold, jewels, damasks, silks, hangings, carpets, scarfs, as living Englishmen have only seen in dreams. To hear that the fleet was safe would have been joy enough; this fiery triumph of our arms, this glow of spoil and conquest, all but drive men mad.

Sept. 9. Most mad of all is Essex. The glory obtained by Raleigh and Effingham chafes his pride; the elevation of Cecil in his absence into First Secretary of State disturbs his power. If much remains to him, much is not enough. A warrior who has pushed through the Puerta de la Tierra, and seen the loveliest city in the west of Europe at his feet, should be suffered, he thinks,

9. Lambeth MSS. 658, fol. 21; Censures of the Omissions in the Expedition to Cadiz, 1596; Camden's Ann. Eliz., 1596; Bacon's Apologie, 19, 20; Devereux, i. 380.

to enjoy a monopoly of power and fame. Yet a senseless country shares the credit with his rivals, while a forgetful Queen has given the most active place in her government to his foe. On every side he is robbed of his due ; getting neither his fair part of the spoil, nor anything like his fair part of the reputation. So he sulks and pouts ; prints his own account of the voyage ; finds fault with the generals and admirals ; tells the sailors of the fleet and the soldiers in the camp that their success would have been far more prompt, their prizes far more abundant, had his command of them been unfettered by such a council of fools and cowards.

But Cecil's rise at home provokes him more than Raleigh's success abroad. This case is a repetition of Bacon's case. Sir Thomas Bodley, that experienced scholar and diplomatist to whose wealth and taste we owe the princely library at Oxford, has, like Bacon, been of use to the Earl. Essex, who pays his debts in offices and grants, has pledged his word that Bodley shall be Secretary of State. The Queen has not kept her kinsman's pledge. On his return from Spain, perceiving that he was sent away from London to give Cecil an open field, he begins to sulk and storm. He will not stay at court to be mocked. He will bury his grief at Wanstead, or rush away to the war, and find peace of heart on the Spanish pikes!

Lady Ann's quick ear and loving eye perceive the change that Cecil's elevation, the Earl's discomfiture, must work at court. Now that her sister's son, who so

IV. 9.
——
1596.

bitterly hates the Earl and so sharply resents the connection of any of his own able kin with the insolent and brainless peer, has come to his height of power, she writes to warn Anthony of the evil days in store for them, now Cecil is greater than before, and of the need for her sons to walk with wary step. It is the last letter from her pen, closing, as a good woman's letters should do, with words of love.

LADY BACON TO ANTHONY BACON.

July 10, 1596.

Now that Sir Robert is fully stalled in his long longed-for secretary's place, I pray God give him a religious, wise, and an upright heart before God and man. I promise you, son, in my conjectural opinion, you had more need now to be more circumspect and advised in your troublous discoursings and doings and dealings in your accustomed matter, either with or for yourself or others, whom you heartily honor, nor without cause. He now hath great advantage and strength to intercept, prevent, and to say where he hath been or is in. Son, be it revelation or suspicion, you know what terms he standeth in towards yourself, and would needs have me tell you so; so very vehement he was. Then you are said to be wise, and to my comfort I willingly think so; but surely, son, on the other side, for want of some experience by action and your tedious unacquaintance of your own country by continual chamber and bed-

keeping, you must need miss of considerate judgment in
your verbal only travailing.   If all were scant sound
before betwixt the Γιαξλ [Earl of Essex] and him,
friends had need to walk more warily in his days; for
all affectionate doing he may hurt though pretending
good.   The father and son are joined in power and
policy.   The Lord ever bless you in Christ.   Still I
hearken for Yates; I doubt somebody hindereth his coming to me.   It were small matter to come speak with me.
You know what you have to do in regard touching the
Spaniard.   I reck not his displeasure; God grant he
mar not all at last with Spanish popish subtlety.   Alas!
what I wrote touching the poor sum of five pounds to
your brother [Francis], I meant but to let you know
plainly.   I would rather nourish than any little way
weaken true brotherly love, as appeareth manifestly to
you both.   God forbid but that you should always love
heartily, mutually, and kindly.   God commandeth love
as brethren, besides bond of nature.   This present time
I am brewing but for hasty and home drinking.   In
truth, if I should purposely make a tierce somewhat
strong for you, I know not how to have carried it
through.   It were pity that you and I both should be
disappointed.   Burn, burn, in any wise.

From your mother,
A. B.

Bacon warns the Earl against hasty speeches and
offensive acts.   Essex swears the rough way is the only

IV. 9. way with Elizabeth. She may be driven, not led. "My
— Lord," says Bacon, "these courses are like hot waters;
1596. they may help at a pang, but they will not do for
Sept. daily use." Essex seems crazed. Bacon seeks to dis-
suade him from this lust of arms; his proper weapon
being a chamberlain's stick. In happy phrase he tells
him that this haughty bearing to the Queen, this craving
for command in camps, may prove to him the two wings
of Icarus, — wings joined on with wax; wings which
may melt as he soars to the sun.

1597. 10. Essex cools to a man whose talk is so very much
June. wiser than he wants to hear. They have no scene,
no quarrel, no parting; for there are no sympathies to
wrench, no friendships to dissolve. Essex ceases to seek
advice at Gray's Inn. They now rarely see each other.
Bacon is writing his Essays, fagging at the bar, slipping
into love; and Essex is still happy to serve him, when
he can do it at anybody's cost but his own.

Francis falls into love. Lord Campbell thinks he
only falls into debt. "He was desperately poor; he
therefore made a bold attempt to restore his position by
matrimony." This is surely in Bantam's vein. "When
one does n't know," asks the cockfighter, "is not it natural to think the worst?" The lady that Bacon courts
is rich and of his kin. Elizabeth Hatton, a granddaugh-
ter of his uncle Burghley, niece of his cousin Cecil, has

10. Essex to Sir Thomas Cecil, June 24, 1597; Bankes's Story of Corffe Castle, 34.

been left a widow, young, lovely, powerful in her friends IV. 10.
and in her fine estate. The mistress of Hatton House,   ——
of Corffe Castle, of Purbeck Isle, a woman whose lovely 1597.
hand is celebrated in Jonson's verse, —   June.

> " Mistress of a finer table
> Hath not history or fable," —

has, of course, crowds of adorers at her feet: among
them men no less renowned than William Earl of Pembroke and Francis Bacon. The lady, or her kinsman
for her, puts aside their suits. Cecil looks on his fair
niece as a thing to be sold for his own gain. Her youth,
her beauty, her great inheritance are precious in his
sight, and the husband for such a woman must be to
him a strong defender or a useful slave.

Essex, on the point of sailing for the Azores, writes
to Sir Thomas and Lady Cecil, saying, if he had a sister to give away in marriage, he·would gladly give her
to his friend If this means more than the cheap generosity of words, it is most fortunate for Francis that
Penelope and Dorothy, the Earl's two sisters, are already
in holy bonds. It would have been bad enough for him
to have won Lady Hatton ; it would have been awful to
have stood in the shoes of Northumberland or Rich.

11. During the Earl's absence at the Azores Effing- Oct. 22.
ham is made an earl : an affront to Essex more galling

11. Patent of the Earldom of Nottingham, Oct. 22, 1597, S. P. O.; Elizabeth
to Essex, Oct. 28, 1597, S. P. O.; Raleigh to Cecil, July 20, 1597, S. P. O.; Cecil to Essex, July 26, 1597, S. P. O.; Devereux, i. 467.

IV. 11. than the rejection, on his suit, of the services of Bacon
———   and Bodley; for this creation robs him, as he thinks,
1597.   of the glory of Cadiz fight, and permits a man whom
Oct. 22. he loathes to walk before him in the Queen's train and
sit above him in the House of Peers. When he hears
of this grant having passed the Seal, he quits his command without leave, hurries up to town, and finding
the thing done, insults the Queen, spurs to Wanstead
House, defying at once the entreaties of the Council
to return, and the advice of his best friends to submit.
A dark and ruinous spirit now stands by his side.
Raleigh screens him from blame in his great failure at
the Azores; pleading for him with the Queen in almost
passionate terms; but Raleigh is the lion in the way
of Blount, his new and most confidential friend. Under the lead of Sir Christopher Blount, Essex parts
from his old Protestant and patriotic allies, from Bacon and Raleigh, from Cecil and Grey, turning his eyes
and ears to the blandishments of loose women and the
suggestions of discontented men; to such wantons as
Elizabeth Southwell, and Mary Howard, to such plotters as Robert Catesby and Christopher Wright. A craze
is in his blood and in his brain. "It comes from his
mother," sighs the hurt and angry Queen.

12. As Lettice Knollys, as Countess of Essex, as Countess of Leicester, as wife of Sir Christopher Blount, this

12. Papers of Mary Queen of Scots, xvi. 7, 15, 16, 17; Camden's Ann. Eliz..
632; Craik's Romance of the Peerage, i. 5, 338.

mother of the Earl has been a barb in Elizabeth's side for thirty years. Married as a girl to a noble husband, she gave up his honor to a seducer, and there is reason to fear she gave her consent to the taking of his life. While Devereux lived she deceived the Queen by a scandalous amour, and after his death by a clandestine marriage with the Earl of Leicester. While Dudley lived she wallowed in licentious love with Christopher Blount, his groom of the horse. When her second husband expired in agonies at Cornbury, not a gallop from the place in which Amy Robsart died, she again mortified the Queen by a secret union with her seducer, Blount.

Her children riot in the same vices. Essex himself, with his ring of favorites, is not more profligate than his sister Lady Rich. In early youth Penelope Rich was the mistress of Sydney, whose stolen love for her is pictured in his most voluptuous verse. Sydney is Astrophel, Penelope Stella. Since Sydney's death she has lived in shameless adultery with Lord Montjoy, though her husband Lord Rich is still alive. Her sister Dorothy, after wedding one husband secretly and against the canon, has now married Percy, the wizard Earl of Northumberland, whom she leads the life of a dog.

Save in the Suffolk branch of the Howards, it would not be easy to find out of Italian story a group of women so detestable as the mother and sisters of the Earl.

13. The third husband of Lady Leicester is her match

IV. 12.
——
1597.
Oct.

13. Craik's Rom. Peerage, i. 127, 208.

IV. 13. in licentiousness, more than her match in crime. By
—— birth a papist, by profession a bravo and a spy, Blount is
1597. incapable either of feeling for his wretched wife the
Oct. manly love of Essex, or of treating her with the lordly
courtesy of Leicester. Brutal and rapacious, he has married her, not for her bright eyes, now dim with rheum
and vice, but for her jewels, her connections, and her
lands. He cringed to Leicester, that he might sell the
secrets of his cabinet and enjoy the pleasures of his bed.
With the same blank conscience, he wrings from the
widow her ornaments and goods. Chain, armlet, neck-
lace, money, land, timber, everything that is hers, wastes
from his prodigal palm. He beats her servants; he
thrusts his kinsfolk upon her; he snatches the pearl from
her neck, the bond from her strong box. A villain so
black would have driven a novelist or playwright mad.
Iago, Overreach, Barabas, all the vile creatures of poetic
imagination, are to him angels of light. What would have
been any other man's worst vice is Blount's sole virtue,
— a ruthless and unreasoning constancy to his creed.
Fear and shame are to him the idlest of idle words; and,
just as he would follow the commands of his general, he
obeys the dictation of his priest. As a libertine and as a
spy, his days have been spent in dodging the assassin or
in cheating the rope. Waite was sent by Leicester to kill
the villain who had defiled his bed; Blount repaid the
courtesy by prompting or conniving at Leicester's death.
Taught by Cardinal Allen, deep in the Jesuit plots, he
has more than once put his neck so near the block, that

a world which neither loves nor understands him hugs
itself in a belief that he must have bought his safety
from arrest and condemnation by selling to Walsingham
or Cecil the blood of better and braver men.

14. This bravo has subdued the imperious Countess of
Leicester to his will. She has been to him an easy, if not
an ignoble prey ; for the profligate woman dotes on her
tyrant ; so that she who could barely stoop to the kiss of
Devereux and Dudley, prides herself on the blessing of
being robbed and cuffed by a wretch without grace, accom-
plishments, or parts. When, for his private gain and the
promotion of his faith, it serves Blount's turn to win over
Essex the same brutal ascendency which he has established over Lady Leicester, he feels no pang of heart
in turning her tenderness as a mother into the abominable instrument of his guile. His bold, coarse arts are
soon successful with the giddy youth ; who draws closer
and closer to his mother's husband, puts him into places
of trust near his person, listens to his counsels, makes
associates of his male and female friends, gets him a command in the army, and gives him a seat in the House of
Commons.

Bacon and Blount propose to Essex the two courses
most opposed to each other : Bacon the abandonment of

14. Devereux, i. 281; Council Reg., Mar. 16, 1600. The frequent recurrence
of the Privy Council Register in these notes reminds me that I ought to express,
and in the warmest manner, my many obligations to Henry Reeve, Esq., of the
Privy Council Office. I owe to his ready and unvarying kindness an easy access to the sources of some of the most important facts in this volume.

IV. 14. his military pomp, of his opposition to the Queen, and the
—— acceptance now and forever of that great part which Lei-
1597. cester had filled for so many years ; Blount the pursuit of
Oct. war and glory, so as to dazzle the multitude, overawe the
Queen, find employments for his companions, and con-
solidate his personal power.   Bacon would make him
chief of the Protestant nation, Blount of a discontented
and disloyal Roman Catholic sect.   One asks him to be
grave, discreet, and self-denying.   The other fires his
blood with maddening and dramatic hopes.   He cleaves
to Blount, who tempts him with the things for which his
restless and evil nature pants.   He begins to toy with
treason.   He admits Roman Catholics of sullied reputation and suspected loyalty into his confidence.   He even
interferes to protect from justice the traitor Sir John
Smyth.

Oct. 24.   15. At the end of those four years for which Bacon
has compelled the Government to accept of subsidies, the
money being spent, writs for a new parliament go out.
Bacon now stands for Ipswich, the family county town
and the aim of his warmest ambition ; having for his
colleague in the representation Michael Stanhope, a
grand-nephew of Lady Ann.   His kinsmen muster strong
in Westminster.   Anthony sits for Oxford, Nathaniel for
Lynn ; Henry Neville, his sister's son, for Liskeard ; Sir
Edward Hoby, his cousin, for Rochester ; Sir Robert

15. Mem. of Stages of Bills in Parliament, Oct. 1597, S. P. O.; Willis, Not.
Parl., iii. 187, 139, 140, 141, 142; D'Ewes, 549; Townshend, 102.

Cecil, also his cousin, for Herts. Benedict Barnham, of Cheapside, whose pretty little daughter, Alice, Bacon will years hence make his wife, is returned for Yarmouth, having represented Minehead in the former Parliament. Raleigh sits for Dorsetshire ; and Christopher Yelverton, the Speaker nominate, for Northants. Sir Christopher Blount, by command from the Earl of Essex, serves for Staffordshire. In this new session the member for Ipswich sits, not, as Lord Campbell writes, a burgess prostrate, penitent, under the royal ban, anxious by his silence and servility to efface the recollection of his former speech. No voice is raised so often or so loud as his. Again he speaks for ample grants ; again he votes with the reforming squires ; again he wages battle of privilege against the Privy Council and the House of Lords. He serves on the Committee of Monopolies. He seconds Sir Francis Hastings's motion for amending the penal laws. But the great contest of this session, the one that makes it memorable in English history, is fought on a bill of his own, framed on the treason of Sir John Smyth, and meant to arrest the decay of tillage, the perishing of the yeomen population from the English soil.

16. Yelverton chosen Speaker, Bacon rises with a motion on the State of the Country. State of the

16. Summary Articles of the Bill for Maintenance of Husbandry, Oct. 1597, S. P. O.; D'Ewes 550 – 53; Bacon's History of the Reign of Henry VII., Works, vi. 94.

IV. 16.
—
1597.
Nov.
Country means to him the relation of the people to the land. The population lives on the soil. Mining is in its cradle, though the iron ordnance of Sussex and Arden has been heard on the Rhine and the Theiss; manufactures are few and scant, though the dyed wools of Tiverton and Dunster have begun to find markets on the Elbe and the Scheldt. To grow corn, to herd cattle, to brew ale and press cider, to shear sheep, to fell and carry wood, are the main occupations of every English shire. The farms are small and many; the farmers neither rich nor poor. The breeder of kine, the grower of herbs and wheat, is a yeoman born; not too proud to put hand to plough, not too pinched to keep horse and pike. A link between the noble and the peasant, he is of the very thew and marrow of the state; a man to stand at your shoulder in the day of work or in the day of fight. This sturdy class is dropping the plough for the weaver's shuttle and the tailor's goose; the rage for enclosing woods and commons, for impaling parks, for changing arable land into pasture, for turning holdings for life into tenancies at will, having driven thousands of yeomen from fields and downs which their fathers tilled before the Conqueror came in. Whole districts have been cleared. Where homesteads smoked and harvests once waved, there is now, in many parts, a broad green landscape, peopled by a shepherd and his dog. Where the maypole sprung, and the village green crowed with frolic, are now a sheep-walk or a park of deer.

17. The loss of this martial race, the bowmen of Cressy, the billmen of Boulogne, is a grievous weakness for the Crown; thinning the musters for defence, swelling the materials for mutinies and plots. Nor has this change escaped the Jesuits, or those who live to watch and thwart the Jesuits. A paper of instructions for the Roman Catholic priests and gentry, On the means of recovering England to the Holy See, lays stress on the discontent caused by these enclosures of commons and village greens. Smyth used this argument at Colchester. The Catholic peers have not been slow to increase an evil which their party treats as a means of future good to the Church. Dr. James, the Dean of Durham, has had to warn Burghley of the consequences of this waste of tillage and population in the two shires of Durham and Northumberland; shires in which two or three Roman Catholic earls own nearly all the soil. The yeomen have embraced the national faith, while most of the old nobility cling to the foreign creed; and a fanatic like Percy or Seymour may often find a legal form of persecution in the pretence of converting his arable land into pasture, or of forming a new park. But if this rage for enclosure is sometimes abused into a means of sectarian spite, it is very far from being confined to the Roman Catholic lords. From Durham to Devon the tenants are chased

17. Discourse of the Providence necessary to be had for the setting up of the Catholic Faith when God shall call the Queen out of this life, Aug. 1600, S. P. O.; Dr. James to Burghley, May 26, 1597, S. P. O.; Stillman to Cecil, Jan 2, 1600, S. P. O.

from their farms that sheep may feed and deer disport. Ire fills and inflames the yeomen's veins. In every park wall they see a menace, in every doe the substitute of a man. They throw down the pales and ensnare the deer. A youth of Stratford-upon-Avon kills his buck in Charlcote Park. A crowd from Enfield scours the preserves of Hatfield Chace. Every spark becomes his own Robin Hood, and cheap haunches of venison smoke on the tables of Cheapside and Paternoster Row. To snare deer is, in all the popular comedies and songs, an heroic protest, not at all a crime.

18. Unlike the Jesuits and the Jesuitized peers, whose purpose it may be to thin the fibre and relax the power of England in the field, Bacon seeks to arrest this evil in its germ. Placed by his birth between the nobles and the commons, he shares neither the pride of the superior nor the envy of the inferior rank. His genius, too, is singularly free from taint of sect or class. He is wholly English. His glory is to reconcile classes through reform, to strengthen the Crown by justice. Concord, tolerance, loyalty at home; sway, extension, trade abroad,—these are the points at which he aims. Not so the Jesuits. They have begun to despair of aid from Spain; after the wreck of the Armada, the sack of Cadiz, they fear lest England may be found too strong for subjection to Rome by either foreign guile or for-

18. Discourse of Providence necessary to be had for the setting up of the Catholic Faith, Aug. 1600, S. P. O.

eign steel. They turn their eyes, therefore, to the men with sore hearts and brawny arms, and, taking note of the discontent among the yeomen, begin to count with confidence on the approaching days of civil war.

19. Bacon's plan for staying the decline of population is to convert this new grass-land into arable, to put these new parks under the plough. A committee of the House of Commons, named to consider this plan, votes in its favor, when the House commissions its author to frame and introduce his bill. He brings in two bills: one for the Increase of Tillage and Husbandry; one for the Increase of People. These bills provide that the more land shall be cleared without special reason and a special license. They provide that all land turned into pasture since the Queen's accession, no less a period than forty years, shall be taken from the deer and sheep within eighteen months, and restored to the yeoman and the plough.

20. If the Commons pass these bills at once, the Peers receive them with amazement. Ask the Shrewsburys, Worcesters, and Northumberlands to dispark their chases and restore the plough! As well ask Regan for the hundred knights. At once they name a committee of Peers to oppose the two bills; which committee calls

19. Summary Articles of the Bill for Maintenance of Husbandry, Oct. 1597, S. P. O.; Breviate of a Bill entitled " An Act for the Increase of People for the Service and Defence of the Realm," Dec. 20, 1597, S. P. O.
20. Lords' Jour., ii. 212, 217.

IV. 20. to its aid the legal dexterity of Chief Justice Popham
——   and Attorney-General Coke.
1597.

Dec.   21. Though the foreign enemy is at the gate and
every true man at his post, Vere in the Low Countries,
Raleigh and Montjoy at Plymouth, Essex still sulks and
pouts at Wanstead. In vain the Lord-Treasurer coaxes.
In vain the Earl's friends remonstrate with him on the
wickedness of dividing or distracting his country at such
a time. In vain they beg him to put aside his wrongs,
if he has any wrongs, until the danger of a fresh invasion from Spain, of a fresh massacre in Ireland, shall
have passed away. The Queen declares herself hurt
more by this desertion than by his failures when at sea.
But nothing moves him until Bacon's patriotic bills come
up before the Peers, when he hastens to town, and,
receiving the nomination of Earl Marshal, takes his seat
in the House of Lords. As he had not been named to
the hostile committee, he begs that his name may be
added to the list.

For this committee Coke draws up thirty-one legal
objections to Bacon's bills. Thus armed to contest his
logic and deny his law, the Peers send Black Rod down
to request a conference with the Lower House.

22. Aware of these hostile preparations in the other

21. Burghley to Essex, Nov. 9, 19, 30, 1597, S. P. O.; Remonstrance with
Essex, Nov. 16, 1597, S. P. O.; Howard, Montjoy, and Raleigh to the Council,
Nov. 9, 1597, S P. O.; Hunsdon to Essex, Nov. 1597, S. P. O.
22. Lords' Jour., ii. 217; Statutes 39 Elizabethæ, c. 1 and 2.

House, the Commons, ere entering into conference, wish
to have a copy of Coke's thirty-one legal objections to
their bills. The Lords refuse to give it. But Bacon,
will not bend ; if the Commons are to meet objections,
they must know what these objections are. No copy, no
conference ! After much debate the Peers consent to
give their written answer to the bills when the gentlemen of the Commons shall come up to confer.

Conference now meets, the burgesses employing Bacon
as their champion, the barons employing Coke. After
day on day of talk, after many proposals and some
amendments, Coke gives way, and the worsted Peers
accept the two bills with some slight modifications of
title and clause.

The bills did not pass, says Lord Campbell.

They are in the Statute Book, 39 of Elizabeth, 1
and 2.

23. No love for enclosures which thin her hamlets of
their strength prevents the Queen from receiving most
graciously and rewarding most nobly this momentous
service to her crown. Bacon knows her well. A law
case having been referred to some of the judges and
counsel, she inquires his mind on the course she is pur-
suing. "Madam," says he, "my mind is known; I am
against all enclosures, and especially against enclosed
justice." Only two weeks after signing her name to his
bill for replacing the yeoman on the soil from which

IV. 22.
——
1598.
Jan.

.

Feb.

Feb. 27.

23. Resuscitatio, 40; Patent Rolls, 40 Elizabethæ, Pars iii. 26.

he has been driven, she sets her hand to the grant of a third estate. This act of her princely grace confers on Bacon the rectory and church at Cheltenham, together with the chapel at Charlton Kings, in the lovely valley nestling under Cleve and Leckhampton hills; a valley not yet famed for those mineral springs, those shady walks, those pretty spas and gardens, which in the days of Victoria have transformed Lansdowne and Pittville into suburbs of delight; yet rich in the voluptuous charms of nature, blessed with a prodigal fertility of corn and fruit, of kine and sheep. The rectory, the chapelry, are noble gifts. With them are granted all the land, houses, meadows, pastures, gardens, rents,— all services, — all views of frankpledge, courts leet, fines, heriots, mortuaries, and reliefs, — all tithes of fruit and grain, — all profits, all royalties, — save only the usual crown rights reserved on crown lands, with a fee to the Archdeacon of Gloucester, and an obligation to support two priests and two deacons, — on the payment of a nominal rent of seventy-five pounds a year.

CHAPTER V.

THE IRISH PLOT.

1. UNDER the eyes of Blount, Essex parts more and more from the good cause and from those who love it. His horses are not now seen in Gray's Inn Square. The correspondence with Anthony Bacon drops. The barges which float to Essex stairs bring other company than the Veres and Raleighs, the Cecils, Nottinghams, and Greys. To sup with bold, bad men; to listen when he ought to strike; to waste his manhood on the frail Southwells and Howards, have become the feverish habits of his life. Sir Charles Danvers, Sir Charles and Sir Jocelyn Percy, Sir William Constable, Captain John Lee, — all discontented and disloyal Roman Catholics, — are now his household and familiar friends. The young apostate Lord Monteagle sits at his board; though merely, as is guessed from what comes after, in the shameful character of Cecil's tool and spy. But in the rear of Danvers and Percy, Constable and Lee, wicked and dangerous as these men are, lurks a crowd of ruf-

V. 1.
——
1598.
Sept.

1. Lodge's Illustrations, ii. 545; Devereux, i. 475; Birch's Memoirs of Queen Elizabeth, ii. 70; Vaughan to Cecil, Jan. 29, 1598, S. P. O.; Vaughan to Hesketh, Jan. 29, 1598, S. P. O.; Council Reg., Mar. 16, 1600.

fians at whose side they seem respectable. Tresham is seen at Essex House. Catesby sits at the Earl's table. All the slums and jails of London stir with a new life. As a Privy Councillor, Essex can send into the prisons and fetch their inmates to his private house. Light breaks into the cells of Bridewell and the Fleet. Sir John Smyth is liberated on bond, Essex himself coming forward as the traitor's friend and surety. Father Thomas Wright, a Jesuit agent, deep in the secrets, high in the confidence, of the Courts of Rome and Madrid, who has been for many months in trouble, at first confined in Dean Goodman's house, but of late transferred to a common jail, steals after dusk from the Bridewell to Essex House for secret interviews with the Earl and Blount. Nor is the bustle limited to the London taverns and the London jails. The cloughs of Lancashire, the ridges and heaths of Wales, send up to London the most restless of their recusants and priests. Vaughan, the Bishop of Chester, notes a mysterious change in that Papist district, and warns the head of the Government that he must look for sudden storms. The recusants of his diocese, he says, refuse to pay their usual fines, defy the clergy and magistrates, and talk of the support which they expect from new and powerful friends. When pressed too hard, instead of bowing to the laws as they have been wont to do, they jump to horse and spur away.

2. The gang of Papist conspirators who now begin

to gather into force round the Earl of Essex, propose
to .themselves not only to escape from fine and imprisonment, but to dethrone the Queen, to restore the
faggot to Smithfield and the mass to St. Paul's. They
hope to effect this change by a military surprise and
a secret understanding with the Pope. Essex tells the
Jesuit Father Wright, in their midnight meetings, that
he could become a Roman Catholic, were it not that
the Roman Catholics have always been against him.
Wright assures him that the Roman Catholics will
now be his best friends. The plotters lay down their
plans. To surprise the Queen they must have the command of an armed force ; Raleigh must be killed ; a
military faction formed, an army raised, and the places
of trust secured to the principal leaders in the plot.

3. As the Queen will trust Essex with no more regiments for Rouen, no more ships for Spain, he begs for
a command against the Irish kernes. Ireland is ablaze.
That Hugh O'Neile, son of the bastard of Dundalk,
who owes to the policy and generosity of Queen Elizabeth his life, his education, his nobility, even his ascendency in his sept, has turned on his benefactress: laying down his earldom of Tyrone ; assuming the sovereign and rebellious style of The O'Neile ; raising the
unkempt, unclothed Ulster savages ; and filling the val-

---

2. Examination of Thomas Wright, July 24, 1600, S. P. O.; Abstract of Evidence against the Earl of Essex [July 22, 1600], S. P. O.

3. Irish Correspondence, 1595 – 98, S. P. O.; Annals of the Four Masters,
591 - 645; Council Reg , Oct. 29, 1595, July 19, 1598.

leys from Inishowen to Monaghan and Down with the tumult of war. Fires burn on the hill-tops. Churches are profaned, innocent homesteads razed. The Gallo-glass, mounted on his brisk marron, pricks through the country, spearing his enemies, driving off their kine. A horde of ferocious kernes, shaggy and ill-fed, their arms a skean and pike, their dress a blanket or a shirt, plunge into the houses of English gentlemen, wreaking such woe and shame on the Protestant settlers as pen of man refuses to describe. An English force keeps front to the rebellious horde, but the fire darts out in a hundred places. Connaught kindles into insurrection ; Munster defies the Saxon ; Ulster presses on the Pale ; Spanish ships stand off the coast ; Spanish regiments are forming at Ghent and at the Groyne. A day may bring the Basques, the Walloons, and Pandours to Kin-sale. Drogheda is in danger. Dublin itself is not safe.

4. Shakespeare gives the English passion voice : —

> " Now for our Irish wars !
> We must supplant these rough, rug-headed kernes,
> Which live like venom where no venom else,
> But only they, hath privilege to live ! "

So cries the English king in that new play of Rich-ard the Second, which is now drawing crowds of citi-zens and courtiers to the Globe. Troops are being

---

4. Shakespeare's Richard II., editions of 1597 and 1598; Camden, Ann. Eliz., 1598; Chamberlain to Carleton, May 4, 17, 30, 1598, S. P. O.; Council Reg., July 19, Dec. 22, 1598.

raised and fines imposed for this new war ; the recusants
who will not fight for their country against their creed,
— such men as Tresham, Talbot, Rookwood, and Throckmorton, — being mulcted in heavy rates. The force is
of imposing strength. Two thousand veterans come
home from the camp of Vere, their ranks filled up by
a levy of youngsters from the loom and plough. In
all, some twenty thousand horse and foot are on the
march.

Who shall conduct them to the coasts of Down, the
passes of the Foyle ?

5. Essex asserts his claim. Those who would see
the fire of the insurrection stamped under foot propose to
send out Raleigh, Sydney, or Montjoy. But events at
Court disturb the preparations against O'Neile. The
great Lord Burghley dies, leaving vacant the Treasury
and the Court of Wards. Essex, as usual, wants them
both; and Cecil, who thinks that offices held by his
father ought to descend upon himself, becomes, as he
has been before, a secret and powerful advocate for his
rival's nomination to a distant post. For a time the
Queen will hear of no such a thing ; yet, as Raleigh
will not go, and Vere is in the field, Essex, with an
underground and treacherous aid from Cecil, gains his
suit.

5. Chamberlain to Carleton, May 30, Aug. 30, Nov. 8, 1598, S. P. O.; Lytton to Carleton, Aug. 29, 1598, S. P. O.; Mathews to Carleton, Sept. 15, 1598,
S. P. O.

V. 6.
———
1598.
Oct.

6. Cecil's beautiful young niece still wears her widow's weeds: a prize with which he may either bribe an enemy or fix a friend. She has rejected Pembroke as well as Bacon. To the surprise of her gay and youthful suitors, she allows her uncle Cecil to buy with her hand the unscrupulous arts and venomous tongue of Coke. A first wife, who brought him love and money, not yet cold in her grave, the grisly old bear of an Attorney-General marries this dainty and wilful dame. How she is persuaded to such a match no soul can tell. Old, grim, penurious, every way opposite to herself and to everything that she seems to like, he has neither the wit that wins nor the fame that fills a lady's ear. Wags whisper that she hopes to be able to break his heart. He, too, is rich. She has got one fortune through Sir William Hatton, why not a second fortune through Sir Edward Coke ? Her kinsman's motives are, no one doubts, coarse. He has need for such an instrument as Coke, — close, supple, learned, grinding, cold to his dependants, cringing to his superiors. Nor is he disappointed in the match. On Coke's marriage into the Cecil house, though the wife whom he vows to love rejects his name and destroys his peace, he becomes to Cecil and to Cecil's faction a brutal and obsequious slave.

7. At a private meeting of the Privy Council held at

6. Autobiographical Notes of Coke in Harl. MSS. 6687, transcribed by John Bruce for the Collectanea Top. et Gen., vi. 108.

Essex House, only Cecil, Fortescue, and Buckhurst present, a commission for the lord-lieutenancy is drawn. Essex has had no speech with Bacon for eighteen months.
Their ways now lie apart. In the conferences on his
bills for restoring tillage and increasing population they
stood in hostile ranks; yet, on the eve of his fatal voyage to Ireland, Essex rides once more, and for the last
time now, to Gray's Inn Square. Had he come to seek
counsel, no man could have given him safer. More than
any one alive — more than Chichester or Montjoy —
Bacon sees through the Irish question. Sure that Ulster
will not be calmed by the sword and the rope, that no
dash from Cork to Coleraine will make a savage sept,
ruled by a Brehon law, prefer husbandry to theft, his
plan is to clear the forests, to drain the bogs, to lay out
roads, to build ports and havens, to plant new towns.
His hope lies in the plough, not in the sword.

> "We must supplant these rough, rug-headed kernes."

He would have the great officers of the Queen's government and army live in the country, build in it their
houses, as Sir Arthur Chichester, whom Cecil has sent
from Flanders to Dublin, afterwards builds his house on
the Lough of Belfast. But a man like the Earl of Essex,
living only in the air of courts and the light of camps,
has neither temper, hardihood, nor patience for such a

---

7. Council Reg., Mar. 8, 1599; Bacon's Remains, 89, 48; Certain Considerations touching the Plantation in Ireland, 1606; Bacon's Apologie, 23; Essex to
Cecil, Mar. 29, 1599, Add. MSS. 4160.

work.　Bacon tells him to give up an enterprise in which he can neither serve his country nor secure himself from shame and loss.　Essex has not come to learn.　With soul corrupted by disloyalty, he turns his back on the one honest voice which even yet might have saved his fortune and his fame from wreck. ·

8. Father Wright consults Cresswell and Parsons, the experienced chiefs of the English conspiracy in Madrid and Rome, on these bold and perilous plots.　The Jesuit Fathers, doubtful if it be not sin and folly to shed Catholic blood to raise Essex to a throne, urge him through Wright to adopt the Infanta's claim in preference to his own ; a course to which Essex, when pressed by Wright, most sternly demurs, as becomes a descendant of John of Gaunt.　Philip and Clement, less deep in guile than the Jesuits, agree to recognize, and if need be to aid, a rebellion of the Earl and his partisans against the Queen, on this understanding, — that Essex, when king, shall become reconciled to the Church, shall leave Ireland to be ruled by O'Neile as viceroy, shall abandon the Protestant Netherlanders, shall yield up Raleigh's conquests and plantations in America, and shall recognize the rights of Spain to an exclusive possession of both the Indies.　It is understood that the Irish army is to effect this plot, of which all the details are to be settled with O'Neile.

8. Abstract of the Evidence against Essex [July 22, 1600], S. P. O.; Examination of Wright, July 24, 1600, S. P. O.

9. Twenty thousand men march to the coast and cross the sea. Lee, Danvers, Percy have all commands in this force. Constable, broken for bad conduct, is restored by Essex to his rank. Father Wright begs hard to be taken with them; but, although a Privy Councillor may fetch a prisoner to his house, a lord-lieutenant of Ireland has no power to empty the London jails. All that he can do for Wright is to get him removed from Bridewell to the Clink.

From the hour of his quitting Whitehall Essex assumes the powers of a sovereign prince. On his way to the coast he sends back Lord Montjoy. Montjoy is his friend; the yet nearer friend of his sister, Lady Rich. For love of her, Montjoy has joined in opposition to Raleigh on the right hand, to Cecil on the left; but neither friendship for Essex, nor love for Lady Rich, would draw a man so firm in faith, so loyal to the Crown, to league with a gang of Papists against the Queen. Essex sends him back.

From Drayton Bassett, where Blount and Lady Leicester live, Essex has the effrontery to write for leave to appoint Blount his Marshal of the Camp. A marshal of the camp is the second in command, the first in activity and influence; to put such a fellow as Blount in such a place, the Queen indignantly demurs. There is Sir Henry Brounker, an officer of talent and experience; let him be our marshal. Essex pouts and sulks. "If she grant me not this favor," he writes to Cecil, "I am maimed

9. Council Reg., Mar. 11, April 2, 1599; Essex to Cecil, Add. MSS. 4160; Abstract of Evidence against Essex, July 22, 1600, S. P. O.

V. 9.
———
1599.

of my right arm." Cecil takes care he shall have his way.

May. 10. When he lands in Dublin he casts to the four winds his commission and instructions. One of his first and most insolent acts is to appoint the young Earl of Southampton his Master of the Horse. This friend and patron of Shakespeare is not a Papist, not an ally of Blount. He is a patriot, though not a wise one; a Protestant, though not a zealous one. Heady, amorous, quarrelsome, swift to go right or wrong as his passions tempt him, he has vexed and grieved the Queen by falling madly and licentiously in love with Mistress Vernon, one of her beautiful maids of honor, and filling her court with the fame of his amours. In this offence against modesty he has been abetted by the young lady's first cousin Lord Essex, himself too frail as regards the passions, and too familiar with his mother's vices and his sister's infidelities to feel the shame brought on his kin by a scandal which after all may end in marriage. Sent away from London, Southampton had returned in secret, and had married the lady without her sovereign's knowledge. For these offences he had been ordered into free custody. Breaking his gage of honor, he has stolen away to Dublin, where the Earl, in place of sending back the Queen's fugitive, gives him the welcome which a prince at

10. Cecil to Southampton, Sept. 3, 1598, S. P. O.; Council to Essex, June 10, 1599, S. P. O.; Elizabeth to Essex, July 19, 1599, S. P. O.; Devereux, i. 474.

war might give to a deserting general from the hostile camp.

11. Every one knows the issue of this Irish campaign : a lost summer, a corrupted army, a traitorous truce. Instead of smiting O'Neile, Lee arranges an interview on the Lagan, at which the English and Irish rebels discuss their terms and enter into league. Blount hails his fellows in the Celtic camp. Like the Irish traitors, he abhors the Protestant Queen, not only as the most powerful enemy of their church, but as an insolent sovereign who has spared their lives. They propose to carry out the Papal scheme, giving England to Essex, Ireland to O'Neile, The Desmonds and Fitzmaurices, not less than the O'Donnels and O'Kanes, are privy to a league in which the Celts drive a bargain with their allies ; for while the Roman Catholics are to get the whole of Ireland to themselves, they claim immunities in England equal to those of the rival creed. They are to enjoy on the Thames, not alone freedom of conscience, but street processions of the host and public performance of the mass.

12. Essex breaks up his camp at Drogheda ; hurries to Dublin, Blount at his side, Danvers, Constable, Lee

11. Annals of the Four Masters, 646 – 654; Blount's Confessions, State Trials, i. 1415.

12. Annals of the Four Masters, 655; Blount's Confessions, State Trials, i. 1415; Bacon's Notes to Camden, Works, vi. 359; Memorandum of Precautionary Measures, Aug. 1599, S. P. O.; List of Army in Kent and Essex, Aug. 1599, S. P. O.

V. 12.

1599.
Sept. at his heels; crosses the sea, leaving Ireland without an army or a government; the English settlers aghast at this desertion, the Ulster rebels elate with joy. At Milford Haven they receive intelligence which breaks down all their plans. The country rings with arms. While they have been conspiring with O'Neile, the Privy Council, under guise of preparing to repel an expected landing of the Spaniards, have drawn out the musters, set the trainbands in motion, filled the city with chosen troops. Wags have mocked and jested over this invisible Armada; but Essex lands at Milford Haven to find his road to London barred by a truly formidable force. Nottingham covers the capital with a camp of six thousand horse and foot. Twenty-five thousand men answer to the roll in Kent and Essex. Under such a change of affairs, even Blount dissuades a march on London. The road is long; halberdiers cannot fly, like Imogen, on the wings of love; and the very maddest of the plotters knows that the Protestant gentlemen of Gloucester, Wilts, and Berks will not stare idly on while gangs of mutinous troopers, led by Papist captains, march past to dethrone their Queen. With the whole army of Drogheda at their backs, they could not force their way through six or eight warlike shires. Better, says Blount, prick on alone. A chance remains that by dash and swiftness Essex may surprise the Queen, put his friends in power, and return to Dublin to mature his plans.

Sept. 28. To horse, to horse! No pause in the ride till he flings himself, splashed and faint, at his sovereign's feet.

13. Lee, Danvers, Constable, Davis, spur into London.
News-writers stare at the swarms of captains and com-
manders from the Irish camp which suddenly hustle
through the taverns of Paternoster Row and fill the pit
of the theatre, where Rutland and Southampton are
daily seen, and where Shakespeare's company, in the
great play of Richard II., have for more than a year
been feeding the public eye with pictures of the deposition of kings. But the plotters have met their
mates. The Earl is in charge. From the presence of
his Queen he has passed into custody; when a solemn
act of the Privy Council having declared him unfit to
discharge the duties of Earl Marshal, Privy Councillor,
and Master of the Ordnance, a writ from the Star-Cham-
ber cites him to answer for his suspicious dealings with
O'Neile. This citation he disobeys. After a brief confinement in the house of Lord Keeper Egerton, he is
placed in permanent free custody in his own great mansion in the Strand.

14. The Council hastens to repair the evil done in
Dublin. Montjoy goes over as Lord Deputy. Stern
letters recall the Lords Justices and magistrates of Ireland to their duty. Threads of the great conspir-

13. Rowland White, Oct. 8, 11, 1599, in Sydney Papers, ii. 130, 132; Devereux's Lives of the Earls of Essex, ii. 76 – 117; Speeches in the Star Chamber
on Essex's Expedition to Ireland, Nov. 1599, S. P. O.; Essex to Eliz., Feb. 11,
22, 1600, S. P. O.
14. Wood's Confessions, Jan. 20, 1599 – 1600, S. P. O.; Council Reg., Feb. 2,
1600.

V. 14. acy soon appear. Among the witnesses against Essex,
——   Thomas Wood, a nephew of Lord Fitzmaurice, makes
1600.
Feb.   this declaration : —

He saith that, happening to be with the Lord Fitzmaurice, Baron of Lixnaw, at his house of Lixnaw, between Michaelmas and Allhallowtide, the said Baron
walking abroad with the said Wood asked him what force
the Earl of Essex was of in England. He answered he
could not tell, but said he was well beloved of the com-
monalty. Then said the Baron that the Earl was gone
for England, and had discharged many of the companies
of Ireland ; and that if her Majesty were dead he should
be King of England and O'Neile to be Viceroy of Ireland ;
and whensoever he should have occasion and could send
for them, he would send him eight thousand men out of
Ireland. The said Wood asked the Baron how he knew
that, and he answered that the Earl of Desmond sent him
word so.

THOMAS WOOD.

This statement, wholly in the handwriting of Wood, remains in the State Paper Office.

Below it Cecil has written : —

This confession and declaration was made before us
whose names are underwritten this 20th of January, 1599
(1600) ; and after being charged of us severally and
jointly to declare nothing but truth upon his soul and

conscience, as he would answer it at the latter day, he V. 14.
hath both protested this to be true that he hath written,
and that he is a Christian and would not say an untruth 1600.
in this kind for all the good in the world ; and for proof Feb.
thereof hath again set his hand in our presence.

THOMAS WOOD.

T. BUCKHURST.
NOTTINGHAM.
ROBERT CECIL.
J. FORTESCUE.

15. The world parts suddenly from the fallen man. March.
Those who know or suspect the depth of his guilt shun
him as one who is lost past hope ; those who see no more
than his disgrace fall off from a losing cause. Cecil
spurns his advances ; when the old Countess of Leicester
begs of him to save her son, Cecil answers her that his
fate is with a higher power. Babington, Bishop of Worcester, glances at him cautiously in a Court sermon ; but
when sent for by the angry Queen he denies that he
pointed to the Earl. Save his cousin, Lady Scrope, and
his sisters, Lady Rich and the Countess of Northumberland, not one of his confederates or companions dares to
speak for him a word. Blount slinks with his wife to
Drayton Bassett. Southampton goes abroad to fight
Lord Gray, breaking his parole for the second time ; an

<hr>

15. Chamberlain to Carleton, Feb. 22, Mar. 5, 1600, S. P. O.; Cecil to Countess of Leicester, Mar. 21, 1600, S. P. O.; Sydney Papers, ii. 132, 213; Council
Reg., Aug. 3, 17, 1600.

V. 15. offence for which the council, though loath to strike the
amiable and misled young gentleman, strips him of his
1600.
March. company of horse. Lee makes no sign. Danvers and
Constable hide their heads. These Bobadils of Drogheda
and Milford skulk about the kens of Newgate Street and
Carter Lane; and only a group of women, kin to the
Queen, who gloom about the court in black, find courage
for even tears and weeds.

Yea; there is one. In this dead silence of despair,
one voice alone dares to breath the Earl's name, to
whisper in the royal ear excuses for his fault, to plead
with that leonine heart for the mercy which becomes
a monarch better than his crown.

April. 16. Any man save Francis Bacon would have left the
Earl to his fate. The connection has been to him waste
of character and waste of time. The hope of making
Essex chief of the national party has come to naught
and their intercourse has ceased. To Bacon, and to
all his kin, the Earl has brought anxiety, grief, and
shame. The loss of rank and power is the least part
of his loss; that loving and beloved brother, to whom
the Essays are so tenderly inscribed, has now sunk
past hope, the victim of his companion's riot and evil
ways. Despite the warnings of the Saint of God, though
Anthony and Essex had both promised her to amend
their ways, they have run from bad to worse, until one

16. Lady Bacon to Anthony Bacon, various dates, in Lambeth MSS. 649,
650; Devereux, i. 406.

is about to sink into political crime, the other into a premature grave.

V. 16.

——

1600.

June.

17. The prospects, the affections of Bacon and Essex now lie apart, distant as the temperate and the torrid zones. For two whole years they have met but once; to part less near in opinions than before. All that Bacon foresaw from the Irish expedition has come to pass. The voyage has failed. More than the visible failure Bacon does not know; nothing of the interviews with Wright; nothing of the understanding with the Jesuits; nothing of the Pope's approval; nothing of the compact with O'Neile. Cecil keeps these formidable secrets close, sharing them, if with any one, only with his creature and dependant Coke. In other business of the Crown, in admiralty affairs, revenue affairs, in debts, in grants, and fines, above all in arbitrations, Bacon is now constantly employed by the Crown. Instructions from the Privy Council run to Yelverton, Coke, Fleming, and Bacon. In cases of dispute, as in those of Blundel, of Perrim, of Trachey, he is often employed alone. But in taking the confessions, in confronting the spies and prisoners of the Irish plot, he has no share. Yet, knowing no more of it than all men know, why should he risk his future to save a man who has covered him with misfortunes, who has sought his advice to cast it in his teeth?

17. Council to Yelverton, Coke, Fleming, and Bacon, Nov. 9, 1600, S. P. O.; Council Reg., Feb. 2, 28, July 6, Sept. 29, Dec. 24, 1600.

18. Bacon is not the man to ask. Seeing the Earl crushed without being charged, supposing him free from crime, he carries his plea of clemency to the throne. Often in the Queen's closet on public duty, he seizes every opening for this plea. Never had such an offender such an advocate. Gayly, gravely, in speech, in song, he besets the royal ear. He kneels to her Majesty at Nonesuch; he coaxes her at Twickenham Park. When she ferries to his lodge, he presents her with a sonnet on mercy; when she calls him to the palace, he reads to her letters purporting to come from the penitent Earl. What Babington dares not hint from the pulpit, Bacon dares to urge in the private chamber. Wit, eloquence, persuasion of the rarest power, he lavishes on this ungrateful cause. At times the Queen seems shaken in her mood; but she knows her kinsman better than his advocate knows him. Spain still threatens a descent; and Ireland rocks with the tumult of civil war. Those scenes of Shakespeare's play disturb her dreams. This play has had a long and splendid run, not less from its glorious agony of dramatic passion than from the open countenance lent to it by the Earl, who, before his voyage, was a constant auditor at the Globe, and by his noble companions Rutland and Southampton. The great parliamentary scene, the deposition of Richard, not in the printed book, was probably not in the early play; yet the

18. Abstract of Evidence against Essex, July 22, 1600, S. P. O.; Shakespeare's Richard II., editions of 1598 and 1608.

representation of a royal murder and a successful usur- pation on the public stage is an event to be applied by the groundlings in a pernicious and disloyal sense. Tongues whisper to the Queen that this play is part of a great plot, to teach her subjects how to murder kings. They tell her she is Richard; Essex, Boling- broke. These warnings sink into her soul. When Lambard, Keeper of the Records, waits upon her at the palace, she exclaims to him, " I am Richard, know you not that ? "

19. Nor does the play by Shakespeare stand alone. One of the Earl's friends publishes on this story of the deposition of Richard a singular and mendacious tract, which, under ancient names and dates, gives a false and disloyal account of things and persons in his own age: the childless sovereign; the association of defence; the heavy burden of taxation ; the levy of double subsidies ; the prosecution of an Irish war, ending in general dis- content ; the outbreak of blood; the solemn deposition and final murder of the prince. The book has no name on the title-page, — that of John Hayward signs the ded- ication. Bolingbroke is made the hero of the tale ; and, that even the grossly stupid may not miss its meaning, this lump of sedition is dedicated to the Earl. In one place it openly affirms the existence of a title to the throne superior to that of the Queen !

19. Hayward's First Part of the Life of Henry IV., 1599; Papers concerning the History of Henry IV., the Letter Apologetical written by Dr. Hayward, 1599, S. P. O.

V. 20.   20. This proves too much for Elizabeth. Packing the
——   scribe in jail, she sends for Bacon to draw up articles
1600.   against him.
June.

Had she sent for Coke!

To Bacon's tenderness of human life the poor scribbler,
Hayward, owes his subsequent length of days and authorship of other books. "There is treason in it," says the
Queen; as indeed there is. "Treason, your Grace?"
replies Bacon; "not treason, Madam, but felony, much
felony." "Ha!" gasps her Highness, willing to hang a
rogue for one crime as for another; "felony, — where?"
"Where, Madam? Everywhere, — the whole book is a
theft from Cornelius Tacitus." A light of laughter breaks
the cloud. "But," says her darkening Highness, "Hayward is a fool; some one else has writ the book; make
him confess it; put him to the rack."

"Nay, Madam," pleads the advocate of mercy; "rack
not his body, — rack his style. Give him paper and pens,
with help of books; bid him carry on his tale. By comparing the two parts, I will tell you if he be the true
man."

July.   21. Aware how strong are Bacon's views on political
crime, some of the conspirators, conscious of their own
guilty thoughts, dread lest in these frequent passages with
the Queen he may be taking part against their lord.

20. Bacon's Apologie, 36; Bacon's Remains, 42; Matters wherewith Dr. Hayward was charged, and Dr. Hayward's Confession, 1599, S. P. O.
21. Bacon's Apologie, 47; Birch, 459; Montagu, xii. 168.

Fear gives suspicion wing. Among themselves they whisper that in the royal presence he has pronounced the offence treason. The true offence *is* treason ; but Bacon has not called it such, for he has no knowledge of its darker facts. He therefore meets and spurns the misrepresentation of his words. In a note to Lord Henry Howard, one of the Roman Catholic friends of Essex, he writes with honest heat: "I thank God my wit serveth me not to deliver any opinion to the Queen which my stomach serveth me not to maintain ; one and the same conscience guiding and fortifying me. The untruth of this fable God and my sovereign can witness, and there I leave it. . . . . For my Lord of Essex, I am not servile to him, having regard to my superior duty. I have been much bound unto him ; on the other side, I have spent more time and more thoughts about his well-doing than ever I did about mine own. I pray God you his friends amongst you be in the right."

22. Affairs grow brighter for the Earl. Good news come in from Dublin and the Hague ; news that Desmond has been taken, and Wexford pacified by Montjoy ; that Vere and Nassau have fought a battle and gained a victory on Nieuport sands. The Queen's heart opens. When the Earl now begs for freedom, she more than ever inclines to hear his prayer. Cecil gets alarmed ; put-

22. Essex to Eliz., June 21, 1600, S. P. O.; Chamberlain to Carleton, July 1, 26, 1600, S. P. O.; Confession of D. Hayward, July 11, 1600, S. P. O.; Abstract of Evidence against Essex, July 22, 1600; Examination of Thomas Wright, July 24, 1600, S. P. O.; Bacon's Apologie, 41, 57.

ting Wright and Hayward under stern examination, he frames from their confessions an indictment against Essex, which, if half of it were proved, would assuredly send him to the block.   But an advocate, stronger than Cecil, stands beside the Queen ; who, in season, as well as out of season, in the midst of a dispute on law, in the turn of an anecdote, in a casual laugh or sigh, searches and finds a way to her heart.   One day she asks him about his brother's gout.   Anthony's gout is sometimes better, sometimes worse.   "I tell you how it is, Bacon," says her sagacious Majesty ; "these physicians give you the same physic to draw and to cure ; so they first do you good, and then do you harm."   "Good God, Madam !" cries Bacon, "how wisely you speak of physic to the body ! consider of physic to the mind.   In the case of my Lord of Essex, your princely word is, that you mean to reform his mind, not to ruin his fortune.   Have you not drawn the humor ?   Is it not time to apply the cure ? "   Another day she tells him the Earl has written to her most dutifully, that she felt moved by his protestations ; but that, when she came to the end, it was all to procure from her a patent of sweet wines !   "How your Majesty construes ! " says Bacon ; " as if duty and desire could not stand together ! Iron clings to the loadstone from its nature.   A vine creeps to the pole that it may twine."   " Speak to your business," says the Queen ; speak for yourself : for the Earl not a word."

Yet drop by drop the daily oil softens her heart.   At

length the Earl is set at large; though as one to whom V. 22.
much has been pardoned; one who shall never again
command armies, or even approach the Court. Eliza- 1600.
July.
beth will see her kinsman's face no more. Shall he go
back to the Irish camp? "When I send Essex back
into Ireland," says the Queen, "I will marry you, —
you, Mr. Bacon. Claim it of me."

CHAPTER VI.

THE STREET FIGHT.

1. WHEN free to plot, Essex, in the secrecy of his own house, and in open breach of loyalty and honor, renews the intrigue with Rome. Blount returns from Drayton Basset to crowd Barns Elms and Essex House, the Earl's head-quarters in and near London, with the most desperate of his Papist gangs. Mad at their loss of time, they propose to do without an army what they failed to do with one. Enough, they say, to raise a troop, to kill Raleigh and Nottingham, to seize the Queen by force, and summon a Parliament of their own. Essex shall be swept to the throne by a street fight and an act of assassination. Yet, if they still pretend to believe him more popular than Elizabeth, they dare not trust his chances and their own safety to an English crowd. Seeking to gain strength elsewhere, they open a deceptive intercourse with James, incite O'Neile to resist by promises of speedy help, raise a band of their sturdy partisans in Wales. One Englishman holding office, Sheriff Smith, of London, prob-

---

1. Nottingham to Montjoy, Goodman, ii. 14; Jardine's Criminal Trials, i. 842; Chamberlain to Carleton, Oct. 10, 1600, S. P. O.

ably a Roman Catholic, alone listens to their schemes. The Earls of Rutland and Southampton sit at the board; Rutland bound, like Southampton, by a pair of bright eyes to follow the Earl's fortunes, being deeply in love with Elizabeth Sydney, daughter of Lady Essex by her first husband Sir Philip; neither of them sharing his insane ambition or suspecting his murderous thoughts. The partners of his secret soul are those Papists, old and new, who have been and will be the terror and shame of England for twenty years. Blount and Danvers, Davis, Percy, and Monteagle are not the worst. From kens like the Hart's Horn and the Shipwreck Tavern, haunts of the vilest refuse of a great city, the spawn of hells and stews, the vomit of Italian cloisters and Belgian camps, Blount, long familiar with the agents of disorder, unkennels, in the Earl's name, a pack of needy ruffians eager for any service which seems to promise pay to their greed or license to their lust.

2. These miscreants are wholly Papists. Four of the five monsters who, some years later, dig the mine in Vineyard House, Robert Catesby, John Wright, Christopher Wright, and Thomas Winter, answer to this call of Blount; while the fifth, Thomas Percy, is with them in the persons of his more reputable kinsmen Jocelyn and Charles. Nearly all their most guilty associ-

VI. 1.
——
1600.
Oct.

2. List of Prisoners in the Compter and the Poultry, Feb. 8, 1601, S. P. O.; Lodge, ii. 545.

ates of the Powder Plot, Throckmorton, Lyttleton, and Grant, join with them; as also Ogle, Baynham, Whitelocke, and Downhall, the dregs and waste of a dozen Roman Catholic Plots.

3. They mean to kill the Queen, — a palace murder if she resist them, a Pomfret murder if she yield. Raleigh and Cecil are to share the fate of Bushy and Green. Is Essex more squeamish than Bolingbroke? Is Blount less bold than Piers of Exton? Though they advance towards their goal under cover of a design to free the Queen from enemies who hold her in thrall, the confession of Blount on the scaffold removes all doubt of a deliberate plan to assassinate her if she stand in their way. "I know and must confess," said the impenitent ruffian, "if we had failed in our end, we should even have drawn blood from herself." Nor is this design of dethronement and assassination a last resource of men at bay. The plan was formed two years before. It lay at the door of all Father Wright's suggestions, inspired the publication of Hayward's tract, controlled the understanding with O'Neile, gave color to the correspondence with King James.

4. At the moment when this faction had been struggling to secure the Irish command, Bacon had been en-

3. State Trials, i. 1415.
4. Scottish Papers of Elizabeth, lxii. 28, 46, 50, 52, 54; lxiii. 13, 15, 22, 29, 31, 45.

gaged with Coke and others in probing a mysterious crime. VI. 4.
A Scot of many names and characters, — Thomas Anderson, Thomas Alderson, Valentine Thomas, a servant, a sol- 1600.
dier, a gentleman, — giving no good account of his journey
to London, had been brought into the Tower. Bread and
water, Bacon and Coke, had brought him to his knees.
He confessed that he had been employed by the King
of Scots to kill the Lord Treasurer Burghley and her
Majesty the Queen. Here is the confession, solemnly at-
tested : —

Collection of the Principal Points in Valentine Thomas's
Confession concerning the Practice against Her Majesty's Person. Subscribed by himself the 20th of December, 1598.

Valentine Thomas, otherwise called Thomas Alderson
or. Anderson, confesseth that his access to the King of
Scotts was principally procured by one John Stewart of
the Buttery, who keepeth the King's door, and that he re-
paired to the King at sundry times and in sundry places ;
and amongst divers speeches of many things concerning
the state of England and her Majesty's person, the King
fell one day into some speech of the Lord Treasurer,
whom he wished Valentine Thomas to kill, as having ever
been his enemy about the Queen, which fact when Valentine undertook to execute, after some speeches how it
might best be done, the King further replied, " Nay, I
must have you do another thing for me, and all is one ;
for it is all but blood. You shall take an occasion to

deliver a petition to the Queen in manner as you shall think good, and so may you come near to stab her." And Valentine told the King that it was a dangerous piece of work, but he would do it, so the King would reward him thereafter, and the King said, " You shall have enough." And after this, Valentine took his leave of the King, and said he was to go to Glasgow for a time to his kinsman's wedding; and the King said, "Go, as you say, to Glasgow, and then come again, when you hear that Sorleboy is come." And so he left the King, and the Laird Arkinglasse came to the King.

> [Signed]   VALENTYNE THOMAS.

[Attested by]   JOHN PEYTON.
                EDW. COKE.
                THO. FLEMYNG.
                FR. BACON.
                WM. WARD.

The Government has kept this story secret. The Queen, indeed, professes to believe it false, and she is wise to do so. James stands beyond her reach; her courts cannot punish him; after her death he must be King. To prove him an assassin is to make of him, and of all who support his claims, the most ruthless of her foes. James, knowing of Thomas's arrest, is anxious to be spared the disgrace of a public trial; yet the knowledge that such a crime has been contemplated helps to nerve the hand of every one who loves his Queen, — the visible embodiment of English virtue and English strength.

5. If only the Papists share the heart of Blount, still,
where he fancies that either private love or lust of spoil
will tempt a man to arm, he throws his line. From
Lancashire, from Norfolk, and from Devon, friends of the
conspirators prick to town. Among them comes Sir
Ferdinando Gorges, governor of Plymouth, a brave and
loyal gentleman, akin to Sir Walter Raleigh, who, seeing
him drawn into a dangerous plot, sends to warn him.
Blount, now ready for the blow that is to make him
father-in-law to a king, persuades Gorges to invite the
Captain of the Queen's Guard to come and speak with
him at Essex House. Raleigh jumps into his barge.
At Essex-stairs the plotters beg him to land; but finding the fox too wise to trust his life in such hands,
Blount, throwing off the mask, sends an armed boat in
chase of him, which failing to catch its prey, fires four
pieces into his barge.

6. The blood of the conspirators mounts with this
attempt at assassination. On Sunday they will rise;
the pretext to be spread through the streets and lanes
being that Raleigh has formed a plot to murder the
Earl. The parts in the play are all given out. While
Smith secures the city in their rear, a force will march
from Essex House and seize the avenues of Whitehall.
Blount is to keep the palace-gates, Davis the hall, Dan-

---

5. Declaration of the Practice of the Earl of Essex, 1601; Gorges's Answer to
certain Imputations, quoted in Cayley, i. 337; State Trials, i. 1424.
6. Jardine's Criminal Trials, i. 320.

VI. 6.
———
1601.
Feb.
vers the entrance of the presence-chamber, while Essex himself, pushing into the royal closet, is to force the aged Queen, sword in hand, to yield.

7. To fan the courage of their crew, and prepare the citizens for news of a royal deposition, the chiefs of the insurrection think good to revive for a night their. favorite play. They send for Augustine Phillips, manager of the Blackfriars theatre, to Essex House. Monteagle, Percy, and two or three more, — among them Cuffe and Meyrick, gentlemen whose names and faces he does not recognize, — receive him; and Lord Monteagle, speaking for the rest, tells him they want to have played the next day Shakespeare's deposition of Richard the Second. Phillips objects that the play is stale, that a new one is running, and that the company will lose money by a change. Monteagle meets his objections. The theatre shall not lose; a host of gentlemen from Essex House will fill the galleries; if there is fear of loss, here are forty shillings to make it up.

Feb. 7.   Phillips takes the money; and King Richard is duly deposed for them and put to death.

Feb. 8.   8. Next morning, after the play, when the conspirators are about to rise, Egerton, Popham, and Knollys knock at the gates of Essex House. This visit of the

---

7. Examination of Augustine Phillips, Feb. 18, 1601, S. P. O. This examination has been printed by Mr. Collier, but with an error in the names.
8. Council Reg., Feb. 14, 1601; State Trials, i. 1333 – 1409.

Lord Keeper, the Lord Chief Justice, and the Queen's Chamberlain, disconcerts their plains. They meant to begin by a street tumult and a march on Whitehall, under cover of a design to punish Raleigh and restore the Queen to her freedom of choice. The arrival of these great officers of State compels them either to lay down their arms and submit to the law, or to rush into the city, raising the cry of war against the Queen. Mad as the action seems, they choose to strike. Putting the Ministers under guard, the Papist rabble, Blount, Catesby, Tresham, Danvers, Davis, Wright, Grant, Lyttleton, Baynham, and their fellows, tear past Temple-bar, yelling to the astonished citizens to arm and follow the young Earl.

9. The Queen sits in her palace superbly calm. Raleigh himself has scarcely her nerve of steel. Told at dinner that her faithless kinsman is in arms against her, she eats her meal, no more disturbed than by a tumult on the stage. When, some minutes later, comes in news that London has risen for the Earl, she proudly puts aside the lie: " He who placed me in this seat will preserve me in it."

10. Essex is no more Bolingbroke than Elizabeth Richard. It is Sunday morning, and the people crowd

9. Birch, ii. 468; Jardine's Criminal Trials, i. 309.

10. Lodge's Illustrations, ii. 545; List of Prisoners in the Poultry and the Compter, Feb. 8, 1601, S. P. O.; Council Reg., Feb. 14, 1601.

VI. 10. the streets; some making holiday, more on their way to
—   church. Yet, though the Earl rides past them, not a
1601.
Feb. 8.   man from Temple Bar to Cheap arms to follow this descendant of John of Gaunt. As the Papists wheel into
the city, the inhabitants shut their gates. Halberds and
lances soon gleam out from city doors; not to guard the
Earl, but to defend religion and the Queen; so that,
when the baffled insurgents, pressed from the upper lanes
about Guildhall, beat a retreat towards St. Paul's, they
find the gorge of Ludgate and the long line of approaches
to Essex House blocked up with pikes. Deceived in the
promises of Smith, the despairing band fall back on Ludgate Hill, where Levison, with a party of soldiers, guards
the pass. Blount sounds a charge. Some fall, some
turn, some cut their way through. Seeing his old adver-
sary, Waite, in the ranks before him, Blount rushes upon
him, and, though faint with wounds, chops the assassin
down. It is the last pang of joy before he yields.

The game is now up. All London is against them in
an hour, as England will be in a week. The gangs dis-
perse. Some crawl into alehouse-vaults; some leap into
boats and drop with the tide; but every honest man's
hand is against them, and at sundown most of the leaders are safe in jail. In less than forty-eight hours from
the first rebellious shout near Temple-bar, Ogle and
Throckmorton are in the Gatehouse; Baynham, Lyttleton, and Percy in the Fleet; Smith and Constable
in the Poultry; Blount in Mr. Newsom's house in Paul's
Churchyard, when his wounds allow, to be carried to

the Tower; Whitelocke in the Marshalsea; Catesby in VI. 10.
the house of Sheriff Gamble; Grant and the two Wrights
in the White Lion; Danvers, Essex, Lee, Southampton,
and Monteagle in the Tower.

11. Swift justice is the only mercy they can now hope
from man.

Never has criminal fairer trial, less partial judges, than
the Earl. His peers, the companions of his youth, the
connections of his blood, are summoned by a special
message from the Crown. The most odious facts against
him are withheld; the Government wishing to spare his
memory, though they cannot in honor, and dare not in
policy spare his life. They shrink from proclaiming to
the world that a kinsman of the Queen has been in
treacherous intercourse with Jesuits and the Pope. Not
a word is said on the trial about his midnight interviews
with Father Wright; not a word about his complicity in
the publication of Hayward's tract. Only the obvious
facts are proved, but these suffice. From the hour of his
rising his fate has been sealed. That girlish romance of
the ring, that still more girlish tale of Elizabeth's weakness and change of mind, are idle mirage of the brain.
Camden, indeed, speaks of her hesitancy; but Camden
wrote after the Queen's death, when it had become fashionable at court to speak well of the Earl. Jardine was
the first to remark that this rumor of her changes and
hesitations is unsupported by any one passage in the

11. Council Reg., Feb. 13, 1601; Jardine, i. 876.

VI. 11. State Papers. In fact, Elizabeth never in her life
— showed less weakness than in the case of her rebellious
1601. kinsman. For a crime like his there was no mercy but
Feb. 19. the grave.

12. Called by the Privy Council to bear his part in
this great drama, Bacon no more shirks his duty at
the bar than Levison shirked his duty at Ludgate Hill,
or Raleigh his duty at Charing Cross. As her Council
Learned in the Law, he has no more choice or hesitation about his duty of defence than her Captain of the
Guard. Raleigh and Bacon have each tried to save
the Earl as long as he remained an honest man; but
England is their first love, and by her faith, her freedom, and her Queen, they must stand or fall.

Never is stern and holy duty done more gently on
a criminal than by Bacon on this trial. He aggravates
nothing. If he condemns the action, he refrains from
needless condemnation of the man. Here is his speech,
(set down, though it has already appeared in print,
that the reader may have the whole case before his
eyes without trouble of turning to another book):—

" My Lord, I expected not that the matter of defence
would have been excused this day; to defend is lawful, but to rebel in defence is not lawful; therefore
what my Lord of Essex hath here delivered, in my

12. Council to Bacon, Feb. 18, 1601, S. P. O.; Abstract of Evidence against
Essex, July 22, 1600, S. P. O.; Jardine i. 316-821, 851, 860.

conceit seemeth to be *simile prodigio*. I speak not to simple men, but to prudent, grave, and wise peers, who can draw up out of the circumstances the things themselves. And this I must needs say, it is evident that my Lord of Essex had planted a pretence in his heart against the Government, and now, under color of excuse, he layeth the cause upon his particular enemies. My Lord of Essex, I cannot resemble your proceedings more rightly than to one Pisistratus, in Athens, who, coming into the city with the purpose to procure the subversion of the kingdom and wanting aid for the accomplishing his aspiring desires, and as the surest means to win the hearts of the citizens unto him, he entered the city, having cut his body with a knife, to the end they might conjecture he had been in danger of his life. Even so your Lordship gave out in the streets that your life was sought by the Lord Cobham and Sir Walter Raleigh, by this means persuading yourselves, if the city had undertaken your cause, all would have gone well on your side. But the imprisoning the Queen's councillors, what reference had that fact to my Lord Cobham, Sir Walter Raleigh, or the rest? You allege the matter to have been resolved on a sudden. No, you were three months in the deliberation thereof. O, my Lord, strive with yourself and strip off all excuses; the persons whom you aimed at, if you rightly understand it, are your best friends. All that you have said, or can say, in answer to these matters, are but shadows. It were your best course to confess and not to justify."

VI. 12.   . What a contrast to the style of Coke! Later in the
——   day, after hours of prevarication on the part of Essex,
1601.   Bacon speaks again, in a warmer tone, but without a
Feb. 19. particle of rancor in his words: —

"My Lord, I have never yet seen, in any case, such
favor shown to any prisoner; so many digressions, such
delivering of evidence by fractions, and so silly a defence
of such great and notorious treasons. Your Lordship
may see how weakly my Lord of Essex hath shadowed
his purpose, and how slenderly he hath answered the
objections against him. But admit the case that the
Earl's intent were, as he would have it, to go as a sup-
pliant to her Majesty, shall petitioners be armed and
guarded? Neither is it a mere point of law, as my
Lord of Southampton would have it believed, that condemns them of treason, but it is apparent in common
sense; to consult, to execute, to run together in num-
bers, in doublets and hose, armed with weapons, what
color of excuse can be alleged for this? And all this
persisted in after being warned by messengers sent from
her Majesty's own person. Will any man be so simple
as to take this to be less than treason? But, my Lord,
doubting that too much variety of matter may occasion
forgetfulness, I will only trouble your Lordship's remembrance with this point, rightly comparing this rebellion
of my Lord of Essex to the Duke of Guise's, that came
upon the barricadoes at Paris in his doublet and hose,
attended upon but with eight gentlemen; but his con-

fidence in the city was even such as my Lord's was; VI. 12.
and when he had delivered himself so far into the shal-
low of his own conceit, and could not accomplish what
he expected, the King taking arms against him, he was
glad to yield himself, thinking to color his pretexts and
his practices by alleging the occasion thereof to be a
private quarrel."

Defence there is none: the peers condemn him to
death.

13. After trial and condemnation, when the Garter is   March.
plucked from his knee and the George from his breast,
the Earl's pride and courage give way.   He closes a
turbulent and licentious life by confessing against his
companions, still untried, more than the law-officers of
the Crown could have proved against them; and, despicable to relate, most of all against the two men who have
been his closest associates, — Blount and Cuffe.   His
confessions in the face of death deprive these prisoners
of the last faint hope of grace.   They go, with Meyrick
and Danvers, to the gallows or to the block.   But the
anger of the Queen being stayed, the rest of the gang
— Catesby, Tresham, Grant, Winter, Baynham, and
their tribe — escape, some with imprisonment, some
with mulct, for future villanies.   At the end of twelve
or fifteen weeks the last of the conspirators leaves the
Tower.

13. Council Reg., Feb. 24, 1602; Jardine's "Criminal Trials," i. 866 - 872;
State Trials, i. 1412, 1414.

VI. 14.　　14. Their fines reward service for which no other sal-
—　　aries are paid.　The Queen, who in the fictions of biog-
1601.　raphers and historians is forever starving Bacon for the
Aug. 6.　good of his soul, now makes over to him, in actual fact,
a considerable share of Catesby's fine.　The manner of
this grant of twelve hundred pounds is not less gracious
than the gift itself.　It is not made in the usual way,
from the Lord Treasurer's office, but as a public act of
the Privy Council and the Queen.

A council meets at Greenwich Palace, Egerton in the
chair.　Around him sit Lord Buckhurst, the delightful
poet ; Nottingham, the great commander ; the Earls of
Shrewsbury and Worcester ; Knollys, Fortescue, and
Cecil.　These councillors draft a letter to Coke, which
stands among the many interesting letters in the Privy
Council register : —

A LETTER TO EDWARD COKE, ESQ., HER MAJESTY'S ATTORNEY-GENERAL.

Aug. 6, 1601.

Forasmuch as her Majesty is pleased to bestow particular reward upon divers of her servants, to be taken out
of such fines as have grown unto her by the offences of
several persons, we have thought good to let you know
particularly who they be that are at this time to receive
several portions in that kind, to the intent that you may
cause some such assurances to be passed over, as the

14. Council Reg., Aug. 6, 1601.

person may be assured to receive those portions as are
allotted to them according to her Majesty's gracious pleasure, in this sort following. When there is an assurance
passed to her Majesty's use of certain lands, for the payment of two thousand at several days by Francis Tresham,
her Majesty is pleased that Mr. Lieutenant of the Tower
shall receive the sum of a thousand five hundred pounds,
assigned him out of that; the other five hundred remaining to be disposed at her Majesty's pleasure. Next, you
shall understand that she is likewise pleased to divide
the fine of Mr. Catesby between Mr. Francis Bacon, Sir
Arthur Gorges, and Captain Carpenter, at Ostend, in this
sort following, for which you are likewise to prepare some
such assurance to be passed from the Queen as the person
may receive those sums, every one pro rata, out of every
portion as it is assigned to be paid at several times,
namely, to Mr. Bacon the sum of a thousand two hundred pounds; to Sir Arthur Gorges a thousand two
hundred pounds; and to Captain Carpenter the rest;
for doing whereof these presents shall be your warrant.

VI. 14.
———
1601.
Aug. 6.

THOMAS EGERTON.
BUCKHURST.
NOTTINGHAM.
SHREWSBURY.
WORCESTER.
KNOLLYS.
ROBERT CECIL.
JOHN FORTESCUE.

VI. 14.
—
1601.
Aug.

Fancy Coke's delight in passing an assurance for twelve hundred pounds to Francis Bacon !

15. One actor in the drama which has shaken London slips mysteriously from public view. Flung into the Tower with Essex and Danvers, as of equal guilt, Lord Monteagle is neither put with them on trial for his life, nor, in the various public investigations, are the damning facts of his having sent for Augustine Phillips and of having paid the Globe comedians to play the deposition of Richard II. on the very eve of the rising, allowed to escape Coke's lips in a public court. That Phillips was sent for to Essex House, and was there paid money to change the play at the Blackfriars theatre, are facts too grave for the prosecution to conceal ; but when Coke rose, with the comedian's evidence in his hand, he dropped the name of Lord Monteagle from the sworn depositions, in-serting that of Meyrick in its place ! Meyrick is hanged, Monteagle only fined.

Oct 24.

Cecil must have his reasons for this strange suppres-sion, this cruel substitution : reasons which become clear from Monteagle's share in the more terrible drama of the Powder Plot.

16. Lord Campbell writes, and many others have written, as though it would have been right for Bacon to have shirked his part in this great act of justice.

---

15. Phillips's Examination, Feb. 18, 1601, S. P. O.; State Trials, i. 1445.
16. Campbell's " Lives of the Chancellors," iii. 37, 39.

Yet this can hardly be his serious meaning. To put Bacon in the wrong, the objector must prove Essex to have been acting in his right. This, it may be safely asserted, they can never do. If all writers must agree that England was justified in crushing with swift, stern hand this peculiarly hideous and unnatural plot, by what path of reasoning can we come to a conclusion that one of the Queen's Counsellors, called to his duty by the Crown was not right?

In Bacon's place, we must assume that Lord Campbell would have done his duty as Bacon did. There is no second course for honest men. Bring the case down. Lord Campbell has had many clients: men who have paid him fees far larger than the patch of meadow tossed to Bacon by the Earl. Imagine events arming the papal powers once more against England; hostile fleets off the coast; O'Donnel or M'Mahon at the head of a successful host in Connaught; Zouaves swarming in Cork; our colonies menaced with fire and sword; a gang of ruffians, spawn of the stews and prisons, abroad in London; the Queen's cousin of Hanover plotting with all those rebels and fanatics against her crown and life; a foreign league resolving to put down our free constitution and our Protestant faith, — imagine, under all these circumstances of alarm, one of Lord Campbell's former clients, a man for whose personal character he felt no respect and whose political conduct he held in abhorrence, joining with John Mitchell, Dr. Cullen, and the disbanded remnants of the Pope's brigade, in

VI. 16. open rebellion against the law, in rousing the dregs of
⸺ the city, in shedding innocent blood at Charing Cross;
1601.
Aug. would not Lord Campbell, under such provocations, do
his duty as a lawyer and as a man?

This was Bacon's case. He owed nothing to Essex
that could have tempted even a weak man to take the
wrong side instead of the right side. He owed alle-
giance to his country and to truth. He was as much
the Queen's officer, armed with her commission, bound
to obey her commands, as her Captain of the Guard.
He had no part in the Earl's crime, and utterly ab-
horred his means, his associates, and his ends. To have
done more than he did in the conduct of this bad drama might have been noble and patriotic; to have done
less would have been to act like a weak girl, not like
a great man.

Oct. 17. That the bearing of Francis Bacon throughout
these mournful events is just and noble is the public
verdict of his time. Lord Campbell talks of his fall in
popularity. "For some time after Essex's execution
Bacon was looked upon with great aversion." But, in
truth, he never loses for a day the hearts of his countrymen. Of this the proofs are incontestable. While
the spirits of men are yet warm with remembrance of
the scenes at Tyburn and on Tower Hill, writs travel
down into the shires for a new Parliament. Now, therefore, comes the proof how far he has fallen. If he be

---

17. Campbell's "Bacon," iii. 43; Willis, "Not. Parl.," 149.

thought of with aversion, as Lord Campbell says, here VI. 17.
arc the means, the opportunities, and the scenery for a
condign revenge. The scot and lot men of Elizabeth
1601.
Oct.
are not nice. A candidate cross to the moods of squire
and freeman often finds himself burned in straw, pelted
with foul eggs, or drummed by humorous rogues from
the county town. Do the friends of Lord Essex rise on
his adversaries? Is the drum beaten against Raleigh,
or the stone flung at Bacon? Just the reverse. The
world has not been with the rebellious Earl; and those
who have struck down the papist plot are foremost in
the ranks of the new Parliament. Four years ago Bacon had been chosen to represent Ipswich, and the chief
town of Suffolk again ratifies its choice. But his public
acts have won for him a second constituency in St. Albans. Such a double return — always rare in the House
of Commons — is the highest compliment that could
have been paid to the purity and popularity of his political life.

CHAPTER VII.

THE NEW REIGN.

VII. 1.   Nor is Bacon's popularity a tide at the ebb. The
—— Queen dies. A King comes in who knows not Joseph,
1603. nor the principles of Joseph. James has secretly prom-
April. ised peace to Spain. A man of weak nerve and small,
quick brain, fond of his ease, a friend of dogmatic con-
troversies, and a stranger to religion, he can neither
tolerate nor understand the passionate fervor of the
realm for this foreign war. By war he sees that he
may offend the Jesuits and the Pope, men who can
put poison into his wine or sharpen against him an
assassin's knife. What are the Dutch to him, that he
should offend for them the masters of a hundred legions
and twenty secret fraternities? Why, these Dutch are
in arms against lawful kings! England, it is true, has
undertaken their defence, and, in league with Henri
Quatre, she has for many years past commanded in
their towns and camps. But the treaties of Elizabeth,
he says, are not his treaties, nor can he hold himself
bound by the acts of a woman and a fool.

But the desertion of a cause which every man between

1. King's MSS. 123; Harl. MSS. 532.

the four seas possessing high spirit and sound faith feels
to be his own, is not the act of a day. A path must
be prepared. The eager spirits must be dispersed or
stunned, the great fighting men must be crushed or
bribed. Cecil adopts this policy of peace, which suits
his genius and secures to himself the foremost place.
Nottingham is won by a youthful bride, and Vere is
recalled from the Flemish camp. A master-work of
political art sends Gray and Raleigh to the Tower. At
the same time Bacon is thrust aside, discredited to the
new sovereign, his usual access to the throne refused,
and his proffered services of tongue and pen disdained.

2. At court he is under a cloud. The patron of Essex, the employer of Valentine Thomas, takes into his
grace all those who shared in the Earl's affections and
in his crime. Southampton is restored in blood. Lady
Rich and the Countess of Northumberland appear at
court. Lady Rich's lover, Montjoy, becomes an earl.
Rutland gets the reversion of a royal park, Monteagle
a grant of land. Among those old partisans of Essex,
who now keep the gates of Whitehall and dispose of
offices and grants, Bacon is undoubtedly unpopular, —
less, however, for his past speech against the Earl than
for his present defence of the dead Queen. In James's
ear the name of Elizabeth is rank ; on Bacon's tongue

---

2. Grant Book of James the First, 2, 3, S. P. O.; Doquets of James the First,
Nov. 13, 1604, S. P. O.; Warrant Book of James the First, 4, S. P. O.; In felicem memoriam Elizabethæ, Bacon's Works, vi. 283; Willis, Not. Parl., 160.

VII. 2.
——
1604.
Feb.

and pen her virtues live and her glories speak. When no man but himself dares breath her name in the court of her successor, he composes that magnificent prose elegy, In felicem Memoriam Elizabethæ, which he himself esteems the most precious of all his works. The cloud is at Whitehall or at Hampton Court, not at Ipswich or St. Albans. To the country his name is dear as ever. When writs go out for the first Parliament of the new reign (one purpose of which is to restore the friends of Devereux in estate and blood), though the King and court bear hard against him, Ipswich and St. Albans send him to London once again by a double return. Nor is this all. So soon as the burgesses meet in Westminster, he becomes again, what he has been before in every session for twenty years, their chief. Some go so far as to use his name for Speaker of the House; a fact unknown to Lord Campbell; yet worth a word in reference to the report of his lying at that very moment under public ban.

Mar. 27.

3. By ancient usage the Crown appointed the Speaker to be chosen by the House. A leave to elect came down, weighted with a particular recommendation ; and, like a dean and chapter in the election of a bishop, the squires and burgesses were expected to adopt the royal choice. A time has now come for trying what force remains in these feudal forms. Some members think

---

3. Com. Jour., i. 141; Bacon's Essays, No. 8; Bacon's Speech on the Naturalization of the Scots, State Trials, ii. 575.

this leave to elect a Speaker should be taken in its open sense : that the House should choose it officers, causing these old pretensions of the Crown to cease. When, therefore, the court proposes Sir Edward Phellippes, a buzz and hum of opposition rises. Why not have a Speaker of their own ? Hastings, Neville, Bacon, each is named. Hastings is a Puritan, Neville an opponent of the court. That each of these men should be deemed fit instruments of opposition to the Crown is susceptible of easy explanation. But Bacon is neither a Puritan nor an enemy of the court. He differs from the Puritans on some of their principles, particularly on their intolerance for errors of faith ; and he supports the King against many of their most obstinate prejudices, particularly their repugnance to a union with the Scots. Yet the gentlemen who live with him and serve with him, who dine at the same tables, laugh over the same jests, and sometimes, it is likely, suffer from his wit, believe he may be played, in a good cause, even against the King. These gentlemen have not discovered that Bacon is a corrupt and obsequious rogue.

4. If the House of Commons, not yet strong enough to give battle to the Crown on such a field as the choice of Speaker, accepts the nomination of Phellippes, it puts Bacon forward as its man of confidence, electing him on the Standing Committee of Privileges, on the Committee of Grievances, of which he is named reporter, on the

4. Com. Jour., I. 142-253; Lords' Jour., ii. 206, 309.

VII. 4. Committee for Conference on the Restraint of Speech,
——. on the Committee for Union with Scotland; in all, on
1604. twenty-nine committees.   All through the session he
April.
speaks with a boldness, an ability, a frequency unri-
valled in the House of Commons before his day or since.
The topics are great and various : abuses in the taverns,
the laws against witchcraft, the license of purveyors, the
election of members, the sin of adultery, the increase of
drunkenness, the sale of Crown offices and lands.   Two
topics stand out from the rest with almost solid bright-
ness of historical outline.   These are the Grievances
and the Union.

On the first he has the disadvantage of differing from
the Crown ; on the second from a majority of those
country gentlemen with whom he usually speaks and
votes.   James will not hear of the List of Grievances,
nor will the burgesses vote his Bill of Union with the
Scots.   Each side has its personal feeling and its nar-
row view.   With a deeper wisdom and a larger patriotism, Bacon, while he sees with the King that these claims
to suspend the penal laws, to grant private monopolies,
to command personal service, to sign away heiresses in
marriage, to supply his kitchen from the poulterer's bas-
ket and his cellars from the vintner's store at his own
price, are each and all incontestably historical, founded
in custom older in date than the oldest statute in the
book, sees also, with the complaining citizen or squire,
that time, by its slow but devouring sap, has hollowed
the ground on which these regal privileges stand, so that

they have no longer a safe foundation on which to rest, VII. 4.
and seeks to improve the old ways before improvement
is too late. But James is deaf. To take from him the 1604.
April
right to reward a barber with a wine patent, to compel
the young noble to hold his reins or feed his dogs, to
match his favorites of the bedchamber with the daughters of English earls, to fetch in ale from Blackfriars
and fish from Billingsgate wharf, to grant leave to his
groom, or the darling of his groom, to vend pardons
for rape and arson, burglary and murder, would, in his
opinion, be to rob him of the most princely attributes of
his high rank.

5. Some among the Commons are not less weak than
James. When they see him break his word, turn his
back on the List of Grievances, nip in the flower their
hopes of a Church reform, begin a secret correspondence with the Cardinal Archduke and with the Pope,
they set themselves to oppose his policy even in the
few particulars on which his policy is just and sound.
In a union with the Scots Bacon finds a measure of
defence against Spain. A dull squire sees in it only an
opening for the rush into London of savages with red
beards, bare legs, and scurvy tongues.

Waiving his own wrongs for the public good, Bacon
draws for the King the draft of a Bill of Union, which he
introduces into the House of Commons in a splendid

---

5. Abstract by Bacon of Objections in the House of Commons, April 25, 1604,
S. P. O.; Speech on the Union, April 25, 1604, S. P. O.

VII. 5.   speech, opening to the view of knight and squire a politi-
—   cal scene, in which he pictures to their minds the con-
1604. tending nationalities and hostile creeds of Europe ; striv-
April   ing, by his bold, persuasive eloquence, to lure them into
pondering less on the ancient feud of Saxon and Scot,
more on the permanent safety of the English faith and
power. With all the lights of fancy, all the subtleties of
logic, he meets on one side the obstinacy of his colleagues, on the other side the perverseness of his prince.
Each, however, holds to his own. The Grievances are
not heard, the Bill of Union does not pass.

July.   6. While Bacon is making these splendid displays of
political wisdom and personal independence in the House
of Commons, Lord Campbell fancies him slinking and
skulking under public odium !

Lord Campbell takes everything on trust. When
Bacon got his knighthood, Lord Campbell says he was
"infinitely gratified by being permitted to kneel down
with three hundred others." Now, Bacon's letters to
Cecil on the knighthood are not only in print, but are
known to every one who reads. In place of being infinitely gratified, Bacon protests against the shame of
being compelled to kneel down with Peter and John. So
again with his marriage to Alice Barnham. Lord Campbell makes merry over his mercenary love and his match
of convenience. Yet from his own text, and from the
pages of Montagu, it is certain that he knows nothing

6. Campbell's Lives of the Chancellors, iii. 49.

whatever of this love or of this match; neither who Alice VII. 6.
Barnham was, nor the circumstances of her parents; ⸺
neither when she became Bacon's wife, nor the amount 1604.
of jointure which she brought home to her lord. He July.
imagines that Alice became Lady Bacon in 1603, shortly
after July 3d. He says she was rich.

In all that relates to Alice Barnham the writers of
Bacon's life have been as much at fault as though she
had been first the love and then the wife of Ward the
Rover or Steer the Leveller, in place of being, as she was,
lady to a man who framed the New Philosophy and held
the Great Seal. Yet some of the facts about her birth,
the associations of her early years, the members of her
family, the circumstances of her love, courtship, marriage,
and wedded life, may still be recovered from the manu-
script mounds of the Bodleian, the State Paper Office, and
the library of Westwood Park.

7. More than a year ago, in writing to his cousin Aug.
Cecil, Bacon mentioned his having found a handsome
maiden to his mind. She loved him and he loved her.
But her mother, a widow and again a wife, having made
two good matches for herself, has set her heart on making
great alliances for her girls. In part to please her, still
.more to glorify his bride, Bacon waits and toils that

7. Bacon to Cecil, July 3, 1603; Notes on the Pakington Family in Wotton's
Baronetage, ed. by Kimber and Johnson, i. 180. Wotton's account was derived
from a MS. History of Sir John Pakington written by the Rev. Mr. Tomkins, a
Prebendary of Worcester, preserved in Wotton's time at Westwood Park. The
MS. is now lost.

he may lay at her feet a settled fortune and a more splen-did name.

The family into which — when he can steal an hour from the courts of law and the pursuits of science — he goes a-courting, and in which he is now an accepted lover, consists of four girls, their pretty mother, and a bold, handsome, heady step-father of fifty-six, — a group of persons notable from their private stories, and of romantic interest from their loves and feuds with the philosopher, and from the part they must have had in shaping his views of the felicities and infelicities of domestic life.

8. The four young girls are the orphan daughters of Benedict Barnham, merchant of Cheapside and alder-man of his ward; an honest fellow, who gave his wife a good lift in the world, and left his children to take their chance of rising among men, who, with all their sins, are never blind to the merits of women blessed with youth, loveliness, and wealth. Alice is the first to fall in love; but the three hoydens who now romp around her, and perhaps get many a hug and kiss from her famous lover, will soon be in their turns followed for their bright eyes and brighter gold. Elizabeth will marry Mervin Touchet, Earl of Castlehaven, that mis-erable wretch who, when his first young wife, the hoyden of to-day, is in her grave, will expiate on the block the foulest crime ever charged against an English peer.

8. Wotton, i. 180–186; Nash's History of Worcestershire, i. 352; Collins's Peerage, art. " Audley."

The two little things now playing at Alice's knee will become, in due time, Lady Constable and Lady Soames.

VII. 8.

——

1604.
Aug.

The mother of these girls was a daughter of Humphrey Smith, of Cheapside, silkman to the Queen. Eager, lovely, and aspiring, she won the alderman of her ward, — an admirable city match; but she meant and means to rise yet higher in the world, and heaven has given her the strength to fight her way. Of the four husbands whom she has made, or has still to make, the happiest of their sex, each is to be in his turn a loftier one than the last. She has buried a citizen. She will, in turn, bury her knight. She will then marry a baron, and, on his death, an earl. Barnham was her early choice. When he left her with the four girls and a great estate, Sir John Pakington, of Hampton Lovet, ancestor of that Worcestershire baronet who is said to have sat to Addison for the portrait of Sir Roger de Coverley, proffered to console her with his hearty affection and his good old name. The widow was not perverse. If she wept for the dear alderman of Cheapside, it was in a coach emblazoned with the mullets and wheat-sheafs, and with a handsome and jovial knight at her side.

9. Sir John has been a father to the four girls; for

---

9. Council Reg., Aug. 24, 1600, June 6, Oct. 13, 1601; Wotton, i. 180; The Camden Society's Miscellany, iv. 50. There is a portrait of Sir John at Westwood Park. My impressions of him are mainly derived from a multitude of

VII. 9. if rough and ready, apt to quarrel, and quick to strike,
—   he has a gentle and manly heart.   A gentleman with due
1604.
Aug.   pride in his long line and his broad lands, in his length
of leg and width of chest, he is known at Christchurch
and on Richmond-green as Lusty Pakington; and the
good old Queen, who liked to see a man a Man, made
him, for his brave looks, a Knight of the Bath.   A great
swimmer, an adroit swordsman, few who can help it
ever care to wait the shock of his hasty temper or his
vigorous thrust.   The great man of his country-side,
he sends his buck for the judges' table at assizes, and
has his name put first on every commission from the
Crown, whether the shire is called to raise forces against
Spain, build light-houses in the Bristol Channel, or provide for the wants of sick and disabled troops ; but when
orders from the Crown oppose his own particular humor,
as they sometimes do, he quietly puts them in the fire.
The Privy Council has to be rather plain and rough
with the jovial knight.   Once he laid a wager to swim
against three stout gallants from Westminster to Lon-
don-bridge ; but the Queen forbade the match, lest some
of the fools should get drowned   He has a passion for
building and digging on a princely scale.   He buys a
whole forest of trees for his salt-pits and for the great
house which he is building at Westwood Park, and he
sinks a great farm of a hundred acres under water

---

private papers preserved at Westwood, free access to which I owe to the obliging courtesies of the Right Hon. Sir John Pakington, Bart., his descendant and
successor.

that he may have room to swim and fish. Debt catches
the generous spendthrift in its claws; and that which
could not force him into meanness, lures him, at the
age of fifty, into love. When maddened by duns, he
swore to be free of such rogues, even if he had to give
up London, and live on bread and verjuice. News that
Sir John was going to forsake the town, to sell horses
and dogs, and, for the time to come, live on his own
estate, shoot in the woods round Hampton Lovet, and
stick to the sessions of Worcester, as his father and
grandfather had done before him, soon got wing; when
sixty stout gentlemen and yeomen of the shire, his
friends and tenants, seated in their own saddles, pricked
up to London, and waited for him at the palace-gates
while he went in to bid the Queen adieu. Sorry to miss
so fine a gentleman from her court, Elizabeth gave him
an estate in Suffolk, worth from eight to nine hundred
pounds a year, of traitor's land. Off he spurred to
take possession; but, on gaining the door of his new
house, he found there a mourning lady with her children in despair. In place of kicking them out into
the street, he ran away himself, nor ever rested in his
bed till he got the Queen to take back her gift and
bestow it on the weeping lady and her little brood.
When a good friend in the city whispered in his ear
the name of widow Barnham, the great affectionate fellow, wanting to dig and build, and having no objection
to four pretty girls to romp with him and love him, as
they were sure to do, dashed into Cheapside, told his

bashful little tale, and the young widow, wooed for the second time in her life, said Yes.

10. A brood of Pakingtons has joined the brood of Barnhams, — Mary, Ann, and John their names. Mary will live to become Lady Brook ; Ann first to become Lady Ferrars, then Countess of Chesterfield ; Jack will be the first baronet of his line ; and his son, Jack also, will be the famous cavalier who sacrificed so much for Charles the First, and who married Lady Dorothy, the friend of Hammond, and the reputed author of " The Whole Duty of Man."

The Barnhams and Pakingtons keep house together ; in summer-time at Hampton Lovet, among the oaks and apple-trees ; in term and sessions, when the world rides up to town, they hire a lodging in the Strand, over against the door of the Savoy church. Their home is in Worcestershire, — a big stone house, in a wooded dell, close by Hampton-brook, and at the foot of Hornsgrove-hill, — a pile with flanking wings, a trim parterre in front, and five huge lanterns on the roof, from which nothing can be seen save the square, plain tower of the village church, the clasping zone of wood, and now and then a curl of ascending smoke from the Droitwich salt-pans. Near a mile from Hampton Lovet lie the ruins of an ancient abbey, which may possibly have been the scene

10. I derive these details from the Westwood MSS., the stained glasses of Hampton Lovet church, and personal inspection of the localities, with the valuable aid of Sir John and Lady Pakington.

of Sir Roger's ghost. A chain of ponds, alive with fish VII. 10.
and fed by natural springs, drips past the ruin, and beyond these slants a bright green grassy upland, bare of 1604.
Aug.
wood, from the top of which, a level table-land, the eye
sweeps lovingly over wood and water, hill and hamlet
and orchard; near it the village spires of Ombersley and
Hampton; far away the cathedral towers of Worcester;
and in the distance, over leagues of country, powdered in
May with the pink and white of innumerable apple-trees,
in autumn warm with the ruddy glow of the ploughed
red land, the bold purple ridge of the Malvern hills. On
this plateau, high above the low-lying woods, Sir John
has begun to build a big house and dig a big lake,—a
house of rough red brick, with a grand hall and a state-
room above it, panelled, carved, and tapestried,—a house
like himself, thoroughly genuine and English, in which
he is to die, and his descendants are to live. His new
lake, close by his house, is the wonder and bugbear of
the shire.

11. Between this proud mother and this burly knight
the course of Bacon's love for Alice has no great hope of
running smooth. Lady Pakington adores great people;
thinking more of Sir Francis Bacon as a friend and
favorite of the Lord Chancellor than she would have
thought of him had he already published the Great In-
stauration. Lady Egerton condescends to keep her in

---

11. Bacon to Egerton, in Tanner MSS. 251, fol. 38 b; Doquets, Aug. 18, Oct.
28, 1604, S. P. O.

VII. 11. good humor while the man of genius waits and labors
—— for a better time.

1604.
Oct. 28.   He has still to wait, even for that rise in his profession
which is incontestably his due. On the death of Sir
William Peryam, Chief Baron of the Exchequer, and the
third husband of his sister, Elizabeth Bacon, Fleming becomes Chief Baron, yet the Solicitorship, vacant once
more, is given over his head to Sir John Dodcridge, sergeant of the coif.

1605.
Nov.   12. A brief reference in the charge against William
Talbot, a phrase here and there in his Essays, have told
the world what Bacon thought of the Powder Plot. It
has not been known that he had any part, slight or serious, in repressing this foul conspiracy, the natural sequel
of the Essex plot.

The new facts are found in an unpublished letter from
Bacon to Cecil.

Nov. 8.   The crime of Essex, the royal patronage of the conspirators, have borne their fruit in the Westminster mine.
It is the eighth of November, four days after the strange
discovery made by Lord Monteagle. Fawkes is in the
Tower. Catesby, Percy, Christopher and John Wright
are riding through the midland shires, flinging away
cloaks and scarfs, the country at their heels. The fight
is not yet won. Jesuits peer from the slums of White-
friars, and many who have come to town for the fifth of

12. Bacon to Cecil, Nov. 8, 1605, S. P. O.; Examination of John Drake, Nov.
8, 1605, S. P. O.

November still lurk among the sheds of Drury-lane.
True citizens keep watch and ward, lest, maddened by
defeat, some desperate villain should commit midnight
murder or scatter midnight fire.

John Drake, serving-man to Reynolds, a gentleman
living in pleasant Holborn, hears a fellow named Beard
declare that the plot was a brave plot, and that he, for
one, regrets it has failed. Drake runs to his master, and
Reynolds repeats to the Principal of Staple Inn the suspicious words his servant has overheard. The Principal
sees that here is no case for a city Dogberry, — Beard must
be a Papist, may be a plotter. Away he posts with the
ancients of his Inn to Bacon's rooms in Gray's Inn
Square. The words are bad, but general, — may mean
little, may mean much. The knave should certainly be
caught and questioned. Bacon sends the examination
of Drake to Cecil, with the following note: —

BACON TO CECIL.

Nov. 8, 1605.

IT MAY PLEASE YOUR LORDSHIP, —

I send an examination of one who was brought to
me by the principal and ancients of Staple Inn, touching
the words of one Beard, suspected for a Papist and prac-
tiser, — being general words, but bad; and I thought
not good to neglect anything at such a time; so with
signification of humble duty, I remain, at your Lordship's honorable commands, most humbly,

F. BACON.

VII. 13.

1606.
Jan.

13. Even the atrocious plot of Fawkes and Garnet, though its success would have been death to him, as to so many more, does not sour Bacon into a persecutor. He classes their crime with the massacres of Paris; but while the bigots find in these monstrous aberrations a plea for hanging and embowelling Roman Catholics who have taken no part in them, he finds, as wise and tolerant men see in them now, after a lapse of two hundred and sixty years, an argument against arming any one sect of men with the persecutor's sword. The traitor he gives up to the law; the heretic is to him a brother who has lost his way. In the noblest and most original of his Essays, penned in the prime of his intellectual powers, he especially explains and defends this principle of toleration. But the doctrine of his book had been previously exercised as a virtue in his life. The lapse of Tobie Mathews from the English Church to Rome puts his tolerant philosophy to the proof. Born on the steps of the episcopal bench, his grandfather a bishop, his father a bishop, four of his uncles bishops, all his connections in the Church, the fall of this young man makes a noise in England loud as the apostasy of Spalatro makes in Rome. The Puritans would cut him off branch and bole. When he comes from Italy to London, having given up all his old delights, cards, wenches, wine, and oaths, some, who are not themselves

13. Mathews to Carleton, July, 1606, S. P. O.; Ap. to Sainsbury's Original Papers relating to Rubens, 341, 343; Bacon's Essays, ed. of 1625, No. 3; Mathews to Bacon, April 14, July 16, 1616, Lambeth MSS. 936.

saints, would fling him into the Tower and leave him VII. 13.
there to die, as Spalatro, venturing into Rome, is sent
to perish in the dungeons of St. Angelo. James is 1606. Jan.
bitterly incensed against him, looking on his fall as that
of a column of his church; his father drives him from
his heart with a curse; yet, when his whole kin spit
on him and cast him forth, Bacon, strong in his sympathy for a scholar and a man who has lost his way,
takes this outcast and regenerate pervert to his house.
Though he fights against his friend's new doctrines,
he never will consent, with the less tolerant world, to
hunt him down for a change in his speculative views,
which every eye can see has made him a better and a
happier man. The philosopher may not be always able,
by any sacrifice of name and credit, to shield this enthu-
siast from the rage of sects, but he comforts him when in
jail, procures leave for him to return from exile, softens
towards him the heart of his father, and obtains for him
indulgences which probably save his life.

14. In the session which meets after the plot Bacon Feb.
plays a most active and brilliant part. The whole world
has come to town, — some to see that the King is safe,
some to see the traitors hang. Among others have come
up Sir John and Lady Pakington, together with the
young ladies from Westwood Park.

---

14. Carleton to Chamberlain, May 11, 1600, S. P. O.; Wotton, i. 184; Heath's
Preface to Bacon's Speech on the Jurisdiction of the Marches, vii. 569; Dom.
Papers, James I., x. 86.

Sir John has left behind him for a few weeks his brine-pits, his great pool, his herds of deer, his new house in the wood, his petty squabbles with the neighboring squires, and penned himself and the young ladies in a lodging of the Strand, not only that he may see the opening of parliament and hear the news, but that he may fight his way through two or three of his ugly scrapes. In digging his huge pond in Westwood Park, he has put under water some part of an old road, never doubting his power to do what he saw good on his own estate, the more so that he has given a turn to the road more convenient for himself and for every one else. A neighbor, between whom and Sir John no love is lost, seeing the flaw in this easy mode of making things straight, procures from the Crown an order to remove the pond and restore the King's ancient highway. This news he sends to Westwood, saying, with a politeness which the hot old gentleman reads for insult, that, though he has such an order in his hands, he shall not use it so long as the knight shall be pleased to live with him on friendly terms. Scorning to owe his pleasures to such a fellow, Sir John breaks down his banks, and, the pool lying high, the waters race and crash through the orchards, strewing the fields with dead fish for a mile or more, and discoloring the Severn as far off as Worcester for a week. Having let out his pool, he has come to answer for himself, and seek power to fill it with water and fish once more.

A yet more serious quarrel with Lord Zouch has

helped to bring him up to town. As President of the
Council of Wales and the Welsh Marches, Lord Zouch
has for a long time claimed a certain jurisdiction over
the four border shires of Gloucester, Hereford, Salop,
and Worcester; a claim which the shires deny and resist, with loud speeches from the gentry, met by threats
of force on the part of Zouch, tumultuous riding, signing, and protesting, ending for a day in solemn appeals
from the four shires to the House of Commons, and from
the angry Council of Wales to the King. Sir Herbert
Crofts, Knight of the shire for Hereford, has the cause
against Zouch in hand. Sir John, who is Sheriff of
Worcester, but not a Parliament man, having no tongue
to wag, has yet a passionate interest in the appeal; for
Lord Zouch not only claims a certain authority in his
county, but shows no sense of the respect due, even from
a peer, to so great a man as Sir John.

15. Alice is now near her lover, whom she may spy
as he trots from Gray's Inn to Westminster, or lounges
from the house towards Chancery-lane. Bacon sees
many a rock ahead. He is still a simple knight, and
he has the misery of differing from Sir John on the
great question of Lord Zouch and the shires.

Sir John can hardly make him out. Pakington is a
Royalist, root and branch, one who has lent money to his
Prince on Privy Seals, and who would draw a sword

15. Com. Jour., i. 286, 299; App. to the Verney Papers, ed. by John
Bruce, 281.

for Church and King with the ready zeal which made his grandson famous among the soldiers of Charles the First; yet this young lawyer, who has spent his life in recommending reforms, presumes to defend against him, loyal Sir John, the prerogatives of the Crown! Wiser heads than that of the warm old Worcestershire knight are often at fault when trying to explain to themselves the relations of Bacon to the Puritan House of Commons and to the episcopal and regal court. Yet they seem to be easy of explanation. It is, indeed, so rare for a man to stand on good terms with a hostile Crown and House of Commons, that it is often thought and sometimes found to be impossible. Winwood tried it. Strafford tried it. Pym would have tried it. But Winwood lost favor with the House when he took office under the Crown; lost favor at Court when he leaned to the Puritan opinions of the House. Strafford and Pym had each to choose a side. Bacon's position was far more lofty, and for years it seemed as if it were more secure. From his height of view and round of sympathy he is unable to throw himself, tongue and pen, into the exclusive and sectarian lines of either camp. His reconciling genius spans the dividing stream of party. Above the foolish Prince and petulent squires, he sees his country; not merely the England of Bancroft, of the Hampton Court Conference, of the Proclamation against Papists; but the England of a thousand years, of Alfred and of Edward, of Cressy and of Cadiz, of Chaucer and of Spenser; the England of a glorious

past and a hopeful future; the land which nurtured
Wycliffe and Caxton, which broke the spiritual bonds
of Leo, which crushed the invincible fleets of Spain.
This country he strives to arm, to free, to guide; now
by aiding the King in questions of revenue and of
union; now by aiding the House in questions of reform
or war. In each he is consistent first and last. His first
votes in the House were for supplies, his last speech will
be for supplies. With no fear of the controversial genius
of Rome, he feels a wholesome dread of the fleets and
regiments of Spain; those tracts by which Parsons,
Schioppius, and Bellarmino sting the sleep from so many
pillows pass him by; but he cannot hear unmoved that
the same Paul who has launched an interdict on Venice
is forming a Roman Catholic League against England;
that the O'Neiles and O'Donnels, driven out from Ireland
by Lord Montjoy, are hurrying home from Brussels and
Madrid; that rebels are drilling in the wilds of Connaught and Ulster; that Fajardo is manning his ships
in Cadiz bay, and Brochero proffering his red hand to
brush away Virginia with steel and flame. Willing to
meet the men of words with words, he is not less eager
to meet the men of war with steel and lead, the midnight assassin with the chain, the gibbet, and the cord.
Now, to starve the Crown is to leave England weak.
True, the Prince is lax, and moneys voted for the musters and the fleets may chance to drop into the pouches
of Hume and Herbert and Carr; yet of two dark evils
he chooses to dare the least, seeing that to pare down

VII. 15. the subsidies, as many virtuous and unreasoning squires
propose, is to subject James and his needy servants to
the magnificent corruptions of Lerma, the great minister
of Spain, already suspected, and with truth, of having
taken the chief men of the Privy Council and the Bedchamber into his pay. Better own the King's debts than
let Lerma pay them. Therefore, while he speaks with
Hastings and Hyde against patents, wardships, private
monopolies, the whole tag-rag of feudal privilege, he
constantly votes with Hitcham and Hobart for those
supplies which are necessary to maintain the splendor
of the Crown and the efficiency of the musters and the
fleet.

VII. 15.
——
1606.
Feb.

Here he parts from the majority; wide as in his vote
for union with the Scots.

16. Cecil, knowing his kinsman free from selfish and
sectarian views, consults him on the money-bills and set-
tlements. The debates on a grant for the new reign are
about to come on; and Cecil, who as Earl of Salisbury
sits in the Peers, has begun to feel his need of a bold and
influential friend in the Lower House. He hints that
the Court shall no longer oppose Bacon's rise at the bar.
On his part, Bacon is ready to assist the Crown in pro-
curing an ample grant; to shape drafts and preambles
such as may disarm the resentment of knight and squire.
Cecil takes him at his word, and Bacon drafts a bill.
Here is a note which shows how he is nearing power: —

16. Bacon to Cecil, Feb. 10, 1606, S. P. O.

Feb. 10, 1606.

IT MAY PLEASE YOUR GOOD LORDSHIP, —

I cannot as I would express how much I think myself bounden to your Lordship for your tenderness over my contentments. But herein I will endeavor hereafter as I am able. I send your Lordship a preamble for the subsidy, drawing which was my morning's labor to-day. This mould or frame, if you like it not, I will be ready to cast it again, *de novo*, if I may receive your honorable directions : for any particular corrections, it is in a good hand ; and yet I will attend your Lordship (after to-morrow's business, and to-morrow ended, which I know will be wearisome to you) to know your further pleasure : and so in all humbleness I rest at your Lordship's honorable commands more your ever bounden

F. BACON.

17. After warm debates in the Lower House a bill goes up to the throne for two subsidies and four fifteenths, Mar. 11. payable in eighteen months. It is not enough. Hitcham, member for Lyme, a patriotic fighting town on the Dorset coast, proposes in committee a second grant of two subsidies, four in all. A dozen members rise at once. Peake will hear no more about the royal debts. Holt declares the proposition of Hitcham dangerous. Paddye will tell

17. Hoby to Edmonds, Mar. 7, 1606; Cecil to Earl of Mar, Mar. 9, 1606, S. P. O.; Com. Jour., i. 281 – 84.

VII. 17. the King that even kings must not do wrong. Noy de
—
1606.
March.
claims against spoiling the poor to gorge the rich. Dyer
and Holcroft hint that more than once demands like these
have been met by the cry, "To arms!" But the warmest speaker is Lawrence Hyde of West Hatch, member for
Marlborough. Courtiers shrink from an unequal contest.
Sir Edward Hoby, an observant politician, friendly to his
kinsman Cecil and the court, notes how poor a figure the
King's official friends make in that masculine and stormy
House.

Mar. 18.   18. Bacon starts to the front. In the midst of a noisy
sitting of the committee, word comes down from Whitehall that James will not wait, — that the bill must be
passed, or the undutiful members shall feel his ire. Such
words, now frequent, make the King odious and con-
temptible. A storm sets in; the members fling back
threat for threat; the bill is lost.

This scene takes place on Tuesday. On Thursday the
committee meets again; the King has not accepted his
defeat, nor will the Commons enlarge their vote. Saturday brings no change of mood. On Monday the committee must report to the House; and Bacon, who has
been made reporter, will have to report against his own
convictions of what is best for the country and the
Crown. He sees the committee sullen, almost savage.
Monday is the anniversary of the King's accession, yet
no one rises to propose a holiday.

18. Bacon to Cecil, Mar. 22, 1606, S. P. O.; Com. Jour., i. 288; Jonson's
Epigrams, 41; a Proclamation touching a Seditious Rumor, Mar. 22, 1606.

Fagged with work, he must ride down to Gorhambury VII. 18.
for a day of rest. He does not wish to appear as if ‾‾
flying from his post, so he takes up his pen and Mar. 22.
writes : —

1606.

BACON TO THE EARL OF SALISBURY.

This Saturday, the 22d of March, 1606.

IT MAY PLEASE YOUR GOOD LORDSHIP, —

I purpose upon promise rather than business to make
a step to my house in the country this afternoon, which,
because your Lordship may hear otherwise, and thereupon conceive any doubt of my return to the pursuance
of the King's business, I thought it concerned me to
give your Lordship an account that I purpose (if I
live) to be there to-morrow in the evening, and so to
report the subsidy on Monday morning ; which, though
it be a day of triumph, yet I hear of no adjournment,
and therefore the House must sit. But if, in regard of
the King's servants' attendance, you Lordship conceive
doubt the House will not be well filled that day, I
humbly pray your Lordship I may receive your direction for the forbearing to enter into the matter that
day. I doubt not the success, if those attend that
should. So I rest, in all humbleness, at your Lordship's honorable commands,

F. BACON.

An hour after this note is penned a rumor rises, none

8 *

L

VII. 18. knows how, that the king is dead. Some say he has
——
1606.
Mar. 22.
been shot; some, stabbed; some, smothered in his bed.
No one asks where the King is; all agree that he is
killed. Members rush to the Council, to the city, — but
the ministers, the aldermen, know as little as themselves.
Some spur for Theobalds, some for Royston. London
yields itself to the wildest terrors. Hundreds of men
concerned in the Powder Plot are still at large. Garnet
is still unhung; the priests are sworn to have blood for
blood; the Jesuits, it is said, have threatened to burn
London to ashes, to massacre all the Protestants, should
that shining example of Christian virtue come to harm.
Citizens bar their doors, and swing on their Toledo
blades.

A horseman, Sir Herbert Crofts, dashes into Palace
Yard. He has seen the King! The King is safe, and
near the town. Fear now mutinies into joy. Bells
laugh over London roofs, crowds ride in procession to
meet their Prince. If he is safe, the realm is safe.
The Peers and Commons go to Whitehall. Ben Jonson bursts into music. As night comes down, the
streets start out with fire, and the taverns of Fleet-
street and Cheapside roar with patriotic songs.

Mar. 25. 19. Sunday and Monday pass in rejoicings and recep-
tions. Tuesday brings up Bacon. He has not, he tells
the House of Commons, drawn a word-for-word report

19. Com. Jour., i. 286, 299; Cecil to Wotton, Mar. 19, June 18, 1606, S. P. O.;
Statutes 3 Jacobi, c. 26.

from the committee, for his soul is shaken with too
much fear and joy. What, he cries, are a few debts to
the exultation now straining every loyal heart? These
debts are less the King's than the late Queen's. The
Queen made war, the country must repair the ravages
of war. Reparation costs money. The Crown debts,
too, must be paid in full, next year if not this year;
and why prefer a vote one session to a vote another
session? The House can name its time; but he says,
Vote to-day! In that rapturous and sacred moment,
when a great alarm has pressed heart to heart, and
made the whole nation one, he calls on the gentlemen
of England to crown their own happy work by voting
the subsidies necessary to support the power of the
country, the independence of the Crown.

His eloquence bears away the House. Hyde fronts
the stream; but the tide has turned towards Whitehall, and he strives against genius and enthusiasm, if
manfully yet in vain. A bill for another subsidy is
passed.

20. In the flush of this triumph, with his fame now
fixed, and with a great place, won by himself, not tossed
to him by a patron, within reach of his hand (not, as
Lord Campbell says, when he is poor and down in the
summer of the Queen's death), he begs the lady of his

20. Bacon to Egerton, Tanner MSS. 251, fol. 88 b; Rawley's Resuscitatio,
41; Domestic Papers, James I., xix. 33; Heath's Preface, Bacon's Works,
vii. 576.

love to name her day. Three years ago they were pledged to each other; he could have made her Lady Bacon, then, or at any time since then; but he has hoped to give to his bride a more settled fortune and a more illustrious name. Renown beyond the dreams of woman he can give her. Nor is he poor in those worldly gifts which girls are taught to covet even more than character and fame. Besides the grants bestowed upon him by Elizabeth, the reversion in the Star Chamber (not yet fallen in), and the leases of Cheltenham and Charlton Kings, of the Pitts and Twickenham Park, the death of poor Anthony (dead of the vices and excesses caught from his noble friend) has given him Gorhambury and the lands about it, where he now lives when not at Gray's Inn, and where, in after years, he will build Verulam House by the pond, taking his house, as he says, to the water, when the water will no longer flow to his house. More than all, the patent of Solicitor-General may be now sealed to him any day or week, a post of not less value than three or four thousand pounds a year, with openings to higher office and greater pay, to the Privy Council, the Peerage, and the Seals. He is rich, too, in genius and in noble friends. If Cecil plays with him fast and loose, the Lord Chancellor pushes his fortunes at the bar, and Lady Egerton smooths his suit with the young beauty and with her domineering kin. Sir John is in high spirits. True, the bill to exempt the four shires from Lord Zouch's jurisdiction has been dropped by the Lords;

but the king has assured Sir Herbert Crofts with his
own lips that right shall be done; and the loyal country
gentleman believes that when a prince promises to do
right he will of course maintain his word.

The day is named; the tenth of May.

21. By help of Sir Dudley Carleton we may look upon
the pleasant scene, upon the pretty bride, the jovial
knight, the romping girls, and the merry company, as
through a glass. Feathers and lace light up the rooms
in the Strand. Cecil has been warmly urged to come
over from Salisbury House. Three of his gentlemen,
Sir Walter Cope, Sir Baptist Hicks, and Sir Hugh Bee-
ston, hard drinkers and men about town, strut over
in his stead, flaunting in their swords and plumes; yet
the prodigal bridegroom, sumptuous in his tastes as in
his genius, clad in a suit of Genoese velvet, purple from
cap to shoe, outbraves them all. The bride, too, is
richly dight; her whole dowry seeming to be piled up
on her in cloth of silver and ornaments of gold. The
wedding rite is performed at St. Marylebone chapel,
two miles from the Strand, among the lanes and suburbs
winding towards the foot of Hampstead Hill. Who that
is blessed with any share of sympathy or poetry cannot
see how that glad and shining party ride to the rural
church on that sunny tenth of May? how the girls will
laugh and Sir John will joke, as they wind through lanes

VII. 20.
——·
1606.

May 10

21. Carleton to Chamberlain, May 11, 1606, S. P. O.; Bacon's Will; Spedding's Bacon, i. 8.

VII. 21.
—
1606.
May 10.

now white with thorn and the bloom of pears? how the bridesmaids scatter rosemary and the groomsmen struggle for the kiss? Who cannot imagine that dinner in the Strand, though the hunchback Earl of Salisbury has not come over to Sir John's lodging to taste the cheer or kiss the bride? We know that the wit is good, for Bacon is there; we may trust Sir John for the quality of his wine.

Alice brings to her husband two hundred and twenty pounds a year, with a further claim, on her mother's death, of one hundred and forty pounds a year. As Lady Pakington long outlived Bacon, that increase never came into his hands. Two hundred and twenty pounds a year is his wife's whole fortune. What is not spent in lace and satins for her bridal dress, he allows her to invest for her separate use. From his own estate he settles on her five hundred pounds a year.

Now, in what sense can a marriage in which there seems to be a good deal of love, and in which there certainly is no great flush of money, be called, on Bacon's side, a mercenary match?

June.

22. A slight more galling than has yet been put on him awaits the close of his honeymoon. Only a few days after his marriage to Alice, Sir Francis Gawdy, of the Common Pleas, stricken with apoplexy, is removed from his chambers at Sergeants' Inn to Easton Hall, where he

22. Foss's Judges of England, vi. 153, 306, 329: Chron. Jurid. 181; Montagu. v. 297; Council Reg., Oct. 14, 1606.

soon after dies. Coke goes up to the bench, and Dod-   VII. 22.
eridge, the Solicitor-General, ought by the custom of the
law to follow Coke, leaving the post of Solicitor void.   1606.
But Sir Francis Gawdy having been a partisan of the   June.
Essex faction, and his daughter married to the son of
Lady Rich, Cecil, either anxious not to offend that powerful faction, which he has made his own by a double contract of marriage, or doubtful of his cousin's subserviency
in office, sets aside the usual order of promotion at the
bar, and raises Sir Henry Hobart, his obscure Attorney   July 4.
of the Court of Wards, over Doderidge's as well as over
Bacon's head, to the high place of Attorney-General.   Oct.
Bacon complains to Egerton and Cecil of the insult even
more than the wrong of such a trick. The Lord Chancellor, who sees the error made by the government in
alienating the most powerful man in the House of Commons, proposes to heal the wound by asking Sir John
Doderidge to yield his patent to Bacon, taking in exchange the place of King's Sergeant, together with a
promise of the first seat that shall fall vacant in the
King's Bench. To this Sir John and Cecil both object.

23. When Parliament meets in November to discuss   Nov.
the Bill of Union, Bacon stands back. The King has
chosen his Attorney; let the new Attorney fight the
King's battle. The adversaries to be met are bold and

23. Carleton to Chamberlain, Dec. 18, 1606, S. P. O.; Foster to Mathews,
Feb. 16, 1607, S. P. O.; Com. Jour., i. 314, 333; Lane's Reports in the Court
of Exchequer, 22, 31; M'Crie's Life of Melville, ii. 234.

VII. 23.　many., During the recess Cecil has imposed on the
—　　country a Book of Rates, pretending that taxes may be
1606.　lawfully laid in the King's ports at the King's pleasure.
Nov.　John Bates, a merchant trading with Venice, resisting a
tax unsanctioned by the House of Commons, has been
condemned in the Court of Exchequer; but this condemnation of Bates rousing a nation of tax-payers, from
every port into which ships can float come protests
against Sir Thomas Fleming's reading of the law. Beyond the Tweed, too, people are mutinous to the point
of war; for the countrymen of Andrew Melville begin
to suspect the King of a design against the Kirk, and
Melville himself, lured by a false pretence from St. Andrew's to London, has been provoked into an indiscretion,
and clapped in the Tower.

Under such crosses, the Bill on Union fares but ill.
Fuller, the bilious representative of London, flies at the
Scots. The Scots in London are in the highest degree
unpopular. Lax in morals and in taste, they will take
the highest place at table, they will drink out of anybody's can, they will kiss the hostess or her buxom maid
without saying, "By your leave." Brawls fret the taverns which they haunt; pasquins hiss against them from
the stage. Such broils distract the poor King, who sees
no way to put them down save by commanding Popham
to whip and pillory the rogues who beat his countrymen
and friends. Three great poets, Jonson, Chapman, and
Marston, go to jail for a harmless jest against these Scots.
Such acts of rigor make the name of Union hateful to the
public ear.

Hobart goes to the wall. James now sees that the battle is not to the weak nor the race to the slow. Bacon has only to hold his tongue and make his terms. Alarmed lest the Bill of Union may be rejected by an overwhelming vote, Cecil suddenly adjourns the House. He must get strength. The plan proposed by Egerton for making Doderidge a King's Sergeant, Bacon the Solicitor-General, is revived. Pressed on all sides, here by the Lord Chancellor, there by a mutinous House of Commons, Cecil at length yields to his cousin's claim, Sir John Doderidge bows his neck, and when Parliament meets after the Christmas holidays Bacon holds in his pocket a written engagement for the Solicitor's place.

VII. 23.
—
1606.
Dec.

24. The Bill of Union, drawn by Egerton, consists of four parts : hostile laws, border laws, laws of commerce, laws of navigation. Three of these parts present no difficulties to the House of Commons. Statutes which forbid a Scot to pass the Tweed, which fill the dales of Ettrick and Yarrow with feud and slaughter, which prohibit the sale of English wool in Scotland and of Scottish furs in England, find no advocates. All the old barbarous laws are at once annulled. But the knights and burgesses resist the King's design of naturalizing the whole Scottish population.

1607.
Feb. 14.

Nicholas Fuller reopens the debate. A union of these two countries, says the uncivil member for London, would be a marriage of the rich with the poor, the strong with

24. Com. Jour.. i. 333–337 ; Lords' Jour., ii. 469, 472 ; Statutes, 4 Jac. c. 1.

VII. 24.
—
1607.
Feb. 14.

the weak. With the pardonable pride of a London burgess he points to the arts, the industry, and wealth of England, to its orchards swelling with fruit, its pastures fat with kine, its waters white with sails, to its thriving people, abundant agriculture, inexhaustible fisheries, woods, and mines. With all these riches he contrasts a land of crags and storms, peopled by a race of men rude as their climate, poor in resources and in genius, a nation with peddlers for merchants, and two or three rotten hoys for a fleet. Such countries, he contends, are best apart. What man in his senses, having two estates divided by a hedge, one fruitful, one waste, will break down his fence and let the cattle stray from the waste into garden and corn-field? Will any one mingle two swarms of bees? why then two hostile swarms of men? England is bare as the land round Bethel; so that nature and God call out to separate the nations, as Lot chose the left hand, Abraham the right. He denies that the King's accession has changed the relations of the Saxon to the Scot; and sits down with demanding whether, if Mary had borne a son to Philip, that son being heir to his father's crowns, an English Parliament would have naturalized the people of Sicily and Spain?

25. The speech makes a deep impression. Fuller speaks to men convinced; men sore from daily wrongs and insults. Bacon, rising to reply, begins with that shower of

25. Speech by Sir Francis Bacon in the House of Commons concerning the Naturalization of the Scots, 1641; Wilson, 37.

image and illustration which his experience tells him is
never lost on a learned and poetic House. He begs his
hearers to forget all private feuds, to raise their minds to
questions of the highest state ; not as merchants dealing
with mean affairs, but as judges and kings charged with
the weal of empires. Glancing in scorn at Fuller, he
passes with his light laugh the moral of that tale of Abraham and Lot, a parting cursed with a cruel war and a
long captivity, to his illustration of the fence. The King,
Bacon says, threw down the fence when he crossed the
Tweed ; yet the flock of Scots has not yet followed through
the rent. Proud and lavish, doting on dress and show,
the Scottish gentleman will rather starve at home than
betray his poverty abroad. The Roman commons fought
for the right to name Plebeian consuls, and, when they
had won the right, voted for Patricians : so with the
Scots : they claim the privilege of coming into England ;
yield the right, and they will not come. It is said the
land is full. London, he grants, is thronged and swollen, — not the open downs and plains. France counts
more people to the mile. Flanders, Italy, Germany exceed us in population. Are there no English towns
decayed ? Are there no ancient cities heaps of stones ?
Why, marsh grows on the pasture, pasture on the
plough-land. Wastes increase ; the soil cries loud for
hands to sow the corn and reap the harvest. But this
bill for naturalizing the Scots stands on a far higher
ground. A people, warlike as the Romans and as ourselves, a race of men, who, like wild horses, are hard to

VII. 25. control because lusty with blood and youth, offer to be
—   one people with us, friends in the day of peace, allies in
1607.   the day of strife.   Take from the Scots this brand of
Feb.
aliens, they will stand by our side, bulwarks and defend-
ers against the world.   Should you shut them out from
England, treating them as strangers and enemies, they
may prove to you what the Pisans proved to Florence,
the Latins to Rome.   In our ancient wars the invader
found the gates of our kingdom open.   France could
enter through Scotland, Spain through Ireland.   Pass
this bill, we close our gates.   No minor argument deserves a thought.   Union is strength, union is defence.
You object that the Scots are poor.   Are not strong
limbs better than riches ?   Has not Solon told us the
man of iron is master of the man of gold ?   Does not
Macchiavelli pour his scorn at the false proverb which
makes money the sinews of war ?   The true sinews of
war are the sinews of valiant men.   Leave, gentlemen, to
the Spaniards the delusion that a heap of gold, filched
from a feeble race, can give the dominion of the world.   If
union with the Scots will not bring riches to our doors, it
will bring safety to our frontiers, will give us strength at
sea and reserves on land.   Alone we have borne our flag
aloft ; with Scotland united in arms, with Ireland settled
and at peace, with our war fleets on every sea, our merchants in every port, we shall become the first power in
the world.   Warmed with such glorious hopes, how can
the gentleman of England stand upon terms and audits,
— upon mine and thine, — upon he knows not what !

26. The House rings with applause. Cecil sends a *VII. 26.*
copy of this speech to James; and, in the midst of his
trials, it is some pleasure to the poor pedant to see *1607.
Feb.*
what splendid things a practical statesman and philosopher can say for his favorite scheme.

If the Union is postponed till another generation,
its eloquent advocate gains his place.

Lord Campbell assumes that Egerton's plan for Ba- *June 25.*
con's promotion failed, and that he rose into office
through the changes on Popham's death. These are
mistakes. Fleming succeeds Popham, Tanfield succeeds
Fleming, and Hobart remains Attorney. To create a
vacancy, Doderidge has to take the coif, when Bacon's
commission as the King's Solicitor-General immediately
passes the Seal.

26. Cecil to Lake, April 16, 1607, S. P. O.; Chron. Jurid., 183.

CHAPTER VIII.

SOLICITOR-GENERAL.

VIII. 1.
——
1607.
June 25.

1. On the twenty-fifth of June, 1607, at the age of forty-six years and five months, Bacon entered office. During the six years which he acted as Solicitor-General, Lord Campbell has found no flaw in his practice, — abstinence which is due in part to the circumstance that for these six years, with the unimportant exception of the trial of Lord Sanquhair for murder, Lord Campbell has overlooked every fact in Bacon's life. If there is nothing to relate, there may be nothing to condemn.

Yet there is much in the story of these six years, — years in which he wrought at the Essays and shaped out the New Philosophy; in which, to his personal disquiet, he resisted the design of Sir John Pakington and his friends to abridge the authority of the Court of Wales; in which, at his personal risk and loss, he aided to plant Virginia and Ulster; in which, against his professional interests, he engaged in many a good fight for popular liberties against the Crown, — which men of sense and spirit will wish for the sake of example to keep alive.

1. Campbell's Life of Bacon, iii. 56.

2. Cecil is now at his height of fortune. On the sudden, dramatic death of Dorset, the most daring of poets, the most prudent of financiers, Cecil takes the White Staff without parting from his office as premier Secretary of State. He is now nearly all in all. Except in naval affairs, in which Nottingham's great age and eminence as a sailor forbid all meddling, no department of the public service, home or foreign, trade, police, finances, law, religion, war, and peace, escapes the quick eye and controlling hand of the tiny hunchback. Every one serves him, every enterprise enriches him. He builds a new palace at Hatfield, a new Exchange in the Strand. Countesses intrigue for him. His son marries a Howard, his daughter a Clifford. Ambassadors start for Italy, less to see Doges and Grand Dukes than to pick up pictures and statues, bronzes and hangings for his vast establishment at Hatfield Chace. Gardeners travel through France to buy up for him mulberries and vines. Salisbury House on the Thames almost rivals the luxurious villas of the Roman Cardinals in wealth of tapestry, of furniture, and plate. Yet under this blaze of worldly success Cecil is the most miserable of men. Friends grudge his rise; his health is broken; the reins which his ambition draws into his hands are beyond the powers of a man to grasp; and the vigor of his frame, wasted by years of voluptuous license, fails him at the moment when the strain on his faculties is at the full.

2. Eure to Cecil, April 27, 1608, S. P. O.; Chamberlain to Carleton, July 7, 1608; Provisoes between Salisbury and Morral, Dec. 1608, S. P. O.

VIII. 3.   3. In this strain of powers no longer fresh, in this
—   solitude of severed friendships, in this misery of broken
1608.   health, Cecil turns to his hale, bright cousin, not for the
Aug.   companionship he will not give, but for· the hints and
helps a lawyer has to sell. Bacon does not love him.
More than Coke, Cecil has been to him a cross and grief;
for, while he can fight with his own weapons the coarse
and spiteful foe, his gentle heart supplies no armory
of defence against the cold and veiled contempt of
his perfidious friend. When this agonized spectre of
success invites him to more frequent consultations on
affairs, instead of gliding into that· kindly and gracious correspondence which is the habit of his pen, he
chooses to stand with him on the ceremonial footing of
good manners and the duties of his place. While writing notes of business like the following, Bacon may
have in mind the day, not long ago, when the Earl
of Salisbury declined to cross the Strand to taste the
hypocras and kiss the bride : —

BACON TO SALISBURY.

Aug. 24.   This Wednesday, the 24th of Aug. 1608.

IT MAY PLEASE YOUR LORDSHIP, —

I had cast not to fail to attend your Lordship to-
morrow, which was the day your Lordship had appointed for your being at London; but having this day
about noon received knowledge of your being at Ken-

---

3. Bacon to Cecil, Aug. 24, 1608, S. P. O.; Essays, xliv.

sington, and that it had pleased your Lordship to send VIII. 3.
——
1608.
Aug. 24. for me to dine with you as this day, I made what diligence I could to return from Gorhambury; and though I came time enough to have waited on your Lordship this evening, yet, your Lordship being in so good a place to refresh yourself, and though it please your Lordship to use me as a kinsman, yet I cannot leave behind me the shape of a Solicitor. I thought it better manners to stay till to-morrow, what time I will wait on you. And, at all times rest, your Lordship's most humble and bounden,

F. BACON.

To the last hour of Cecil's life, Bacon keeps this ceremonial style. No kindness flows between the cousins; they talk of business, not of love; and when Cecil passes to his rest, a new edition of the Essays, under cover of a treatise on Deformity, paints in true and bold lines, but without one harsh touch, the genius of the man.

4. The feud of the four shires is again ablaze. Sir Nov. John Pakington has found that the King's promise to do right has borne no fruit for him or for his friends sweeter than the sour crabs of his own orchard. Lord Zouch is gone, and Lord Eure, with a new set of standing orders, reigns in his stead; yet the Court of Wales,

<hr>

4. Cott. MSS. Vit., c. 1; Dom. Papers of James the First, xxviii. 48, xxxii. 13, 14, S. P. O ; Heath's Preface, Bacon's Works, vii. 584.

M

under this new President, is no less warm to maintain its right than under the old. Indeed, in the belief of wise and practical men, the time has not arrived for either abolishing the court or interfering with its powers.

This Court of Wales and the Welsh Border, like the more important Court of the North, was erected as a defence against Papist Missionaries and Papist plots. The gentry of Wales and of the Border shires were mainly Roman Catholic; and every villain who in Elizabeth's time disturbed the public peace, and brought shame or punishment on the members of the Roman Church, reckoned on the aid of an army of fighting and fanatical Sir Hughs. The Court of Wales kept them under. The poor, who wished to smelt the iron-ore, to feed their sheep, to dredge their streams for pearls, and net their bays for fish, in peace, blessed it for this boon, and not for this alone; for this royal Court gave them such cheap and speedy justice as could not be obtained in counties governed by the ordinary courts under the common law. If prompt and stern, its rule was national in spirit, popular in aim. The abuses which crept in a few years later, and which caused its fall, were of a kind unknown in the days of Elizabeth, and only just beginning to be known in the days of James. Charles the First gave a new aim to the Court, perverting the power created by Henry and fostered by Elizabeth as a defence of the national sentiment and national faith, into instruments of attack upon them; then, indeed, but not till then, the Court of Wales fell under public odium, and

was swept away in the revolutionary storm.   But the
men who destroyed it under Charles were not the men
who complained of it under James.   The Crofts, Hop-
tons, Pakingtons, Sandys, Lees, Sheldons, Blounts, and
Corbets who contested the authority of Lord Eure, were
afterwards no less hot on the other side, voting and fighting against popular rights under Charles.

5. To Sir John, and to country gentlemen like Sir
John, the Court of Wales is not so much a national
grievance as a personal offence.   It takes from his place
and dignity; and he instructs his under-sheriff to refuse
obedience to the precepts of such a Court.   The gentry
of Herefordshire are up in arms; but people in the
southern and middle shires suspect, as proves to be the
fact ere long, that these loud cries against the Court of
Wales come mainly from a wish on the part of a few
magistrates to get rid of a popular and successful local
power, which curbs for the common good their private
feuds, and keeps a bright eye on the movements of their
missionary priests.   Many of those who cry loudest
against the Court are said to find reasons for their discontent in the commands of their confessors.   Most of
them are Papists, open or concealed.   Sir Herbert Crofts,
long passing for a firm Protestant, has within the year
avowed himself a convert to the Church of Rome.   Sir

5. Eure to Salisbury, Jan. 26, 1608, S. P. O.; Eure to Pakington, Jan. 3,
1608, S. P. O.; Pakington to Eure, Jan. 17, 1608, S. P. O.; Council Reg.,
Nov. 2, 1613.

VIII. 5. John adheres to the Church, but his near kinsman,
—— Humphrey Pakington, is an active and dangerous re-
1608. cusant, whose name is constantly before the Privy Coun-
Nov. cil. Lord Eure complains to Sir John. Sir John flatly
refuses to obey his precepts. Eure writes to Lord Salisbury that his powers must be preserved in full, or he
shall feel it a duty to resign his place.'

6. Cecil consults Bacon, now become chief adviser
of the Crown in all affairs of law, and finds his opinion
on the jurisdiction of the Court of Wales, as in most
things, the reverse of that pronounced by Coke. Coke
is against Eure. A dry, stiff formalist, wanting the
warmth of heart, the large round of sympathies which
enable his illustrious rival at the bar to see into political questions with the eyes of a poet and a statesman,
Coke can only treat a constituted court as a thing of
words, dates, readings, and decisions; not as a living
fact in close relation to other living facts, and having
in itself the germs of growth and change. A point of
law is taken for debate before the judges, when Bacon
appears in opposition to Sir John and his friends, and
pronounces that argument on the Jurisdiction of the
Marches which is printed in his works. After this hearing a proclamation from the King announces the confirmed authority of the Court of Wales; but the mag-

6. Dom. Papers James the First, xxxvii. 53, 54, 56, S. P. O.; Bacon's Works,
vii 587; Proclamation for the Continuance of the Authority and Jurisdiction
of the Presidencies of the North and of Wales [Nov. 1608].

istrates of the four shires continue their opposition, and
the case drags on for nine or ten years, until these magistrates drop the agitation in presence of more solemn
facts.

7. In no History of America, in no Life of Bacon,
have I found one word to connect him with the plantation of that great Republic.   Yet, like Raleigh and
Delaware, he takes an active share in the labors, a conspicuous part in the sacrifices, through which the foun-
dations of Virginia and the Carolinas are first laid.

Like men of far less note, who have received far
higher honors in America, Bacon pays his money into
the great Company, and takes office in its management
as one of the Council.   To his other glories, therefore,
must be added that of a Founder of New States.

8. The causes which led Bacon, with most of his parliamentary and patriotic colleagues, to join the Virginia
Company with person and purse, are the same causes
which move him to fight for the Union and the Subsidies.   The plantation of Virginia is a branch of the
great contest with Spain.

England and Spain have long been rivals in plantation and discovery.   Neither may claim for itself the
wide continents of America by the happy exercise of

7. Virginia Charter Book, May 23, 1609, S. P. O.
8. Fernando Gorges's Brief Relation, 3, 10; Charters of Virginia, April 10,
1606, Mar. 9, 1607, May 23, 1609, S. P. O.

VIII. 8. native genius; for while a Genoese gave the south to
Spain, a Venetian conferred the north on England. Frobisher and Gilbert followed in the wake of Cabot, though
in a different spirit and working to another end. Inflamed by tales of the Incas' shining palaces, Frobisher
went forth in search of mines and gold; Gilbert, who
revived the spirit of the Great Discoverer, sailed to the
far west and gallantly gave his life, not for the rewards
of wealth and fame, but solely in the hope of extending
English power and of converting souls to God. When
he sank in the Golden Hind he left these tasks to his
young half-brother, Sir Walter Raleigh, who lived to be
the true Founder of the United States.

Raleigh, trained to politics under the eyes of Elizabeth,
saw that the battle-field of the two maritime powers lay
in the waters and along the shores of the New World.
Europe was peopled. But the prairie and the savannah,
the forest and the lake of America were virgin fields, the
homes of an expanding race, the seats of a mighty empire
in the time to come. Who shall occupy this splendid
scene? Shall the New World become mainly English or
mainly Spanish? Shall the original type and seed of her
institutions be a Free Press or a Holy Office? Such questions throb and thrill in the veins of Englishmen of every
rank.

9. They answer with one voice. While the Queen
lived and Raleigh was free to spend his genius and his

1609.
May 23.

9. Smith's History, 88, 90; Nova Britannia, 1609; Jourdan's Discovery of the

fortune on the work of discovery and plantation, it never VIII. 9.
flagged. But when James came in, and, with his dread
of heroism and adventure, flung the explorer of Guiana, 1609.
May 23.
the founder of Virginia, into the Tower, as a first step
towards receiving the Spanish ambassador, Velasco, with
proposals for a shameful peace, the old English spirit appeared to droop. Velasco for a time said little of Virginia, for the fires of the Armada and of Nieuport burned
in many hearts; but Lerma, in his letters to the King,
reserved an exclusive right of the Spanish crown, based
on a Papal bull, to all the soil of the New World from
Canada to Cape Horn. When his agents in London
found their season they made this claim; when his admirals in the Gulf of Mexico felt their strength they chased
the English from those seas as pirates. If the Spanish
cruisers caught an English crew, they either slung them
to the yard-arm or sent them prisoners to Spain.

Ruled by a corporation of adventurers, tormented by
these Spanish cruisers, unprotected by the royal fleets,
the settlement on the James River falls to grief. A man
of genius, Captain John Smith, more than once snatches
it from the jaws of death. But the planters fight among
themselves, depose Smith from power, and send back
nothing to the Company save miserable complaints and
heaps of glittering dust. The colony is on the verge of
failure, when a threat from Spain to descend on the
Chesapeake shoots new life into the drooping cause. All

Barmudas, otherwise called the Isle of Divels, by Sir T. Gates, Sir G. Sommers,
and Captain Newport, with divers others, 1610.

VIII. 9. generous spirits rush to the defence of Virginia. Bacon

——

1609.

May 23.

joins the Company with purse and voice. Montgomery, Pembroke, and Southampton, the noble friends of Shakespeare, join it. Nor is the Church less zealous. The ardent Abbott, the learned Hackluyt, lend their names. Money pours in. A fleet, commanded by Gates and Somers, sails from the Thames, to meet on its voyage at sea those singular and poetic storms and trials which add the Bermudas to our empire and The Tempest to our literature.

10. One hundred and seventy-five years after Walter Raleigh laid down his life in Palace Yard for America, his illustrious blood paid for by Gondomar in Spanish gold, the citizens of Carolina, framing for themselves a free constitution, remembered the man to whose genius they owed their existence as a state. They called the capital of their country Raleigh. The United States can also claim among their muster-roll of Founders the not less noble name of Francis Bacon. Will the day come, when, dropping such feeble names as Troy and Syracuse, the people of the Great Republic will give the august and immortal name of Bacon to one of their splendid cities ?

1610.

April.

11. The session of 1610 shows Bacon in a characteristic scene. Bound by the traditions of his place to support

10. Statutes of North Carolina, c. xiv.

11. Add. MSS., 11, 695; Lords' Journals, ii. 574.

the King's measures in the House of Commons, when the VIII. 11.
session opens, with a freedom which surprises the King's
friends, and which Coke and Doderidge have never dared
to take, he both speaks and votes against the superior
law-officers of the Crown.

The List of Grievances has at length been shaped into
a proposition, and laid before the House.   This Great
Contract, as the people call it, offers to buy from the
Crown, either for a fixed sum of money to be paid down,
or for a yearly rental, certain rights and dues inherited
by the King from feudal times, which the change of manners and the refinements of society have made abominable
to rich and educated men.   Escutage, Knight-service,
Wardship of the body, Marriage of heirs and of widows,
Respite of homage, Premier seizin, every knight and squire
in the land longs to suppress, as things which yield the
King an uncertain income, but cover themselves with a
certain shame.   A group of feudal tenures which concern
the dignity of the Crown, such as Sergeantry, Homage,
Fealty, Wardship of land, and Livery, they propose to
modify, so as to satisfy just complaints while preserving to
the King all services of honor and ceremonial rite.   Aids
to the King they limit in amount; suits, heriots, and
escheats they leave untouched; monopolies for the sale
of wines, for the licensing of inns, for the importation of
coal, they abrogate.   In lieu of these reliefs, they offer
the King one hundred thousand pounds a year.

12. At first James will not listen.   The terms of such a

9 *

VIII. 12. contract touch, he says, his honor. These privileges may be of no moment to the Crown; to part with them may neither lower its dignity nor abate its pride; yet why should he be asked to part with them? Elizabeth had them. All the Plantagenets, all the Tudors had them. Why should the first of the Stuarts strip his Crown of privileges held by his predecessors for five hundred years? But James is not true to his own folly. To resist a sale of the rags and dust of feudal power, if done on the ground of conscience, would to many seem respectable, to some heroic; but the offer of a hundred thousand pounds a year tempts a man dogged by duns to compromise with his sense of right. He lends his ear; he hints his willingness to treat. Will the Commons give a little more? Will they take a little less? If so, he will hear them; if not, not. Cecil asks Fleming and Coke to declare whether James can lawfully sell the burdens on tenures, yet preserve to his Crown the tenures themselves.

13. The chance of hurting Bacon, who pleads in office, as he always spoke when out of office, for the full surrender of these feudal dues, is too much for Coke. Their feud has, indeed, grown fiercer as they have grown in years, flashing out even in the courts of law. "The less you speak of your own greatness," says Bacon in open court, "the more I shall think of it, and the more, the less." As Bacon contends that a sale of the burdens on

Side note:
1610.
April.

---

12. Add. MSS., 11, 695; Com. Jour., i. 419, 420.
13. Spedding's Bacon, vii. 177; Add. MSS., 11, 695.

tenures is in fact a sale of the tenures, Coke answers VIII. 13.
Cecil that the King may, if it shall please him, sell the
burdens, yet keep the tenures intact. James therefore
sends to tell the Commons that he will sell to them for
six hundred thousand pounds paid down, and a rental of
two hundred thousand pounds a year, his rights of marriage, wardship, premier seizin, respite of homage, and
reliefs.

1610.
April.

14. In these debates, the Solicitor-General, brushing
away the distinctions of Coke and Fleming, urges on the
House of Commons and on the Crown the wisdom of
abolishing these feudal tenures both in name and fact.
Tenures in capite and by knight-service, he says, have
lost their virtue. When the sovereign summoned his
liegemen to the field, Reason might have cried, — Hold
fast all tenures which augment the national force ! But
the King no longer leads his armies in the field or
calls his vassals round his flag; war has grown into a
science, arms into a profession ; if an enemy should
appear at Dover or Berwick, no man would now wait
for the King's tenant to strike. In the musters for defence, holders in soccage stand foot to foot with holders
by knight-service. In feudal ages the tenures meant
defence ; but the usage and the idea has alike gone by ;
and tenures no longer represent either force, honor, or
obedience.

15. Bacon pleads so well that after warm debates the July 23.

14. Bacon's Speech, April, 1610; Lords' Jour., ii. 580.

VIII. 15. King consents to reduce his demands, the House of Commons to raise their price. The two powers draw nearer
1610.
July 23. to each other, and a happy resolution seems about to
cleanse away some of the very worst abuses of the feudal
state. For two hundred thousand pounds a year the
Crown agrees to renounce forever these feudal rights.

How this Great Contract comes to an abrupt and ignominious end, how King and Commons wrangle over
the Book of Rates, and how a session that began so pros-
perously closes in open strife between the people and
their prince, not a single bill receiving the royal signature, all this, though full of constitutional, and even of
romantic interest, is a tale for the historian of England,
not for the critic of Bacon's life.

1612.
May. 16. So long as his kinsman Cecil lives, Bacon sees no
hope of rising in the world. In May, 1612, the Earl of
Salisbury, Lord Treasurer of England, premier Secretary of State, and Master of the Court of Wards,
worn out by fag of brain not less than by disease of blood,
dies, and a burst of gladness breaks over court and country at the news. His companions of the Privy Council
traduce his fame, his tenants at Hatfield attack his park.
Of all men living, the cousin he so deeply hurt is the least
unjust. In an edition of the Essays, now in the press,
Bacon paints him to the life: every one knows the por-

---

15. King's Proclamation, Dec. 31, 1610; Add. MSS., 11, 695; Lords' Jour., ii.
666-86; Statutes of the Realm, iv. 1207.
16. Bacon's Essays, xliv.; Apophthegms, Works, vii. 175.

trait; yet no one can pronounce this picture of a small,
shrewd man of the world, a clerk in soul, without a spark
of fire, a dash of generosity in his nature, unfair or even
unkind. The spirit of it runs in a famous anecdote.
" Now tell me truly," says the King, " what think you
of your cousin that is gone ? " " Sir," answers Bacon,
" since your Majesty charges me, I 'll give you such a
character of him as if I were to write his story. I do
think he was no fit councillor to make your affairs better.
But yet he was fit to have kept them from growing
worse."

" On my so'l, man ! " says James, " in the first thou
speakest like a true man, in the second, like a kinsman."

17. From the day of Cecil's death, his prospects,
clouded till now, begin to clear. If promotion pauses,
it is only because the crowds of suitors perplex the
King. Carr and Northampton claim the Treasurer's
staff. Everybody begs the Court of Wards and Liveries.
Sir Thomas Lake, Sir Henry Wotton, Sir Ralph Winwood, Sir Henry Neville, each aspires to the rank of
Secretary of State. The patriots put up Bacon's name
for this great office, and shrewd observers fancy him
nigh success. Poor James, unable to decide, hankering,
though afraid, to make Carr his chief minister, puts
the Treasury into commission for six months, gives the
Wards to Carew, and startles the gossips of Whitehall

17. Chamberlain to Carleton, Nov. 26, 1612, S. P. O.

VIII. 17. by announcing that, instead of employing either Bacon
—   or Wotton, Winwood or Lake, he means for the future
1612.   to be his own Secretary of State.

Nov.   18. Carew dying suddenly six months after his nomination, Bacon applies for the Court of Wards. His
pay as Solicitor-General is only seventy pounds a year.
Promised for his service to the Crown a place of profit,
he points out in a letter to Carr that the Court of
Wards is one for a lawyer rather than a courtier to
hold.

BACON TO LORD ROCHESTER.

Nov. 14, 1612.

IT MAY PLEASE YOUR GOOD LORDSHIP, —

This Mastership of the Wards is like a mist, — sometimes it goeth upwards and sometimes it falleth down-
wards. If it go up to great lords, then it is as it was
at the first; if it fall down to mean men, then it is
as it was at the last. But neither of these ways concerns me in particular, — but if it should in a middle
region go to lawyers, then I beseech your Lordship have
some care of .me. The attorney and solicitor are as
the King's champions for civil business, and they had
need have some place of rest in their eye for their en-
couragement. The Mastership of the Rolls, which was
the ordinary place kept for them, is gone from them.

18. Bacon to Carr, Nov. 14, 1612, S. P. O.; Lake to Carleton Nov. 19, 1612,
Venetian MSS., S. P. O.

,If this place should go to a lawyer, and not to them, VIII. 18.
their hopes must diminish. Thus I rest, your Lordship's affectionate, to do you humble service,

1612.
Nov.

F. BACON.

He feels so certain of this suit that he orders the
new clothes for his servants; yet the suit fails. He
wants the Court of Wards and Liveries as a right, and
will not buy it. Sir Walter Cope, a man of larger
fortunes and smaller scruples, while Bacon alleges service, tells down his money and buys the place. The
wags of the Mitre have their laugh. "Sir Walter,"
they say, "has got the Wards, Sir Francis the Liveries."

19. If he sue without success for the Court of Wards, 1613.
he is constantly consulted or employed in the most   Aug.
weighty, the most delicate business of the Crown.
Most conspicuous, perhaps, of the cases which now engage his mind is the old, old story of Irish broils.

Of Ireland itself he never speaks but in words of
tenderness and grief. With him the green, lustrous
island is "a country blessed with almost all the dowries
of nature, — with rivers, havens, woods, quarries, good
soil, temperate climate, and a race and generation of
men, valiant, hard, and active, as it is not easy to find
such confluence of commodities, if the hand of man
did join with the hand of nature; but they severed, —

<hr>

19. Bacon to Carr, Nov. 14, 1612, S. P. O.

the harp of Ireland is not strung or attuned to con-cord." More the pity, thinks its generous and sagacious friend !

20. Sir Arthur Chichester, the wisest, firmest man ever sent from England to rule the Celt, — after driv-ing out the rebels O'Neile and O'Donnel, crushing O'Dogherty and the assassins who ravished and de-stroyed Derry, — has built a new city on Lough Foyle, garrisoned and calmed Strabane, Ballyshannon, Omagh, and the forts along the lines from Kerry to Inishoan, and peopled with the germs of a new race the wastes of Antrim and Down, of Londonderry and Coleraine. Strong in his genius and in his success, after founding an English state in Ulster on the ruins of the great Celtic insurrection, he calls a Parliament in Dublin to sanction what has been done, and to resume, for the first time in the remembrance of living men, a regular mode of civil and popular government. For seven years he has ruled by the sword. He wishes to lay it down. But blood is hot and feuds run high. The Saxon and the Celt, the Protestant and the Papist, meet in Dublin, less disposed to sit on the same benches and hear each other prate than to pluck out the sharp skean and fly at each other's throats. At the first meeting they fall to blows. One party says Sir John Everard shall be

20. An Account of the Right Hon. Sir Arthur Chichester, Lord Belfast, Lord Deputy of Ireland; by Sir Faithful Fortescue: with Notes and a Memoir of the Writer by Lord Clermont; 1858. Ellis's Orig. Letters, Third Series, iv. 173.

Speaker; the other, Sir John Davis. Everard is in VIII. 20.
opposition, Davis the Irish Attorney-General; Everard
the candidate of the monks, Davis of the Crown. Chichester can but follow the Imperial law. Usage good
in Westminster must be held good in Dublin. Davis
must be Speaker. Indeed, the majority elect him. But
a crowd of men, summoned from the Bog of Allen,
from the banks of Lough Swilly, from the wilds of
Sligo and Mayo, — representatives of the MacOiraghtys
and MacCoghlans, of the O'Doghertys, O'Donnels, and
O'Concannons, — who have scarcely ever heard of a precedent, have not learned to respect a majority of votes.
When the Protestants file into the right lobby, instead
of filing into the left the Roman Catholic members seat
Everard in the chair. They refuse to move or to be
counted like a drove of sheep! Davis, voted into the
chair by a majority of twenty-eight, is taken up to his
seat by two members, as in the English House of Commons. Everard will not stir. Davis plumps into his
lap. In a wild Irish uproar, Everard, caught by the
crowd, is thrust out neck and crop. The Celtic members grasp their skeans. If Chichester, wise in time,
had not prudently set them in a ring of steel, the members, instead of hearing each other's grievances, would
have cut each other's throats. Such a House of Commons is an impracticable instrument for preserving the
peace of Ireland, and Chichester dissolves it. On the
evening of the row, to show his scorn of such brab-
bles, the Lord Deputy goes out to play his usual rubber.

1613.
Aug.

VIIL 21.
—
1613.
Aug 13.

21. Everard and his friends come over to complain at Whitehall. They talk of their wrongs. They object to the new boroughs planted by the English; they require that these boroughs shall not be allowed to send representatives to an Irish House of Commons! They whine of danger to their persons, of a Gunpowder Plot to blow them into the sky.

The King consults Bacon. Anxious for Parliaments, but aware that Parliaments presuppose habits of order and discussion, respect for opinion, submission to majorities, Bacon gives the King this advice: —

BACON TO JAMES.

Aug. 13, 1613.

MAY IT PLEASE YOUR MOST EXCELLENT MAJESTY, —

I was at my house in the country what time the commission and instructions for Ireland were drawn by Mr. Attorney, but I was present this day the forenoon, when they were read before my Lords and excepted. to, some points whereof use was made, and some alterations followed, but I could not in decency except to as much as I thought there might be cause, lest it might be thought a humor of contradiction or an effect of emulation, which, I thank God, I am not much troubled with, for, so your Majesty's business be well done, whosoever be the instrument, I rest joyful. But because this is a tender piece of service, and that which was well directed by

21. Abbot, Aug. 4, 1613, S. P. O.; Add. MSS. 19, 402, fol. 37.

VIII. 21.

1613.
Aug. 13.

your Majesty's high wisdom may be marred in the manage, and that I have been so happy as to have my poor service in this business of Ireland, which I have minded with all my powers, because I thought your estate labored, graciously accepted by your sacred Majesty, I do presume to present to your Majesty's remembrance (whom I perceive to be one of the most truly politic princes that ever reigned, and the greatest height of my poor abilities is but to understand you well) some few points in a memorial enclosed which I wish to be changed. They tend to this scope principally, that I think it safest for your Majesty at this time, *hoc agere*, which is to effect that you may hold a parliament in Ireland with sovereignty, concord, contentment, and moderate freedom, and so bind up the wound made without clogging the commission with too many other matters ... whereas these instruments are are so marshalled as if the grievances were the principal. The grievances which were not commended to these messengers from the party in Ireland, but slept at least a month after their coming hither, and ... are divers of them of so vulgar a nature as they are complained of both in England and Ireland, and both now and at all times. For your Majesty to give way upon this ground, to so particular an inquiry of all these points, I confess I think is unworthy of majesty, for they are set down like interrogatories in a suit in law. And my fear is they will call up and stir such a number of complaints and petitions, which not being possible to be satisfied, this commission, meant for satisfaction, will

VIII. 21. end in murmur. But these things which I write are per-
—
1613.
Aug. 13.
haps but my errors and simplicities. Your Majesty's
wisdom must steer and ballast the ship. So most humbly craving pardon, I ever rest your Majesty's most devoted and faithful subject and servant,

FR. BACON.

Government acts on this counsel of maintaining in
Dublin a firm and inflexible justice. A Parliament meets
within twelve months, the members of which quarrel
indeed among themselves, as is only national and natural; but which proves itself as capable of transacting
public business as almost any Parliament in Palace Yard.
It gives peace to Ireland for thirty years.

For nearly all that is most gracious and noble, most
wise and foreseeing in the Irish policy of the Crown in
this reign, thanks are due, next after Arthur Chichester,
to Francis Bacon. Yet Lord Campbell, a statesman and
a lawyer, has not one word on this theme!

Oct. 21. 22. Two years of fag and moil cure James of his ambition to be thought the best scribe in Christendom.
Dissolving the commission of the Treasury, he gives the
Staff to Northampton. He brings Winwood forward as
Secretary of State; but ere passing his commission under
the Seal, James raises his great competitor for that post
a step in his profession; Coke going up to the King's

22. Chamberlain to Carleton, Oct. 14, 27, 1614, S. P. O.; Grant Book, 102;
Bacon's Apophthegms in Resuscitatio, 38.

Bench, Hobart to the Common Pleas, and Bacon to the VIII. 22.
Attorney's place.   Coke huffs at the King's Bench, a

1613.
court of higher dignity than the Common Pleas, but of
Oct. 27.
fewer fees.   James has to interfere.   " This is all your
doing, Mr. Attorney," says the irascible Lord Chief
Justice ; " it is you that have made this great stir."
With the light laugh that has so often maddened Coke,
he answers, " Your Lordship all this while hath. grown
in breadth ; you must needs now grow in height, or you
will be a monster."

23. Lord Campbell sees in these promotions, not the   Nov.
natural changes brought about by time, such as every
year occur at the bar, but a mean trick, a court intrigue,
an affair of secret letters, of back-stairs interest, in short,
a dodge and a cheat!   To this reading of events may be
opposed the judgments of those among Bacon's contemporaries who know him best, the electors of the University
of Cambridge, the members of the House of Commons.
Their judgments, happily for us, are given in a very
conspicuous and decisive way.

Bacon's first advice to the Crown in his new office is to
abandon its irregular, unproductive methods of raising
funds, inventions of the Meercrafts and Overreaches of

23. Mem. of Burgesses chosen for more than one place, April, 1614, S. P. O.
Bacon's biographers have been misled about his seat in 1614 by an erroneous
conjecture of Willis (Not. Parl., iii. 173).   There is a list of the Parliament of
1614 among the valuable MSS. at Kimbolton Castle, for which, as for many
other courtesies, I am indebted to the obliging friendship of his Grace-the Duke
of Manchester.

VIII.23. the court; to call a new Parliament to Westminster, to
—   explain frankly the political situation, and to trust the
1614.   nation for supplies. The advice, though hotly opposed
March.
by Northampton and the whole gang of Spanish pension-
ers, men paid to provoke hostility between the Commons
and the Crown, so far prevails that writs go down into
the country. For thirteen years Bacon has represented
Ipswich in the House of Commons. Ipswich clings to
him with the love of a bride. But Cambridge, a more
splendid and gracious constituency, claims him for its
own. In the ambition of a public man there is nothing
more pure than the wish to represent in Parliament the
University at which he has been trained; nor is there
for the scholar and .the writer any reward more lofty
than the confidence implied in the votes of a great constituency of scholars and gentlemen. In Bacon's case
there are peculiar obstacles. He left Cambridge early
and in disdain; he has kept no friendly intercourse with
its dons; the business of his intellectual life has been to
destroy the grounds on which its system of instruction
stands. Yet the members of the University feel that as
a writer and a philosopher he is not only the most brilliant Cambridge man alive, but the most brilliant Englishman who ever lived. They elect him.

The burgesses of Ipswich also elect him. The burgesses of St. Albans also elect him. Such a return is
unprecedented in parliamentary annals. Only the most
popular and patriotic candidates are rewarded in this
Parliament by double returns. Sandes is elected for

Hendon and Rochester, Whitelocke for Woodstock and VIII. 23.
Corffe Castle. No one save the new Attorney-General
can boast of a triple return.

Of course he sits for Cambridge ; a fact, overlooked by
his biographers, from Rawley to Lord Campbell, which
connects his fame in a gentle and gracious form with
the political history of Cambridge.

24. Nor is this gracious confidence of his University
the most striking proof of popularity which he now receives. When the Houses meet in April, a whisper
buzzes round the benches that the elections for Cambridge, Ipswich, and St. Albans are null and void. No
man holding the office of Attorney-General has ever been
elected to serve in Parliament, and some of the members
seem resolved that so powerful an officer of the Crown
never ought to sit, and never shall sit, in that House.
The Attorney-General is the Crown trier ; he sets the law
in motion ; he gathers the evidence, weighs the words,
sifts the facts for prosecution. Unless scrupulous beyond
the virtue of man, such an officer, hearing everything,
noting everything, forgetting nothing, may become, in a
House of Commons bent on free speech as its sacred
right, the worst of inquisitors and tyrants. He shall not
sit. Yet, notwithstanding their jealousy of power, the
representative gentlemen of England have no heart to
put the wisest and best among them to the door. They

24. Chamberlain to Carleton, April 14, 1614, S. P. O.; Com. Jour., i. 456;
Statutes of the Realm, iv. 1207.

seek for precedents, that he may sit. No case is on the rolls. An Attorney-General, chosen after his nomination, cannot sit by precedent. What then ? They waive their right. They take him as he is. Crown lawyer or not Crown lawyer, he is Sir Francis Bacon. As Sir Francis Bacon he shall sit. But the case shall stand alone. This tribute paid to personal merit and public service must not be drawn, say the applauding members, into a precedent dangerous to their franchise. He is the first to sit, he must be the last.

That an exception in favor of the new Attorney-General should have been made by men so hostile to the court that they broke up at last without passing a single bill which the Crown could assent to, is most strange. The results are yet more strange. As if to witness to the latest generations the profound estimation in which Bacon was held by a House of Commons which had known him closely for thirty years, and which had seen him vote and act under every form of temptation that can test the virtue and tax the genius of a public man, this exception, made in his favor solely, became the rule for his successors and for succeeding times. Once only has the restriction been referred to in the House. That was in the case of his immediate successor. Since his time the presence of the Attorney-General among the representatives of the people has been constant. This fact suggests not only that a change has taken place in public thought, but that the character of the Crown official has undergone a change. Such is the truth.

Before Bacon's day the Attorney-General was the personal servant of the prince: from Bacon's day he has been the servant of the State. Bacon was the first of a new order of public men. The fact is scarcely less creditable to his political purity than the composition of the Novum Organum is glorious to his intellectual powers. Bad men kill great offices. Good men found them.

10

.

CHAPTER IX.

ST. JOHN AND PEACHAM.

1. If Lord Campbell has not one word to say on Bacon's part in the plantation of Virginia, in the regeneration of Ulster, he has room for page after page of statement, more or less false in fact, wholly false in spirit, on the examination into the contempt of Oliver St. John, and on the trial for libel of Edmond Peacham.

Happy the great lawyer who in passionate times can give up office with no worse recollection on his soul than having conducted two such cases for the Crown !

2. First of Oliver St. John. In the session of 1614, as in every session when he was out of office, Bacon puts his strength to the supplies. The day which he has so long feared has come ; the Papal powers, united over the corpse of Henri Quatre, have formed their league ; Spinola's Pandours and Walloons are crushing out the free, industrial, and religious life of the Lower Rhine. A dozen cities lift their hands for help. Battalions clash down the passes of the Alps and the Pyrenees, armadas

---

1. Campbell, Life of Bacon, iii. 62 – 66.
2. St. John to Mayor of Marlborough, Oct. 11, 1614, S. P. O.

IX. 2.

1614.
Oct. 11

ride in the roads of Sicily and in the bays of Spain. The English fleet is rotting in port. Only ten or twelve ships are in commission; four in the Thames or the Downs, one or two at Portsmouth and Plymouth, four in the Irish seas. The Crown is deep in debt. To a man not mad with jealousy of power such a political situation must be intolerable, and it is intolerable to Bacon. But the Puritans are deaf. They fear the King even more than the Roman League. They will not give. Unable to procure grants from Parliament, James tries to raise money by a benevolence; when the lords, the bishops, and archbishops, come to his aid, bringing cups, rings, and golden angels into the Jewel House of the Tower. All mayors of towns are ordered to receive such gifts as may be offered. No rate is laid; no one is forced to give; at least, so say the officers of the Crown. In loyal shires persuasion may be used to swell the lists; but where the magistrates are not loyal, the benevolence flags. Many of the Puritans, all the Papists, close their hands; those distrusting the court; these wishing well to the foe. The benevolence fares best in the Protestant shires; worst in the Catholic shires. Kent, Surrey, Middlesex, Herts, Berks, Essex, and Norfolk yield an army of subscribers. Sussex sends up only three; Durham, Cumberland, Westmoreland, not one. Now, it is clear that those who oppose a Parliamentary vote may fairly decline to make a free gift. But Oliver St. John, Black Oliver his contemporaries call him, from his bilious temper and dark complexion, is not content merely to decline. A man of a

IX. 2.
———
1614.
Oct. 11.

stormy and yet slavish spirit, he must denounce this measure of the government by voice and pen. He will not let the people give. In a public letter to the Mayor of Marlborough he declares that the King, in asking his people for a free gift of money, is violating his oath, committing a perjury more gross than that for which more than one English monarch has lost his crown!

Dec.

3. It is impossible for the Privy Council to overlook such a contempt. The lawfulness of a Benevolence may be open to debate; no true Englishman can doubt that St. John's letter is in the highest degree scandalous to the King, and in the highest degree injurious to the national force. Lord Campbell (who confounds this Oliver St. John with the famous Lord Chief Justice of the Commonwealth, now a boy of sixteen!) appears to regard St. John as an earlier Hampden. A closer reading of the time would show that he was one of those loud and lying politicians who are the disgrace of every cause. Instead of being the Hampden, Black Oliver was the O'Brien or the O'Connor of his time; though he had neither Smith O'Brien's abilities nor Feargus O'Connor's dash. When the Marlborough bully is cited into the Star Chamber, Coke condemns him to five thousand pounds fine and imprisonment for life. Yet even the Tower, which so often elevates a fool into a martyr, fails to make St. John

---

3. Council Reg., Nov. 19, 25, Dec. 4, 9, 1614, Feb. 3, May 31, 1615; Chamberlain to Carleton, Jan. 5, Feb. 9, 1615, S. P. O.; Council to James, Feb. 8, 1615, S. P. O.; Add. MSS. 19, 402.

appear, even to the undiscerning mob, either a wise or a brave man. When the gate of his cell creaks on its hinge he begins to whine and cry. He repents his sally, recants his words. He goes on his knees, he pledges his future fame. He begs, fawns, groans to be let out. Even those who make an idol of every one barred in the Tower turn from this pusillanimous and crouching prisoner in disgust.

4. One of St. John's letters to the King is so amazingly abject as to constitute a curiosity in literature. In England we are not used to such a style of prison supplication, for the men who go wrong generally have the merit of going wrong in good faith, and when called to the martyr's crown wear it as a crown. It may be well to give a passage from this document (now for the first time printed), that the world may note, under his own seal, what kind of hero this Oliver St. John is, whom Lord Campbell mistakes for the great Chief Justice !

OLIVER ST. JOHN TO THE KING.

Most High and Mighty King, my alone virtually and rightfully dread Lord and Sovereign (after God my Maker and my Saviour Jesus Christ), my hearty chief joy, love, slave, and delight !

In all humbleness of soul and spirit showeth unto your sacred Majesty your poor distressed subject and

4. Add. MSS. 19, 402, fol. 62.

faithful servant, sometimes long close prisoner in the Tower of London; that whereas it graciously pleased your said Majesty, on humble submission and petition to consider and commiserate the lamentable condition of the poor petitioner, censured in the Star Chamber for a letter written to the Mayor of Marlborough in October 1614, and therewith showed your princely and Royal heart so moved to mercy, that as the then Lord Chancellor said you had out of admirable and more than kingly benignity and bounty so remitted the same that I had not any more to starve, although my fine, together with my submission, remained on record. . . . . . But my great and brain-sick offence against your Most Excellent Majesty, my right dear Sovereign (for which phrase at your Highness's feet my broken heart again and again most humbly and instantly asketh your most gracious pardon), forbidding me your awful presence . . . . . on my bended knees, in all humility of heart and spirit, [I] beseech your great, imperial, and sacred Majesty, first gracious remission and pardon, both of the fault and pain, as also, most gracious King and my dearest liege lord, that you will further be graciously pleased to show your most admirable goodness and mercy (if it may stand with due order of state policy) in commanding a removal or deleator of the whole record thereof; that so great an ignominy remain not on the name of him who, having been now received your Majesty's sworn servant, is still resolved ever to receive therein that fatal arrow in his breast (with loyal

Hugo de St. Clara) than once admit into his heart the
least disloyal thought against your sacred person, dignity, or fame; the very least of us whoso shall seek
to impeach, let God from Heaven shoot sharp arrows
into his heart, that all the King's enemies may fall
before him. So prayeth, from his inmost heart,

Your Majesty's humble, faithful, and
obedient vassal,
OLIVER ST. JOHN.

5. Lord Campbell, who brands the conduct of Bacon
in officially aiding to silence this impudent and whining
demagogue, is more than usually infelicitous in the
grounds of his charge. He says that Bacon in his
speech against Oliver St. John strenuously defends the
raising of money by benevolences. Now, he does no
such thing. He never once touches the law of these
free gifts. He proves, and proves most clearly, that the
particular benevolence denounced by St. John to the
Mayor of Marlborough as a violation of the King's oath,
has no character of a forced loan. The question tried,
if one may say so to a nobleman who has been a Lord
Chief Justice and is now a Lord Chancellor, was not
one of law, but one of fact, — not whether a benevolence was, in the reign of James the First, legal, but
whether St. John had been guilty of a grievous contempt in publishing his letter to the Mayor. The trial
of John Bates for refusing to pay the taxes levied by

5. State Trials, ii. 899.

IX. 4.

1614.
Dec.

the Book of Rates was a trial of law ; the trial of Oliver St. John for calling the King forsworn was a trial of fact. St. John was condemned, not for refusing to subscribe his money, but for publishing a letter in contempt of the Crown.

6. Pass to the case of Peacham, — a case which Lord Campbell has taken less pains to understand than even that of St. John. " Fine and imprisonment," he writes, " having no effect in quelling the rising murmurs of the people, it was resolved to make a more dreadful example, and Peacham, a clergyman of Somersetshire, between sixty and seventy years of age, was selected for the victim. On breaking into his study, a sermon was there found, which he had never preached, nor intended to preach, nor shown to any human being, but which contained some passages encouraging the people to resist tyranny. He was immediately arrested, and a resolution was taken to prosecute him for high treason. But Mr. Attorney, who is alone responsible for this atrocious conduct, anticipated considerable difficulties both in law and in fact before the poor old parson could be subjected to a cruel and almost ignominious death."

In every line of this passage there is error ; indeed, the whole passage is an error. No murmurs arose in the country on account of St. John. No one at court ever dreamt of making Peacham a victim, for no one out of Somersetshire had ever heard his name. His

6. Peacham's Examination, Aug. 31, 1615, S. P. O.

study was not broken into for the purpose of finding treason in it. It was not a sermon that had been found. It is ridiculous to say that the papers seized in his desk were not intended to be shown to any human being, for they had been written for publication and had in truth been shown to several persons. Peacham was not arrested immediately on the seizure of his papers; he was already in custody for offences less dubious than a political crime. Mr. Attorney was not alone responsible for his prosecution. He was not at all responsible. The prosecution was ordered by the Privy Council, of which he was not a member. It was conducted by Winwood, the Puritan Secretary of State.

7. Not much has been left to us by the writers about Edmond Peacham; yet evidence remains in the books at Wells, and in the records of Her Majesty's State Paper Office, to prove that he was one of the most despicable wretches who ever brought shame and trouble on the Church. It is there seen that he was a libeller. It is there seen that he was a liar. It is there seen that he was a marvel of turbulence and ingratitude; not alone a seditious subject, but a scandalous minister and a perfidious friend. It is in evidence that he outraged

7. Sentence of Deprivation against Peacham, Dec. 19, 1614, S. P. O.; Presentation Books at Wells. I am indebted for many particulars respecting Peacham to the friendly inquiries made for me by Lord Auckland, Bishop of Bath and Wells. A brief inspection of the papers preserved in the old gate-tower at Wells convinces me of their very great value for ecclesiastical and family history.

IX. 7. his bishop by a scandalous personal libel; and that he
——   did his worst to get the patron to whom he owed his
1614.
Dec.   living hung.

8. Hallam tells us how hard it is for him to see any
way in which this poor parson, in a wild part of the
west country, far from a large town, could have fallen
into the clutches of the law. The reader of Hallam
will be glad to find that Peacham fell into grief, not
on account of his politics, but for an unbearable ecclesiastical offence.

For several years Peacham had been rector of Hinton St. George, a parish in the wildest part of Somersetshire, and in the diocese of Bath and Wells. James
Montagu, Dean of the Chapel, was bishop. The lord
of the manor and patron of the living of Hinton St.
George was John Paulett, grandson of Bacon's old
friend and guardian, Sir Amias Paulett, and founder
of the noble line of that name and place. Margery, a
sister of this John, married Sir John Sydenham of
Combe, one of his political friends. Paulett represented the county in Parliament, in which he distinguished himself by a firm, yet far from disloyal opposition to the court.

The papers at Wells still prove that Peacham had
been very troublesome to the Church. There had been
irregularities in his institution. There had been libels

8. Wells MSS.; Collins's Peerage, art. Pawlett; Council Reg., Dec. 9, 16,
1614.

and accusations in the Bishop's Court. At length, there .IX. 8.
came from Hinton St. George a foul and malignant libel
against the bishop himself; when Montagu appealed to
his primate, and Archbishop Abbott cited the offender
to appear before him at Lambeth and purge his fame.
His character and his cause appeared so bad that, on
his arrival in town, Abbott lodged him in the Gatehouse,
among the herd of recusants, monks, and priests.

9. Many a Puritan preacher, silenced for a word on Dec. 19.
copes and stoles, on the closed book or the unlit candle,
must have envied this libeller such a hearing as the
Church condescends to grant him. Ten commissioners,
one of them an archbishop, four of them bishops, meet
to try his case. If Abbott and King lean to Puritan
views, Andrews and Neile incline towards Rome. In
such a tribunal there is sure to be sympathy for any
excess of zeal. Yet these four men, as well as the other
six, condemn him. Ecclesiastics who differ from each
other on every point of doctrine and discipline agree to
find Peacham guilty of composing, writing, or causing
to be written, a defamatory libel against his ordinary,
contrary to his canonical obedience and reverence and
to the virtue of his oath, and of writing, or causing to
be written, a scandalous libel against the laws, statutes,
and customs of the Church and the ecclesiastical jurisdiction, defaming the clerical order and the national
rite. By a solemn act they cast him from the Church.

9. Sentence of Deprivation against Edmond Peacham, Dec. 19, 1614, S. P. O.

Margin notes: IX. 8. — 1614. Dec. — Dec. 19.

10. Among the papers seized in his house at Hinton St. George, and brought up with him to London, is a mass of political writings scrawled on loose sheets, sewn together so as to make a book. Glancing through these sheets, the commissioners find them stuffed with defamatory attacks on the Court, the Government, the Prince of Wales, and the King, so sharp and savage that they must have been either meant for the signal of a rising or have been composed by a man drunk or mad. The King is charged with falsehood, his ministers with fraud. Peacham treats the King with no more reverence than his bishop. He has felt himself moved to say that James might be smitten of a sudden, in a week, like Ananias and Nabal; that the Prince will want to take back the Crown-lands sold by his father, when men will rise up against him, saying, — This is the heir, let us kill him. He has declared the King's officers so vile that they should be set upon and put to the sword; the King himself a creature not alone unfit to reign, but unworthy to bear the name of Christian or of man, — a thing too abject to crawl on earth or be redeemed in heaven.

These passages are not only meant for the public eye, but are ready for the press.

11. Winwood, who, if not a Puritan, is a protector

---

10. The true State of the Question whether Peacham's Case be Treason, State Trials, ii. 878.

11. Council Reg., Nov. 2, Dec. 9, 1614, Feb. 25, 26, 1615.

of the Puritans, by whose help he holds his place at
court, sees no cause in this depraved and convicted man's
religion to stay his hand. If Peacham is a Puritan,
the lay chief of the body does not seem to know it.
Winwood puts him under question; when the vicious
old sinner falls into deeper and more odious sin. From
either demoniacal spite at his recent loss, or from utter
callousness of heart, he accuses John Paulett, the patron to whom he owes his living in the Church, of a
treasonable knowledge of the contents of his book.
And not only John Paulett, but his sister's husband,
Sir John Sydenham, whom he charges, not alone with
criminal silence, but with a positive share in the composition. Nor do the wretch's lies end here. Among
the most intimate friends of Paulett is Sir Maurice
Berkeley, a politician and a reformer, who plays a
conspicuous part in London life, and who divides with
him the representation of the shire; him also Peacham charges as a confederate. Winwood gets alarmed.
A sedition of which Paulett, Berkeley, and Sydenham
are the accomplices may be fraught with peril. He
sends Peacham to the Tower, brings Paulett and Berkeley before the Privy Council, and calls up Sydenham
from Combe.

12. All three gentlemen scout with indignation this
abominable lie. Paulett and Berkeley say they have
never heard one word of the scandalous and seditious

12. Council Reg., Jan. 18, 1615.

IX. 12.

1615.
Jan.

Jan. 18.

book; Sydenham says he never wrote a line of it. And they tell the truth. If they speak against the Crown on questions of prerogative and grievances, they say what they have to say in the House of Commons. If they are hostile to the court, these men are neither libellers nor traitors.

Where lies the truth?

Here are the seditious libels against the Crown, of which Peacham asserts that he shares the authorship with Sydenham and the privity with Paulett and Berkeley. How is Winwood to probe the mystery? The law has but one course. Peacham must be interrogated as Fawkes was interrogated.

The Crown sends down a commission to the Tower, consisting of Winwood, Secretary of State; Cesar, Master of the Rolls; Bacon, Attorney-General; Yelverton, Solicitor-General; Montagu, Recorder of London; Sergeant Crew; and Helwys, Lieutenant of the Tower, to put him to the question. An extract from the Council Register will show the order under which they act: —

THE COUNCIL TO WINWOOD, MASTER OF THE ROLLS, LIEUT. OF TOWER, AND OTHERS.

"After our hearty commendations. Whereas Edmond Peacham, now prisoner in the Tower, stands charged with the writing of a book or pamphlet containing matters treasonable (as is conceived), and being examined thereupon refuseth to declare the truth in those points whereof he hath been interrogated. For so much as the same doth concern his Majesty's sacred person and government, and doth highly concern his service, to have many things yet discovered touching the said book and the author thereof, wherein Peacham dealeth not so clearly as becometh an honest and loyal subject. These shall be therefore in his Majesty's name to will and require you and every of you to repair with what convenient diligence you may unto the Tower, and there to call before you the said Peacham, and to examine him strictly upon such interrogatories concerning the said book as you shall think fit and necessary for the manifestation of truth; and if you find him obstinate and perverse, and not otherwise willing or ready to tell the truth, then to put him to the manacles as in your discretion you shall see occasion; for which this shall be to you and every of you sufficient warrant."

13. That these instructions were obeyed by the commissioners there is no room to doubt. A man of gentle heart may regret that commands so savage and so futile should proceed from the English Crown; but while grieving that our ancestors were either less wise or less compassionate than ourselves, no candid mind will consent to assess the fault of an entire generation on the character of a single man. A belief that truth must be sought by help of the cord, the maiden, and the wheel, was in the opening years of the seventeenth century uni-

13. Dom. Papers James the First, lxxx. 6, 26, 88.

IX. 13. versal. It had come down with the codes and usages of
— antiquity, sustained by the practice of every people on
1615. the civilized globe; most of all by the practice of those
Jan. wealthy and illustrious communities which had kept most
pure the traditions of Imperial Roman law. Men who
agreed in nothing else, agreed in seeking truth through
pain. Nations which fought each other to the knife over
definitions of grace, election, and transubstantiation, had
a common faith in the possibility of discovering truth by
the rack, the pincers, and the screw. There were torture-
chambers at Osnaburgh and Ratisbon, no less hideous
Feb. than those of Valladolid and Rome. The same hot bars,
the same boots, the same racks, were found in the Piombi
and the Bastile, in the Bargello and the Tower. Nor
was the Church one whit more gentle or enlightened than
the civil power. Cardinals searched out heresy in the
flames of the Quemadero, as the Council of Ten tracked
treason in the waves of the Lagune. Bacon was not
more responsible for the universal practice than for the
particular act. To have set himself against the spirit of
his time he must have mounted St. Simeon Stylites's column, or shrunk into St. Anthony's cave. If he chose to
live among men, he must discharge the duties of a man.
There lies a deep gulf between acts of duty and acts of
the will. One who from morbid mind, or from love of
pain, must follow the death-cart to Tyburn, is not performing a noble or necessary deed; yet the chaplain who
has to recite the prayer, the sheriff who has to signal the
drop, go free from blame. So in truth with Bacon. If

he were present at the question of Peacham, he was
there as one of a commission acting under special commands from the Privy Council. It is silly to say he was
responsible for what was done. He was not chief of the
commissioners. He was not even a member of the high
body in whose name they spoke. His official superiors,
Winwood and Cesar, were on the spot. Does Lord
Campbell think the Attorney-General should have declined to act with them, thrown up his commission, and
refused to obey the Crown ?

14. Bear in mind the age in which he lived. The
cry of pain, the gasp of death, were no such shocks to
the gentle heart as they would be in a softer time. Men
had been hardened in the Smithfield fires. Minds were
infected by the atrocities of Papist plots. The ballads
sung in the streets were steeped in blood, and the plays
which best drew audiences to the Globe theatre were
those in which fewest of the characters were left alive.
Hamlet, Pericles, Titus Andronicus, were the Shake-
sperian favorites. No man is known to have felt any
sickness of the heart in presence of judicial torture.
Egerton often saw men on the rack. Winwood stood
by while Peacham, under torture, told his tale. James
was present when Fawkes was stretched. A feeling, it
is true, was beginning to quicken in society against this
use of the rack. Both Coke and Bacon disapproved its
use ; but this merciful sentiment of a few jurists and
philosophers was unshared by the multitude of men who

IX. 14. made the laws. Until the Crown should see fit to aban-
—
1615.
Feb.
don this old plan of seeking truth through crushed feet
and dislocated joints, the officers of the Crown had no
choice but to read their commission and execute their
trust.

15. This truth is so clear that it ought to need no
illustration. Take a fact from our own time. More
than one living judge is supposed to be adverse to trial
by jury. Yet the judges sit in courts where property
and life are daily exposed to the mercy of a dozen illog-
ical and prejudiced men. Are they responsible for the
wrong done? Again, it is conceivable that a judge might
feel uneasy on the score of capital punishments. It is
inconceivable that any judge on the Bench would refuse
to hang a Palmer or a Rush so long as the law continues
to declare wilful murder worthy of death. Bacon told
the King that he misliked the use of torture in judicial
inquiries. He told him so in this very case of Peacham.
Further than that expression he could not go.

Bacon's case in 1860 may possibly become Lord Campbell's case in 1960. Let the public heart go on soften-
ing for a hundred years, fast as it has softened from the
early days of John Howard, and the whole civilized
world may come by 1960 to regard the strangling of a
human being, on any pretext whatever, as a monstrous
crime. Would such a change of public feeling lay Lord
Campbell open to the charge of judicial murder? Would
it be just in a writer of that compassionate age to relate

with " horror " that Lord Campbell prostituted emi- IX. 15.
nent parts and sullied an honorable name by sitting for
many years in a court of justice where life was taken
in the name of law, with his own lips delivering man
after man, and even woman after woman, to be strangled in presence of a brutal crowd, by a wretch who received his blood-money for every loathsome job?   Would
it be fair to say that Lord Campbell in his thirst for
blood took the life of Sarah Chesham, a poor woman
sentenced to death on circumstantial proof, who protested her innocence with the rope round her throat?
Would it be fair to say that with savage glee he ordered
Emma Mussett to be strangled on pretence of child-
murder, even though obliged to confess that the evidence was full of doubt?   Would it be honest in the
writer of a future century to say that in 1860 Lord
Campbell stood alone on the bench in his resolute practice of hanging women, — while, under such humane
judges as Crompton and Cresswell, the lives of Celes-
tina Sommers and Elizabeth Harris, criminals of whose
guilt no man could doubt, were spared?   We think the
writer who should say this, or anything like this, in
1960, would be as unfair to Lord Campbell as Lord
Campbell has been to Francis Bacon.

16. How Peacham lies and swears, now accusing   Aug.

16. State Trials, ii. 870; Diary of Walter Yonge, 27; Chamberlain to
Carleton, Feb. 9, Mar. 2, Aug. 24, 1615, S. P. O.; Council Reg., July 12,
1615.

IX. 16.
——
1615.
Aug.

others, and now himself, anon retracting all that he has said, denying even his handwriting and his signature, one day standing to the charge against Sydenham, next day running from it altogether; how he is sent down into Somersetshire, the scene of his ignoble ministry, to be tried by a jury of men who will interpret his public conduct by what they know of his private life; how he is found guilty by the twelve jurors and condemned by Sir Lawrence Tanfield and Sir Henry Montagu, two of the most able and humane judges on the bench; how his sentence is commuted by the Crown into imprisonment during the King's pleasure; and how he ultimately dies in Taunton jail, unpitied by a single friend, I need not pause to tell.

Aug. 31.

17. After sentence of death has been recorded against him, he offers to tell the truth, if the King will only spare his life. The written confession, twice signed by his hand, which remains in the State Paper Office, tells in his own words how he came to utter that lie about Sir John Sydenham. A question being put to him:—

"He answereth that all the said words wherewith he charged Sir John Sydenham were first written by himself, this examinate, only; and, afterwards hearing these same words delivered unto him by Sir John Sydenham, they were, to this examinate, a confirmation of that which he had formerly written. And, being further asked how he

17. Peacham's Examination, Aug. 31, 1615, S. P. O.

could so strongly father those words upon Sir John Sydenham, seeing he now confesseth himself to be the
author, and Sir John Sydenham but only to confirm him
in them, he answereth that, when he made this answer,
he understood not that distinction betwixt the author and
confirmer, but that they were both taken for one to his
understanding.   And, being asked as before, what was
his reason and end in charging Sir John Sydenham, he
answereth he did it to satisfy his Majesty and the Lords
with the truth."

Being asked his motives and intentions in writing the
pamphlet : —

" He answereth that, first, it was compiled without any
knowledge of evil (?) on his part, either against the King
or estate ; and, secondly, after good and advised deliberation, he would have taken out all the venom and poison
thereof, before ever he would have published the same.
And, being asked in what manner he would have published it, — either by preaching it, or delivering copies of
it, or by printing it, — he protesteth that his intent was
never either to publish, or to give copy, or to print, but
only in private, for his own study, to reduce it into heads,
that he might make use thereof for such particulars as he
out of the text observed, whensoever he should have occasion to speak of any such matter, when all the evil was
taken out."

He pronounces this a true confession ; saying he should

abhor telling a lie to his sovereign, and should think himself guilty of his own blood if he kept back anything after having been promised his life for revealing the truth.

18. One more charge. Bacon, it has been said, not only stands by while the prisoner undergoes examination, but, on the King's command, consults the judges as to whether this crime of seditious writing amounts to treason by the law. In the wake of Macaulay, Lord Campbell says that a private consultation with the judges was an act most scandalous and most unusual. The scandal of such proceedings may be matter of opinion; their frequency is beyond denial. The Kings of England always enjoyed, and constantly exercised, the right of consulting their judges on the statutory bearing of political crimes. These judges had always been the King's judges; holding their commissions at his pleasure; bound by their oaths to advise him on points of law. Macaulay says there is no instance of the Crown privately consulting with the bench: " Bacon was not conforming to an usage then generally admitted to be proper. He was not even the last lingering adherent of an old abuse. It would have been sufficiently disgraceful to such a man to be in this last situation. Yet this last situation would have been honorable, compared with that in which he stood. He was guilty of attempting to introduce into the courts of law an odious abuse, for which no precedent could be

18. Macaulay's Essay on Bacon; Campbell's Life of Bacon, iii. 65.

found." Why, the law-books teem with precedents.
One will serve for a score. It happens, indeed, that
there is one precedent so strange in its circumstances,
and so often the subject of legal and historical comment,
that it is amazing how it could have slipped the recollection of any lawyer, and most of all a lawyer writing of
the times of James the First.

19. Peacham's arrest occurred in 1614. In 1612, Bartholomew Legate, a poor Arian preacher, of simple nature
and extreme dogmatic views, was tried by a consistory
of divines, then sitting at St. Paul's, condemned for ten
separate heresies, and sentenced to be burnt alive. King,
his ordinary, turned him over to the secular arm. But,
as an Act of the first year of Elizabeth had repealed the
Statute of Heresy, leaving errors of faith to the more
merciful ruling of the common law, a question arose as
to whether the Crown had power to execute this abominable sentence of the divines. James thought he had
full powers. The judges were consulted one by one.
Abbott instructed Egerton how to act; and the Lord
Chancellor conferred in private with his legal brethren,
Williams, Croke, and Altham being sounded by him or
by his orders. As they all agreed that James, despite
the repeal of the Statute of Heresy, had power to burn,
the King, on their authority, issued his warrant under
the sign manual to Egerton, Egerton sent his writ to

19. Chamberlain to Carleton, Feb. 26, Mar. 25, 1612, S. P. O.; Sign Manuals,
i. No. 15; Egerton Papers, 447.

IX. 19.

——

1615.

Sept.

the sheriff, and thus, without condemnation in any civil court, Bartholomew Legate perished in the Smithfield flames.

This is the precedent Macaulay seeks.

20. It is right to add that the Privy Council abandoned all proceedings against Paulett and Berkeley at an early date, and that Sydenham was restored to his freedom purged in fame. It is also right to add that the notion of treating Edmond Peacham as though he were in some sort a Puritan martyr is an aberration of the modern biographical mind. The Puritan writers say nothing for him; he has no place in the pages of Toulmin or of Neale. He was degraded by a Puritan Archbishop, prosecuted and condemned by a Puritan Secretary of State.

20. Council Reg., Mar. 26; Chamberlain to Carleton, Mar. 2, 1615, S. P. O.

CHAPTER X.

RACE WITH COKE.

1. LORD CAMPBELL accuses Bacon of having fawned on Somerset in his greatness, of having abandoned him in his fall. Part of this accusation was made by Coke; not all of it; and in a whisper, not in boldly-spoken words. A glance at the facts, as they stand in the registers of the Privy Council and the archives of the State Paper Office, will suffice, it is thought, to convince an impartial reader that Bacon's course through these proceedings against the Earl and Countess of Somerset was in the highest degree noble and humane. Such a reader will see that he was neither obsequious to Somerset in his pride, nor insolent to him in his disgrace.

2. Somerset had not been friendly to Bacon's suit. Not that the young Scottish favorite was wholly wanting in sympathy for merit. His own abilities were not vast,

X. 1.
—
1615.
Sept.

---

1. Campbell, iii. 66; Yelverton to Bacon, Sept. 3, 1617, Lambeth MSS. 936.

2. Bacon to Carr, Nov. 14, 1612, S. P. O. Mr. Amos, in his Great Oyer of Poisoning, 1846, and Dr. Rimbault, in his Introduction to the Miscellaneous Works of Sir Thomas Overbury, 1856, have thrown light on the story of Somerset; but the true history can be traced in its minute details nowhere save in the State Papers of 1612-15. These papers are far too numerous to cite.

nor his tastes, except in dress, refined; yet he was very far from being the abject creature that Lord Campbell says. Abject of nature he was not; guilty of murder he was not. More than one popular poet found in him a patron and a friend. He was kind to Jonson, more than kind to Donne. For years he maintained the closest intimacy with Overbury; a connection not to have been kept with that haughty and sensitive man of genius had Somerset been the fool in feathers and rosettes he is commonly made. But Bacon's policy was not his policy. Blown about with every wind, the favorite swayed from west to east, now moored among the extreme Puritans, now among the most bigoted of the Papists. When he at length chose a side, it was with the party against which Bacon had spent the best of his days and the most brilliant of his powers; for he suffered his name to be used, and his influence over James to be abused, by that iniquitous Spanish faction of which Sir William Monson was the pensioned agent, Lord Northampton the pensioned chief.

A nature proof against gold was not proof against love. A pair of bright eyes, which, in the language of Donne,

" Sowed the court with stars,"

turned upon him; the eyes of Lady Essex, Lord Northampton's niece. Her uncle set her on; that venal old pander putting the young wife of Essex in Somerset's way, tempting her virtue to break its vows, and lending his house to the profligate pair for their stolen kisses. Soft of heart, inclined by youth and rivalry to vice, Somerset

fell into the snares laid for him by wily graybeard and
the shameless girl.

3. Somerset won to their side, the Romanist party
ruled the state. All that a doting prince has in his gift
— rank, places, pensions, grants, monopolies, embassies,
mitres — for a time were theirs. They gave to whom
they would, and they sold to whom they could. They
refused to give Bacon the Court of Wards. They sold it
to Cope. But their reign was short; for the actors in
this drama of unholy love fell from their odious profligacy
into a diabolical crime. Overbury, whom they feared,
not only for his influence over Carr, but for the English
vigor of his Protestantism, was done by them to death.
At first they kept their secret; and in truth the accusation
against them was of a kind which defies belief. That
three great earls, with three or four distinguished knights
holding high positions in the country, should league themselves with wizards, harlots, quacks, 'prentice-boys, and
grooms, to murder a private gentleman for a few verses of
reproof addressed to a friend in love, required the bold
and morbid imagination of a Webster even to conceive.
Poisoning, too, was rare: " It is neither of our country
nor of our church," said Bacon; " you may find it in
Rome or Italy; there is a region or perhaps a religion for
it." People forgot that Northampton was of that religion,

8. Wake to Carleton, Venice Correspondence, Nov. 18, 1612; Chamberlain
to Carleton, Nov. 26, 1612, S. P. O.; Bacon's Speech in Star Chamber, Nov. 10,
1615, S. P. O.

X. 3.
———
1615.
Sept.

that his associates were Italians and Jesuits, and that his early days had been spent in Florence and Rome.

4. Yet suspicion spread. The poet's kinsmen murmured. Some who understood his character, many who admired his writings, spoke of his sudden death, his singular interment. Then, the publication of "The Wife," a poem which charmed all hearts by its wisdom and poetic beauty, kindled a burning wish to inquire into the poet's fate. Five editions of The Wife were sold in a year; five thousand voices began to call his enemies to account. The cry could not be stifled. Men forgot their affairs to ask about the poisoners of Overbury; the ordinary courts of law, even the playhouses, were abandoned for the development of a more striking drama. Term, says Bacon, was turned into a justicium or vacancy by it. Yet, who was to set the law in motion? Those to be touched by the officers of justice, perhaps by the hangman, stood among the highest in the land. Who would lay finger on the Howards and the Carrs?

5. Men sprang up for this desperate duty. By his union with the wife of a living man, Somerset grieved the church of which Abbott was the hierarchical head, not

---

4. A Wife, now a Widowe, 1614; A Wife, now the Widow of Sir Thomas Overburye, 1614; Do., in three subsequent impressions, 1614; Bacon's Speech in Star Chamber, Nov. 10, 1615.

5. Archbishop Abbott's Narrative, in Rushworth, i. 460; Bacon's Speech in Star Chamber, Nov. 10, 1615; Weston's Examination, Sept. 28, 29, Oct. 2, 3, 5, 6, 1615, S. P. O.; Sir Thomas Monson's Examination, Oct. 5, 1615, S. P. O.

less than the Puritan congregations of which Winwood
was considered the parliamentary chief.   The Archbishop,
having strained his strength and jeopardized his life to
prevent the divorce, was ready to fight, with such allies
as God might send him, against the malign ambition and
insatiable greed of Lady Somerset's kin.   Therefore, when
the cry for justice on the murderers of Overbury rose to
heaven, he offered his high rank and holy character as a
shield to such witnesses as, without this august protection,
would scarcely have dared to wag their tongues.   Winwood, Egerton, Zouch, Southampton; Essex, Pembroke,
and Montgomery, all the more patriotic peers, the friends
of poets, the founders of Free States, joined hands with
the brave Archbishop in this crusade against vice and
crime.   Bacon, who had known the poet and admired
the qualities of his genius, went with the English churchman and the English peers.

The bright eyes and soft cheek of George Villiers, a
prettier man than even Carr, reconciled the King's heart
to a general arrest and rigorous examination of his old
favorite's bosom friends.   Coke managed the case against
them.

Soon the confessions of Franklin, Weston, and Anne
Turner implicated high persons.   Northampton was be-
yond the reach of law; but his tools or dupes, Sir
Gervase Helwys, Sir Thomas and Sir William Monson,
were still alive.   Coke lodged them in the Tower; sent
Helwys to the gallows; got a true bill found against Sir
Thomas Monson at Guildhall, and would have put him

to death, with or without evidence of his guilt, but for the necessity of keeping him, an unconvicted man, as evidence against Carr.

6. In these trials of the assassins, it is remarkable that Bacon, though holding office as Attorney-General, has no share. Either his gentle nature shrinks from the horrors of a criminal prosecution, or Coke excludes him from proceedings in which he expects to find abundant profit and fame. Either supposition may be true. It is obvious from the record of the criminal courts that Bacon must often have left to others, when he might have taken the part himself, the dramatic and exciting task of chasing criminals to death. None of Coke's thirst for blood parched up his soul: the trials of Essex and Sanquhair are almost the sole cases in which Bacon took part that ended in the loss of life. Coke, bent on hanging and bowelling all these miserable wretches, may have feared his tender heart and his respect for the forms of law. Certain it is that Sir Lawrence Hyde acts as Crown prosecutor, and that one at least of the prisoners, that one a woman, is hurried to the gallows in a way which no lawyer can now defend.

7. In the more important trials of the Earl and Countess of Somerset, not before Coke, but before the highest

---

6. State Trials, ii. 911-948; Welden, 101.

7. Sherburne's Report of Lady Somerset's Trial, May 24, 1616, S. P. O.; Winwood to Wotton, May 2, 1616, Venice Correspondence, S. P. O.; Bacon's Charge, in Montagu, vi. 235.

court in the realm, the House of Peers, Bacon assumes
his place. Lady Somerset pleads guilty, throwing herself on the mercy of God and the King, — drawn to that
course by an understanding, or a promise, that her appeal to the Crown shall be mercifully heard. Bacon is
prepared for either course : the notes of a speech intended to have been made against her are preserved among
his works. They are singularly merciful and gentle.
Somerset's case comes last. Lord Campbell assumes his
guilt ; but such a study of the confessions as he gave to
the evidence against Sarah Chesham or William Palmer
would convince him that, though guilty of some depravity of heart and understanding, as well as of criminal
weakness towards his wife and her associates, it is very
far indeed from sure that he was guilty of any share in
Overbury's death. No proof was given, nor has any
proof been yet found, that Somerset knew of Weston
being put into the cell to kill Overbury, or of the Countess sending the relays of poisoned tarts and soups. It is
certain that he was deceived throughout by Lord Northampton. Yet, on the other hand, it is not to be denied
that his indolent selfishness led him to the very verge of
connivance in the crime. It was a case of doubt, and
will remain so to the end of time. Bacon claimed strict justice from the Peers, while he left the gates of mercy open
to the Crown. The Peers condemn Somerset, but with a
tacit understanding that his life shall not be taken away.

8. When Somerset has been sent to the Tower, — when

the Howards are cast down from their bad eminence, and the flagitious Spanish clique seems broken by their fall, — Bacon's voice is raised for clemency. When he has done his duty as Attorney-General, he remembers his privileges as a Christian and a man. Life enough has been taken. Helwys, Weston, Franklin, Anne Turner, all the more active agents in the deed, are gone. The Countess has a baby at her breast, — that little girl who, born in shame, will live to become the mother of William Lord Russell. She has confessed her guilt, she has been awfully punished, and the remnant of her years is doomed to obscurity and shame. The Earl maintains his innocence ; the world has not been satisfied of his guilt. Humanity and Law alike concede to him the protection of every doubt. Bacon's counsel to the Crown must be allowed to be pure. He owes nothing to Somerset in the past, — he can have nothing to hope from him in the time to come.

9. He has some domestic and rather humorous trials of his own. Sir John and the lady in Worcester break his rest. Having put his scorn upon Lord Eure, and worried him into selling his place to Lord Gerard ; having got, with the help of Gervase Babington, Bishop of Worcester, a grant from the Crown to restore his pool ; having finished his house in the middle of Westwood

---

8. Bacon to James, April 28, 1616.
9. Council Reg., Mar. 7. 1615; Dom. Papers James the First, lxxxvii. 67, S. P. O.; Wotton, i. 186.

Park, and given a banquet to Lord and Lady Compton
and their train in honor of the event, which has been the
talk of neighboring shires, the warm old knight, having
no one left to fight with, has begun to fuss and wrangle
with his wife. The widow, on her side, is now perverse.
Sir John has to turn her out of doors. When she leaves
the park and rides up to town, her clothes and trinkets,
sent on before her, are stolen on the way. In the full
belief that Sir John has caused her to be plundered, Lady
Pakington sends her wrongs to the Privy Council, and
begs to have a general warrant of search for her stolen
trunks. This piece of domestic comedy stands solemnly
recorded in the Council-books : —

X. 9.
——
1616.
May.

March the seventh, 1615.

Present :

George Abbott, Archbishop of Canterbury.
Thomas Howard Earl of Suffolk, Lord Treasurer.
Edward Somerset Earl of Worcester, Lord Privy Seal.
William Herbert Earl of Pembroke, Lord Chamberlain.
The Earl of Dunfermline.
The Bishop of Winchester.
Lord Knollys.
Sir Ralph Winwood, First Secretary of State.

A GENERAL WARRANT DIRECTED TO ALL HIS MAJESTY'S
PUBLIC OFFICERS.

" Whereas complaint hath been made unto us by the

11 *

X. 9.
———
1616.
May.

Lady Pakington, wife to Sir John Pakington, knight, that, having occasion to repair to London, and sending up divers trunks of apparel and other necessaries for the use of her person, the same was carried aside, and as yet detained from her, to her great hindrance and prejudice. These are therefore to will and require you to make search in all places where you shall be directed by this bearer for apparel belonging to the Lady Pakington, and the same being found to cause it to be delivered to this bearer for her use."

This warrant to search for Lady Pakington's hoods and jerkins, fans, ruffs, and farthingales, is signed by the Archbishop, the Lord Treasurer, and the rest!

10. It may for charity be hoped the poor lady finds her trunks, though the Council-books say no more about them. Certain it is that when she again goes home to Westwood Park she nags and frets Sir John, and not Sir John alone. Two of her girls are now married, and she does her very worst to make their husbands as miserable as her own. How Mervin Touchet bears her tongue we are not told; but this young lord being rather crazed, and exceedingly vicious and tyrannical, it is likely enough that he submits, as such men do, to the woman's cold, dry, dogged will. Not so, Francis Bacon, who insists to her surprise and rage, on being the master in his own house. When she tries on him the arts which have some-

10. Montagu, xiii. 63.

times roused, but more frequently have tamed Sir John, X. 10.
he tells her in the plainest words to mind her own business, and mind it better than she has done. He even 1616.
May.
shuts his door upon her when he finds her naught. If
she hints in her own sweet way that, should he turn his
wife out of the house, as she supposes he soon will, now
that he has turned his deaf side to her mother's counsels,
she will receive her back from him, and give her, the poor
outraged thing, a home, Bacon quietly reminds her that,
considering what is passed, and who has been already cast
off once, it is more likely that she will come to beg a room
at Gorhambury than that Lady Bacon will need to seek
one at Westwood Park.

This letter is in Montagu ; but though curious to the
last degree, it has passed unnoticed the eye of every
writer of Bacon's life, because the relation of Bacon to
Lady Pakington has not been known. I reproduce it in
connection with the domestic facts to which it belongs,
and which it helps to explain.

To my Lady Pakington, in answer to a Message by
her sent.

Madam, —

You shall with right good-will be made acquainted
with anything that concerneth your daughters, if you
bear a mind of love and concord, otherwise you must be
content to be a stranger unto us; for I may not be so unwise as to suffer you to be an author or occasion of dissen-

X. 10.
———
1616.
May.

sion between your daughters and their husbands, having seen so much misery of that in yourself. And above all things I will turn back your kindness, in which you say you will receive my wife if she be cast off; for it is much more likely we have occasion to receive you being cast off, if you remember what is passed. But it is time to make an end of those follies, and you shall at this time pardon me this one fault of writing to you; for I mean to do it no more till you use me and respect me as you ought. So, wishing you better than it seemeth you will draw upon yourself,

I rest yours,

FR. BACON.

11. The merciful part which Bacon, as Attorney-General, plays in the release of Sir William Monson and Sir Thomas Monson from the Tower, having escaped the researches of Basil Montagu, has escaped the criticisms of Lord Campbell. Yet the facts of this interference embrace a continuation of the duel with Coke, and are essential to an understanding of some of the remoter causes of Bacon's fall.

In the first warm days of discovery the two Monsons were flung into the Tower. The proof would have gone hard against them. They were Papists. They were friends of Northampton. They were intimate with Lady

<hr>

11. Waad's Statement, Sept. 1615, S. P. O.; Coke's Memorandum, Sept. 11, 1615, Jan. 8, 1616, S. P. O.; James to the Commissioners, Oct. 21, 1615, S. P. O.; Coke to the King, Dec. 4, 1615, S. P. O.; Sir Thomas Monson to Coke, Dec. 5, 1615, S. P. O.

Somerset. Sir William Monson was the secret agent X. 11.
of the Spanish Ambassador. Sir Thomas had been the ——
means of placing Weston in Overbury's cell. Any actual
participation in the murder has never yet been proved
against either of them; yet in the flush and anger of
the public, more could have been brought against them
than any twelve Protestant jurors would have asked in
order to their condemnation. Guildhall would have pronounced them guilty, as King's Bench had pronounced
Anne Turner guilty, and Coke would most gladly have
sent them to the gallows or the block.

But Bacon feels that, now the King has resolved to
pardon Somerset and his guilty wife, the Monsons cannot
be put to death without shocking all reasonable, con-
scientious men. They are Catholics; but he cannot treat
their religion as a crime. Coke is furious. As one of
the four commissioners for the prosecution, he has made
a vast collection of secret papers on the subject; these
papers he refuses to give up; and from threats which
he has used on hearing that he may be balked of his
prey, it is feared that in his fury he may send them to
the press.

12. The advocates of mercy hie to the King. James
commands Bacon to require from Coke the surrender
of all these documents for his Majesty's use. The Attorney-General thereupon writes to the Lord Chief
Justice : —

12. Bacon to Coke, April 16, 1616, S. P. O.; Carew to Roe, Jan. 18, 1617,
S. P. O.

X. 12.

1616.
May.

BACON TO COKE.

MY LORD, —

I received yesternight express commandments from his Majesty to require from your Lordship, in his Majesty's name, all and every such examinations as are in your Lordship's hands of Sir William Monson for his Majesty's present service. Therefore, I pray your Lordship either send them presently, sealed up, by your servant, or, if you think it needful, I will come to you myself and receive them with mine own hands. I rest, your Lordship's loving friend, to command,

FR. BACON.

This Tuesday, at seven o'clock in the morning, 16th of April, 1616.

Imagine the rage of Coke! No evidence to connect Sir William with the murderous scenes in the Tower has been discovered, while the proofs of his connection with the Spanish Ambassador, and of his disbursements of money to the partisans of Spain, are of a kind not to be produced by the king in a court of law.

13. Sir Thomas Monson's case is far more difficult than Sir William's; for Sir Thomas was in daily communication with Helwys when the poisons were being

13. Coke to the King, Feb. 8, 1616, S. P. O.; Queries by Coke, Feb. 1616, S. P. O.; Chamberlain to Carleton, June 8, 1616, S. P. O.

given, and his warm recommendation of Weston first
encouraged Helwys to permit and then to share the
crime. Yet a careful examination of the mass of evidence in the State Paper Office must convince a lawyer
that Monson was no worse than Northampton's tool and
dupe. He was guilty of Romanism, — a crime which
Coke, and many bigots like Coke, would have punished
with the drop. He was guilty, too, of grave indiscretion
and of crawling subserviency towards Northampton.
How could the Crown lawyers deal with such a case ?
Monson had undergone a public examination, not a
public trial. Coke would have his life.

14. But while the two Monsons lie in the Tower, each
loud in his denial of guilt, yet scared in soul by the
violence and injustice of his adversaries, Coke himself,
the most eager and malicious of those adversaries, crashes
down suddenly from his high place.

That command to give up the confessions and examinations of Sir William must have gone to the quick ; as it
not only robs him of the power to bully and hang a man
for whose creed he has no tolerance, but takes from him
a case in which he feels a lawyer's pride, to give it over
to one whom of all living man he most loathes and fears.
This wrong he resents in word and deed. Seeing scorn
and insult on the brow of a prince from whom he hoped
to win smiles and bounty, he droops into discontent and
opposition. In the great case of Commendams he comes
into fatal collision with the King.

14. Carew to Roe, Jan. 18, 1617, S. P. O.

15. The case of Commendams, on the law of which Egerton and Bacon differ from Coke, may be explained in a few words. A living in commendam was in the same position as a ward in custody; it was committed to some one's care. The custom of such holdings in the church arose in troublous times, when a Genseric was in Rome or an Attila in Gaul; then sees and parishes, left without occupants, were given in commendam to the nearest bishop or the nearest priest. In time the Popes discovered in this system of holding sees or livings a means of rewarding a loyal friend or buying off a formidable foe. In England, too, the plan had its use and its abuse. Some of the livings were so rich, while some of the sees were so poor, that a clergyman might lose in worldly state by his translation to the bench of spiritual peers. Such a fact, it is obvious, must have limited the choice of the Crown, in case of vacancy among the bishops, to the lower or less fortunate ranks of the clergy,— a limitation not to be desired or endured, had not the Crown, when succeeding to the rights of the Holy Chair, inherited the power of granting livings in commendam. Yet such a power was open to grave abuse. Paulo Sarpi has denounced the evils which it brought upon Roman Catholic communities, where a Pope's bastard or a Cardinal's nephew, under the title of a holder in commendam, swept the revenues of a province into his private purse.

15. Storia del Concilio Tridentino, 1629; Collier's Ecclesiastical History of Great Britain, vii. 389; Council Reg., June 6, 1616.

While Coke is in his rage, the case of a living held in commendam comes before the King's Bench. It is a private cause; but Sergeant Chibborne, in the course of his speech, goes out of his way to contest the King's power to grant commendams at all. Fearful lest the angry Chief Justice may pronounce a verdict touching the Crown, without the Crown being heard in its defence, James mounts a messenger for London commanding Bilson and Winwood to attend the next sitting of the Court of King's Bench and report to him the arguments there used. Winwood being sick, Bilson, Bishop of Winchester, is the sole witness; but his report alarms the King in high degree, for he hears Chibborne contend that the Crown has no power to grant livings or sees in commendam save in cases of extreme need; and that no such need can arise in England, where no man is bound to keep hospitality beyond his means.

16. Informed by Bilson of what has passed in the King's Bench, James sees the gravity of his position, and commands Bacon to write and require Coke to put off the further hearing of this case until he, the King, can come to town and consult the judges. This command a servant carries from Gray's Inn to the Lord Chief Justice's room in Sergeants' Inn; when Coke, who is just setting out for Westminster Hall, sends his own man to Gray's Inn to beg that Mr. Attorney

16. The Judges to James, April 27, 1616, S. P. O.; James to the Judges, Council Reg., June 6, 1616.

Q

will give to each of the twelve judges a copy of his note.

Coke's presence has been required in the Court of Chancery to assist in hearing a case for the Crown; but setting the immediate duty of the day aside, defying the royal command, as conveyed through Bacon, he goes down to Westminster, takes his seat in the King's Bench, and calls the forbidden· case. After a further hearing he takes the judges to his rooms in Sergeants' Inn, where he persuades them to sign a letter to the King, throwing the blame of his disobedience on Bacon, whose request for a posponement of the trial they condemn as contrary to law and to the oaths of a judge.

17. James reads this letter with amazement. If his rage against Coke, and his fears of encroachment, do not lure him one day sooner from his dogs and deer, he pens a smart rebuke to the judges, who, when they see how the tide sets,· begin to feel heartily ashamed of what they have signed. They know, indeed, that the reasons given by Coke are a mere pretence; that Bacon's letter was sent by command; that the Crown has power by law to grant livings in commendam; and that to delay the hearing until James could arrive in town and lay his arguments before them would neither interfere with justice nor disturb their oaths. All these points of the case the King sets forth in his

17. Council Reg., June 6, 1616.

note with unsparing ire. He ends by once again, in
his own words and in his own name, insisting that the
hearing shall be stayed, referring them, with a good
sense of which he is seldom capable, to his Attorney-
General for his opinions on particular points.

18. Ambling to town for the Whitsun games, he
sends for his twelve judges to the palace. Of the
many comedies played in that superb political theatre,
few have been so droll as this trial of the judges by
the King. All the great officers of state are present;
the King himself, Archbishop Abbott and Bishop Bilson, Lord Chancellor Egerton and Lord Treasurer Suffolk, Winwood Secretary of State, and Zouch Lord
Warden of the Cinque Ports, together with a host of
inferior councillors and clerks. Bacon stands there to
defend himself. Coke, a member of the Privy Council,
takes his seat.

The men whose lives have been one long duel, who
have pleaded in the same courts, who have made love
to the same woman, who have served in the same House
of Commons, who for thirty-five years have been at guard
and thrust, appear in a scene which can only end in disaster for one of them, perhaps in ruin for both. James
opens the inquiry. Bilson states what he heard in the
King's Bench. Bacon's letter and Coke's reply are put
in as evidence and read. Eleven of the judges see their
error. Falling on their knees, they confess their fault

18. Council Reg., June 6, 1616.

X. 18.
——
1616.
June 6.
and implore the King's most gracious pardon. Coke alone, if wrong at first, has courage enough to be wrong at last; maintaining that the facts of his note were true, and that Mr. Attorney's message was against his oath.

James turns to his Chancellor; but Egerton, before pronouncing judgment, begs, as the case involves points of law, that Bacon may first be heard.

19. Bacon rises. In the portrait of Van Somers, painted a few weeks later, we see him as he stands confronting Coke. Thirty-six years have passed since he entered on the fag and contest of the world; but thirty-six years of toil, thought, study, disappointment, and success, have neither soured his blood nor disturbed the beauty of his face. The bust of Somers is the bust of Hilyard come to its perfect growth. Brow broad and solid; eye quick yet mild; nose straight and strong, of the pure old English type; beard trim and dainty, as of one to whom grace is nature; over all the countenance a bold, soft, kindling light; an infinite sense of power and subtlety and humor, unmixed with any trace of pride.

20. Turning to the King he shows, by proofs which seem superfluous, that in staying the hearing Coke would have hurt no law, broken no oath. The Lord Chief

19. The portrait of Van Somers is at Gorhambury.
20. Council Reg., June 6, 1616; Sherborne to Carleton, June 12, 1616, S. P. O.; Gerard to Carleton, June 14, 1616, S. P. O.

Justice starts to his feet; the King's counsel, he says, X. 20.
may plead before the judges, they must not dispute with
them.   Bacon answers for his order and for himself, that
a King's counsel is, by his office and his oath, free to
proceed or declare against any man, against the greatest lord in the kingdom, even against any body of men,
though they were peers and judges; and he demands
from the King's justice that this spirt of bad temper
and worse law shall be withdrawn. James sides with
his Attorney-General, and Coke has to eat his words.

The Lord Chancellor now asks that the oath of a
judge may be read; and when Yelverton has done this,
he pronounces judgment wholly against Coke. In Egerton's verdict the judges all concur; promising for themselves to respect all future messages from the Crown.
Coke alone answers that he will do what he shall find
fit for a judge.

The fall of this arrogant man is soon noised in the
Strand and at St. Paul's.

21. Bacon is sworn a member of the Privy Council;   June 9.
as in every stage of his rise, without a bribe. The
very first act of this new Councillor, who, on grounds
of humanity, is moving heaven and earth to save a couple
of Papists from the gallows, is to induce the favorite and
his master to restore the famous Puritan preacher Doc-   June 16.
tor Burgess to his ministry in the Church. Burgess

21. Council Reg., June 9, 1616; Montagu, xliii. 233; Carew to Roe, Jan. 18,
1617, S. P. O.; Chamberlain to Carleton, July 5, 1617, S. P. O.

X. 21.
——
1616.
June 16.

has long been silenced. Many congregations wish to hear him ; among others, the Honorable Society of Gray's Inn. Bacon prevails, and the thunders of the great preacher are again heard at St. Paul's Cross.

June 30.

22. Bacon is nominated one of a commission, with the Lord Treasurer, Chancellor of the Exchequer, and other ministers, to consider a plan for raising funds by selling the old feudal right of homage and by disafforesting the distant and unprofitable Crown-lands.

More than sufficient offences are soon discovered against Coke — frauds, contempts, and disobediences — to insure a condemnation either in the Star Chamber or in any court over which the Crown can name the judge. When he hears of this investigation into his past life, the bully of Westminster Hall lowers his tone. Not that his course on the bench has been impure ; it has, in fact, as all the world knows, been ostentatiously the reverse of impure ; yet the practice of all the courts is so unsafe, the system of fees so lax, that no man on the bench can stand up against an accusation brought by the Crown. No judge on the bench knows better than Coke that to be tried for a Crown offence is to be condemned. In the most grovelling key he prays to be spared the shame of a public trial ; on his knees he implores the Council to protect him ; saying, and very

22. Council to the Commissioners, June 30, 1616, S. P. O.; Council Reg., June 26, 30, 1616; Chamberlain to Carleton, June 22, 1616, S. P. O.; Sherborne to Carleton, June 29, 1616, S. P. O.

truly saying, that any man in place, however high his
state, however clean his hands, may be crushed by an
indictment laid in the royal name. Again and again
he appears before the Privy Council, under his rival's
eyes, in the same ignominious attitude, begging for
mercy in the same miserable tone.

X. 22.
——
1616.
June 30.

The woman who in his prosperity was the torment
of his life no sooner finds him grovelling on his knees
before men deaf to his groans, and the savings of his
long practice at the bar menaced with fine and forfeit,
than she bounds to his side, makes his suit her own,
worries her kinsmen for help, besieges the Queen with
petitions, and declares that, come evil or come good to
her husband, she will share his fate.

July

23. Though Anne puts forth her weakness in his
cause, Coke is degraded from the Council, forbidden to
travel circuit, commanded to revise his Reports. Vil-
·liers against him, the poor Queen is snubbed; and Lady
Hatton, in place of conciliating those who might help
her suit, insults the favorite's mother, and on her complaint gets sent away from court. Coke humbles his
pride, confesses his fault, nay, darkens his fame as a
jurist and a judge, by stooping, on the King's demand,
to alter his Law Reports; a confession of guilt if his

Oct.

.

23. Villiers to Bacon, Oct. 3, 1616, Lambeth MSS. 936; Williams to Carleton, July 3, 1616, S. P. O.; Chamberlain to Carleton, July 6, Oct. 26, Nov. 9,
14, 23, 1616, S. P. O.; Sherborne to Carleton, July 11, Oct. 5, 1616, S. P. O.;
Winwood to Carleton, July 13, 1616, S. P. O.; Egerton's Speech to Montagu,
Nov. 18, 1616, S. P. O.; Grant Book, 197, 198.

X. 23.
———
1616.
Oct.

cases are false, a dishonest compliance if he believes them true. Even this last concession is made in vain. ·

When stripped of his office and deposed from the bench, his wife, who was going to make his cause her own, packs up her furniture and plate, leaps into her coach, and leaves him to his loneliness and rage. His seat in the King's Bench is offered to Bacon and declined. Sir Henry Montagu, Recorder of London, a man of very great wealth and very high abilities as' a lawyer, grandson of Bluff King Hal's famous Lord Chief Justice, and founder of the ducal line of Manchester, gets his place.

Nov.

24. The fall of Coke throws light into the Tower. Sir Thomas Monson gains the liberty of that fortress. Sure that Monson ought not to be tried, since it has become improbable that he could be convicted and impossible that he could be hung, Bacon is not the less sure that for the King's credit and for Monson's own safety he ought not to be merely set free. He proposes, therefore, with the full concurrence of Sir Henry Yelverton, that a pardon shall be granted under the Seal, reciting Monson's plea of innocence, the dubious proofs against him, and the gracious clemency of the King. Egerton backs this compromise ; for he too, though himself a convert from the Church of Rome, believes with Bacon that a gentleman may be a Papist without

24. Council Reg., Aug. 10, 1616; Bacon to James, Dec. 7, 1616, S. P. O.; Statement of the Case of Sir Thomas Monson, Feb. 12, 1617, S. P. O.

being a traitor.   In his own name and that of Yelverton, Bacon communicates this plan to James : —

BACON TO KING JAMES.

IT MAY PLEASE YOUR MOST EXCELLENT MAJESTY, —
According to your pleasure, signified unto me, your
Attorney, by word of mouth, we have considered of the
state of Sir Thomas Monson's case, and what is fit further
to be done in it, and we are of opinion, — first, that it is
altogether unfit to have a proceeding to a trial, both because the evidence itself (for so much as we know of it)
is conjectural, as also for that to rip up those matters now
will neither be agreable to the justice nor to the mercy
formally used by your Majesty towards others ; secondly,
to do nothing in it is neither safe for the gentleman, nor
honorable (as we conceive) for your Majesty, whose care
of justice useth not to faint or become weary in the latter
end.   Therefore we are of opinion that it is a case fit for
your Majesty's pardon, as upon doubtful evidence, and
that Sir Thomas Monson plead the same publicly, with
such protestations of his innocency as he thinks good,
and so the matter may come to a regular and just period,
wherein the very reading of the pardon, which shall recite the evidence to be doubtful and conjectural, added to
his own protestations, is as much for the reputation of
the gentleman as we think convenient, considering how
things have formerly passed.   Hereupon we have advised

12

with the Lord Chancellor, whom we find of the same opinion. All which, nevertheless, we, in all humbleness, submit to your Majesty's better judgment.

Your Majesty's most humble

and most bounden servants,

FR. BACON,

HENRY YELVERTON.

The advice is welcome. A pardon, drawn up in this sense, passes under the Seal. Monson, brought up at the bar of the King's Bench and this paper read to him, declares his innocence once more, protests that his pardon should be read as evidence of his innocence, not of his guilt. Montagu, now Chief Justice, tells him it may be read in this sense, and Monson with a joyful heart goes home from the Tower.

25. Egerton is sick. Though he will not give up the Seals, as Villiers presses him to do, while he can sign his name, he begins to divest himself of the minor offices and responsibilities of the world ; among other changes yielding the Stewardship of St. Albans to the friend who now sits by his bed, lightening his pains and cares, and whom he, like all the world, has sealed for his successor in the Court of Chancery. Among the public affairs in which Bacon is employed are, the Disorders in our Trade with Spain, and a Report touching a child supposed to have

25. Add. MSS. 19, 402; Sherborne to Carleton, Feb. 8, 1617, S. P. O.; Council Reg., Feb. 2, 1617.

been left by Lady Arabella Stuart. The first is referred X. 25.
to Bacon alone, with power to collect evidence and to
offer remedies for the wrong. The second concerns the 1617.
Feb. 12.
King more nearly than the murder of English crews, the
confiscation of English goods. This story of a royal child
he refers to four commissioners, the highest functionaries
of the state — Abbott, Suffolk, Winwood, and Bacon ;
Bacon, on whom the burden of inquiry falls, representing the great lawyer now lying sick at York House.

26. After Lady Arabella's death in the Tower a whis- Feb. 2.
per flew abroad that her romantic marriage had not been
altogether barren ; that she had given birth to a child
while confined in Sir Thomas Parry's house at Lambeth ;
and that this heir of the Seymours was still alive. The
story has a deep and romantic interest. If there be such
a child, it stands very near the throne, — uniting, as it
must, in one head the rival claims of the Seymour and
Lennox lines of descent from Henry the Seventh ; therefore a rival, as some folks think, to the King's own children, and one who may become truly formidable should
the rickety Prince of Wales not live. Such a birth was
not unlikely in itself. The Lady Arabella was only
thirty-six when she fell in love and secretly gave her
hand to William Seymour. They were married weeks
before their amour was discovered. Even when parted
by force, their love and wit found means for meeting.
Even when Seymour was in the Tower, he so far won

26. Council Reg., Feb. 2, 16, 1617.

upon his jailer by his youth, his misery, or his gold, that he was frequently allowed to go up the river and see his wife. Nothing, therefore, in the tale of a child having been born to all this love appears improbable to men who fear or hate the King, while the motives for concealment, if it has been born, are clear to all. James is profoundly moved. A new Perkin Warbeck menaces his throne.

True or false, the story is a serious fact for James and for his dynasty: not less grave for them if false than true; unless it. can be wholly and forever rooted out from the minds of men. Hence the commission. For a time the mystery defies even Bacon's subtlety of search and proof. It is always hard to prove a negative, — most hard in such a case as this. The commissioners may convince themselves ; they have to convince a credulous world, at the risk of leaving that world open to seduction by any knave who may choose to play his head against a crown. They send for Seymour, who knows nothing or will tell them nothing. They send for Sir John Keys and Doctor Mountford, physicians to the royal lady. They question Edward Kirton and Edward Reeves, her body servants. None of these will own to knowledge of the birth of any child. Such evidence is, however, far from decisive. Where are Lady Arabella's waiting-women ?

It is known that, while imprisoned in Parry's house, Arabella's waiting-woman was called Ann Bradshaw. Ann has dropped out of sight, though no one thinks that she is dead. Where is she ? The Seymours don't know.

Her old friends and fellow-servants don't know. Such
a fact is of itself suspicious. Is the missing maid watch-
ing over the missing child? There must be an end of
these questions. If alive, and between the four seas, Ann
must be found; for on her testimony hang the chances
of a civil war.

X. 26.

1617.
Feb. 2.

A search through every shire from Exe to Tweed dis-
covers her in Duffield, — an obscure village lost among
the snows of the Peak. Though old, full of aches and
pains, her memory is good: she remembers everything
about her unhappy mistress, was with her day and night
in Parry's house, and is positive she never had a child.
The local magistrates dare not jolt her off to London
through the winter cold, the doctors saying she would
die on the road. A message speeds to Bacon. Not an
hour is to be lost; the weal of millions hangs on the
words of this sick creature; so he mounts for Duffield
Sir Clement Edmondes, a trusty Clerk of the Privy
Council, to see the woman and take her important evidence on oath. Clement sends in his report. The tale
sworn by the waiting-woman convinces the commissioners and the Council that the rumor of a young Seymour, born of Lady Arabella, being in existence is a lie.
In witness of this inquiry, and of this result, James
causes an elaborate statement of the facts to be inserted
in the Council Register, signed by George Abbott,
Thomas Howard, Ralph Winwood, and Francis Bacon.
The search which satisfies the Council seems to satisfy
mankind. It is, indeed, amazing that, during all the

X. 26.
———
1617.

troubles aud illusions of the succeeding forty years, no one ever assumed the character of Lady Arabella's son.

Mar. 7.

27. Four weeks after closing this delicate inquiry Bacon receives the Seals. Egerton's love bears fruit; but the risks of failure in his suit have indeed been great for Buckingham makes no secret of his wish to ruin the old Chancellor and sell his place. While the favorite haggles with aspirants for the office about its price, the King himself puts the Seals into Bacon's hands.

Riding down to York House, he thanks his old friend, and in his Majesty's name presents him with the patent of an Earl. He now turns to the Court of Chancery, not in despair at the long arrears, but with confident sense of his power to conquer the vast accumulation of work. The rules which he lays down; the spirit in which he decides, are beyond all praise. Nor do the labors of his Court, the ceremonial of his rank, and the sittings of the Council consume his strength. He instructs Buckingham in the arts of government. He toils at his Novum Organum. Within a week of his investiture the

Mar. 17

King leaves London for the Northern Kingdom, calling Bacon to the exercise of very extraordinary powers. In commission with Pembroke, Suffolk, and a single secretary, he receives power to pardon able-bodied offenders under sentence of death, save only those convicted of

27. Council Reg., Mar. 7, 24, 1617; Grant Book, 200; Chamberlain to Carle ton, Mar. 15, 1617, S. P. O.; Commission to Abbott, Bacon, and others, Mar. 17, 1617, S. P. O.

rape, burglary, witchcraft, and wilful murder, and send X. 27.
them over sea. In commission with Abbott and others,
he is authorized to pass securities for loans, to issue
proclamations, to conduct the Irish business, to perfect
the ecclesiastical commission, and generally to conduct
the government of the realm. Yet, in spite of this
enormous addition to his active duties, he clears off the
whole arrears of Chancery causes by the end of June.

CHAPTER XI.

LORD CHANCELLOR.

XI. 1.
—
1617.
July.

1. In striding over Coke's head to the Mace and Seals, Bacon puts the crown to his many offences against that wealthy and vindictive foe. Their lives have been spent in a daily contest for rank, love, place, and power. Up to the present year Coke has been able to keep in front. He made more money, he won Lady Hatton, he first got office under the Crown. *He went up to the Common Pleas while Bacon was fighting for his promotion at the bar. Before the great philosopher was commissioned as Attorney-General, the great jurist had been seated on the King's Bench. For the three years and four months that Bacon, as Attorney, waited in the Council anteroom, Coke sat at the board. The scene is now changed, the characters reversed. Within a few weeks Coke has been degraded from the Council to make way for Bacon, and reduced from the King's Bench that his rival may feel the insolent joy of refusing to accept his place. The humiliation has now been capped by Bacon filching from him, at the very moment of his

1. Council Reg., Nov. 4, 1613; Yelverton to Bacon, Sept. 3, 1617, Lambeth MSS. 836.

negotiation with Villiers, the Mace and Seals, without
paying for them one shilling of those irregular sums
which he himself was told he must lay down. Such a
success enrages the miser even more than it galls the
man.

2. How can he drag this rival down? The way is but
too easy. Gain the favorite. Virtue is no protection to
men in power. He has been thrown. Egerton only
escapes an ignominious fall by the approach of death.

The story of Egerton's latter days has never yet been
told. As an illustration of the time, it is in the highest
degree important for a clear comprehension of his successor's fall.

As Egerton grew old a host of lawyers and ecclesiastics
began to crave the Seals; conspicuous among these were
Bilson and Bennett, Hobart and Coke. The Great
Seal, though held like the White Staff during pleasure,
changed hands so rarely that the possession was regarded
as one for life. Pickering, Hatton, Bromley, Nicholas
Bacon, kept the Seals to the last, as Northampton, Salisbury, Dorset, and Burghley kept the Staff. The rule
applied to every office in the Household and the State.
Now this appearance of a permanent possession gave to
each holder of office a vested right in it, which had a
market value. No man ever yielded his place without
being paid for it, any more than a colonel of the line

---

2. Sherborne to Carleton, Feb. 23, 1617, S. P.).; Lovelace to Carleton, Mar.
11, 1617, S. P. O.

12 *   R

gives up his commission without his price. Death only could deprive him. As Egerton would not die though he had held the Seals longer than any Chancellor since the Conquest, nor yield his place except on reasonable terms of surrender, those who meant to make a purse by the transfer began to brood over the possibility of forcing him to yield by means of a criminal prosecution. A sentence in the House of Lords would be legal death. Once it were pronounced the Seals would fall into the King's gift. This was a new and perilous game to play; but the plan seemed easy, the profits vast. A trial might be made. Any old lawyer learned in the vices of the times, could get up an accusation. Buckingham could secure a majority in the House of Lords. The temptations which drew Buckingham into this odious and criminal course were very great. Sir John Bennett offered for the Seals no less a sum than thirty thousand pounds.

3. This scheme of a criminal information quickened into life on Egerton's refusal to pass under the Seal some patents in which the Villiers family had a share. Famous among these was a grant to Sir Giles Mompesson for the manufacture of gold and silver thread. Everybody wore lace. In the comic writers of James's reign, in Jonson, in Webster, in Massinger, the young gallants strut in lace, — not in the tawdry stuff sold by Autolycus as a present from country lads to country lasses, but in

3. Sign Manuals, vi. 109; Com. Jour., i. 530–576.

glinting silver and gold ; the metals dropping in threads
from the ruff, or wrought into the doublet and hose, the
cloak and cap. Venice could not supply the want. The
price of gold and silver lace ran high ; and the profits of
the trade all went abroad. A Licenser of Inns, Sir Giles
Mompesson, a man of energy and wealth, conceived a
scheme for introducing this profitable manufacture into
England. There were serious difficulties. Silver and
gold were scarce ; sometimes not to be bought except
on ruinous terms. The patent under which he was to
work must not alone protect his trade, but allow him to
take up gold and silver for his need, even the coin of
the realm. By giving two of Buckingham's brothers a
share in the business, Mompesson hoped to secure protection for his enterprise.

4. Blind to the lights of trade, Egerton refused to seal
this grant. Not that he perceived and lamented the true
evil of monopolies ; every profession was then a guild ;
and without a monopoly there could be no trade. The
grocer, the perfumer, the vintner, the tailor, was each
invested in a charter or a patent. Egerton, during his
long reign as Chancellor, passed hundreds of patents,
some of them far more mischievous than the one for
enabling the London spinners to rival their Venetian
brethren in the production of gold and silver thread.
His repugnance to it sprang from the contempt of an
old man for new fripperies of dress and show, and from a

4. Chamberlain to Carleton, Mar. 8, 1617, S. P. O.

fear that Mompesson would ruin the Crown by withdraw-
ing the coinage from circulation into trade.

5. Buckingham was furious. Urged by his own vexation and by his complaining brothers, he swore to ruin
the old Chancellor. Agents sneaked about the Inns of
Court speaking evil of the great lawyer, now on his bed
of death, provoking all who had suffered wrongs, or who
fancied they had suffered wrongs, in his court, to rise up
against the tyrant. Men soon answered to the call. A
blameless life, a sick-bed, were no protection against this
outrage. One said he had given money into the court;
another said he had given a ring, a cabinet, a piece of
plate. In substance and form these tales were true, in
spirit and intention they were false. Charges enough
were gathered: charges more numerous, said Sir William Lovelace, than those which had recently crushed
Coke; charges as flimsy and as fatal, I may add, as those
which four years later served to overwhelm Egerton's
successor. Buckingham sent to the sick man's room
the news of this flagitious inquisition and its triumphant
close; it is greatly to be feared that the blow broke the
old man's heart.

6. It needs no magician to see that he who nearly slew
Egerton might just as easily slay the successor of Egerton.

---

5. Lovelace to Carleton, Mar. 11, 1617, S. P. O.
6. Chamberlain to Carleton, Mar. 11, 1617, S. P. O.; Gerard to Carleton, Mar.
20, 1617, S. P. O.

Buckingham is cheated of his profit; for though Bacon
pays to Egerton eight thousand pounds for the surrender
of his legal rights, not a shilling of this money flows into
the favorite's purse. The Villiers people are not pleased
with a Chancellor who refuses to push their fortunes and
feed their pride; nor is Buckingham a man to forget
that, if Egerton had been chased into the House of Lords,
as Coke had been into the Star Chamber, he might have
put into his own pocket from the transaction a good many
thousand pounds.

XI. 6.
—
1617.
July.

7. The loss is great. It is Coke's business to show
Villiers how it may be recovered. Bacon is not robust
nor likely to live long. He works too much, and lives
too well, for vegetable length of days. Gout racks his
joints; being the first beggar, as he jests, who ever had
it. If he dies, well; if not, he may be ruined. Coke,
who begins by collecting scandals against him, whispers
to the favorite that the new Chancellor is no true friend
to him; that he is not zealous for the advancement of
Sir Christopher Villiers and Sir John Villiers; that he
has been already false to Somerset, and may end by
playing false with his Lordship. Buckingham lies open
to such hints; his family more open to the direct persuasion of angels and double angels. Coke gets Lady
Buckingham on his side. If he could only part with his
hoards, his day of revenge might be near; happily he

---

7. Yelverton to Bacon, Sept. 3, 1617, Lambeth MSS. 936; Carleton to Chamberlain, May 24, 1617, S. P. O.

XI. 7.
——
1517.
July.

cannot pay down his money even to assuage the rancor of his heart.

He thinks of a plan by which he may gain his end, yet save his pelf.

8. A daughter has been born to Coke of his second wife. This wife and he never pulled together, and of late their wrangles have been louder than at first. Their marriage was a scrape, their wedded life has been a quarrel and a jest. She disdains to bear his name, she slams her door in his face. She gives entertainments in Holborn, from which he and his friends are insolently shut out. Their tastes are in the strongest degree opposed.

He is penurious, she profuse. He loves folios and a farthing candle; she lights and revels, masques and plays. By day and night a rout of fiddlers, dancers, wizards, lovers, and magicians pours through the galleries of her great mansion looking on the Fleet. Coke slinks in shame from the sight of all this devilry to his den in Sergeants' Inn. Their misery makes the sport of wits and gallants; while in their quarrels and their unhappiness Bacon (though he has not himself escaped the common lot, — a mother-in-law) has nevertheless, in his own modest and tranquil home, good reason to thank heaven night and day for his escape from such a wife.

8. Jonson's Metamorphosed Gypsies; Bankes's Story of Corffe Castle, 35 – 44; Lady Hatton to Cecil, undated Papers, xl. 6, S. P. O.

9. The child of this dismal pair is blossoming into a beauty and a toast, whose sensuous loveliness Jonson depicts in some of his most luscious lines : —

> " Though your either cheek discloses
>   Mingled baths of milk and roses;
> Though your lips be banks of blisses,
>   Where he plants and gathers kisses;
> And yourself the reason why
>   Wisest men of love may die ! "

Yet the beauty of her cheek and lips is the smallest part of Frances Coke's charms. As Lady Hatton's only child, she is heiress of Hatton House, of Corffe Castle, of Purbeck Isle. Coke privately offers this wealthy girl to Buckingham's mother for one of her pauper sons. A bargain is soon struck. Sir John Villiers is to take her with twenty thousand pounds dower and a settlement of two thousand marks a year. Buckingham is to pardon all Coke's offences, and use his power to restore him to high place and confer on him high rank.

To this huckstering Frances Coke is much averse, her mother still more averse. The young lady hates Sir John, a man old enough to be her father, without person or talents, and poor as a church mouse. Her mother huffs at a contract made at her expense, without her leave. That Coke should propose a scheme is

9. Jonson's Gypsies Metamorphosed; Sherborne to Carleton, Dec. 7, 1616, S. P. O.; Chamberlain to Carleton, Dec. 21, 1616; June 4, July 19, 1617, S. P. O ; Winwood to Lake, May 27, 1617, S. P. O.

XI. 9.

1617.
July.
enough to make her loathe it. But in such a scheme as this match with Sir John Villiers she has better grounds for hesitation than a woman's whim. She very justly fears the tenure of a favorite's place. Has she not witnessed Somerset's golden rise and stormy end? A twinge of gout, a saucy word, a prettier cheek, may turn the King's eye another way. What then? With Buckingham's fall may come down all his house. Even now sharp eyes are turned on the rising star of Lord Mordaunt. Some note how James of late has begun to ogle a youth named Coney. Bets are made that Buckingham's fortunes are on the wane. Lady Hatton will not hear of such a match for her only child. Husband and wife dispute and quarrel, as they have always done over lesser things; and when the Lord Keeper and the Council, anxious for peace, interpose between them, it is only, as results soon prove, to procure a reconciliation in which Coke tries to deceive Lady Hatton and Lady Hatton succeeds in deceiving Coke. Each plots to outwit the other; Coke bent on winning the good-will of Buckingham; his wife on disposing of her daughter and her property as she herself thinks best. Each plays the spy, makes friends among the servants, gets up factions in the house. Her people take Lady Hatton's part, more because they scorn the penurious old curmudgeon than because they like his prodigal and imperious wife.

She steals a march upon him while he sleeps. Putting her child into a coach at dead of night, she slips

away to Oatlands, where she hides from pursuit in her
cousin Sir Edward Withipole's house.

10. These domestic broils occur while James and
Buckingham are in the north, — setting up organs in
churches, wrangling over Kirk discipline, consecrating
bishops in the land of Knox. The Lord Keeper is
acting as a sort of regent. To him, therefore, in Council, Coke, when he has traced his wife and child, applies for warrants of arrest. Bacon refuses. Coke flies
to Sir John's mother; his wicked wife, he tells this
lady, has stolen his child, has poisoned her affections
towards Sir John, and means to carry her into France
to avoid the match with her ladyship's son.

Her cupidity aroused, the great lady writes to command the Lord Keeper to arm Coke with full powers
of search and arrest. Bacon again refuses. What he
feels it right to deny in one quarter, he has courage
to deny in another; though aware that his duty may
be represented as an insult to Villiers, as an usurpation
to the King.

His refusal to do wrong at her bidding transforms
Lady Buckingham into a ruthless and inexorable foe.

11. Safe in the strength of his great patroness, Coke,
defying the Lord Keeper and the Privy Council, arms

10. Council Reg., July 11, 14, 1617; James to Bacon, July 25, 1617, in Birch,
133.
11. Chamberlain to Carleton, July 19, 1617, S. P. O.; Gerard to Carleton,
July 22, 1617, S. P. O.; Council Reg., July 14, 1617.

XI. 11. a dozen of his servants, rides down to Oatlands, runs
a beam against Withipole's door, and, smashing into his
wife's retreat, without warrant of arrest, without a constable, he seizes the fainting girl, tosses her into his
coach, and hurries her away to Stoke.

A universal howl pursues the perpetrator of this outrage on the public peace. The Council meet to consider this violation of domicile. As they are rising for
the day, Lady Hatton raves to the door. How can they
they decline to see her? She is a woman and in dis-
tress; she is of kin by blood or marriage to the Lord
Keeper, to the Lord Treasurer, to half the Council;
she is pleading in her right. When admitted to the
Council chamber, she describes with consummate art the
outrage she has suffered, the confinement of her daughter in a lonely house, her sickness to the point of death,
and she implores the lords, as only mothers robbed of
their children can implore, that the child may be sent
for, that her story may be heard, that a physician may
see her lest she die.

The Council grant her prayer. An officer of the court
rides down to Stoke, takes the girl from her imprisonment, and lodges her in town.

July 21. 12. The Lord Keeper summons Coke to attend the
Council and answer for this breach of the King's peace.
With an insolence which his secret understanding with

12. Council Reg., July 21, 1617; Chamberlain to Carleton, June 4, 1617,
S. P. O.; Yelverton to Bacon, Sept. 3, 1617, Lambeth MSS. 936.

XI. 12.
——
1617.
July 21.

the favorite's kin makes safe for him, Coke declares that he has done his duty, that his wife meant to break the match with Sir John Villiers, that she would have carried his daughter away to France, that she herself traduced and set on her servants to traduce Sir John. Bacon, who may object to a marriage between Frances Coke and Sir John Villiers, — a marriage projected for his own humiliation and for the recovery of power by the late Chief Justice, — feels, as one of the Commissioners governing the realm, the gravest objection to such acts as those of Coke. He replies, therefore, in the name of the Council, that Villiers, as a gentleman worthy of the young lady, would have sought her in a noble and religious fashion, not with a gang of armed men, in a midnight brawl, in contempt of natural and statute law.

Yelverton, the Attorney-General, declares that the late Lord Chief Justice, in violating Withipole's house without warrant or constable, has grievously offended against the law. None of the Council, certainly not the Lord Keeper, has any wish to weigh upon the irascible old man ; but when he fails to justify by witnesses any one allegation against his wife, they are compelled to file an information against him in the Star Chamber for breach of the peace, and allow his daughter the shelter of the Attorney-General's house.

Coke shudders at this order for his appearance in the Star Chamber. Recently fined four thousand pounds in that court for taking bail of a pirate, he fears lest a

XI. 12.
——
1617.
July 21. second accusation should end in a second fine. He cannot count on either gratitude or wisdom in the Villiers people. These thriftless adventurers may think it safer to take his money than wait for the chance of obtaining his wife's broad lands. He finds it wiser to defer to the Privy Council. With a rancorous animosity in his heart towards Bacon, and with fiery rage against Yelverton, he bends so far as to undergo a pretended reconciliation with his wife. Bacon joyfully announces to the King that peace is made.

July 25. 13. A line of writers closing in Lord Campbell represents Bacon as first selfishly striving to thwart the match; then, finding Buckingham bent on it, as plotting with Lady Hatton by underground and criminal practices to defeat it; next, after bearing with abject spirit the most provoking taunts and threats from the favorite, as meanly condescending to eat his words and to forward a match which he must have detested with all his soul. The dates supplied by the Council Register correct these errors. Bacon's first note to Buckingham on the match has the date of July twelfth, his first note to the King that of July twenty-fifth. Before the earlier date, Lady Hatton and her daughter ran away, the ex-Chief Justice broke into Withipole's house, the Council met to consider his offence, and Clement Edmondes, their clerk, took charge of the girl. Before the later date, and before a single word was heard from Buck-

13. Bacon to Buckingham, July 12, 25, 1617; Bacon to James, July 25, 1617.

ingham in answer, Bacon calmed the outrage, recon- XI. 13.
ciled husband and wife, and restored Frances Coke to ___
her father's house.

14. After all this was done, he wrote to Buckingham
and the King the reasons which, in his opinion, made
a marriage between John Villiers and Frances Coke
undesirable ; the refusal of Lady Hatton, the depend-
ency of the young girl on her mother, the quarrelsome
temper of the two parents, the notoriety and scandal
of their domestic feuds, the disapproval of leading men
in the Government, the recent disgrace of Coke, the
divisions which his return to the Council would bring
with it, — sage and honest reasons, one and all, which
received the most prompt and signal justification from
events. But Buckingham was blind. The King himself forbade Bacon to oppose the favorite's schemes of
family aggrandizement. Unable either to resist his Majesty's commands, or to close his eyes on the coming
evil, he accepted the duty laid upon him : "For my
Lord of Buckingham, I had rather go against his mind
than against his good. Your Majesty I must obey."

15. Lady Hatton, on publishing a prior contract be-

---

14. Vere to Carleton, Aug. 12, 1617, S. P. O.; Gerard to Carleton, Aug. 18,
1617, S. P. O.

15. Council Reg., Sept 24, 1617; Obligations and Oaths of Frances Coke to
become the Wife of Henry Vere, July 10, 1617, S. P. O.; Gerard to Carleton,
Aug. 18, 1617, S. P. O.; Herbert to Carleton, Oct. 6, 1617, S. P. O.; Vere to
Carleton, Oct. 20, 1617, S. P. O.

XI. 15.

1617.
Oct.

tween her daughter and the young Lord Oxford, is put into arrest, and the marriage of Sir John and Frances celebrated with regal pomp. It begins in misery to end in shame. Lady Hatton resists every persuasion to appear, nor is there a single Cecil present at the rite. James makes the bridegroom Viscount Purbeck; but he cannot make the young bride love or respect a man to whom she has been sold. Coke is content. To the chagrin of the Lord Keeper, to the terror of Yelverton, he returns to the Privy Council, — a lawyer out of work, — the situation in which his enmity can oftenest wound and his activity oftenest thwart the detested rival who holds the Seals. Expecting a coronet, Coke chooses for himself the title of Lord Stoke. He believes, as the world believes, that his rise will be the signal for Bacon's fall; yet such are the suavity and zeal, the splendor and success of the new Lord Keeper, —such his popularity on the bench and at Whitehall, — that, in spite of new scandals brought upon him and his family by Sir John and Lady Pakington, he is able to defy the malice of his enemies and to soar above every storm.

16. When her daughter's husband received the Great Seal, Lady Pakington supposed that her day of deliverance from Sir John was at hand. The lusty knight, who has sunk her rents in his brine-pits and fish-ponds, has now grown old, verging on seventy years of age, while she is still young and hale. But time, which slackens his thews,

16. Dom. Papers James the First, xcii. 88.

has left untamed his temper and his pride. The mother XI. 16.
of a Lord Keeper's wife can surely get justice done to her
at last against the tyrant! She appeals to the law, and 1617.
Oct.
brings him before the Court of High Commission, where
her cold, easy manner tells in her behalf, and his fluster
and violence get him sent to jail and put under lock and
guard. To Bacon's deep mortification, and despite his
strenuous efforts to avoid the case, this domestic broil is
referred to him.

Under trials of excessive difficulty and delicacy, he bears
himself between husband and wife, in this miserable stage,
in a way to extort the praise of even those news-writers
and gossips who are in other matters the harshest critics
of his life. He tells Lady Pakington she is in the wrong,
and that she ought to yield. He warns her against the
hope of finding in him a lenient judge so long as she follows her cold, unbending course.

This is the testimony of an unfriendly hand : —

CHAMBERLAIN TO CARLETON.

July 5, 1617.

There be great wars betwixt Sir John and his lady,
who sues him in the High Commission; where, by his
own wilfulness, she hath some advantage of him and
keeps him in prison. But the Lord Keeper deals very
honorably in the matter, which, though he could not com-
pound being referred to him, yet he carries himself so
indifferently that he wishes her to yield, and tells her

XI. 16. plainly and publicly that she must look for no counte-
—
1618.

nance from him as long as she follows this course.

Jan.

17. Notwithstanding these scandals and vexations in his own family, the Lord Keeper rises in power, expands in fame. In January, 1618, he attains the higher grade of Chancellor. In July of the same year he becomes a Peer. His slanderers sink beneath his feet. No severity seems to the Privy Council too great for those, however high in rank, who menace his person or dispute his justice. For a saucy word they send Lord Clifton to the Fleet: for a complaint against one of his verdicts they commit Lady Ann Blount to the Marshalsea. In 1620 he publishes his Novum Organum, — a book which has in it the germs of more power and good to man than any other work not of Divine authorship in the world. He is now at the height of earthly fame. First layman in his own country, first philosopher in Europe, what is wanting to his felicity? Neither power, nor popularity, nor titles, nor love, nor fame, nor obedience, nor troops of friends.

1620. All these he has, — no man in greater fulness. If his heart has other longings, he has only to express his wish.

1621. In January, 1621, he receives the title of Viscount St.
Jan. 27.
Albans, in a form of peculiar honor, — other Peers being created by letters-patent, he by investiture with the coronet and robe.

17. Council Reg., Dec. 30, 1617, Mar. 17, 27, 1618; Grant Book, 241, 283; Herbert to Carleton, Dec. 30, 1617, S. P. O.; Chamberlain to Carleton, Feb. 3, 1621, S. P. O.

18. Yet, only seven months after printing the Greatest XI. 18.
Birth of Time, only three months after receiving in the —
King's presence the robe and coronet, he is stripped of 1621.
his honors, degraded from his great place, condemned to Jan. 27.
a monstrous fine, and flung into the Tower.

The tale of this fall is the most strange and sad in the
whole history of man.

18. Lords' Jour., iii. 105.

CHAPTER XII.

FEES.

XII. 1.
———
1620.
Nov.

1. To see why the threat of prosecution so deeply disturbed Egerton, and how easy it may be for unscrupulous
men to frame a charge of corruption against his success-
or, a reader who is not a lawyer should remind himself
of the state of society in the days of James the First.

There is no civil list. Few men in the court or in the
Church receive salaries from the Crown; and each has to
keep his state and make his fortune out of fees and gifts.
The King takes fees. The archbishop, the bishop, the
rural dean take fees. The Lord Chancellor, the Lord
Chief Justice, the Baron of the Exchequer, the Master of
the Rolls, the Attorney-General, the Solicitor-General,
the King's Sergeant, the utter barrister, all the functionaries of law and justice, take fees. So in the great offices
of state. The Lord Treasurer takes fees. The Lord Ad-
miral takes fees. The Secretary of State, the Chancellor
of the Exchequer, the Master of the Wards, the Warden
of the Cinque Ports, the gentlemen of the Bedchamber,
all take fees. Everybody takes fees, everybody pays fees.

2. In some public offices and courts the amount to

XII. 2

162?.
Nov.

be paid is fixed, either by ancient usage or by such a common understanding as in modern times controls a railway or steamboat fare. In some, particularly in the courts of justice, it is open. Bassanio may present his ducats; three thousand in a bag. The judge may only take a ring. A fee is due whenever an act is done. The occasions on which, by ancient usage of the realm, the King claims help or fine are many: the sealing of an office or a grant, the knighting of his son, the marriage of his daughter, the alienation of lands *in capite*, his birthday, New Year's Day, the anniversary of his accession or his coronation, — indeed, at all times when he wants money and finds men rich enough and loyal enough to pay. In like manner the clergy levy tithe and toll; fees on christenings, fees on churchings, fees on marriages, fees on interments; Easter offerings, free offerings; charities, church reparations, church extensions, pews, and rents.

In the government offices it is the same as in the palace and the church. If the Attorney-General, the Secretary of State, the Lord-Admiral, or the Privy Seal puts his signature to a sheet of paper, he takes his fee. Often it is his means of life. To wit, the retaining fee paid by the King to Cecil, as premier Secretary of State, is a hundred pounds a year. But the fees from other sources are enormous. These fees are not bribes.

3. The same at the Bar and on the Bench. The Bar is a free profession, — a member of the Temple or of Lin-

coln's Inn being bound to plead, as the knights whose swords are rust were bound to fight, in love and faith, taking no purse nor scrip. It is an order of courtesy and chivalry ; its members the soldiers of justice, pledged to protect the weak, to help the needy, to defend the right. Now, all this service is by law and usage free. A barrister may not ask wages for his toil, like an attorney or a clerk, nor can he reclaim by any process of law, as the clerk and the attorney can, the value of his time and speech. If he lives on the gifts of grateful clients, these gifts must be perfectly free. This theory of a counsel's hire, though old as our language and our institutions, is of course a sham. No junior on the Oxford circuit dreams of succoring damsels from love of Dulcinea, or freeing galley-slaves from the obligations of knighthood. No guineas, no speech. The shifts by which lax attorneys are tickled into passing the fees which no law compels them to pay are droll as anything in the immortal laws of Barataria.

4. Now, the rules which continue under Victoria to govern the Bar, under James the First governed the Bench. The Lord Chief Justice or the Lord Chancellor, like the Secretary of State, is paid by fees. The King's judge is neither in deed nor in name a public servant; he receives a nominal sum as standing counsel for the Crown ; and for the rest he depends on the income arising from his hearing of private causes. These facts appear in a comparison of the amounts paid by the

Crown to its great legal functionaries, with the estimated
profits of each particular post. Thus the Seals, though
the Lord Chancellor had no proper salary, were in Egerton's time worth from ten to fifteen thousand pounds a
year. Bacon valued his place as Attorney-General at six
thousand a year; of which princely sum (twenty-five
thousand a year in coin of Victoria) the King only paid
him eighty-one pounds six shillings and eight pence.
Yelverton's place of Solicitor brought him three or four
thousand a year, of which he got seventy pounds from
James. The judges had enough to buy their gloves and
robes, not more. Coke, when Lord Chief Justice of England, drew from the State twelve farthings less than two
hundred and twenty-five pounds a year. When travelling circuit, he was allowed thirty-three pounds six shillings and eight pence for his expenses. Hobart, Chief
Justice of the Common Pleas, had twelve farthings less
than one hundred and ninety-five pounds a year; Tanfield, Lord Chief Baron of His Majesty's Court of Exchequer, one hundred and eighty-eight pounds six shillings a year. Yet each of these great lawyers had given
up a lucrative practice at the Bar. After their promotion to the Bench, they lived in good houses, kept a
princely state, gave dinners and masques, made presents to the King, accumulated goods and lands. Their
wages were paid in fees by those who resorted for justice
to their courts.

5. These fees were not bribes. If the satirists, from

5. Dom. Papers James First, i. 68, S. P. O.

Latimer to Nashe, described the Bench of Bishops and the Bench of Judges as taking bribes, it was only in the vein common to lampooners in every age of the world; the vein in which Boccaccio describes his Friars, and Jonson his Justice Overdos. Serious men made no complaint. Judicial corruption was not a grievance in 1604. In 1606 an attempt to reduce the fees in one department of Chancery business was rejected by the popular party in the House of Commons.

In the Great List of Grievances, drawn up in 1604, we find complaints that Cecil lives in adultery, that Parliament is packed with courtiers, that the Forest Laws have been revived, that pardons are sold to cutthroats and felons, that monopolies are granted to duns, and patents bestowed on extortioners and pimps; not that the great lawyers are thought corrupt, or that justice is supposed to be bought and sold.

Nor is such a grievance felt though undescribed. In the List of Grievances there is one charge against the Lord Chancellor Egerton. Had there been a second, it would certainly have been named. In 1604 the charge which law reformers made against Egerton was that he held the two offices of Master of the Rolls and Keeper of the Great Seals. It never occurred to these men to complain that he took his wages in the shape of fees.

6. In 1606 a bill was laid before the Commons, by a disappointed jobber, to reduce some of the fees for

6. Tanner MSS. 169, fol. 42; Com. Jour., i. 259, 268, 279.

copies in the Court of Record. In the debates on this XII. 6.
bill Bacon assumed a leading part. The argument of
counsel was against the interference of Parliament in
the unfair fashion of the bill, with what Bacon called
the freeholds of the officers in that Court. The notes
of his speech, which are in the Bodleian Library, and
have not been printed, put the case as it appeared to
the best minds in England in 1606, a year before he
held any office under the Crown. Bacon showed that
the bill to reduce the fees for copies originated in a
spirit, not of reform, but of revenge; that a similar
bill had, in years gone by, been promptly rejected by
the House; that such a law to cut down fees was unprecedented; that the bill was retroactive, against all
law and justice; that a man's right in his fees was sacred as his right in his goods and lands. Remembering
all that is to follow, with how much curiosity one reads
these nineteen heads of a discourse against the bill!

1620.
Nov.

Sir Francis Bacon's Speech.

First: It hath sprung out of the ashes of a decayed
monopoly by the spleen of one man; that, because he
could not continue his new exactions, therefore would
now pull down ancient fees.

Second: It knows the way out of the House; for in
the xxxv Eliz. the like bill was preferred, and much
called upon at the first, and rejected at the engross-
ment, not having twenty voices for it.

XII. 6.
——
1620.
Nov.

Third : It is without all precedent ; for look into former laws and you shall find that, when a statute enacts a new office or acts to be done, it limits fees, as in case of enrolment, in case of administration, &c., but it never limits ancient fees to take away other men's freeholds.

Fourth : It looks extremely back, which is against all justice of Parliament, for a number of subjects are already placed in offices : some attaining them in course of long service ; some in consideration of great sums of money ; some in reward of service from the Crown, when they might have had other suits and such offices again allied with a number of other subjects, who valued them according to their offices. Now, if half these men's livelihoods and fortunes should be taken from them, it were an infinite injustice.

Fifth : It were more justice to raise the fees than to abate them, for we see gentlemen have raised their rents and the fines of their tenants, and merchants, tradesmen, and farmers their commodities and wares ; and this mightily within c. years. But the fees of offices continue at one rate.

Sixth : If it be said the number of fees is much increased because causes are increased, that is a benefit which time gives and time takes away. It is no more than if there were an ancient toll at some bridge between Berwick and London, and now it should be brought down because that, Scotland being united, there were more passengers.

Seventh : Causes may again decrease, as they do already begin ; and therefore, as men must endure the prejudice of time, so they ought again to enjoy benefit of time.

Eighth : Men are not to consider the proportion between the fee and the pains taken, as if it were in a scrivener's shop, because in the copies (being the principal gain of the officer) was considered ab antiquo his charge, his attendance, his former labors to make him fit for the place, his countenance and quality in the commonwealth, and the like.

Ninth : The officers do many things sans fee, as in causes in forma pauperis, and for the King, &c., which is considered in the fees of copies.

Tenth : There is great labor of mind in many cases, as in the entering of orders, and in all examinations. All which is only considered in the copies.

Eleventh : These offices are either the gift of the King or in the gift of great officers, who have their office from the King, so as the King is disinherited of his ancient rights and means to prefer servants, and the great offices of the kingdom likewise disgraced and impaired.

Twelfth : There is a great confusion and inequality in the bill, for the copies in inferior courts, as for example the Court of the Marches, the Court of the North (being inferior courts), are left in as good case as they were, and high courts of the kingdom only abridged, whereas there was ever a diversity half in half in all fees, as Chancellor's clerks and all others.

Thirteenth : If fees be abridged as too great, they

13 *

ought to be abridged as well in other points as in copies, and as well in other offices as in offices towards the law. For now prothonotories shall have their old fees for engrossing upon the roll and the like, and only the copies shall be abridged; whereas, if it be well examined, the copies are of all fees the most reasonable; and so of other offices, as customs, searches, mayors, bailiffs, &c., which have many ancient fees incident to their offices, which all may be called in question upon the like or better reason.

Fourteenth: The suggestion of the bill is utterly false, which in all law is odious. For it suggesteth that these fees have of late years been exacted, which is utterly untrue, having been time out of mind and being men's freehold, whereof they may have an assize, so as the Parliament may as well take any man's lands, common means, &c., as these fees.

Fifteenth: It casts a slander upon all superior judges, as if they had tolerated extortions, whereas there have been severe and strict courses taken, and that of late, for the distinguishing of lawful fees from new exactions, and fees reduced into tables, and they published and hanged up in courts, that the subjects be not poled nor aggrieved.

Sixteenth: The law (if it were just) ought to enter into an examination and distinction what were rightful and ancient fees and what were upstart fees and encroachments, whereas now it sweeps them all away without difference.

Seventeenth : It requires an impossibility, setting men
to spell again how many syllables be in a line, and puts
the penalty of **xxs.** for every line faulty, which is xviii*l.*
a sheet. And the superior officers must answer it for
clerks' faults or oversight.

Eighteenth : It doth disgrace superior judges in court,
to whom it properly belongeth to correct those misde-
meanors according to their oaths and according to discretion, because it is impossible to reduce it to a defi-
nite rule.

Nineteenth : This being a penal law, it seems there
is but some commodity sought for, that some that could
not continue their first monopoly might make themselves
whole out of some penalties.

These arguments prevailed. A committee being named
to report on the bill, they reported against it, and the
bill was laid asleep.

7. A few years later, mainly through the speeches
and the writings of Bacon himself, a feeling began to
show itself against the payment of judges, registrars,
and clerks, by uncertain fees. Each new Parliament saw
the subject stirred. In the sessions of 1610 and 1614
bills were introduced and dropped. But the argument
for a great and just change of the old system grew
under debate. The business of the courts increases
daily, and the private causes have long ago become
more numerous and important than the King's causes.

7. Com. Jour., I. 427, 489.

A plan, therefore, which may have done very well under Edward or Henry, may be a very great evil under James. An unpaid Bench, though all that society wished for its defence under feudal or Brehon law, may obviously become a dangerous power in a highly artificial and litigious age. Such is the reasoning of many wise men. Not that justice is less purely dispensed under Bacon than of yore; the reverse is a conspicuous fact. The improvement has been slow and safe. Hatton danced through his duties with more credit than Bromley; Puckering surpassed Hatton, and Egerton eclipsed Puckering. The last Chancellor of all is the best; in character as in intellect Bacon tops the list. A desire to change the fee system is not the child of discontent, but of growth. Under Edward or Richard the Commons would have refused a salary to the judge; for a magnificently paid Bench would have seemed, and probably would have behaved, as the ministers of a despotic prince, eager only for their master's work, contemptuous of the intrusion of private causes, callous to the concerns of common men. The profits from private suits quickened the stream of justice; helped to maintain the independence of the upright judge. Yet many men see that a time must come, some think it has come, when, through the growth of riches and the purification of law, the system of various and precarious fees may be wisely abandoned for a system of payments by the State.

8. An old lawyer like Coke knows how to turn this

war between an old system and a new sentiment to account. Time has neither cured his jealousy of Bacon nor cooled his resentment towards Yelverton. If the alliance with Buckingham has not yet brought him the Mace and Seals, nor even the barony of Stoke, it has given him the favorite's mother for a friend. Lady Buckingham is busy for her kin ; her son John married and made a peer, she wants an heiress for her son Christopher, two or three rich husbands for her penniless nieces, a suitor, may be, for herself. A wife for Kit she may buy with honors, just as she bought Frances Coke for John. But husbands for her neices, men of high rank and wealth, she can only tempt into the noose with offices and power. She has bought Sir Lionel Cranfield up for one niece. For another she · has fixed her eye on James Ley, the rich Attorney of the Court of Wards. Cranfield's wooing has been comic as a play. Falling in love with Lady Effingham, he proposes to her, and is about to marry her, when the news reaches Lady Buckingham, who instantly warns her miserable dependant that if he hopes to thrive at court he must give up Lady Effingham, and marry a young person, who is certainly poor in purse, but rich enough for two in friends. Cranfield takes the wife offered to him, with a seat at the Privy Council, and a promise of one of the highest places in the sovereign's gift.

8. Harwood to Carleton, Feb. 6, 1619, S. P. O.; Brent to Carleton, May 29, 1619, S. P. O.; Nethersole to Carleton, Jan. 18, 1620, S. P. O.; Chamberlain to Carleton, July 14, 1621, S. P. O.; Sign Man., Nos. 44, 53.

XII. 8.

1620.
Nov.

To lure him on, James Ley is made a baronet, and a special act under the Sign Manual remits to him the usual fees for the escutcheon of the bloody hand.

These promotions, moreover, are but stepping-stones to place. What great offices can be got?

9. A beginning has been made with the White Staff.

Suffolk was unpopular. The father of Lady Somerset, an avowed Roman Catholic, a suspected pensioner of Spain, he was hated while in power with such bitterness of hate, that when Buckingham's tools charged him with extortion, false dealing, bribery, and embezzlement, to none of which accusations he lay fairly open, no one felt either surprise or pity at the fate of this pernicious peer; and when the Court of Star Chamber, with the sham proofs of his guilt before it, deprived him of the Staff, fined him thirty thousand pounds, and flung him during pleasure into the Tower, the whole country, which knew him to be a Papist and believed him to be a spy, felt the sentence which deprived him of power to do harm run through its veins, — a shock of joy.

10. The profits of this transaction only kindle the greed for more. Yelverton's turn comes next.

If not a Puritan in religion, Sir Henry Yelverton has

9. Proceedings against the Earl of Suffolk, Nov. 13, 1619, S. P. O.

10. Bacon's Notes, Lambeth MSS. 936, fol. 133; Chamberlain to Carleton, June 28, 1620, S. P. O.; Archæologia, xv. 27.

generally spoken and voted with the Puritan party. A
man of good parts and unbending character, he has lived
on friendly terms with Bacon, with whom he kept his
terms at Gray's Inn and served in the House of Commons. His popularity in the House, like the popularity
of Bacon, kept him out of office. In the debates, for
many years his name stood side by side with that of
Bacon, with whom he spoke for the subsidies and for the
Union. The same breeze of favor brought them both
into power. When Bacon became Attorney-General he
used his influence to procure the Solicitorship for Yelverton. Since then they have acted constantly together,
most of all so in the effort to prevent Frances Coke from
being forced to marry a man she could not love. Buckingham and the faction of Buckingham have never liked
Yelverton. They have not been able to forget the circumstances of his rise, to forgive the obstinacy of his
demeanor, or the way in which he has exercised towards
them his power. When Bacon got the Seals, Sir James
Ley, who wanted to succeed him as Attorney, offered to
pay Buckingham ten thousand pounds for the post. Lady
Buckingham supported the lover of her niece; but the
King, when he put the Seals into Bacon's hands, himself
passed the patent of office to Yelverton; who refused to
contract an obligation to Villiers, though urged by Archbishop Abbott and the Duke of Lenox to conciliate the
chief authority in the bedchamber and the closet. Yelverton's offences are that he has been very manly, and
that he occupies a very high post.

XII. 11.   11. Unhappily, in the exercise of powers not well de-
____   fined, he has given an advantage to his hot and unscru-
1620.
Nov. 10. pulous enemy, Coke.   A new charter has been lately
passed to the city of London, with clauses favorable to
the citizens, which Coke has no trouble in persuading
James trench on the prerogatives of his Crown.   It is
not pretended that Yelverton took money for inserting
these clauses, though it is admitted for the defence that
in putting them into the charter he went beyond his
powers.   Sir Henry submits his error to the King's judgment.   Such a course suits neither Buckingham nor
Coke, who want his fine and the profits on his place.
Cited into the Star Chamber, over which Bacon, as Lord
Chancellor, presides, Yelverton admits his indiscretion,
and Bacon, who cannot deny his fault, essays to soften
his judges.   The notes for his speech, written in his
own hand, remain at Lambeth Palace.   They stand as
under : —

BACON'S NOTES ON YELVERTON'S CASE.

" Sorry for the person, being a gentleman that I lived
with in Gray's Inn, served with when I was Attorney,
joined with since in many services, and one that ever
gave me more attributes in public than I deserved ; and,
besides, a man of very good parts, which with me is friend-

____

11. Lambeth MSS. 936, fol. 188 ; Yelverton's Speech in the Star Chamber,
Nov. 10, 1620, S. P. O. ; Locke to Carleton, Nov. 11, 1620, S. P. O. ; Dom. Papers, cxvii. 76.

ship at first sight, much more joined with an ancient XII. 11.
acquaintance. But, as a judge, I hold the offence very
great, and that without pressing measure ; upon which I
will only make a few observations, and so leave it. First,
I observe the danger and consequence of the offence ; for
if it be suffered that the Learned Counsel shall practise
the art of multiplication upon their warrants, the Crown
will be destroyed in small time. The Great Seal, the
Privy Seal, Signet, are solemn things, but they follow the
King's hand. It is the bill drawn by the Learned Counsel
that leads the King's hand. Next, I note the nature of
the defence ; as, first, that it was error in judgment. For
this, surely, if the offence were small though clear, or
great but doubtful, I could hardly sentence it. For it is
hard to draw a straight line by steadiness of hand, but it
could not be the swerving of the hand. And herein I
note the wisdom of the law of England, which termeth
the highest contempts and excesses of authority misprisions, which (if you take the sound and derivation of the
word) is but mistaken. But if you take the use and ac-
ceptation of the word, it is high and heinous contempt
and usurpation of authority. Whereof the reason I take
to be, and the same excellently imposed, for that main
mistaking it is ever joined with contempt; for he that
reveres will not easily mistake ; but he that slights and
thinks of the greatness of his place more than of the
duty of his place will soon commit misprisions."

Coke, furious at the sound of such mild, soft words,

XII. 11. demands from the Court a sentence of imprisonment
—— for life and a fine of six thousand pounds. Even the
1620.
Nov. judges of the Star Chamber will not go his length.
They condemn Yelverton to a fine of four thousand
pounds.

Dec.　　　12. Two great offices, the Treasury and the Attorney-
Generalship, are now for sale. Buyers crowd in ; for
this system of ruining men in order to vend their posts
is new, and no one yet perceives that to purchase a great
office is to be in future the first step towards destruction.
Montagu bids for the Staff; and as the purchase, if
made, will cause him to leave the King's Bench, Lady
Buckingham promotes his suit, that she may raise Ley
to the rank of Lord Chief Justice and marry him to her
pauper niece. On going down to Newmarket to see the
King, Montagu calls to tell Bacon he hopes to bring back
with him the Staff. "Take heed what you do, my
Lord," says the Chancellor ; "wood is dearer at Newmarket than at any other place in England." The Treasury, with the title of Mandeville, costs Sir Henry Montagu no less than twenty thousand pounds.

13. Coventry buys the Attorney's office, and Heath
becomes Solicitor in his place. At both ends Buckingham makes his profit. Not to speak of present bribes, he

12. Apophthegms in Resuscitatio, 42; Locke to Carleton, Dec. 2, 1620,
S. P. O.
13. Woodford to Nethersole, Feb. 2, 1621, S. P. O.; Chamberlain to Carleton,
Feb. 3, 1621, S. P. O.

so arranges the game that these two removals bring him,
or save him, eight hundred pounds a year. Lady Buckingham presents the King's Bench to Ley.

These profits and promotions edge the tooth for more.

14. In the crowd of able and unscrupulous men who
wait in the anteroom of Villiers, and who build their
fortunes on him, there is none more able or more unscrupulous than Sir Lionel Cranfield. He had risen from
the grade of a London apprentice, through the useful and
unclean offices of a receiver, a contractor, and a surveyor
of public income, to the rank of a Knight, a member
of Parliament, and a Master of Requests, before he got
introduced to the Villiers gang. His life, indeed, has
been a study of safe and decorous villany. He got his
first step by making love to his master's daughter; he
grew rich by cheating the customs; he won notice from
the Council by telling them how to squeeze rich aldermen
while lightening the load on such poor devils as himself; he secured the protection of Lord Northampton by
a bribe of land which was not his own; he pleased the
King by a plan for jobbing away the Crown lands on a
more extensive scale; he fixed himself on Buckingham
by betraying to him, or to his cause, his first patrons, the
Howards. Cranfield was the chief instrument in de-

14. Doquets, April 1, 1605, Dec. 20, 1607, May 31, 1610; Sign Manuals, No.
49; Minute, Undated Papers of 1607, xxviii. 81; Northampton to Lake, Aug.
12, 1612, S. P. O.; Winwood to Lake, Mar. 29, 1617, S. P. O.; Brent to Carleton, Jan. 31, 1618, May 29, 1619, S. P. O.; Nethersole to Carleton, Jan. 18,
1620, S. P. O.

XII. 14. nouncing Suffolk and placing the Staff in Buckingham's
hands for sale. To reward this service, Suffolk's son-in-
1620.
Dec.
law, Viscount Wallingford, was compelled by threats of
prosecution, fine, and ruin, to surrender to Cranfield the
Court of Wards. Only a villain of stony heart and
brazen cheek could have either done this deed or taken
this reward ; for these Howards whom he betrayed and
spoiled were the very men who brought him into notice,
presented him at court, and procured for him a seat in
the House of Commons. But, in truth, there is no act
of turpitude, short of the vulgar crimes for which men
are hung, at which Cranfield, when his interests call,
would stop.

15. Bishop Goodman, who knew him well, and who
has left a defence of him, such as it is, confesses for
him to more dubious conduct and to more safe rascal-
ities than would have blasted the credit of ten ordinary
men. Courting the society of wits and scholars, pretending to wit himself, he has no true knowledge of
letters, no true sympathy for such weak fry as poets
and playwrights. Pelf is his god. His greed of money
is a brisk passion, and he has a perfect familiarity with
the crooked ways in which money can be got. No rogue
can deceive Cranfield. "Tush man !" he will say, "I
was bred in the city." His hand is in every one's purse ;
and woe to the man on whose place he has set his

15. Goodman, I. 295–308; Coryat's Description of a Philosophical Feast,
Dom. Papers, lxvi, 2. S. P. O.

heart! To pull down judges and councillors, for his own advancement and for his patron's gain, is the task to which he has now devoted a busy and teeming brain. Since his marriage with Lady Buckingham's niece, he has been suffered to mulct and plunder at his ease; and though some of his victims, mad with their losses, threaten to cut his throat, the audacious speculator in human roguery holds his course as though there were no retribution for injustice, either in this world or in the next. A loftier vista opens to his sight; the Staff and the peerage seem within his reach; but he can only grasp them by the help of that powerful and vindictive woman to whom he lately owed the pleasant alternative of destruction or a wife.

16. This great lady, if old enough to have grand-children, is not, in her own belief, too old to have a lover; and one more subtle than a serpent is at her side. John Williams was the chaplain to Egerton when Egerton held the Seals; but while blessing his master's meat and wine, he kept an eye on business; and when Bacon, coming to York House, offered to continue him in his post, the divine refused, having begun to dream of recovering the custody of the Great Seal from the lawyers to the churchmen. In the face of candidates like Bacon, Montagu, and Coke, such a hope would seem to most men vain; not so to one versed in the

arts by which a low order of monks and priests have in all ages striven to enslave the world. He makes court to Buckingham's mother; convinced that no woman is insensible to the flatteries of love, least of all an ambitious woman, greedy for pleasure and past her prime. When he has interested her passions in his career, his fight is wellnigh won. She puts him in the way to rise. She recommends him to her son; so shaping his course that, as either Lord Chancellor or as Archbishop of Canterbury, he may soon appear to the world in rank and power a husband less unworthy of herself.

Buckingham finds in Williams a divine of easy virtue and specious talents; who never prates to him about reform, who pays no homage to the primate, who detests the House of Commons with all his soul. At a word from his new mistress or from her son, Williams would not scruple to send his archbishop to the Fleet, or to resist and insult the whole Puritan parliament. A man capable of rising through an old woman's folly and a young man's vices has not been slow to rise. The needy chaplain has become Dean of Salisbury and Dean of Westminster. He is to have the first mitre that falls into the King's gift. If Bacon can be ruined, he is to have the Seals.

17. To three such schemers as an old Chief Justice, a

17. Gerard to Carleton, May 9, 1617, S. P. O.; Chamberlain to Carleton, May 10, 1617, S. P. O.; Proposals concerning the Chancery, 1650; Council Reg., Sept. 28, 1622.

Master of the Court of Wards, and an ex-chaplain to the
Lord Chancellor, urged by the sharpest passions of cupidity and revenge, and backed by the whole tribe of
Villiers, an accusation against the holder of the Seals is
easy enough to frame. The courts of law are full of
abuses. The highest officer of the realm has no salary
from the state. Custom imposes on him a host of servants ; officers of his court and of his household ; masters, secretaries, ushers, clerks, receivers, porters, none
of whom receives a mark a year from the Crown ; men
who have bought their places, and who are paid, as he
himself is paid, in fees and fines. The amounts of half
these fees are left to chance, to the hope or gratitude of
the suitor, often to the cupidity of the servant or the
length of the suitor's purse. The certain fines of Chancery, as subsequent inquiries show, are only thirteen
hundred pounds a year, the fluctuating fines still less ;
beyond which beggarly sum the great establishments of
the Lord Chancellor, his court, his household, and his
followers, gentlemen of quality, sons of peers and pre-
lates, magistrates, deputy-lieutenants of counties, knights
of the shire, have all to live on fees and presents. The
causes heard are many, — five or six hundred in every
term ; the servants of the court are not all honest ; some
indeed are flagitious rogues. The Chancellor has not
taken them voluntarily into his service, nor can he always turn them adrift : their places are their freeholds.
Among thousands of suitors, all of whom must have paid
fees into the court, half of whom must be smarting under

XII. 17. the pangs of a lost cause, it will be strange indeed if cun-
——   ning, malice, and unscrupulous power combined, cannot
1620.   find some charge that may be tortured into the appear-
Dec.   ance of a wrong.

18. They find a fitting instrument for this nefarious
search. John Churchill is a wretch whose days have
been spent in the most sordid tricks and chicaneries of
law. His father was a defaulter in the Court of Wards,
he himself was early in life concerned in a most infamous fraud. Ten years before he lends his services to
the enemies of Lord St. Albans he sold to Sir John
Bourchier, for a thousand pounds down and eighty
pounds a year for life, a manor which Bourchier found
that he had previously conveyed to his two uncles for
twenty shillings.

Bacon, who found this rascal occupying a place of
trust in the Court of Chancery, detecting him in an act
of forgery and extortion, has been compelled to turn him
into the street. Broken for his bad faith, liable to severe
punishment for his fraud, sore against his superior, he
is just the man for Williams and Coke. Familiar with
the court and with its clients, every vicious witness, every
maddened loser, every knave who has been exposed,
every dupe who has been hurt, are known to him by

18. Grant Book, 62; Crump to Churchill, April 14, 1605, S. P. O.; Acton to
Churchill, April 14, 1605, S. P. O.; Mabel to Churchill, Aug. 28, 1605, S. P. O.;
Ellis Churchill to Churchill, Aug. 29, Sept. 19, 20, Oct. 3, 1605, S. P. O.;
Bourchier to Cecil, June 16, 1611, S. P. O.; Chamberlain to Carleton, Mar. 24,
1621, S. P. O.

name and sight. A promise of protection from the law,
with a restoration to his place on Bacon's fall, sharpens
at once his greed and his hate. He hunts among the
victims of Chancery law. Every one who has a grievance,
or who fancies he has a grievance, against the Lord
Chancellor, he persuades or compels to set down his
tale.

19. Ever since the day when Bacon got the Seals,
Coke has been scoring up accusations against him. Lists
were framed by the Villiers clan, ready to lodge with the
King, before the Chancellor had been a year in office.
Every month has helped them to new matter. By the
industry of Churchill they are now prepared to go before
the Star Chamber; but a patriotic proposal, made and
pressed on the Crown by Bacon himself, shifts the scene
of their accusation from the Star Chamber to the House
of Peers.

19. Yelverton to Bacon, Sept. 3, 1617, in Birch, 138.

14

CHAPTER XIII.

THE ACCUSATION.

1. IT is no easy berth that Lord Mandeville has bought for his twenty thousand pounds. Soon he becomes aware that greedy eyes are on the Staff, that Buckingham is restless, and the Villiers clan hungry. The more he tries to please, the faster he multiplies his foes. Worse than all an empty exchequer gapes and yawns. " There is not a mark in the Treasury," he says to Bacon. " Be of good cheer then, my Lord," laughs the Chancellor ; " now you shall see the bottom of your business at the first."

2. Something must be done. Bacon says, Call a parliament. The spirit of reform runs high and grievances groan on every tongue. To meet the country is to court complaint and risk collision ; yet Bacon presses this counsel on the King, for a series of astounding events

---

1. Bacon's Apophthegms, in Resuscitatio, 42.

2. Council Reg., Dec. 27, 1620; Teynham to Edmonds, Dec. 23, 1620, S. P. O.; Howard to Naunton, Dec. 26, 1620, S. P. O.; Replies of Peers and Bishops on the Palatinate Contributions, Undated Papers, cxviii. 43, 44, 45, 57, 58, 59, 60, S. P. O.; Chamberlain to Carleton, Dec. 22, 1620, S. P. O.; Com. Jour., i. 507, 508.

abroad makes a prompt and permanent reconciliation

of the English King and Commons a statesman's gravest care. The Reformed Religion is at stake. Deploying her troops and the troops of her Austrian and Bavarian allies into line, Spain has enveloped Germany in cloud and flame, opening the **Thirty Years' War** with the sack of the Palatinate and the occupation of Prague. Max is master of the Hradshin, Spinola of the Rhine.

England, not less than the Protestant faith, is smitten by this blow; for Frederick and the Queen of Hearts are fugitives from Prague; the Winter King and Queen, as the fanciful Germans call them, owning neither principality nor kingdom, not even a home, on German soil.

James, fooled by the Spanish Jew, Gondomar, is mumbling about a Spanish match for his son Charles when surprised in his cups by news that Max and Spinola have robbed his daughter and her children of their native and elective crowns. What can he do? His purse is empty, —his credit gone. The goldsmiths of Lombard-street will not cash his bonds. He tries, indeed, to beg funds from a patriotic and warlike people for the recovery of the Palatinate, making of the great Protestant question a small affair of his own household; but the trick is stale, the confidence of his people gone. No man will give or lend. Used as the King is to evasion, he is startled by the shabbiness of his peers in this great need. The Roman Catholic lords refuse on the ground of sickness, debts, and out of town; their true reason, as he ought to know, is their secret sympathy for Spain

XIII. 2.
——
1621.
Jan.

and Bavaria as the armed protectors of the Roman Church; but the bishops, the deans, the English clergy, with rare exceptions, close their fists with the same hypocritical lies. The goldsmiths speak like men; they will not part with their money because they feel no confidence in the securities offered for their gold. They will send the King, they say, ten thousand pounds as a free gift, rather than lend him a hundred thousand with his crown for pledge.

3. Under such discouragements from his courtiers, James listens to the voice of his Chancellor. If Lord St. Albans, in his earlier days, often had to differ from the House of Commons on subsidies and grants, it had never been through want of patriotism in the knights and burgesses; only through their fears lest the moneys granted by them should be wasted, not on the regiments and fleets, but on the Herberts and Carrs. In the hour of peril St. Albans feels that he can trust their patriotism for supplies. The success of Max on the Weissenberg, the devastations of Spinola on the Neckar and the Main, disasters the most signal which have yet befallen the cause of God and the cause of freedom, bring the external danger to our doors. The nation feels its loss. Men mourn the King's indifference to the cries of religion and the claims of nature; and a popular frenzy

3. Thomas Scot's Vox Populi, 1620; Second edition of the same, revised, 1620; Undated Domestic Papers, cxviii. 102, 105, S. P. O.; Murray to Morton, Jan. 11, 1621, S. P. O.

breaks into accusing prose and song, pouring its subtle
fire through the veins and arteries of the land in de-
fiance of the most rigorous proclamations and the most
savage censorship of the press.

Bacon would meet the people. Let the King call a
parliament together, state. the situation, and throw himself heart and soul into the religious war!

4. This time there should be no mistake. The sessions of 1610 and 1614 were lost through quarrels;
not one Act passed in either. Grievances must now be
met; reasonable men must be gained over to support
the Crown. The enemy must see in England only one
party, one flag. Therefore let the King become the
leader of the Commons, let the Government adopt the
business of reform!

Many voices in the Council rise against these proposals
of the Lord Chancellor. But the Queen of Hearts cries
loud for help; the bankers will lend no more, the nobles
will give no more; so James, with many a pause and
doubt, with many a sigh for the days, now gone forever,
when he could chase the stag and quaff his strong Greek
wine untroubled by the clash of arms or the brawl of
tongues, consents to Bacon's plan.

The Chancellor, with the help of four great lawyers,
including Montagu and Coke, draws up a scheme to pro-

4. Bacon to James, Oct. 10, 1620, Mar. 11, 1621; to Buckingham, Oct. 19,
Dec. 19, 1620, printed in Birch, 1763, orig. at Lambeth Palace, 936; Statutes
of the Realm, iv. 1207.

mote a safer feeling between the House of Commons and the Crown ; a scheme of reform as well as of defence ; involving an immediate issue of writs, an honest hearing of public complaints, an abolition of unjust or unpopular monopolies, a withdrawal of some of the more obnoxious patents, above all an instant increase of the royal fleet.

5. This statement, addressed through Buckingham to the King, and signed by Bacon, Montagu, Heath, Coke, and Crewe, has not heretofore been printed : —

November 29, 1620.

MY VERY GOOD LORD, —

It may please his Majesty to call to mind, that, when we gave his Majesty our last account of Parliament's business in his presence, we went over the grievances of the last Parliament in 7mo., with our opinion, by way of probable conjecture, which of them are like to fall off, and which may perchance stick and be renewed. And we did also then acquaint his Majesty that we thought it no less fit to take into consideration grievances of like nature which have sprung since the said last session, which are the more like to be called upon by how much they are the more fresh, signifying withal that they were of two kinds. Some proclamations and commissions, and many patents, which, nevertheless, we did not then trouble his Majesty withal, in particular ; partly, for that we were not then fully prepared (it being a work of some

5. Tanner MSS. 290, fol. 33.

length), and partly for that we then desired and obtained
leave of his Majesty to communicate them with the council-table.   But since, I the Chancellor received his Majesty's pleasure by Secretary Calvert that we should first
present them to his Majesty with some advice thereupon
provisional, and as we are capable, and thereupon know
his Majesty's pleasure, before they be brought to the
table, which is the work of this despatch.   And herein
his Majesty may be likewise pleased to call to mind that
we then said, and do now humbly make remonstrance to
his Majesty, that in this we do not so much express the
sense of our own minds or judgments upon the particulars, as we do personate the Lower House, and cast with
ourselves what is like to be stirred there.   And, therefore,
if there be anything, either in respect of matter, or the
persons that stand not so well with his Majesty's good
liking, that his Majesty would be graciously pleased not
to impute it unto us, and withal to consider that it is to
this good end that his Majesty may either remove such
of them as in his own princely judgment, and with the
advice of his council, he shall think fit to be removed, or
be the better provided to carry through such of them as
he shall think fit to be maintained in case they should be
moved, and so the less surprised.

First, therefore, to begin with the patents.   We find
three sorts of patents (and those somewhat frequent since
the session of 7mo.) which *in genere*, we conceive, may
be most subject to exception of grievance ; patents of old
debts, patents of concealments, and patents of monopolies

XIII. 5. and forfeitures of, or dispensations with, penal laws, together with some other particulars which fall not so
properly under any one head.

1621.
Jan.

In these three kinds we do humbly advise several
courses to be taken. For the first two, of old debts and
concealments, for that they are in a mode legal (though
there may be found out some point in law to overthrow
them), yet it would be a long business by course of law,
and a matter unusual by act of council, to call them in.
But that truth moves us chiefly to avoid the questioning
them at the council-table is because if they shall be taken
away by the King's act it may let in upon him a flood of
suitors for recompense ; whereas, if they be taken away at
the suit of the Parliament, and a law thereupon made, it
frees the King, and leaves him to give recompense only
where he shall be pleased to extend grace. Wherefore
we conceive the most convenient way will be, if some
grave and discreet gentlemen of the country, such as
have at least relation to the court, make at fit times some
modest motions touching the same : That his Majesty
would be graciously pleased to permit some laws to pass
(for the time past only), nowhere touching his Majesty's
legal power to free his subjects from the same, and so his
Majesty, after due consultation, to give way unto them.
For the third, we do humbly advise that such of them as
his Majesty shall give way to have called in may be
questioned before the council-table, either as granted
contrary to his Majesty's Book of Bounty, or found since
to have been abused in the execution, or otherwise by

experience discovered to be burdensome to the country.

. But herein we shall add this further humble advice, that it be not done as matter of preparation to a Parliament, but that occasion be taken, partly upon revising of the Book of Bounty, and partly upon the fresh example in Sir Henry Yelverton's case of abuse and surreption in obtaining of patents, and likewise that it be but as a continuance in conformity of the council's former diligence and vigilance, which hath already stayed and revoked divers patents of like nature, whereof we are ready to show the examples. Thus, we conceive, his Majesty shall keep his greatness, and somewhat shall be done in Parliament and somewhat out of Parliament, as the nature of the subject and business requires. We have sent his Majesty herewith a schedule of the particulars of these three kinds, wherein for the first two we have set down all that we could at this time discover. But in the latter we have chosen out but some that are most in speech, and which do most tend either to the vexation of the common people, or the discontenting of the gentlemen and justices, the one being the original, the other the representative of the Commons. There be many more of like nature, but not of like weight, nor so much rumored, which to take away now in a blaze will give more scandal that such things were granted than cause thanks that they be now revoked. The council may be still doing. And because all things may appear to his Majesty in the true light, we have set down as well the suitors as the grants, and not only those in whose names the patent came to our knowledge.

14 *   U

XIII 5.
—
1621.
Jan.

For proclamations and commissions, they are tender things, and we are willing to meddle with them sparingly; for, as for such as do but wait upon patents (wherein his Majesty, as we conceived, gave some approbation to have them taken away), it is better they fell away by taking away the patent itself than otherwise, for a proclamation cannot be revoked but by a proclamation, which we would avoid. For the Commonwealth Bills which his Majesty approved to be put in readiness, and some other things, there will be time enough hereafter to give his Majesty account, and, amongst them, of the extent of his Majesty's pardon, which, if his subjects do their part, as we hope they will, we do wish may be more liberal than of later times, pardons being the ancient remuneration in Parliament. Thus, hoping his Majesty, out of his gracious and accustomed benignity, will accept of our faithful endeavors and supply the rest by his own princely wisdom and direction ; and also humbly praying his Majesty, that, when he hath himself considered of our humble propositions, he will give us leave to impart them all, or as much as he shall think fit, to the lords of his council, for the better strength of his service, we conclude with our prayers for his Majesty's happy preservation, and always rest

Your Lordship's, to be commanded,

FR. VERULAM, Canc.
H. MONTAGU,
HENRY HEATH,
EDW. COKE,
RAN. CREWE.

6. The King adopts, or appears to adopt, this scheme, XIII. 6.
and writs go out for the elections. To Bacon's grief,
the nation, mad with news from Prague and the Palatinate, sends up to Westminster four hundred of the
most violent men who have ever met in the Great Council; yet, with straight, swift meaning to do right, to
purge abuses in church and state, to launch the army
and the fleet against an insolent enemy, even a parliament of fanatics may be turned to good. James, unhappily, loses heart. Fitful and feverish in his moods, he
gets alarmed by the returns, puts off the opening, stoops
to Gondomar's tales potters once more about a match in
Spain for young Prince Charles. Gondomar regains his
power. While Spinola cleanses Cleves and the Palatinate
with fire, and the Dutch burghers, smitten into warlike
rage, rush to the help of violated cities, James suspends
Sir Robert Naunton, Secretary of State, writer of the
admirable Fragmenta Regalia, from his public functions,
for merely giving some hope of English aid to the Protestants of the Rhine!

7. When allowed to meet, the knights and squires Jan. 30.
come together in a turbulent, almost in a savage mood.
They listen with bent brows while the poor King maun-

6. Bacon to Buckingham, Dec. 16, 1620; Chamberlain to Carleton, Jan. 20,
1621, S. P. O.; Lake to Carleton, Jan. 20, 1621, S. P. O.; Bacon's Declaration,
Jan. 16, 1621, S. P. O.

7. James's Speech on opening Parl., Jan. 30, 1621, S. P. O.; Note of Sir
George More's Report, Feb. 6, 1621, S. P. O.; List of Sub-Committee on Papists, Feb. 5, 1621, S. P. O.; Chamberlain, Feb. 17, 1621, S. P. O.; Com. Jour.,
i. 508, 512, 515, 525.

XIII. 7.

1621.

Jan. 30.

ders about his love for the Church and his hopes of obtaining a Spanish wife for his son, about his dislike for the doings of the Bohemian Protestants and his willingness to spill his own blood in defence of those of the Rhine, and when he goes away to his palace they proceed, in stern, bright haste, to purge their benches from any suspicion of Popish taint. A committee searches the vaults. The whole House takes the sacrament in public. A second time, and with added solemnity and publicity, the members swear the oaths of supremacy. Hollis and Britton, Roman Catholics of good family, are excluded from Parliament. Shepherd is expelled for a jest against the Puritans. A sub-committee revises and edges the penal laws.

Feb.

Burgess and knight are now in fearful earnest. No more weakness, no more tolerance! Max and Spinola are at our gates.

8. Coke, returned for Liskeard in Cornwall, offers himself as the champion of every fanatical cry, of every mad antipathy of the hour. He yells for the blood of Papists, for the hoards of monopolists, for the license of free speech. His age, his rank, his experience of the world, his powers of debate, impose on many of the untried members, now serving their maiden session in the House of Commons. Some take him for a guide; still more accept his aid.

8. Com. Jour., i. 510, 514, 519, 523; Chamberlain to Carleton, Feb. 10, 17, 1621, S P. O.; Locke to Carleton, Feb. 16, 1621, S. P. O.; Statutes, iv. 1208.

The money bills pass at once. The Chancellor has XIII. 8. not reckoned on the patriotism of the land in vain. Indeed, in their haste to man the fleets, to put a moving fort between the coast of Essex and the camps of Calais and Ostend, the burgesses vote the King two subsidies without a dissenting voice.

1621.
Feb.

9. James takes this money, not without joy and wonder; but when they ask him to banish recusants from London, to put down masses in ambassadors' houses, to disarm all the Papists, to prevent priests and Jesuits from going abroad, he will not do it. In this resistance to a new persecution, his tolerant Chancellor stands at his back, and bears the odium of his refusal. Bacon, who thinks the penal laws too harsh already, will not consent to inflame the country, at such a time, by a new proclamation; the penalties are strong, and in the hands of the magistrates; he sees no need to spur their zeal by royal proclamations or the enactment of more savage laws. Here is a chance for Coke. Raving for gibbets and pillories in a style to quicken the pulse of a Brownist, men who are wild with news from Heidelberg or Prague believe in his sincerity and partake his heat. To be mild now, many good men think, is to be weak. In a state of war philosophy and tolerance go to the wall; when guns are pounding in the gates, even justice can be only done at the drum-head.

9. Com. Jour., 518, 523; Speech of a Privy Councillor in the House of Commons, Feb. 16, 1621, S. P. O.; Locke to·Carleton, Feb. 16, 1621, S. P. O.; Murray to Carleton, Feb. 17, 1621, S. P. O.

10. Feeding these fiery humors, Coke gets the ear
of an active section of the House, who push him on,
their orator of hate, as in happier times they have made
his great compeer their advocate of charity and peace.
Coke pours on them his gall. No one in the House
yet dreams of attacking persons under cover of a wish
to expose abuses. Even in the case of Mompesson,
whose manufacture of gold and silver thread is supposed
by country gentlemen to have raised the price of beer,
they declare in their first petition to the King that they
want measures of redress, not injury to particular men.
But a moderation that might end in real good to the
country is foreign to the nature and designs of Coke.

11. Sure of the ears of a sect, Coke suggests, as a
branch of the Grievances, that inquiry should be made
into abuses in the courts of law, with a view to limit
the duration and cost of suits, more especially in the
Chancery and the Court of Wards. Doubts arise on
this as to whether Parliament has any power over the
King's courts; when Bacon, though he fears and dis-
trusts Coke, and complains to the King of his insolence,
meets the inquiry with open heart. The Commons are
helping to do his work. Reform of the law, and of the

10. Request concerning Sir Giles Mompesson, Feb. 27, 1621, S. P. O.; Locke
to Carleton, Feb. 24, 1621, S. P. O.

11. Chamberlain to Carleton, May 10, 1617, S. P. O.; Ordinances made by
the Rt Hon. Sir Francis Bacon for the better Administration of Justice in the
Court of Chancery, 1642; Locke to Carleton, Feb. 24, 1621, S. P. O.; Com.
Jour., i. 519, 525.

courts of law, has been his theme for thirty years. XIII. 11.
When he got the Seals, his very first speech in Chancery
proposed a scheme for removing abuses in fees and suits.
His rules for conducting business were in themselves
the best of reform bills. More than all, he has introduced into that slow and despotic court the substantial
amendments of patience, courtesy, and speed. Not a
cause is on the lists unheard. Vices remain ; vices of
form, of persons, of constitution ; vices too strong for
a single man, however prompt and powerful, to subdue.
If the House of Commons have any search to make into
his court he offers them full leave ; if they have anything
to say on it he bids them freely speak their mind. Without this leave they could not move one step.

Blind to the plot against him, the Chancellor knows no
cause why he should fear their search.

12. While Coke, under cover of the public good, is
slowly sliming round his prey, the Chancellor, called by
his place to decide between the quarrels of two peers,
has the honorable misfortune to offend in a peculiar
manner the pride of Lady Buckingham and her obedient
clan.

This scheming mother has fixed her eyes on Elizabeth Norreys, daughter of Francis Baron Norreys of
Rycote, as a wife for her son Kit. Elizabeth is rich, for
her mother was an heiress, and she is an only child. To

12. Lords' Jour., iii. 19, 20; Locke to Carleton, Feb. 16, 24, 1621, S. P. O.;
Chamberlain to Carleton, Mar. 30, 1621, S. P. O.

Margin note: XIII. 11. — 1621. Feb.

XIII. 12. soften Lord Norreys, he has been created Viscount
Thane and Earl of Berkshire. But these Villiers peers,
1621.
Feb. these Purbecks and Berkshires, gall the more ancient
nobles. Berkshire either pushes or strikes Lord Scrope,
a haughty peer, whose ancestors have been in the House
of Lords since the days of Edward the First. The
eleventh Baron of his line complains of this rude and
upstart earl. Berkshire being in the wrong, Bacon despite
his known connection with the Villiers people, has the
courage to send him to the Fleet prison till he repents
his sally and apologizes to Lord Scrope.

In a few days Berkshire, on submission to Scrope,
regains his freedom, and returns to his seat; making for
the upright Chancellor one vindictive enemy the more.

Mar. 2. 13. Free from the personal malevolence and from the
virtuous starts which harass Coke, bent on pleasing his
great patroness and on winning a rich reward, Cranfield
goes straight and swift to the point; attacking Bacon,
Montagu, and Yelverton by name, and proclaiming that
he does so from a sense of duty to the King. Some one
speaks of abuses in the Courts of Wards. Cranfield
springs to his feet, and with brazen brow admits the
existence of abuses in his court, but impudently declares
that the corruptions of the Court of Chancery far exceed
the corruptions in the Court of Wards.

14. Time has now come for the Villiers faction to show

13. Com. Jour., i. 525, 535; Locke to Carleton, Mar. 3, 1621, S. P. O.

their game. While Cranfield and Churchill have been
hunting the dens of London for accusations against the
Chancellor, Buckingham has been frequent in his calls
at York House. Bacon is sick and nigh to death. Pains
rack his head, and gout torments his feet. Yet up to the
11th of March he continues to meet the Council, sitting
face to face with Coke and Cranfield, who watch his
looks and weigh his words with all the vigilance of
spite. At length the treachery of Buckingham grows
too plain for even Bacon's eyes to blink. If the House
of Commons is slow to strike, it must be whipped into
the mood for framing accusations and demanding victims. So Coke brings down a message to the Commons,
the most extraordinary and the most criminal ever sent
down by a subservient House of Peers. Coke tells the
burgesses that the King is pleased with what they have
done and what they are doing; that the King advises
them to strike while the iron is hot, not to rest content
with shadows, but to demand real sacrifices. He tells
them, too, that Buckingham has fallen in love with Parliaments; that he urges them to go on, and gives up
his brother, a partner with Mompesson, to their wrath.
No one mistakes the drift and scope of these words.
Up to the date of this extraordinary and wicked speech,
no one has breathed a word against Bacon's fame.
Chancery, not the Chancellor, has been in fault. Now
the plot breaks.

XIII. 14.
—
1621.
Mar. 2.

Mar. 13.

14. Council Reg., Mar. 11, 1621; Com. Jour., i. 552, 555; Lords' Jour., iii.
42, 50.

XIII. 14.

1621.
Mar. 18.

Two days after Coke's message, Sir Robert Phillips, chairman of the committee, informs the House that two witnesses, Kit Aubrey and Edward Egerton, are ready to make complaints against the Lord Chancellor. These men come up to the bar and tell their tale.

Aubrey having a suit in Chancery against Sir William Brouuker, says he was advised by his counsel to send a present of a hundred pounds to the court; which money he paid to Sir George Hastings, who thanked him for it in his master's name, and wished him better speed in his suit. Egerton, feeling grateful to the Lord Chancellor for a service done to him while Bacon was Attorney-General, sent him, on his going to live at York House, through the hands of Sir George Hastings and Sir Richard Young, a basin and ewer, together with a purse of four hundred pounds.

Each complains that, though he paid his money, he took nothing by his gift.

15. Such charges against the Lord Chancellor are in the last degree frivolous. Fees and gifts like Aubrey's and Egerton's are common as sun and rain. A barrister or a judge, set apart from the world, with no salary from the State, receives, as a rector or a prelate might receive in his day of furnishing or feasting, aid from the public and from his friends. Indeed, the

15. Goodman's Memoirs, i. 295–6; A Selection of the Proceedings of the House of Commons against the Lord Verulam, Lord Chancellor of England, Mar. 15, 17, 19, 1621; Com. Jour., i. 552–563.

higher clergy growl that the great lawyers get a larger XIII. 15.
share of this help in need than the zealous servants of —
God. Bishop Goodman has a curious paragraph in 1621.
point : — March.

"I did once intend," he says, "to have built a church;
and a lawyer in my neighborhood did intend to build
himself a fair house, as afterward he did. One sent
unto him to desire him to accept from him all his timber; another sent unto him to desire him that he might
supply him with all the iron that he spent about his
house. These men had great woods and iron-mills of
their own. The country desired him to accept of their
carriage. What reason had this man not to build?
Truly I think he paid very little but the workmen's
wages. Whereas, on the contrary, in the building of
my church, where it was so necesssary, for without the
church they had not God's service, and no church was
near them for nearly four or five miles, truly I could
not get the contribution of one farthing. Lord! how
are the times altered! It was not so when St. Paul's
Church in London and other cathedrals were built.
God's will be done!"

When Bacon got the Seals his friends and admirers
clothed York House for him with plate, arras, furniture,
and pictures; some sending books, some money, some
cups of silver and gold. In the crowd of presents came
Egerton's ewer and purse; came as an expression of
gratitude and friendship. No reference was made when
they were given to any future act; nor had the Chan-

cellor any knowledge of Egerton's having a suit in court. These facts are stated in the House by Sir Richard Young.

In Aubrey's case it is clear that the fee was paid in the usual way; openly paid; paid by advice of his own counsel; paid to the proper officer of the court. It is no less clear that the Lord Chancellor could have no special personal knowledge of this payment. He does not keep the accounts of his court. Hastings tells the House of Commons that though he paid in Aubrey's money he never mentioned to the Chancellor Aubrey's name. The truth of this story is confirmed in a singular way. When Bacon, on his sick couch, first hears of this payment, by Aubrey of a hundred pounds, he pronounces it a lie, and declares that he shall deny it on his honor before the world. He is not aware that it was paid to his clerk.

16. Such charges are too flimsy to stand alone. Except the tools of Coke, of Cranfield, and of Buckingham, men who have received their cue, and the herd who, without opinions of their own, are ever to be found on the stronger side, no one in the House of Commons pretends to believe that such facts establish a case against the Lord Chancellor, fit to be sent before the House of Lords. Heneage Finch, Recorder of London, next to Coke himself the most learned jurist in the house, declares that the evidence brought in support of the accusation frees the Lord Chancellor from blame.

16. A Collection of the Proceedings, &c., Mar. 17, 1621.

17. Churchill now comes up. Meautys protests that a
dismissed servant, an extortioner, a forger, with no hope
of escaping pillories and jails except by lies against the
Chancellor, shall not be heard against his lord. But
Coke and Phillips get him sent, together with a wretch
named Keeling, a low solicitor, a partner in Churchill's
villanies, to the committee, which comprises the Chancellor's most eager foes. In secret, and without cross-exam-
ination, Churchill and Keeling tell their tales, and the
hostile members of the committee frame their grand indictment, charging Bacon with bribery and fraud.

The cases on which they count are in number twenty-
two. It is amazing they should be no more. In his four
years of Chancery business, Bacon has pronounced about
seven thousand verdicts ; each verdict must have hurt
some man in fame or purse ; must, by a law of nature,
have seemed to the losing man unjust. Does any one
love the judge who has pronounced against him ? Would
the most upright judge feel easy on having to put his
honor or estate at the mercy of a jury, each of whom
had been mulcted in his court ? Yet out of these seven
thousand sufferers, the skill of Coke, and the roguery of
Churchill can only frame an accusation of twenty-two
particulars, not one of them to the point !

18. At first the Chancellor only smiles. Charges

17. A Collection of the Proceedings, &c., Mar. 20, 21, 1621; Com. Jour., i.
564.
18. Council Reg., Dec. 30, 1617, Mar. 17, 27, 1618, June 19, 1619, Jun. 20,
1620; Bacon to Buckingham, in Montagu, 33.

XIII. 18. against the court over which he sits he expects to hear,
1621. and will be glad to consider; charges against himself
Iar. 20. personally he knows must be malignant, and he supposes must be vain. The Council guards the high place
he fills with as much care as it guards the Crown.
The fate of Lord Clifford and Lady Blount is before
the slanderer's eye; and a word from the King or
from Buckingham would send Churchill to be whipped
through Cheap and fettered in the Clink. When he
finds the case go on, he expresses to Buckingham his
indignation at the course of Coke: "Job himself, or
whoever was the justest judge," he writes, " by such
hunting of matters against him as hath been used
against me, may for a time seem foul. If this is to
be a Chancellor, I think if the Great Seal lay upon
Hounslow Heath, nobody would take it up." But he
is not alarmed. " I know I have clean hands and a
clean heart."

19. As the case proceeds, — as Ley, and Coke, and
Cranfield, all the tools of Lady Buckingham, take part
in it, — he begins at length to perceive the bearing of
the charge and the purpose of his enemies. The facts
of the accusation are nothing, the fact of it is much.
As he lies sick at York House, or at Gorhambury, hearing through his friend Meautys of the moil and worry
about him in the House of Commons, he jots on loose
scraps of paper at his side his answers and remarks.

19. Bacon Memoranda, Lambeth MSS. 936, fol. 146.

These scraps of paper are at Lambeth Palace. Their XIII. 19.
contents are embodied in letters to Buckingham, to the
House of Lords, and to the King: yet they possess an
1621.
March.
original and abiding interest in their first rude drafts;
a stamp of honesty and sincerity which the eye cannot
help but see or the heart but feel. On one of these
sheets he writes : —

" There be three degrees or cases, as I conceive, of
gifts or rewards given to a judge.

" The first is, — of bargain, contract, or promise of
reward, pendente lite. And this is properly called ve-
nalis sententiæ, or baratrîa, or corruptelæ munerum.
And of this my heart tells me I am innocent; that I
had no bribe or reward in my eye or thought when I
pronounced any sentence or order.

" The second is, — a neglect in the judge to inform
himself whether the cause be fully at an end or no
what time he receives the gift, but takes it upon the
credit of the party that all is done, or otherwise omits
to inquire.

" And the third is, — when it is received, sine fraude,
after the cause is ended ; which, it seems, by the opinions of the civilians, is no offence."

Only the first of these three cases, a contract to defeat justice for a personal gain, implies moral guilt or
invites legal censure.

Bacon adds : —

" For the first, I take myself to be as innocent as
any babe born on St. Innocent's day in my heart.

XIII. 19.   "For the second, I doubt in some particulars I may
be faulty.

1621.
March.   "And for the last, I conceive it to be no fault."

20. The evidence produced against him, as Heneage
Finch has told the House of Commons, proves his case
and frees him from blame. Of the twenty-two charges
of corruption, three are debts, — Compton's, Peacock's,
and Vanlore's : two of these, Compton's and Vanlore's,
debts on bond and interest. Any man who borrows
money may be as justly charged with taking bribes.
One case, that of the London Companies, is an arbitra-
tion, not a suit in law. Even Cranfield, though bred in
the city, cannot call their fee a bribe. Smithwick's gift,
being found irregular, has been sent back. Thirteen
cases — those of Young, Wroth, Hody, Barker, Monk,
Trevor, Scott, Fisher, Lenthal, Dunch, Montagu, Rus-
well, and the Frenchmen — are of daily practice in every
court of law. They fall under Bacon's third list, common fees, paid in the usual way, paid after judgment
has been given. Kennedy's present of a cabinet for
York House has never been accepted, the Chancellor
hearing that the artisan who made it has not been paid.
Reynell, an old neighbor and friend, gave him two hundred pounds towards furnishing York House, and sent
him a ring on New Year's day. Everybody gives rings,
everybody takes rings, on a New Year's day. The gift

20. A Collection of the Proceedings, &c., Mar. 20, 21, 1621; Com. Jour.,
l. 563, 578.

of five hundred pounds from Sir Ralph Hornsby was

made after a judgment, though, as afterwards appeared, while a second, much inferior cause, was still in hearing. The gift was openly made, not to the Chancellor, but to the officer of his court. The last case is that of Lady Wharton ; the only one that presents an unusual feature. Lady Wharton, it seems, brought her presents to the Chancellor herself ; yet even her gifts were openly made, in the presence of the proper officer and his clerk. Churchill admits being present in the room when Lady Wharton left her purse ; Gardner, Keeling's clerk, asserts that he was present when she brought the two hundred pounds. Even Coke is staggered by proofs which prove so much ; for who in his senses can suppose that the Lord Chancellor would have done an act known to be illegal and immoral in the company of a registrar and a clerk ?

It is clear that a thing which Bacon did under the eyes of Gardner and Churchill must have been in his mind customary and right.

It is no less clear that if Bacon had done wrong, knowing it to be wrong, he would never have braved exposure of his fraud by turning Churchill into the streets.

Thus after the most rigorous and vindictive scrutiny into his official acts, and into the official acts of his servants, not a single fee or remembrance traced to the Chancellor can, by any fair construction, be called a bribe. Not one appears to have been given on a promise ;

not one appears to have been given in secret; not one is alleged to have corrupted justice.

21. Very few knights or burgesses take part in the debate : on one side Cranfield, Coke, and Phillips; on the other side Sackville, Meautys, and Heneage Finch, make nearly all the list. This charge against Bacon is regarded by citizens and country gentlemen as a mere theme for lawyers, — a charge of technical corruption more than of moral guilt. They may very well stand aloof when Coke and Finch, the two most eminent lawyers in the House, express on it the most diverse views. Coke construes every fee into a bribe; Finch denies that any fee can be called a bribe unless it can be shown to have been taken as part of a contract to pervert justice. Finch does not admit of Bacon's three distinctions, — he only knows of fees and bribes. A fee paid at an improper time is not a bribe ; for how, he asks, can a judge retain in his recollection the name of every suitor in his court ? The House consents to let the case go up to the Lords, though as an inquiry, not as an impeachment. If they wish the system of Fees amended, as they wish that of Patents, of Protections, of Pardons, of Personal Service, or of Wards and Liveries amended, they do not load the Chancellor with a personal charge. Otherwise Coke. They want to cleanse the court ; he to destroy the judge. They see a grievance in the Chancery, as they see one in the Rolls, the Wards,

21. Com. Jour., i. 564-67; Proceedings, &c., Mar. 20, 21, 1621.

and the King's Bench; he finds the most noxious grievance in the Lord Viscount St. Albans, holder of the
Great Seal.

22. To drag the House of Lords on the way down
which they have thus far lured the House of Commons,
the gang of conspirators procure from James a commission for Sir James Ley to execute the office of Lord
Chancellor. Though not a peer, such a commission
will make Ley the leader and spokesman of the peers.
Seeing what means are used against him, Bacon is
warned by a friend to look about him. He calmly answers, " I look above."

23. He knows now that his ruin is meant, — that the
peers who are to try him will pronounce as Buckingham points. Two or three learned, independent men
may protest by their votes or absence against these
scandalous proceedings; the majority, who wish to
dance at Whitehall, — to enjoy the favorite's smiles
and partake the gifts of his master, — will have to
speak and act under the eyes of Prince Charles, who
is not so much Buckingham's partisan as his slave. It
is with Ley and Williams not a question of Bacon's
guilt so much as of his place. But his own courtesy
and generosity blind him to the vile motives of his
persecutors. In the loose sheets at his bedside, and
afterwards in letters to the King, he writes: —

22. Lords' Jour., iii. 51.
23. Bacon to James, Mar. 25, 1621; Montagu, 999.

XIII. 23.

—

1621.
March

"When I enter into myself, I find not the materials of such a tempest as is now come upon me. I have been never author of any immoderate counsel, but always desired to have things carried suavibus modis. I have been no avaricious oppressor of the people. I have been no haughty, intolerable, or hateful man in my conversation or carriage. I have inherited no hatred from my father; but am a good patriot born. Whence should this be ?"

That eye, so quick to see the power of truth, the beauty of nature, cannot see that it is crime enough that he has vexed Lady Buckingham by his independence, and that Williams wants his place.

Yet, knowing his own heart, he can say with honest pride : —

" I praise God for it, I never took penny for any benefice or ecclesiastical living.

" I never took penny for releasing anything I stopped at the Seal.

" I never took penny for any commission, or things of that nature.

"I never shared with any reward for any second or inferior profit."

Mar 19.

24. Ley presides over the peers. On the House resolving themselves into committee, a preliminary fight takes place, which shows the strength of this Villiers gang. When the House is in committee, it is the rule

24. Lords' Jour., iii. 55; Lambeth MSS. 936, fol. 146.

that the Lord Chancellor shall move to his place, and sit XIII. 24.
as a simple peer. Ley, therefore, drops from the woolsack to the back benches, where he must sit, while the
Lords are in committee, as a mere assistant, without a
vote. His friends propose that he shall resume the chair,
even while the House is in committee; and after a strong
opposition, though the Prince and Buckingham are present to support their friends, these last carry their proposal, and Ley resumes the chair. This vote decides
Bacon's fate.

In a private interview James now urges the Chancellor
to trust in him; to offer no defence; to submit himself to
the peers; to trust his honor and his safety to the Crown.
It is only too easy to divine the reasons which weigh with
Bacon to intrust his fortunes to the King. He is sick.
He is surrounded by enemies. No man has power to help
him, save the sovereign. He is weary of greatness. Age
is approaching. In his illness he has learned to think
more of heaven and less of the world. His nobler tasks
are incomplete. He has the Seals, and the delights of
power begin to pall. To resist the King's advice is to
provoke the fate of Yelverton, still an obstinate prisoner
in the Tower. Nor can he say that these complaints
against the courts of law, against the Court of Chancery,
are untimely or unjust. So far as they attack the court,
and not the judge, they are in the spirit of all his writings
and of all his votes. In his soul, he can find no fault
with the House of Commons, though the accidents of
time and the machinations of powerful enemies have

XIII. 24. made him, the Reformer, a sacrifice to a false cry for
——   reform.
1621.

April. 28.   25. In answer to a statement sent to him from the
Lords, he confesses, as the King has begged him to confess, to the receipt of the several fees and gifts, and to a
trust in the servants of his court, often most unwise.
Most of the cases fall under his third division ; two or
three under his second ; none under his first. Beyond
this point his confession and submission do not run. If
he takes to himself some share of blame, he takes to himself no share of guilt. He pleads guilty to carelessness,
not to crime. But he points out, too, that all the irregularities found in his court occurred when he was new in
office, strange to his clerks and registrars, overwhelmed
with arrears of work. The very last of them is two years
old. For the latter half of his reign as Chancellor, the
vindictive inquisition of his enemies, aided by the treachery of his servants, has not been able to detect in his
administration of justice a fault, much less a crime.

May 3.   26. The peers condemn. The Villiers faction move
to suspend during life his titles of nobility. Abbott
and the bench of bishops oppose this motion. Fine,
imprisonment, loss of office, are the forms of a political
sentence ; degradation from nobility is a moral censure.
One is only loss of power, the other is loss of honor. A

25. Lords' Jour., iii. 99, 100.
26. Chamberlain to Carleton, May 2, 5, 1621, S. P. O.; Lords' Jour., iii. 105.

majority of two defeats this scheme of adding infamy to XIII. 26.
punishment. The second motion passes. Ley has the
satisfaction of declaring to his partisans in the House of
Peers that the greatest man who ever sat upon its benches
is ignominiously expelled, deprived of the Seals, fined
forty thousand pounds, and cast into the Tower.

XIII. 26.

1621.
May 3.

CHAPTER XIV.

XIV. 1.
——
1621.
May.

1. BACON makes no complaint. He feels that he is made a sacrifice, an innocent sacrifice, for what he hopes may turn out to be the public good. The court is corrupt, though the judge is pure. In a few brave words he states the case: " I was the justest judge that was in England these fifty years, but it was the justest censure that was in Parliament these two hundred years."

2. With the sentence on Lord St. Albans ends the ministerial passion for reform. No further search is made into Chancery iniquities, nor does the House remember to proceed with its inquiry into the evil practices of the King's Bench and the Court of Wards. The Crown makes a feeble effort of investigation, but only, like the House of Commons, to let the question drop. If the new Chancellor names a commission to report on Fees, nothing comes of their report. All that is irregular in the mode of conducting legal business grows

1. Apophthegms, Spedding's Works of Bacon, vii. 179.
2. Statutes of the Realm, iv. 1208; Welden, 130; King's Proclamation, July 10, 1621; Proposals concerning the Chancery, 1650.

to be more irregular. Instead of being a court without XIV. 2.
arrears, it is soon blocked up with clients. The new men —
invent new methods of extortion. 1621.
May.

With the fall of the Reformer ends the immediate prospect of reform. The very topic is adjourned to the times
of Naseby and Dunbar.

3. All the agents of this memorable persecution get July.
their share of spoil, except the man to whose invention
and persistence its success is due. Coke is in disgrace ;
for the match between his daughter and Sir John Villiers,
though crowned with a peerage, has turned out a dismal
work. Ley, if he misses the Seals, which Lady Buckingham reserves for the one nearer and dearer, obtains a wife,
with the prospect of promotion and a peerage, for which
indeed he has not long to wait. Churchill goes back to
the trust which he so shamefully abused. Williams steps
into the Privy Council and receives the Seals. " I should
have known my successor," says Bacon, on receiving this
extraordinary news. Some of the great peers demur
to the nomination of such a fellow as Williams to the
presidency of their lordships' house; and the King only
quells this clamor of the Howards and De Veres by
threatening them, if they object to Williams, with the
nomination of Richard Neile. To give dignity to Lady
Buckingham's friend, he is named successor to Dr. Moun-

3. Chamberlain to Carleton, June 23, July 14, Oct. 13, Nov. 10, 1621, S. P. O.;
Locke to Carleton, Sept. 29, 1621, S. P. O.; Lords' Jour., iii. 42, 81; Paul to
Buckingham, July 12, 1621, S. P. O.; Sign Manuals, xii. No. 66; Grant Book,
309; Doquet, Sept. 12, 1622.

XIV. 3. tain in the see of Lincoln. Cranfield's merits demand
and receive no less magnificent a prize.

1621.

July.   Some of the Villiers gang proposed to attack Montagu, the Lord Treasurer, while their friends were pushing the charge against Bacon. Coke hinted a fault before the House of Peers, while Sir George Paul, one of Lady Buckingham's crew, whose zeal had been inflamed by the gift of a lucrative office under Ley, petitioned the House of Commons against him. But there was danger in attempting too much ; and a word from Buckingham put a stop to the indiscreet initiative of Paul, his new clerk of the King's Bench. The attack is but deferred. When Bacon is in the Tower, Cranfield, now a baron, opens his siege against the Treasury. Montagu is rich and timid, and Cranfield offers him no choice but that of a cutthroat on Stamford Hill, — Your office or your life ! Where Bacon has gone down Montagu cannot hope to stand. If he will allow himself to be robbed of a post which has cost him twenty thousand pounds, and of places about it which have cost his kinsmen and servants twenty thousand pounds more, the victorious party promise to secure him the undisturbed enjoyment of his peer-

Sept. 29. age, and to cover the shame of his fall by reviving for him the old office of President of the Council. Montagu succumbs. Cranfield gets the White Staff, and, after the birth of a son, the Earldom of Middlesex.

1622.

March.   4. These ends of the conspiracy attained, the prose-

4. Meautys to Bacon, Mar. 3, 1622, Lambeth MSS. 936; Spedding's Note, i. 9; Rushworth's Historical Collections, i. 31.

cution of Bacon, the heat of the Government for reform, XIV. 4.
dies off.   Buckingham has no implacable resentment
against the great Chancellor ; he only wanted the Mace
and Seals.   When he has got these baubles into the
hands of Williams, he continues to express, and probably
to feel, the warmest affection for Bacon's person, the
most unbounded admiration for his parts.   Indeed, he
wishes to be thought the friend of Lord St. Albans, as
Greville was the friend of Sir Philip Sydney.   Meautys,
the faithful henchman, in his notes to his master,
hints at something savoring of an intrigue to procure from him confessions of friendship and obligation to the powerful favorite.   Bacon's situation grows
less painful ; his fine is remitted, his freedom restored.
An attempt to overthrow some of his judgments fails.
Of the thousands of decisions pronounced by him in
the Court of Chancery not one is reversed.

1622.
March.

5. Among his books and his experiments, with his
horse and his game of bowls, he soon in the country air
recovers his health, and with his health his spirits and
his wit.   He enriches the Essays with a thousand ex-
quisite touches.   When the Jew, Gondomar, recalled
to Spain by an order from the King, sends to wish Bacon
a good Easter, the wit replies, "Tell the Count I return
him the compliment and wish him a good Passover."
Montagu comes to Gorhambury to complain how ill he

5. Apophthegms, in Spedding's Bacon, vii. 181; Bacon to James, Mar. 25, 1623;
Lambeth MSS. 936; Bacon to Conway, Mar. 25, 1623, S. P. O.

XIV. 5. has been used by the Villiers faction; "Why, my Lord,"

1622.
March.

says Bacon, "they have made me an example and you a president." Poor in everything but his good spirits and his capacity for work, he toils at his History of Henry the Seventh, at the new edition of his Advancement of Learning, at his Advertisement touching a Holy

1623. War. These writings, and the works which have gone before them, extend his fame throughout Europe. But his debts weigh on him. He is anxious for work, even for work of the humblest kind. In 1623 Thomas Murray, secretary to Prince Charles, and Provost of Eton, falls sick and is like to die. Bacon offers himself as a candidate. Sir William Beecher, clerk of the Privy Council, a creature of Villiers, and Sir Henry Wotton, poet, wit, ambassador, are his opponents. Beecher has a promise from Buckingham of the succession to Murray; Buckingham is away in Spain with the Prince of Wales, fanning his face at bull-fights, leering at Castilian dames. Sir Edward Conway, Secretary of State, is now the immediate influence near the King; and Bacon, who comes back to London, to his old lodgings in Gray's Inn, writes to solicit his good-will: —

BACON TO CONWAY.

Gray's Inn, 25th of March, 1623.

GOOD MR. SECRETARY, —

When you did me the honor and favor to visit me you did not only in general terms express your love unto me, but as a real friend asked me whether I had

any particular occasion wherein I might make use of
you. At that time I had none; now there is one fallen.
It is that Mr. Thomas Murray, Provost of Eton (whom
I love very well), is like to die. It were a pretty cell
for my fortune. The college and school I do not doubt
but I shall make to flourish. His Majesty, when I
waited on him, took notice of my wants, and said to me
that as he was a king he would have care of me. This
is a thing somebody must have, and costs his Majesty
nothing. I have written two or three words to his Majesty, which I would pray you to deliver. I have not
expressed this particular to his Majesty, but referred it
to your relation. My most noble friend the Marquis
is now absent. Next to him I could not think of a
better address than to yourself, as one likest to put on
his affections.

I rest your very affectionate friend,

FRANCIS ST. ALBANS.

Conway supports the suit.

6. James allows of Bacon's great claims. He will
think of it; he even hopes to arrange it; satisfying
Beecher with another place. But Beecher is Buckingham's creature; Buckingham is away; till he comes
back nothing can be done. Conway's answer is in the
State Paper Office; its spirit may be guessed from the
following note of Bacon in reply to it: —

6. Bacon to Conway, Mar. 29, 1623, S. P. O.; Do., Mar. 31, 1623, Lambeth
MSS. 936.

BACON TO CONWAY.

Gray's Inn, 29th of March, 1623.

GOOD MR. SECRETARY, —

I am much comforted by your last letter, wherein I find that his Majesty of his great goodness vouchsafeth to have a care of me, a man out of sight and out of use, but yet his (as the Scripture sayeth, "God knows those that are his"). In particular, I am very much bounden to his Majesty, and I pray (Sir) thank his Majesty most humbly for it, that, notwithstanding the former designment of Sir A. Beecher, his Majesty (as you write) is not out of hope in due time to accommodate me of this cell and to satisfy that gentleman otherwise. Many conditions (no doubt) may be as good for him, and his years may expect them. But there will hardly fall (especially in the spent hour-glass of such a life as mine) anything so fit for me, being a retreat to a place of study so near London, and where (if I sell my house at Gorhambury, as I purpose to do, to put myself into some convenient plenty), I may be accommodate of a dwelling for the summer-time. And, therefore, good Mr. Secretary, further this his Majesty's good intention by all means if the place fall. For yourself you have obliged me much ; I will endeavor to deserve it. At best nobleness is never lost, but rewarded in itself. My Lord Marquis I know will thank you. I was looking over some short papers of mine touching usury, how to grind the teeth of it, and yet to make it grind to his Majesty's mill in good

sort, without discontent or perturbation : if you think XIV. 6.
good I will perfect it, as I send it to his Majesty as some
fruits of my leisure. But yet I would not have it come   1623.
as from me, not from any tenderness in the thing, but
because I know well in the courts of princes it is usual
non res, sed displicet auctor. — God keep you.

I rest your very affectionate friend, much obliged,

FR. ST. ALBANS.

Two days later he writes again. What a mournful, yet
what a manful tone ! He has sold York House, the place
of his birth ; he must now sell Gorhambury, the scene
of his happiest hours and most splendid toils. Yet how
inspiring, in the depths of sorrow, to see the great man
bear his burden bravely: no false pride ; no arrogant
remembrance of the Mace, the Seals, the Privy Council,
the Royal table ; only a simple hope of finding in his old
age a sphere of duty in which he can win bread by honest
work !

7. He writes to the King : —

BACON TO JAMES.   Mar. 29.

IT MAY PLEASE YOUR MOST EXCELLENT MAJESTY, —
Now that my friend is absent (for so I may call him
still, since your Majesty, when I waited on you, told me

7. Bacon to James, Mar. 29, 1623, S. P. O.; Bacon to Conway, April 7, 1623,
S. P. O.

XIV. 7.
—
1623.
Mar. 29.

that fortune made no difference) your Majesty remaineth to me king and master, and friend and all. Your Beadsman, therefore, addresseth himself to your Majesty for a cell to retire unto. The particular I have expressed to my very hon. friend, Mr. Sec. Conway. This help (which costs your Majesty nothing) may reserve me to do your Majesty service, without being chargeable unto you, for I will never deny but my desire to serve your Majesty is of the nature of the heart, that will be *ultimum moriens* with me. God preserve your Majesty, and send you a good return of your treasure abroad, which passeth your Majesty's Indian fleet.

Your most humble and devoted servant,

FRANCIS ST. ALBANS.

Murray grows daily worse. Bacon writes again to Conway : —

April. 7.

BACON TO CONWAY.

Gray's Inn, 7th of April, 1623.

GOOD MR. SECRETARY, —

I received right now an advertisement from a friend of mine who is like to know it, that Mr. Murray is very ill (and that, so are the words of his letter) not only his days but his hours are numbered. You have put my business into a good way, and (to tell you true) my heart is much upon this place, as fit for me, and where I may do good. Therefore, Sir, I pray you have a special eye

to it, and I shall ever acknowledge it to you in the best **XIV. 7.**
fashion that I can.   Resting your very affectionate friend, —

Fr. St. Albans.   1623.

8. Murray dies   Time passes on.   Buckingham still   Sept.
away, the King can form no resolution.   Six months later
the place is still vacant.   Bacon writes again : —

BACON TO CONWAY.

Gray's Inn, this 4th day of September, 1623.

Good Mr. Secretary, —

Let me, now his Majesty is in sight of Eton, make my
most humble claim to his Majesty's gracious promise by
you signified, which, as I understand it, was, that if Mr.
Beecher, who had a promise upon my Lord of Buckingham's score, might otherwise be satisfied (which his
Majesty would endeavor), I should have my desire.   Mistake me not, as if I expected this should be done and
perfected till my noble, true friend comes back.   But I
pray refresh it only in his Majesty's memory.   It were
strange if I should not do as much good to the College as
another, be it square cap or round.

I always rest your affectionate friend and servant,

St. Albans.

Buckingham is adverse to his suit.   In small things,   **1624.**
as in great things, though he professes a boundless ad-

---

8. Bacon to Conway, Sept. 4, 1623, S. P. O.; Sign Man., xvi., No. 42.

W

XIV. 8. miration for Bacon's parts, he chooses to have about
— him men more pliable and more frail.　Sir William
1624. Beecher, a gentleman unfit for such a post as Murray's,
takes a promise of 2,500*l.* in lieu of the succession ; but
Sir Henry Wotton, an honorable man and a good scholar,
though of far less various learning and far less exalted
virtue than Lord St. Albans, gets the Provostship of
Eton.

9. It is the last time he troubles Buckingham or
James.　Henceforth he devotes himself to his experiments and his books; to the collections for the Sylva
Sylvarum ; to his Historia Vitæ et Mortis ; to the construction of his new Atlantis ; to the enlargement of
his Essays.　He is a greater man now in his study than
when the Mace was borne before him, and the Lord
Treasurer and Secretary of State rode on his right hand
and on his left.　He lives in seclusion ; but his writ
ings fill the whole world with his fame.

10. From the seclusion of Gorhambury or Gray's Inn
he watches the men who have ruined his fortune and
stained his name fall one by one.　Before their year of
triumph ran out, Coke's intolerable arrogance plunged
him into the Tower, from which he escaped, after eight
months' imprisonment, to be permanently degraded from

10. Council Reg., Dec. 27, 1621, Aug. 6, 1622; Chamberlain to Carleton, Aug.
18, Dec. 1, 1621, June 8, 1622, S. P. O.; James's Reply to the Commons, Dec.
11, 1621, S. P. O.; Locke to Carleton, Jan. 1, 1622, S. P. O.; Buckingham to
Crew, Feb. 11, 1625, S. P. O.

the Privy Council, banished from the court, and confined to his dismal ruin of a house at Stoke. The sale
of Frances Coke to Viscount Purbeck is a dismal failure. She makes the man to whom she was sold perfectly miserable; quitting his house for days and nights;
braving the public streets in male attire; falling in guilty
love with Sir Robert Howard; shocking even the brazen
sinners of St. James's by the excessive profligacy of her
life. Purbeck steals abroad to hide his shame. At last
he goes raving mad. In less than three years from the
day of that gorgeous feast as court, Buckingham would
have given his marquisate to untie the knot. All that
Bacon foresaw has come to pass. Sir Robert Howard,
a son of that Earl of Suffolk whom Buckingham broke
and disgraced, pursues his pleasure and his revenge in
the amour with Lady Purbeck, willing to vindicate by
his sword the injury done by his lawless love. Buckingham, who lacks courage either to defend his family
honor or to renew the scandalous scene of the Essex
divorce, in place of crossing blades with Howard in Marylebone Park proceeds against his sister-in-law for in-
continence, and procures from the Ecclesiastical Court
a sentence condemning her to stand in a penitential
white sheet at the door of the Savoy church. It is
easier to condemn than to catch the nimble profligate,
an accomplished player at hide and seek. Once the
pursuivants catch a glimpse of her near an ambassador's
house; they chase; she slips from her coach, runs
through the gates, changes clothes with a page, who

XIV. 10. minces like a lady into her seat, and tears down the
—　　Strand with Buckingham's men at the wheels.　She
1624.　trips laughingly away, while the officers of justice follow the coach and seize the boy.

May.　　11. The very next Parliament which meets in Westminster strikes down two of his foes.　Three years after
his return to that trust he so grossly abused, Churchill
comes before the House of Commons as a culprit.　He
has been at his tricks again, and is now solemnly convicted of forgery and fraud.　Two months after Churchill's condemnation Cranfield is in turn assailed.　Charges
of taking bribes from the farmers of customs, of fraudulent dealing with the royal debts, of robbing the magazine
of arms, are proved against him ; when, abandoned by
his powerful friends, he is sentenced by the House of
Commons to public infamy, to loss of office, to imprisonment in the Tower, to a restitutionary fine of two hundred thousand pounds !　"In future ages," says a wise
observer of events, "men will wonder how my Lord St.
Albans could have fallen, how my Lord of Middlesex
could have risen."

1625.　　12. The most subtle of his enemies falls the last.
Nov. 1.　After his promotion to the Seals and mitre, Williams,

11. Com. Jour., i. 591, 766; Nicholas to Nicholas, Mar. 17, 1624, S. P. O.;
Chichester to Carleton, May 12, 1624, S. P. O.; Locke to Carleton, May 13,
1624, S. P. O.
12. Suckling to Buckingham, Oct. 24, 1625, S. P. O.; Williams to Goring,
Oct. 30, 1625, S. P. O.

silly enough to dream that he could stand alone, began XIV. 12.
to neglect Lady Buckingham for younger and less exact-
ing women. Murmurs now rise against him; slowly at 1625.
Nov. 1.
first, but gathering strength as his ingratitude, his arrogance, and his cupidity prove themselves month by
month. When Lady Buckingham withdraws from him
her countenance, he falls at once from his fatal height —
is stripped of the Seals with every mark of ignominy —
and is driven, with a sullied reputation, though with
sharpened powers for mischief, from the Court of Chancery into the more settled scenes of ecclesiastical strife.

13. Were there space in his generous heart for ven-
geance, how the passions of the great Chancellor would
glow and leap as these adversaries fall before his eyes
like rotten fruit! Never was the wisdom of counsel
proved more signally, the vindication of conduct more
complete. All that he foresaw of evil has come to pass.
He does not, indeed, live to behold that fiery joy which
lights and shakes the land when Buckingham's tyranny
drops under an assassin's knife; but he lives long enough
to find himself justified by facts on every point of his
opposition to the scandalous family policy and private
bargains of the Villiers clan. Frances Coke has made
Sir John a perfectly bad wife. Elizabeth Norreys has
run away from Sir Christopher, giving up her beauty
and her fortunes to Edward Wray. Lady Buckingham

---

13. Chamberlain to Carleton, Mar. 30, 1622, S. P. O.; Bacon's Will; Montagu, xvi. part ii. 447; Dom. Papers of Charles the First, xxiv. 59.

XIV. 13.
———
1625.
Nov. 1.

herself, after moving earth and hell to pull down Abbott and make her lover an archbishop, has had to endure the pain and mortification of seeing the creature of her fantasy neglect her charms. Coke, Cranfield, Churchill, Williams, have been alike overwhelmed with misery and shame. But he feels no quickening pang of joy at the discomfiture of these enemies. From the moment of his own trial, he has accepted the position of a necessary sacrifice. He breathes no word against the House of Commons, nor questions the justice of the House of Lords. He speaks no evil word of the men who made themselves the instruments of his fall. But he holds to his nobler intellectual work, and the Father of Experimental Philosophy dies at last in the very act of an experiment, quitting the world in peace with all men, leaving a young widow, who, like her mother, will marry again, and appealing for the vindication of his fame to time.

APPENDICES.

APPENDICES.

No. I.

LADY ANN BACON TO LORD BURGHLEY.

(Original in Lansdowne MSS., xliii. 48.)

Feb. 26, 1585.

I KNOW well, mine especial good Lord, it becometh me not to be troublesome unto your honor at any other time, but now chiefly in this season of your greatest affair and small or no leisure ; but yet, because yesterday morning, especially as in that I was extraordinarily admitted, it was your Lordship's favor, so, fearing to stay too long, I could not so plainly speak, nor so well receive your answer thereto, as I would truly and gladly in that matter, I am bold by this writing to enlarge the same more plainly, and to what end I did mean.

If it may like your good Lordship, the report of the late conference at Lambeth hath been so handled, to the discrediting of those learned that labor for right reformation in the ministry of the Gospel, that it is no small grief of mind to the faithful preachers ; because the matter is thus by the other side carried away, as though their cause could not sufficiently be warranted by the word of God. For the which proof they have long been

16

sad suitors, and would most humbly crave still both of God in heaven, whose cause it is, and of her Majesty their most excellent Sovereign here in earth, that they might obtain quiet and convenient audience either before her Majesty herself, whose heart is in God's hand to touch and to turn, or before your honors of the Council, whose wisdom they greatly reverence. And if they cannot strongly prove before you out (of) the Word of God that reformation which they so long have called and cried for, to be according to Christ's own ordinance, then to let them be rejected with shame out of the Church forever. And that this may be the better done to the glory of God and true understanding of this great cause, they require, first, leave to assemble and to consult together purposely, which they have forborne to do for avoiding suspicion of private conventicles. For hitherto, though in some writing they have declared the state of their, yea God's cause, yet were they never allowed to confer together, and so together be heard fully. But now some one, and then some two, called upon a sudden unprepared, to four prepared to catch them, rather than gravely and moderately to be heard to defend their right and good cause.

And, therefore, for such weighty conference they appeal to her Majesty and her honorable wise Council, whom God hath placed in highest authority for the advancement of his kingdom, and refuse the bishops for judges, who are parties partial in their own defence, because they seek more worldly ambition than the glory of Christ Jesus.

For my own part, my good Lord, I will not deny but as I may I hear them in their public exercises as a chief duty commanded by God to widows; and also I confess, as one that hath found mercy, that I have profited more in the inward feeling knowledge of God's Holy will (though but in a small measure) by such sincere and sound opening of the Scriptures by an ordinary preaching, within these seven or eight years, than I did by hearing odd sermons at Paul's wellnigh twenty years together. I mention this unfeignedly, the rather to excuse this my boldness towards your Lordship, humbly beseeching your Lordship to think upon their suit, and, as God shall move your understanding heart, to further it. And if opportunity will not be had as they require, yet I once again in humble wise am a suitor unto your Lordship that you would be so good as to choose two or three of them which your honor liketh best, and license them before your own self, or other at your pleasure, to declare and to prove the truth of the cause with a quiet and an attentive ear.

I have heard them say ere now they will not come to dispute and argue to breed contention, which is the manner of the bishops' hearing; but to be suffered patiently to lay down before them that shall command (they then excepted) how well and certainly they can warrant, by the infallible touchstone of the Word, the substantial and main ground of their cause. Surely, my Lord, I am persuaded you should do God acceptable service herein; and for the very entire affection I owe and do bear unto your honor I wish from the very heart that, to your other rare gifts sundrywise, you were fully instructed and satisfied in this principal matter so contemned of the great Rabbis, to the dishonoring of the Gospel so long amongst us.

I am so much bound to your Lordship for your comfortable dealing toward me and mine, as I do incessantly desire that by your Lordship's means God's glory may more and more be promoted, the grieved godly comforted, and you and yours abundantly blessed. None is privy to this ; and, indeed, though I hear them, yet I see them very seldom. I trust your Lordship will accept in best part my best meaning.

In the Lord dutifully and most heartily,
A. BACON.

For thinness of the paper I write on the other leaf for my ill eyes.

No. II.

LADY BACON TO ANTHONY BACON.

(Orig. Lambeth MSS. 648, fol. 110.)

May 29, 1592.

I am glad and thank God of your amendment ; but my man said he heard you rose at three of the clock. I thought that was not well, so suddenly from bedding much, to rise so early newly out of your diet. Extrem-

ities be hurtful to whole, more to the sickly. If you be
not wise and discreet for your diet and seasoning of your
doings, you will be weakish I fear a good while. Be wise
and godly too, and discern what is good and what not for
your health. Avoid extremities. What a great folly were
it in you to take cold to hinder your amendment, being
not compelled, but upon voluntary indiscretion, seeing the
cost of physic is much, your pain long, and your amendment slow, and your duty not yet done! Give none
occasion by negligence. You go, as is commonly said,
of your own errands. I like not your lending your coach
yet to any lord or lady; if you once begin you shall
hardly end; but that in hope you shall shortly use it, I
would it were here, to shun all offending. It was not
well it was so soon seen at the Court, to make talk,
and at last be mocked or misliked. Tell your brother
I counsel you to send it no more. What had my
Lady Shrewsbury to borrow your coach! Your man
for money, and somebody else for their vain credit, will
work you but displeasure and loss, and they have thanks.
Learn to be wise in things of this sort, and do nothing
rashly. In haste. Late this Sabbath. Farewell. Take
care of your health and please God.

A. B.

LADY BACON TO ANTHONY BACON. II. 2.

(Orig. Lambeth MSS. 649, fol. 65.)

April 15, 1593.

My neighbor upon going to London for his own business told me of it suddenly after this Sabbath forenoon

sermon that he must go to London, and that early to-
morrow. I am desirous to know how your health is;
how matters after Parliament go to private folk, namely,
as concerns your cousin Hoby; and, if you will, your
brother too. God grant us all faithful hearts in piety
and religion, and wise and discreet in godly practices.
If any lack wisdom, ask of the Lord, and receive, as
saith the Apostle James, his grace with all Christian
fortitude to bear up a good conscience. I haste to the
church again. God make you able to hear public instructions to your great comfort! I could willingly hear
of Barly proceedings; for your state of want of health
and of money, and some other things touching you
both, gives me no quiet. God bless you both with good
and godly increase in Christ.

Easter, as they say.

Your mother,

A. B.

II. 3.   LADY BACON TO ANTHONY BACON.

(Orig. Lambeth MSS. 649, fol. 100.)

Gorhambury, June 26, 1593.

SON, —

Goodman Grinnell of Barly came this morning hither
very sad upon a speech he had heard you were about
to let his farm to another, yet hopeth better, both for
your promise and the receipt of some money upon it.
Good son, keep your word advisedly spoken; it is a
Christian credit. Be not suddenly removed nor believe

hastily, but know whom and how. Sure, if that dis- App. II. 3.
position be found and observed in you once, it will be
wrought upon to your hindrance in estimation and profit,
besides that the grandfather, father, and son have there
continued, — I think once upon a sale of wood in your
absence I heard that the Grinnells had dwelled there
above a hundred and twenty years. The man is willing to do as much as another ; the same person that
now would I wot not. What reversion in your absence
was backward, and rather hindered wood sales and other
things, he would fain have had Goodman Fynch with him
to you, but I can in nowise now spare him. Mowing
and other businesses come on ; it is here marvellously
hot and dry, and grass burnt away. God help us ! I
pray you comfort Grinnell's heart and keep just promises justly, and be not credulous lightly ; and so the
Lord bless you and guide you with His Holy Spirit in
His fear ! Be not too frank with that Papist ; such
have seducing spirits to snare the godly. Be not too
open. Sit not up late, nor disorder your body, that
you may have health to do good service when God shall
appoint.

Your careful mother,

A. BACON.

LADY BACON TO ANTHONY BACON. II. 4.

(Orig. Lambeth MSS. 649, fol. 232.)

Oct. 8, 1593.

I pray God keep you safe from all infection of sin and
plague. It hath pleased the Lord to put me in remem-

brance, on both sides of me, by taking two of the sickness, very necessary persons to me, a widow, specially
the goodman Fynch, whose want I shall have cause to
lament daily. His careful, and skilful, and very trusty
husbanding my special rural businesses every way procured me, and that even to the very last, much quiet of
mind and leisure to spend my time in godly exercises,
both public and private. I confess I am so heartily sorry
for his death as I cannot choose but mourn my great
loss thereby, and now in my weakish sickly age ; but the
Lord God doth it to humble His servants and teach them
to draw nearer to Him in heart unfeignedly, which grace
God grant me to be effectual in me. I humbly beseech
His pity. Surely, son, one cannot value rightly the
singular benefit of such a one in these dissolute and
unfaithful days, but by wise consideration and good experience. It may be you know it ere this, by somebody's
posting in jollity ; but be wise and learn in time to your
own good estimation, and be not readily carried either
to believe or do upon unthrifts' pleasing and boasting
speeches, and but mockeries, in order to make their
profit of you and to bear out their unknown to you
disordered unruliness. Among their peradventure pot-
fellowship companions there will be craving of you, and
I wot not what. Promise not rashly, be hic juris ; you
shall be better esteemed both of wise and unwise before
that punitive experience shall teach you to your cost.
It is said that Thistleworth is visited. Some talk how
Fynch should take it there in baiting his horse ; but now

he is gone. So was the will of God, who bless you and
send you much good of all your bodily physic, and make
you strong to do His holy will to your comfort. Be slow
in speaking and promising, lest you repent when it is too
late. Commend me to your brother. Look well to your
house and servants. Fear late and night roads, now
towards winter.

App.
II. 4.

Your sad mother,

A. BACON.

LADY BACON TO ANTHONY BACON.   II. 5.

(Orig. Lambeth MSS. 650, fol. 223.)

Sept. 7, 1594.

I send you herein Crosby's letter, because you may
better understand by it the words of the Sheriff to himself, if the State be brought in question. I am sorry of
the last act you so earnestly required, whereto I was
hardly drawn, as you know, for doubt of danger. Doubtless your brother Nic hath done somewhat in the Exchequer. You thought it could not come to his ear so
soon ; but you see you are deceived. You shall do well
to send for the attorney and mine, — Marsh I do mean.
If he should strain upon the manor to trouble me and
my tenants, I have brought myself in good case by your
means. Mr. Crew is not in city I hear. It is the worse.
The Sheriff threateneth to strain before the next audit,
which is before Michaeltide, which is not three weeks
hence at uttermost. You had not need to slack this, as
Brocket's matter is to my hinderance. Some money I

16 *   x

had need of for to have pay the suit by his cousin. I
have not of mine own at this present for my house
and other charges 6*l.* in money : I am ready to borrow
10*l.* of my neighbors if I can. I send purposely. I
pray you let me know certainly what way you take to
help it with speed. If it once come in Exchequer suit,
one trouble will follow another. Prevent therefore. I
would fain have gone to London for physic next week,
but I perceive I cannot, being weakish to ride so far,
and the way is but ill for a coach for me, besides the wet
weather. I will desire Mistress Morer to be with me here
for that time. If you prove your new in hand physic,
God give you good of it. My Lord Treasurer about five
years past was greatly pressed by the great vaunt of a
sudden start-up glorious stranger, that would needs cure
him of the gout by boast ; " but," quoth my Lord, " have
you cured any ? Let me know and see them." " Nay,"
said the fellow, " but I am sure I can." " Well," concluded my Lord, and said, " Go, go, and cure first, and
then come again, or else not." I would you had so done.
But I pray God bless it to you, and pray heartily to God
for your good recovery and sound. I am sorry your
brother and you charge yourselves with superfluous
horses. The wise will but laugh at you both ; being but
trouble, besides your debts, long journeys, and private
persons. Earls be Earls. Your vain man straitly by
his sloth and proud quarrel-picking conditions sets all
your house at Redbourn out of quiet order by general
complaint, as I hear. Lately young Morer was smote in

the eye by him, and I pray God you hear not of some
mischief by him. But my sons have no judgment.
They will have such about them, and in their house, and
will not in time remedy it before it break out in some
manifest token of God's displeasure. I cannot cease to
warn as long as I am a mother that loveth you in the
Lord most dearly, and as Seneca by philosophy only
could say, in warning a friend I would rather lack
success (which yet I deprecate) than fidelity.

Your mother,

A. BACON.

The heavenly preacher saith, Each thing hath his opportunity and due season : well may you do as blessed
in the Lord !

LADY BACON TO ANTHONY BACON. II. 6.

(Orig. Lambeth MSS. 650, fol. 75.)

March 1595.

One of the prophets, Nahum I think, saith that the
Lord hath His way in the whirlwind, the storm, and
tempest, and clouds are the dust of His feet. The
wind hath had great power, — it hath thrown off a number of tiles, some fruit-trees, and one or two other pales,
posts and all, and stone pinnacle ; and that I am sor-
riest for, hath blown up a sheet of lead on one side of
the gate where the dial stands. But, in my conscience,
your French cattle, Jaques and all, had before loosened
it with hacking lead for pellets. I pray burn this. Let

them not see it; but hurtful they were. I desire to
know how you did and do. I pray be careful to be
well to your own comfort and good desire of your
friends, with avoiding cold-taking continually and pre-
venting by wariness. Sustain and abstain, and be cheer-
ful and sleep in due time. I liked nothing my cousin
Kemp's horse I sent you. I will not Graham's. My
time is in God's hand, and not at his appointment:
he ever stood upon a month's warning in my life.
Some unknown trick there is; it will not serve with
me doubtless. And shall Elsdon and Brocket thus dally
and mock still? If God give me strength I will to
London for these two causes, by His merciful guiding.

A. B.

LADY BACON TO ANTHONY BACON.

(Orig. Lambeth MSS. 650, fol. 69.)

March, 1595.

I came yesterday home, I thank God well, though
very weary, by that missing the right way we roved
and made it longer. I found a very sick and sore
altered man. One might by him see what is the change
wrought by the hand of the Highest in correcting. He
hath been, as you know, a strong-armed man, and active
in such exercises of strength as shooting, wrestling, cast-
ing the bar; and whilst he was with me I never used
footstool to horseback; but now, God help him, weak
in voice, his flesh consumed, his hands, bones, and sinews; but his belly up to his very chest swollen and

hoved up, and as hard withal as though one touched wainscot. I thank the Lord that put me in the mind to visit him with a Christian desire to comfort his soul, which I trust Mr. Wilblood's spiritual counsel and comfort, with hearty prayer, was a mean to it; God, I trust, working with his admonitions in the sick body to the reviving of his soul. He hath his memory perfect, and well and glad of godly correction. God grant him and myself also his continual sweet comfort and feeling mercy to the end! Amen.

For your going you spoke of to London, and will have the two beds hence for your servants, let me know in time. I would you had here tarried till that remove; you should have spared much waste expense, which you need not, and have been better provided. Surely, if you keep all your Redbourn household at London, you will undo yourself. Money is very hard to come by, and sure friends more hard; and you shall be still in other folk's danger, and not your own man, and your debts will pinch you, though you may hope; but your continual sickliness withal is a great hindrance; and if you make show of a housekeeping in the city, you shall quickly be overcharged, much disquieted, and brought not over the ears but over shoulders. Therefore at the beginning be very wary and wise, as it is said. "Learn to be wise for yourself," one said......
Consult the Lord, and do nothing rashly. I could not choose but advise as heretofore. God guide you to safe age's rest, and best course.

App
II. 8

LADY BACON TO ANTHONY BACON.

(Orig. Lambeth MSS. 651, fol. 66.)

March 30, 1595.

I mean, if God will, to come hither again before Easter; but you are going farther hence than my ableness will endure to travel, either by water or by land, and know not when I shall see you any more. I pray God to go before you, and to be with you ever, to heal you, to help you, and to counsel and comfort you continually with His fatherly love in Christ Jesus our Lord. Amen.

I wrote yesterday to my Lady Walsingham and by her to the Countess [of Essex]. She took it well, and thanked me. The Countess is very near her travailing time. I beseech God of His goodness make her a joyful mother, with daily increase of God's blessing upon her and hers. Beware in anywise of the Lord H. [Howard]! He is a dangerous intelligencing man; no doubt a subtle Papist inwardly, and lieth in wait. Peradventure he hath some close working with STANDEN and the SPANIARD [Perez]. Be not too open; he will betray you to divers, and to your AUNT RUSSELL among others. The Duke had been alive but by his practising and still soliciting him, to the double undoing. And the EARL of ARUNDEL, avoid his familiarity as you love the truth and yourself. A very instrument of the Spanish Papists. I pray you no creature know or see this I write; but burn it with your own hands. And remember; for he, pretending courtesy, works mischief devilishly. I have long known him and

observed him; his workings have been stark naught.
Stand at a distance! I am sorry I cannot speak with
Dr. Fletcher for your horse. I would certainly know.
It is not like you will brew hastily. Send me word what
time you guess, because of mine absence if God let me
live. But vessels and carriage must surely be provided;
for indeed I have none for malt. If you tell Crosby your
mind, I will pay for it when I have received rents. Gryst
is very dear methinks, but he denieth. If you had taken
your physics here in your well-warmed house, it had been
better I think. God be your guide in all your ways, and
take heed of cold-taking upon remove and after physic.
Call for your own necessaries; you may forget you, and
you smart for it. Use your legs as you may, daily; they
will else be the feebler, and the sinews stark and
strengthless. It is true, I fear, there is no ordinary
preaching ministry at Chelsea. I cannot tell how to
lament it; but both my sons, methinks, do not care for
it where they dwell. Greater want cannot be. We had
needs watch continually to be well armed against evil
days, imminent to be feared; for of all sorts we wax
worse and worse. London waxeth straitlaced, urging
that slavish pleasing will not salve his hard-cured sore.
Burn this. The God of mercy, health, and peace compass you about with His heavenly favor wheresoever.
Farewell in Christ now and ever.   Your mother,

A. B.

My grief is great about Essex, and truly I fear lest

opportunity should have given rise to most shameful and
grievous adultery and the midst of evils and —— (Here
follow five words much blotted and very indistinct.)

LADY BACON TO ANTHONY BACON.

(Orig. Lambeth MSS. 657, fol. 54.)

Gorhambury, April 1, 1595.

I send between your brother and you the first flight of
my dove-house: the Lord be thanked for all: ij dozen
and iiij pigeons, xij to you, and xvj to your brother, because he was wont to love them better than you from a
boy.   Marvellous hard, snowy, haily, and strong, windy
weather here, and great scarcity.   I have had more toil
in my body few days since I came last hither than in
above twice as long at London.   I wish myself there
again, and peradventure, if God will, I will before Easter
as now minded.   I am glad your beer was sent so soon.
To-day, upon occasion of a maid sending to Redborn, but
none of my servants, I hear Mistress Read and Henry are
malcontent for certain implements; specially, as they say,
in the best reserved chamber for your friends, noble or
not noble, a carpet, and other things filled with birds,
hunting or hawks or dogs.   Mr. Lawson was the nobleman
lodged there, I ween; and like enough, for he is
subtle, vainglorious, and makes you bleared still to
insure all, and pay for all ; and further, as was reported,
that Norris was discontented for your requiring to Mr.
Read, he not made privy before.   Thus they talk, and

something else, now you are gone; and one that tames
the bit is become a tippler and will be overseen with
drink, but an ill servant in your house, the fruit of idleness.

Large was here this day. I told him it was honesty
and Christian duty to dwell at home with his wife. I
would, I said, be loath that my son should bear the blame
of his being an ill husband, and leave his first calling to
labor, for to leave over to be a good thriving fellow. I
used him so still, though other civil service, washing
among. It is commonly spoken that Fynch of Woodend
and Guaram are joint companions in all ill fellowship.
Use them thereafter, and take no luck by such. You
and your brother have taken much discredit by not
judging wisely and rightly of those; yea, both of you,
over-credit to your willing hinderance. I pray the Lord
give you both good understanding by His word and spirit,
and health to serve Him in truth, to your good estimation, with increase of His blessed favor. Let not your
men be privy hereof. As your good mother, I thus
certify. Think of it.

Your mother,

A. B.

Use your legs betimes, for fear of losing by disuse.

Good Rolf was here to-day to speak with me, and very
sadly said thus to me, that he had before now, and presently again did hear that his farm should be let from
him; whereupon his ancient wife and he both were much

grieved. I told him I never heard any tittle of it, and thought it was nothing; so it will be worse, I wis, for you to make a change for Humphrey. He hopes you will at least let him tarry iij years longer after his present state. Finished scamblers are easily had everywhere, but discreet, honest, sufficient farmers would be continued; they serve the country and countenance their landlord indeed. Guaram will prove stark naught if you suffer him to let the ground from Pleatah farm; you are marvellously abused by him and misled; some in my house are too often with him. I will look better to them for it. Yet by them I hear of these his naughty doings, both for himself and you. God be with you, and make you able to every good duty, and guide you all ways to your comfort. God knows when I shall see you. I am therefore more careful to advertise you to beware. Remember Groome I pray you. Brocket will make jest of us both. Keep not superfluous servants to mar them with idleness and undo you. Let Large live at home; best for him, a married man. Nobody see this, but burn it, or send it back; and so commend you to the Lord.

LADY BACON TO ANTHONY BACON.

(Orig. Lambeth MSS. 651, fol. 65.)

April 1, 1595.

SON, —

Woodward told me you required a hogshead of beer. I will, if it please God I come well and in time home to-morrow, I will send you one by the cart of my best

ordinary beer ; the rest remaining is March. I pray you
let me have another hogshead for it. I shall lack else ;
and let one be ready with a car, because of double jum-
bling. I think, well used, you may drink it after five
days' settling at least ; but that, as you see, being above
iiij months old, after it is broached it will not last above a
fortnight because of turning.

This bearer I have newly taken into my house.

A. B.

LADY BACON TO ANTHONY BACON.

(Orig. Lambeth MSS. 657, fol. 64.)

Gorhambury, April, 3, 1595.

I thank you for your horses. I send you a hogshead
of November beer, methinks good, and a barrel also of
the same brewing which I did cause the brewer then to
tun of the first tap of the same brewing, and so strong,
because at that time it was thought you would come to
Redburn, and I meant it to you : it is so strong as I
would not drink ordinarily to my meals, but do you use
it to your most good ; in any wise, when these two vessels
be empty let them be returned by the cart. I cannot
want [do without] them indeed, and they be strong,
besides divers other vessels of mine sent to your sundry
places. I did at one time send six together, if not seven,
to Redburn, and I paid vii s. for heading and hooping and
seasoning of them ; howsoever they made you pay afterward. I did so in truth. I pray remember Groom's
ill handling, and curb it well for all his naughty and

tippling mates. I wrong my men, living well and Christianly in their honest vocation, to suffer them to be ill
entreated and myself contemned; I mean not so. Crosby
purposeth to be with you on Monday if God will, and
your corn ready.

Your mother,

A. B.

Yesterday, seeing my sister Russell at the Blackfriars
house, after the sermon, I found her very much grieved,
and her words charging my Lord Treasurer of very unkind dealing in a matter very chargeable to [her], and a
slight end procured, she said to her hurt, with tears on
account of him. I saw her so lamenting, I said I would
write to Sir Robert Cecil. "No, no," said she; "it is
too late; he hath marred all, and that against my counsel's liking at all." But [do] not you nor your brother
intermeddle in it nor be a knowing of it. I pray you
show your brother this, and let him not take knowledge
lest you both set on work; and for that HOWARD, once
again be very ware as of a subtle serpent. Burn all, for
fear of the servants. Be not hasty to remove. Your
drink well used, and not set abroach all at once, above
the bung first, then by degrees lower once or twice, will
be better and last long, saith the brewer. York House
lease is not here, as I said to my cousin Kemp. Mr.
Bayley hath seen every place purposely to satisfy my
Lord Keeper. I do not remember that ever I saw any
lease from the Bishop sealed, but by parley and trust

betwixt both. Farewell. The brewer, who is now here,
saith that your beer now sent, well handled, will drink
well a month's space. Let not your servants beguile
you secretly or openly. Use your legs in any wise and
daily, lest they fail you when you would ; neglect not in
time, and serve the Lord with all your heart.

LADY BACON TO ANTHONY BACON.

(Orig. Lambeth MSS. 651, fol. 102.)

May 15, 1595.

Grace, and the love of the Lord in Christ. — Your
beer, well handled I trust, is meant to be sent to-morrow
early. The brewer hath been careful himself. I had no
brewing, I dare say these twelve months, more diligently
attended upon of my servants ; if the carriers do their
part, and all were well watched and looked to in the
cellar, it is thought for your own special use it will last
till nigh Michaeltide, both for quantity and quality. As
you appointed it is brewed, 8 hogsheads in all, and of the
chiefest beer 2 hogsheads, marked with an S on each
side of the wheel mark ; the third, somewhat less strong,
being a second, is marked, likewise with chalk, with a
smaller wheel-mark, and one only S, by it to know it
rightly. All the other five alike. God give you the
right use of all His gifts to God's glory and your own
farther advancement and true comfort.

The rowelled horse I had no mind to indeed, nor the
horse Master Spencer rode on. Lawson thrust in here
his and others smuttled and spoiled beast. The horse is

full of windgalls, a token of very spoiling in riding and dressing. Grass is here yet but poor and scant, and I must turn out shortly my two service geldings of necessity. I will not change my own faulty husband's horse for yours, both heavy and stumbling, and never broken for such a toward horse when you first had him. Diverse of my folk now sickly. God increase your health I pray God, and be merciful to us both.

I thank you for your comely mastiff; it is supposed he will hunt after sheep; he is too old; I durst not prove him yet.

Your mother,

A. BACON.

LADY BACON TO ANTHONY BACON.

(Orig. Lambeth MSS. 657, fol. 144.)

3 June, 1595.

SON, —

You had a mind to have the long carpet and the ancient learned philosopher's picture from hence; but, indeed, I had no mind thereto, yet have I sent them, very carefully bestowed and laid in a hamper for safety in carriage.

For the carpet, being without gold, you shall not I think have the like at this time in London, for the right, and not painted, colors; which is too common in this age in more things than carpets, and such it is for all not of late bought worth you to buy. Such implements as your father left I have very diligent locked

in and kept. You have now bared this house of all
the best; a wife would have well regarded such things,
but now they shall serve for use of gaming or tippling
upon the table of every common person, your own men
as well as others, and so be spoiled as at Redburn. I
would think that John, your tailor, should be fittest
to look well to your furniture. God, I humbly beseech
Him, increase in you daily spiritual store, and also the
comfort of bodily health and other comforts of this
life to his own good pleasure, to whose fatherly love
in Christ I commend you.

Arr.
II. 13.

I wish the hamper were not opened till yourself were
at Chelsea, to see it done before you; for the pictures
are put orderly within the carpet. You have one long
carpet already. I cannot think what use this should
be. It will be an occasion of mockery that you should
have a great chamber, called and carpeted. What I
say is not foolish. Draw no charge till God better enable you; but observe narrowly both for your health
and purse. Surely your vi' beer is no ordinary drink
for your house no time of the year specially, and usually
too strong for you; but Podagra will bestir him. Seeing God hath given you some good abilities, I would,
I trow, watch over my diet and everything to put them
in use by health to God's glory and your own more
credit.

If her Majesty have resolved upon the negative for
your brother, as I hear, truly, save for the brust a little,
I am glad of it. God, in His time, hath better in store

I trust. For, considering his kind of health and what
cumber pertains to that office, it is best for him I hope.
Let us all pray the Lord we make us to profit by
His fatherly correction; doubtless it [is] His hand,
and all for the best, and love to His children that will
seek him first, and depend upon his goodness. Godly
and wisely love ye like brethren, whatsoever [happen],
and be of good courage in the Lord with good hope.

Farewell! take diligent heed of your health; be master
of yourself and act most prudently.

Your mother,

A. BACON, Widow.

Do not readily relinquish or grant your town house to
any one.

LADY BACON TO ANTHONY BACON.

(Orig. Lambeth MSS. 657, fol. 203.)

Gorhambury, July 30, 1595.

I most humbly thank God and much rejoiced when
I heard by Crosby you do more exercise your body and
your legs, and that in your course you go to the Earl
yourself at occasions; surely soon, by the grace of God,
you shall find great help by bodily exercise in season,
and much refreshing both to body and mind, and be
more accepted of. I would advise you went sometimes
to the French church, and have there, and bash not your
necessaries for warmth to hear the public preaching of
the word of God, as it is His own ordinance, and, armed

so with prayer for understanding, it maketh the good App.
hearers wise to God, and enables them to discern how to II. 14.
walk in their worldly vocation, to please God, and to be
accepted of man, indeed, which God grant to you both.

Truly, son, the miller's last coming to you was but of
a craft to color his halting touching his secret consenting
to steal, as cause hath been given to suspect him, not
lately alone, but long : he waxeth a subtle fellow, and
hath a cunning head of his own, now he goeth with meal
to London and to some other places hereabout, and will
mar the mill, I doubt, by his flitting. Wherefore should
he have a net ? himself confessed about the scouring of
the mill, but lately, that there was store of trout, and
now almost none, because Bun and others did lately rob,
as you know. I took the miller's part in defending his
right dealing, and so the justices have bound Bun to
good a-bearing till next sessions ; but that same Bun said
earnestly that the miller could join and bear with some,
and he could abide by it, and so hath Mr. Coltman said
when I have blamed him but for angling. Certainly, son,
where he bringeth you, though I would they were more
for you, he carrieth to Mr. Preston and others twice as
many, but say yet not so to him. I mean to take his net
from him, he is waxen so heady, new-fangled, that the
mill goeth to wreck, and customers begin to mislike and
to forsake it, which will hinder our living and discon-
tinue it. I will cause Humphrey to be paid as you order
with Crosby ; surely set aside my poor mortmain, but
200*l.*, or little above, a small portion for my continuance.

17   Y

I thank the Lord for all : spending money goeth but from
hand to mouth, as they say, with me. I gave your brother
at twice 25*l.* for his paling, the rather to cheer him since
he had nothing of me. Crosby told me he looked very
ill ; he thought he taketh still inward grief ; I fear it may
hinder his health hereafter. Counsel to be godly wise
first, and wise for himself too, and both of you look to
your expenses in time, and oversee those you trust how
trustily, for I tell you plainly it hath been long commonly observed that both your servants are full of money.

My Lord Chief Baron's marriage with your sister I
never [had] any inkling of before Crosby told. I pray
at your leisure write to me some circumstance of the
manner, and God bless it. I send Winter purposely,
because you should not send your boy. Gorhambury,
penultima of July.

Your mother,

A. B.

Nobody but yourself see my letters, I pray you.

After harvest some venison would do well here. God
bless you daily with good increase.

LADY BACON TO ANTHONY BACON.

(Orig. Lambeth MSS. 651, fol. 211.)

7 of Aug. 1595.

For your bottles I thank you. The malmsey I tasted
a little ; very good. Humphrey shall, God willing, be

answered ; but with a sight of his reckoning he asketh
for 20 neats' tongues at once, not very seldom neither ;
for Mr. Barber Crosby will go within these 3 days to
keep your credit with him, and such is a very Christian duty. Owe nothing to any, saith the Lord in his
word, but to love one another. I would I were able
to help you both out of debt; but set apart my poor
mortmain, which I certainly have vowed for any ac-
knowledgments to God, I am not worth 100*l*. Yea and
specially you have spent me quick ; nothing can therefore remain after I am dead. God bless you ! I had not
sent now but for this cause, by your message by Wyn-
ter. The two countess sisters will neighbor you ; both
ladies that fear God and love his word ; indeed zeal-
ously, specially the younger sister. Yet upon advice
and some experience, I would earnestly counsel you
to be wary and circumspect, and not to be too open
nor willing to prolong speech with the Countess of War-
wick. She, after her father's fashion, will search and
sound and lay up with diligence, marking things which
seem not courtly, and she is near the Queen, and follows her father's example too much in that. This is
the cause of my now writing. Another matter is, that
now the marriage of your sister is well, by God's appointment, I trust [you] use not such broad language upon
mislike of unkindness. Your men and others, how
peradventure you mark not, may hurt you very much.
Surely if such phrases as you wrote in your letter or
such deriding should come to his ear, it would be very

hurtful to you more than one way, which you need not, being never abroad amongst them. Your sister's nature is but unkind, and at that time of her marriage could not herself think of such things. I pray hearken to him with all courtesy; he is of marvellous good estimation for his religious mind in following his law-calling uprightly; beware, therefore, in words and deeds and speeches at table before him. There is scarce any fidelity in servants. I write more hereof, because others write your letters and not yourself.

I am sorry your brother with inward secret grief hindereth his health. Everybody saith he looketh thin and pale. Let him look to God and confer with Him in godly exercise of hearing and reading, and continue to be noted to take care: I had rather ye both, with God's blessed favor, had very good healths and were well out of debt, than any office. Yet, though the Earl showed great affection, he marred all with violent ·courses. I pray God increase his fear in his heart and a hatred of sin; indeed, halting before the Lord and backsliding are very pernicious. I am heartily sorry to hear how he [the Earl of Essex] sweareth and gameth unreasonably God cannot like it. I pray show your brother this letter, but to no creature else. Remember me and yourself.

Your mother,

A. B.

Gorhambury, 5th August, '95.

With a humble heart before God, let your brother be of good cheer. Alas! what excess of bucks at Gray's

Inn, and to feast it on the Sabbath. God forgive and
have mercy upon England!

LADY BACON TO ANTHONY BACON.

(Orig. Lambeth MSS. 652, fol. 86.)

Gorhambury, Oct. 21, 1595.

Since it so pleaseth God, comfort your brother kindly
and Christianly, and let me, mother, and you, both my
sons, look up to the correcting hand of God in your
wants every way, with humble hearts before Him, and
with comfort, and procure your health by good means
carefully. If I did not warily sustain and abstain, I
should live in continual pain pitifully. For set sickness,
to speak of, I have not now, I thank God, but very cum-
bersome troublous accidents to keep me to exercise mortification. Remember, her Majesty is, they say, now at
Richmond. God preserve her from all evil, and rule her
heart to the zealous setting forth of his glory! Want
of this zeal in all degrees is the very ground of our honest trouble. We have all dallied with the Lord, who will
not ever suffer himself to be mocked. I send you xij pigeons, my last flight, and one ringdove beside, and a black
coney taken by John Knight this day, and pigeons, too,
to-day. Lawrence can tell you my Lady Stafford's
speech was of you, as she hath heard from her Majesty
marvelling you came not to see her in so long space.
Consider well and wisely; for I sent him to her to know
of her Majesty's good estate to Nonsuch, according to my

duty, and to Mr. Doctor Smith. He came not home by London, as I bade him: do what you may for health, piously and diligently, out of question. Where you be you must needs disorder your time of diet and quiet; want of which will still keep you in lame and uncomfortable. I hear the Lord Howard is too often with you. He is subtilely deceitful. Beware! beware! Burn this. The Lord of heaven bless you from heaven, in Christ our Lord and hope.

Your mother,

A. Bacon.

Burn, I pray, but read well first.

LADY BACON TO ANTHONY BACON.

(Orig. Lambeth MSS. 657, fol. 113.)

Gorhambury, June 15, 1596.

By the good hand of the Lord I am come well to Gorhambury, where I find my household well and in good order. I thank God my sister my Lady Russell's coach is far easier than either of yours, and her man, a comely man withal, did it with care and very well; and your brother's footman did very diligently go by me. Here be no strawberries nor fish to send; and for beer, son, I have none ordinary under five weeks, at least above a month, brewed the first week of May, which now carried, after so long settling and in the heat of summer, must needs be spoiled, which were great pity this dearth time. Truly, son, as yet I know not when to brew, by my provision not this ij weeks at least, as well as for vessels. I have tierce of last March beer; but surely, being yet unripe and carried this heat, it will be utterly marred. Paying Mr. Moore's bill for my physic, I asked him whether you did owe anything for physic? He said he had not reckoned with you since Michaelmas last. Alas! why so long, say I? I think I said further it can be muted, for he hath his confections from strangers; and to tell you truly, I bade him secretly send his bill, which he seemed loth but at my pressing, when I saw it came to above xv *l.* or xvj *l.* If it had been but vij or viij, I would have made some shift to pay. I told him I would say nothing to you because he was so unwilling. It may be he would take half willingly, because "ready money made always a cunning apothecary," said covetous Morgan, as his proverb. For Lange, I cannot tell what you would have me do for him: he finds I do not recompense evil with evil. I have at times given him, he knoweth; but he is but whining, and a companion too much with naughty Goodram, though not at Redborn, but to his hurt. Let him ply his labor, in God's name, and not a busybody and secret quarrel-picker, as he is partly suspected. I use charity to him, though I like not his crafty soothing nature. With thanks for your horse J. C. . . . th heed all your infirmities to your comfort. Be zealous over your health. Hours sink away unseasonably. Farewell.

Your mother,

A. BACON.

No. III.

Lady Anne Bacon, Jun., to her brothers Francis and Anthony Bacon.

(Orig. Lambeth MSS. 648, fol. 10.)

Guilford, 16th March, 1592.

Good Brothers, —

Being very desirous to see you both at Redgrave, and yet loth to put you to that pain which might by my desire impair your healths by entreating your repair into this country, yet can I not refrain, upon this occasion offered of the marriage of my daughter, heartily to pray you both to bestow your travels to Redgrave to the same, where, if it shall please God so to dispose of your business and healths as I may see you, I shall think myself greatly beholden to you, and the feast greatly honored by your presence. I hope also it will be comfortable to you, both in rejoicing with my husband and me in the action itself, and also in the intercourse and meeting of many good friends which you there shall see and meet with, especially your brother Anthony, having been so long absent from us all, and by that means have not seen sundry of those good friends of yours which I hope you shall there see. The day is appointed to be on the Thursday, the 6th of April; and even so, with my very hearty commendations to you both, and wishing you all good as to myself, I cease to trouble you.

Your very loving sister,

Anne Bacon.

No. IV.

Francis Bacon to Thomas Phillips.

(Orig. in State Paper Office.)

Sir, —

I congratulate your return, hearing that all is passed on your word. Your Mercury is returned, whose return alarmed us upon some great matter which I fear he will not satisfy. News of his coming came before his own letter, and to other than to his proper street, which maketh me desirous to satisfy or to solve. My Lord hath required him to repair to me, which, upon his Lordship's and my own letter received, I doubt not but he will with all speed perform, when I pray you to meet him if you may, that, laying our heads together, we may maintain his credit, satisfy my Lord's expectations, and procure some good fruit. I pray thee rather spare not your travail, because I think the Queen is already party to the advertisement of his coming over, and, in some, suspect, which you may not disclose to him. So I wish you as myself, this 15th of September, 1592.

Your ever assured,

Fr. Bacon.

Francis Bacon to Thomas Phillips.

(Orig. in State Paper Office.)

[1593.]

Mr. Phillips, —

I send you the copy of my letter to the Earl touching the matter between us proposed. You may perceive what

17 *

APP. IV. 2. expectation and conceit I thought good to imprint into my Lord, both of yourself and of this particular service. And as that which is in general touching yourself I know you are very able to make good, so in this beginning of intelligence I pray spare no care to conduct the matter to sort to good effect. The more plainly and frankly you shall deal with my Lord, not only in disclosing particulars, but in giving him caveats and admonishing him of any error which in this action he may commit (such is his Lordship's nature), the better he will take it. I send you also his letter, which appointeth this afternoon for your repair to him, which I pray, if you can, perform ; although, if you are not fully resolved of any circumstance, you may take a second day for the rest, and show his Lordship the party's letter. If your business suffer you not to attend their Lordships to-day, then excuse it by two or three words in writing to his Lordship, and offer another time.

In haste, your ever assured,

FR. BACON.

Whereas I mention in my letter an intelligence standing in Spain of my brothers, I pray take no knowledge at all thereof.

IV. 3. FRANCIS BACON TO THOMAS PHILLIPS.

(Orig. State Paper Office.)

[1593.]

MR. PHILLIPS, —

I have excused myself of this progress, if that be to excuse to take liberty where it is not given. Being now

at Twickenham, I am desirous of your company. You
may stay as long and as little while as you will; the
longer the better welcome. *Otia colligunt mentem?*
And, indeed, I would be the wiser by you in many
things, for that I call to confer with a man of your fulness. In sadness come, as you are an honest man. So
I wish you all good. From Twickenham Park this 14th
of August.

Yours, ever assured,

Fr. Bacon.

Francis Bacon to his Aunt Cooke. IV. 4

(Orig. at Lambeth Palace, 649, p. 237.)

Windsor Castle, 29 Oct., 1593.

Aunt, —

I had spoken a good while since with my Lord-Treasurer, whose Lordship took pains to peruse the will which
I had with me, and in conversation was of opinion that,
if the younger children wanted reasonable allowance, it
should be supplied, and the other parties to be stored for
their advancement: of the same mind I ever was and am,
and there is nothing in my cousin Morise's note against.
Accordingly I have enclosed a note, of a proportion
which I think you cannot dislike, and which I pray
communicate with my cousin Morise and the rest of
the executors. For my part, I wish you as a kind alliance. But the question is not between you and me, but
between your profit and my trust. I purpose as soon as
I can conveniently to put the money I have into some

other hands, lest you think the case of the money prevaileth with me; but I will endure in a good cause, and wish I you right well.

In haste, your loving nephew,

FRA. BACON.

FRANCIS BACON TO SIR THOMAS CONINGSBY.

(Orig. at Lambeth Palace, Vol. 649, p. 236.)

[Oct. 1593.]

MY VERY GOOD COUSIN, —

Whereas this gentleman, Mr. Nicholas Trot, one to whom, besides familiar acquaintance, I am much beholden, hath conveyed unto him for his money a lease of the prebend of Withington, under the title of Mr. Heyghton, that was sometimes of the counsel of the Marches, a man not like to have been overreached in his bargains, against the which one Wallwyne claimeth by a former deed of gift, supposed to be forged and appearing to be fraudulent, because the same party undertook afterwards to sell it, and his interest hath been quietly missed by twenty years' space, I am earnestly to recommend the assistance of this my friend, according to the equity of the cause, to your good favor, whereof there will be the more need, both because he is a stranger in the country, and because the adverse party, as I understand, hath used force about the possession; and therefore, good cousin, let him use your experience and careful countenance for direction and help, according to that good affection which

I persuade myself you bear me, and which I am ready to answer in all kindness.   And so I wish you as

Your assured loving cousin,

FR. BACON, &c.

FRANCIS BACON TO SIR FRANCIS ALLEN.

(Orig. at Lambeth Palace, 649, 309.)

Edborne, this 25th of December, 1593.

SIR, —

I accept with all kindness and thanks possible the demonstrations you make from time to time of a sincere affection and singular respect towards me, namely, in your last letter to myself, and approve wholly yours to my brother, even to the least and last tittle thereof, wishing as a brother, for his own sake, that he had had but half as good a ground and reason for his demand as you have for your answer.   Protesting unto you with a sincerity very present to the merit of your own touching me without prejudice, that the scanty link of German consanguinity should never have prevailed so far with me as to have once moved me to have given my clear consent to my brother for such his request or recommendation. Touching your particular business, I will not fail, by God's grace, in my next to our most honorable Earl, to perform my uttermost, and will not forget to acknowledge to our good friend Mr. Standen, that whatsover friendly office he shall have rendered by his assistance to do to you, that same is done to myself.   And so, with most hearty wishes of your health and contentment, I

commit you to the protection of the Almighty, remaining
always inviolably

Your most entire friend and servant,

F. B.

IV. 7.   FRANCIS BACON TO SIR FRANCIS ALLEN.

(Orig. at Lambeth Palace, 649, 310.)

Hampton Court, Dec. 20, 1593.

SIR FRANCIS ALLEN, —

I do so much favor this gentleman, Mr. Garret, who
from my praise entered a course of following the wars,
which hath succeeded unto him as to his good commendations, so yet nevertheless not hitherto to his settling
in any place answerable to his desert and profession. In
regard whereof, understanding of the nomination and
appearance of employment in Ireland, he conceiveth it
will be some establishment to him if he may receive your
favor, being by you accepted in the place of your lieutenant, your own virtue and reputation answered, and
the uncertainty of the French employment. Of his proof
and sufficiency to serve I write the less because I take it
to be well known to yourself, but for my particular I do
assure you I can hardly imagine a matter wherein you
shall more effectually tie me unto you than in this. I
wished him to use me but as a mean of my brother's
commendation, which I esteemed to be of extraordinary
weight with you. But because this was the readier and
that the entireness between my brother and myself is

well known to you, he desired to begin with this. Thus
I wish you all protection.

Yours in unfeigned good affection,

F. Bacon.

I was sorry to hear from Mr. Anthony Standen so
sharply and unseasonably you were afflicted by the gout.
But you have of him a careful solicitor, and if I can
come in to him with any good endeavor of mine, you may
reckon of it.

Francis Bacon to the Masters of Requests. IV 8.

(Orig. in the Record Office.)

[?1593.]

After my hearty commendations. At the request of
this bearer, Mr. Edward Cottwin, an ancient follower and
well-willer to my name and family, I have considered of
a suit of his depending before you for the recovery of
certain rents due unto him for divers years past, and
detained from him only upon a strained construction of
extreme law. And finding the honesty of the man and
the equity of his cause to deserve favor, considering that
the main matter (which is the sum in demand) is freely
acknowledged, I could do no less than recommend him
unto your good discretions, desiring you in regard of his
great loss and troubles to afford him, that which you
deny to no man, lawful favor and expedition, which I
shall be always ready thankfully to acknowledge by such

APP.
IV. 8. friendly offices as shall fall within my compass. And so
I leave you to God's safe tuition.

　　　　　Resting your very loving friend,

　　　　　　　　　　　　　　　Fr. ⌐Bacon.

IV. 9.　　　　　FRANCIS BACON TO MR. SKINNER.

　　　　　(Orig. at Lambeth Palace, 650, 143.)

　　　　　　　　　　　　　　　July 29, 1594.

　Sir, —

　I hope you will not find it strange nor amiss if the confidence I have in your kind affection makes me so bold
as most earnestly to request you to pleasure me with the
loan of five hundred pounds for a year. My occasion to
employ the same presently is important. My meaning
(though I say it myself) is entirely, as it ought to be, to
satisfy you without fail at the day, and your assurance
shall be my brother A. Bacon's and my own bond.

　The occasion, my good cousin, and my meaning being
by you believed, as I assure myself they shall and most
heartily pray they may you, I cannot doubt of the friendly assistance of my request as a form of assurance, but
look for such a special favor at your hands, which I shall
be always ready and glad to acknowledge when and
wherein soever it shall please you to employ my true
good will and sincere affection. And so desiring your
answer, which I hope shall be no less to my contentment
than my resolution of full acknowledgment to yours, I
commit you to the protection of the Almighty,

　　　　　And rest your entire loving cousin to use,

　　　　　　　　　　　　　　　F. B.

FRANCIS BACON TO MR. YOUNG.

(Orig. at Lambeth Palace, 650, 186.)

Gray's Inn, Sept. 2, 1594.

MR. YOUNG, —

I shall desire your friendly pains in the repairing and punishing of an outrage offered by one Thomas Lewys, dwelling near Whitechapel, upon a French gentleman of very good quality and honorable, and my special acquaintance, and upon his company, not in terms alone, but in very furious assailing them. My request to you is the rather for the good report of our nation, whither this gentleman is come only for his own satisfaction and experience, that he may have experience of the good policy amongst us in correcting such insolences, specially upon strangers of his respect. And therefore desire you so great an abuse may be examined and corrected. And so in haste I wish you very well.

Your very loving friend,

FR. BACON.

The French gentleman's name is Mr. Corugues, son to the principal treasurer of Guienne, and this bearer shall relate to you the particularities of the abuse.

FRANCIS BACON TO ANTHONY BACON.

(Orig. at Lambeth Palace, 650, 227.)

Gray's Inn, Dec. 10, 1594.

BROTHER, —

I moved you to join with me in security for 500*l.*, which I did purpose then decidedly to have taken up;

z

300*l.* odd secure, and 200*l.* by way of forbearance, both
to the satisfaction of Peter Van, our servant. I thank
you, you assented. I have now agreed with Peter for the
taking up of the whole of one man's, according to which
I send you the bonds and securities. You shall find the
bond to be of 600*l.*, which is one hundred more than it
was at first. The jewel cost 500*l.* and odd, as shall appear to you by my bond. Next I send you immediately
for use an agreement, so to free you of one hundred, for
which you stand bound to Mr. Willis Fleetwood. So in
haste I commend you to God's good preservation.

Your entire loving brother,

Fr. Bacon.

FRANCIS BACON TO ANTHONY BACON.

(Orig. at Lambeth Palace, 650, 237.)

[Dec. 1594.]

GOOD BROTHER, —

If you leave the matter to me, I am like both to deal
with my Lord of Essex in it, attending the first occasion, and to fortify it otherwise, as I will hereafter give
you account. And where I doubt, acquaint you in
particular beforehand. For Mr. Sugden, I had rather
have brought payment than allegation. I ever doubt-
ed the resting upon [him] would come to nothing, and
I desire you to do as you wish; and yet I will endeavor to speed my part nevertheless, and the whole
if I can.

Mr. Trott I have desired to be here after to-morrow

to see her. He taketh this his second chance. I desired Dr. Hammond to visit you from me, whom I
was glad to have here, he being a physician, and my
complaint being want of digestion.

I hope by this Sir Ant. Perez has seen the Queen
dance. That is not it, but her distraction of body to
be fresh and good, I do pray God· both subjects and
strangers may long be witnesses of. I would be sorry
the bride and bridegroom should be as the weather
hath fallen out: thus, it goes to bed fair, and rises
lowering. Thus I commend you to God's best preservation.

Your entire loving brother,

FR. BACON.

FRANCIS BACON TO THE EARL OF SALISBURY.   IV. 13.
(Orig. in State Paper Office.)

[1607.]

IT MAY PLEASE YOUR LORDSHIP, —
I send the two bills according to your Lordship's
pleasure signified to me, hoping your Lordship will pardon me that they come not precisely at the hour. The
book is long and full of difficulty ; and a business such
as this is, I do not much trust to servants or precedents. I found it more convenient to put one payment more upon the Privy Seal than your Lordship
directed, and to take it from the rent; because else,
the grant must have been for ten years and a half,
which is not formal. So I most humbly leave,

And rest your Lordship's most humble and bounden,

F. BACON.

FRANCIS BACON TO THE EARL OF SALISBURY.

(Orig. in the State Paper Office.)

* 28th October, 1608.

IT MAY PLEASE YOUR LORDSHIP, —

According to your Lordship's warrant on the 15th of June last I made a book ready for his Majesty's signature to the use of Mrs. Ellis of the benefit of an extent of the lands and goods of Richard Yonge her father, extended for a debt of 3,000*l.* upon recognizances; which book is since past the Great Seal. And now having received order from your Lordship for amendment of the defects in that patent, I find the case to be thus: That she has since discovered two other debts of record, the one of 8,511*l.* 19*s.* 4*d.*, the other of 2,100*l.*, remaining upon account in the Pipe Office. And though it be true that she shall reap no benefit by the former grant, except these debts be likewise released, on regard the King may come upon the said lands and goods for these debts, — and it may be the meaning was in Queen Elizabeth to free and acquit Mr. Yonge of all debts; for else *Quid te exempta juvat spinis de pluribus una?* — yet do I not see how I may pass the book again, with a release of these two debts, without your Lordship's further warrant, which I humbly submit to your honorable consideration.

Your Lordship's most humble and bounden,

FR. BACON.

FRANCIS BACON TO THE EARL OF SALISBURY.

(Orig. in the State Paper Office.)

Gray's Inn, the 6th of July, 1609.

IT MAY PLEASE YOUR LORDSHIP, —

The assurance which by your Lordship's directions was to be passed to his Majesty by Richard Forebenche, one of the yeomen of the guard of Potter's Park, within the parish of Chertsey, in the county of Surrey, is thoroughly perfected; so if your Lordship so please he may receive the money your Lordship agreed to pay for it.

Your Lordship's most humble and bounden,

Fs. BACON.

FRANCIS BACON TO THE EARL OF SALISBURY.

(Orig. in the State Paper Office.)

IT MAY PLEASE YOUR GOOD LORDSHIP, —

Though Mr. Chancellor and we rested upon the old proclamation which Mr. Attorney brought forth, for matter of transportation of gold and silver, yet because I could not tell whither it were that your Lordship looked for from us, and because if you should be of other opinion things might be in readiness, I send your Lordship a draught of a new proclamation, wherein I have likewise touched the point of change in that manner as was most agreeable to that I conceived of your intent; the Frenchman, after I had given him a day, which was the morrow after your Lordship's departure, never attended nor called upon the matter since. Sir Henry Nevill has sent up a solicitor of the cause, to whom I perceive by Mr. Calvert your Lordship is pleased a copy of his answer when it shall be taken may be delivered. So, praying for your good health and happiness, I humbly take my leave from Gray's Inn, this 10th of August, 1609.

Your Lordship's most humble and bounden,

Fs. BACON.

IV. 17.   FRANCIS BACON TO THE EARL OF SALISBURY.

(Orig. in State Paper Office.)

Gray's Inn, the 13th of Sept. 1609.

IT MAY PLEASE YOUR LORDSHIP, —

According to your Lordship's letter, I send an abstract of the bonds and conditions touching the depopulation, whereby it will appear unto your Lordship that all the articles and branches of the condition consist only of matter of reformation in the country, and not of any benefit to the King, otherwise than that the forfeiture in point of law belongeth to his Majesty; but then the reformation is at large. So I very humbly take my leave.

Your Lordship's most humble and bounden,

Fs. BACON.

IV. 18.   FRANCIS BACON TO SIR JULIUS CÆSAR.

(Orig. in State Paper Office.)

August 23, 1610.

IT MAY PLEASE YOUR HONOR, —

In answer of your letter of the second of this present, but not delivered to my hands till the 20th thereof, concerning Sir Robert Steward his petition exhibited to his Majesty in the name of Edward Williams, for the new founding of the Hospital of St. John's in the town of Bedford, I have examined the state of the cause, as far as information may be expected by hearing the one side; and do find: That this hospital passed divers years since by a Patent of Concealment to Farneham, from whom the petitioner claimeth. That thereupon suit was commenced in the Exchequer, wherein it seemeth the Court found that strength in the King's title, as it did order the hospital should receive a new foundation, together with divers good articles of establishment of the good uses, and an allowance of stipend unto the master. Nevertheless, I find not this order to be absolute or merely judicial; but in the nature of a composition or agreement; and yet that but conditional: for it directeth a course of judicial proceeding, in case the defendants shall not hold themselves to the agreement. And yet notwithstanding this order had this life and pursuance, as I find a letter from the Lord-Treasurer, his Lordship's father, to the then Attorney, for drawing up a book for the new foundation. After which time nothing was done for aught that to me appeareth: no patent under seal, no stirring of the possession, no later order: neither doth it appear unto me likewise in whose default the falling off was. But now of late, some four years past, and about fourteen years after the former order, upon information given of the King's right to the late Lord-Treasurer, Earl of Dorset, his Lordship directed a sequestration of the possession, and that without any mention of these former proceedings ; but that, being as it seemeth swiftly granted, was soon after by his Lordship revoked. The pretenders unto the right of this hospital (with whom likewise the possession hath gone) are as it seemeth the master of the hospital (at this time one Dennis) and the town of Bedford, who claim the patronage of it. But in what state the hospital is for repair, or for employment according unto the good uses, or for government, I can ground no certificate. And therefore it may please you to signify unto his Lordship as well the state of the cause heretofore opened, as my opinion, which is that it were great pity that this hospital should continue either not well founded, or not well employed, the rather being situate in so populous and poor a town ; and that, nevertheless, herein some consideration may be had of the patentee's right ; but for the present, that which is first meet to be done, I conceive to be that the other party be heard ; and to the end to avoid a tedious suit (which must be defended with the moneys that should go to the sustenance of the poor), his Lordship may be graciously pleased to direct his letters as well to the town of Bedford as to the present incumbent, that they do attend a summary hearing of this cause (if his own great business will not permit), before some other that he shall assign ; in which letters it would be expressed that they come provided to make defence and answer to three points : that is, the King's title now in the patentee ; the order and agreement in the Exchequer, why it was not performed ; and the estate of the

hospital, whether it be decayed and misemployed? And App.
so I leave to trouble your Honor from Gray's Inn, 23d IV. 18.
August, 1610.

Your Honor's, to do you service,

FR. BACON.

FRANCIS BACON TO THE EARL OF SALISBURY.   IV. 19.

(Orig. in the State Paper Office.)

London, the 7th of May, 1611.

IT MAY PLEASE YOUR GOOD LORDSHIP, —

Understanding that his Majesty will be pleased to sell
some good portion of wood in the forest of Dene, which
lies very convenient to the company's wireworks at Tyn-
terne and Whitbrooke, we are enforced to have recourse
to your Lordship as to our governor of the said company,
humbly praying your Lordship to afford us some reasonable quantity thereof, the better to uphold the said works,
whereof by information from our farmers there we stand
in such need as without your Lordship's favor we shall
hardly be able to subsist any long time. We do not
entreat your Lordship for any other or more easy price
than that your Lordship directs the sale of it to other,
only we humbly pray for some preferment in the opportunity of the place where the woods lie and in the quantity, as it may answer in some proportion to our wants.
Herein, if your Lordship will be pleased to favor us,
then we humbly pray your Lordship to direct us to some
such persons as your Lordship resolves to employ in the

18

APP.
IV. 19.
business. And so we humbly take our leaves of your Lordship.

Your Lordship's humbly at command,

FR. BACON.

IV. 20. FRANCIS BACON TO THE EARL OF SALISBURY.

(Orig. in State Paper Office.)

October, 1611.

IT MAY PLEASE YOUR LORDSHIP, —

I return your good Lord's minute, excellently, in my opinion, reformed from the first draught in some points of substance. I send likewise a clause warranting the subject to refuse gold lighter than the remedies expressed, which is no new device, but the same with 29th Eliz. I find also Mr. Dubbleday to make it a thing difficult to name the pieces of more ancient coin than his Majesty's, for which I have likewise sent a clause. This last clause is immediately to follow the table of the coins expressed. The clause of the weight is to come last of all. So, with my prayers, I rest

Your Lordship's most humble and bounden,

FR. BACON.

IV. 21. FRANCIS BACON TO KING JAMES.

(Orig. in the State Paper Office.)

January 31st, 1615.

Though I placed Peacham's treason within the last division, agreeable to divers predecessors, whereof I had the records read, and concluded that your Majesty's safety, and life, and authority was thus by law instanced and quartered, and that it was in vain to fortify on three of the heads and leave you open on the fourth, it is true he heard me in a grave fashion more than accustomed, and took a pen and took notes of my divisions; and when he read the precedent and records would say, That you mean falleth within your first or your second division. In the end I expressly demanded his opinion as that whereto both he and I was enjoined. But he desired me to leave the precedents with him that he might advise upon them. I told him the rest of my fellows would despatch their part, and I should be behind with mine, which I persuaded myself your Majesty would impute rather to his backwardness than my negligence. He said as soon as I should understand that the rest were ready he would not be long after with his opinion or answer. For St. John's your Majesty knoweth the day draws on, and my Lord Chancellor's recovery the season and his age promiseth not to be hasty. I spoke with him on Sunday, at what time I found him in bed, but his spirits strong and not spent or wearied, and spake wholly of your business, leading me from one matter to another, and wished and seemed to hope that he might attend the day for St. John's, as it were (as he said) to be his last work, to commend his service and express his affection towards your Majesty. I presumed to say to him that I knew your Majesty would be exceeding desirous of his being present that day, so as it might be without prejudice to his continuance; but that otherwise your Majesty esteemed a servant more than a service, specially such a servant. Surely, in my opinion, your Majesty had better put off the day than want his presence, considering the cause of the putting off is so notorious, and then the capital and the criminal may come together the next term. I have not been unprofitable in helping to discover and examine within these few days a late patent by surreption obtained from your Majesty of the greatest forest in England, worth 30,000*l.*, under color of a defective title, for a matter of 400*l.* The person must be named, because the patent must be questioned. It is a great person, my Lord of Shrewsbury, or rather, as I think, a greater than he, which is my Lady of Shrewsbury. But I humbly beg your Majesty to know this first from my Lord Treasurer; who me thinketh groweth ever studious in your business. God preserve your Majesty.

Your Majesty's most humble and devoted
subject and servant,
FR. BACON.

The rather in regard of Mr. Murray's absence, I humbly pray your Majesty to have a little regard to this letter.

FRANCIS BACON TO THE COUNCIL.

(Orig. in State Paper Office.)

January 27, 1616 [1617].

IT MAY PLEASE YOUR LORDSHIPS, —

According to your Lordships' preference of the 12th of June last, I have considered of the patent of Clement Dawbeny, gent., for the slitting of iron bars into rods. And I have had before me the patentee that now is, and some of the nailers and blacksmiths that complained against the same. Whereupon it pleased your Lordships to call in the said patent. But upon examination of the business I find the complaint to be utterly unjust, and was first stirred up by one Burrell, master carpenter to the East India Company, who hath already of himself begone to set up the like engine in Ireland, and therefore endeavored to overthrow the said patent, the better to vent his own iron to his further benefit and advantage, whereas the nailers and blacksmiths themselves do all affirm that they are now supplied by the patentee with as much good and serviceable iron, or rather better, than heretofore they have been, and that the said patent hath been of much use to the kingdom in general, and likewise very beneficial to themselves in their trades. And, therefore, your Lordships may be pleased to suffer him quietly to enjoy it without any further interruption, and to this did Burrell himself and the opposers willingly condescend, which nevertheless I submit to the wisdom of this most honorable Board.

FR. BACON.

FRANCIS BACON TO KING JAMES.

(Orig. in State Paper Office.)

March, 1617.

The gracing of the Justices of Peace. That your Majesty doth hold the institution of Conservators and Commissioners or Justices of the Peace to be one of the most laudable and politic ordinances of this realm or any other realm. That it is not your own goodness or virtues, nor the labors of your counsel or Judges, that can make your people happy, without things go well amongst the Justices, who are the conduits to convey the happy streams of your government to your people. That your Majesty would as soon advance and call a knight or gentleman that liveth in an honorable and worthy fashion in his country ; and it were to be of your counsel or to office about yourself, your Queen, or son, or an Ambassador employed in foreign parts, or a courtier bred an attendant about your person. That your Majesty is and will be careful to understand the country as well as your court for persons, and that those that are worthy servants in the country shall not need to have their dependence upon any the greatest subject in your kingdom, but immediately upon yourself.

FRANCIS BACON TO LORD ZOUCH.

(Orig. in State Paper Office.)

Gorhambury, 3d August, 1619.

Whereas there are processes gone out, at Mr. Attorney-General's prayer, against Hugh Hugginson and Josias

Ente, concerning the business against the Dutchmen in
Star Chamber; out of a desire to preserve the ancient
privileges and customs due to your place, not to serve
such process within your jurisdiction without your leave
and consent, I thought good hereby to desire your Lordship for his Majesty's service, that you would cause
them forthwith to be sent up to answer Mr. Attorney's
bill, and abide such further proceedings as their case
shall require.

FRANCIS BACON TO KING JAMES.   IV. 25.

(Orig. in State Paper Office.)

Oct. 1626 [? 1620].

MAY IT PLEASE YOUR MAJESTY, —

According to your commandment I have considered
of your patent granted about the time of your going
into Scotland unto Mr. Murray and Sir Robt Lloyd, of a
custom or duty detained from your Majesty of one shilling four pence upon the cloth and 2s. in the pound upon
certain Northern cloth, by color of a Privy Seal [of]
Queen Elizabeth and of a former Seal certificate made by
the Earl of Suffolk, then Lord Treasurer, Mr. Chancellor
that now is, and myself, then your Attorney-General,
upon which certificate the patent did pass. And do find
that the said certificate is very true and well grounded,
wherein I have strengthened myself with the opinion of
your new Solicitor, so that there is no doubt but the right
was and is in your Majesty, and the third part thereof
was sufficiently granted unto them, who nevertheless sub-

mit their interest (being for one-and-twenty years) unto your Majesty. But to suffer the patent to go on to operation, either for your Majesty's two parts or their third part, considering that the merchants have been in long past of that ease, and that cloth is now loaden with the pretermitted duty which was not before (and of which this is no part), and [damaged] the state of the trade of cloth hath been weakened [damaged] for that is con cerned the cost of some of the out ports . . . . . not in any sort advise it, but humbly leave it to your Majesty's . . . r judgment.

IV. 26.

FRANCIS BACON TO SECRETARY CONWAY.

(Orig. in State Paper Office.)

January 21, 1623.

GOOD MR. SECRETARY, —

When you visited me you expressed in so noble a fashion a vif sense of my misfortunes, as I cannot but express myself no less sensible of your good fortune, and therefore do congratulate with you for your new honor now settled. The excellent Marquis brought me yesterday to kiss the King's hands, so as now methinks I am in the state of grace. Think of me and speak of me as occasion serveth. I shall want no will to deserve it. At best, nobleness is never lost. I rest your affectionate friend, to do you service,

FRANCIS ST. ALBANS.

FRANCIS BACON TO SECRETARY CONWAY.

(Orig. in State Paper Office.)

Gray's Inn, 3d of June, 1624.

GOOD MR. SECRETARY, —

This gentleman, Mr. Richard Gilman, who hath been (?) towards me, hath served formerly in Scinde and Russia and the Low Countries, and is suitor now for a lieutenant's place in these succors which are now to be sent. I recommend his suit unto you, and shall give you very hearty thanks if, for my sake, you will pleasure him.

I rest your very affectionate friend,

Fs. St. Albans.

No. V.

V.

ANTHONY BACON TO FRANCIS BACON.

(Orig. at Lambeth Palace, 650, fol. 221.)

BROTHER, —

I thought it meet to advertise you that my Lord of Essex, being come expressly yesterday, after dinner, to speak with the French ambassador and Sir Anthony Perez, not finding Sir Anthony Perez at his house, but word that he should repair to Walsingham House with all speed; where he had two hours' conference with him, and, and amongst other things, urged the matter you wot of at large, with no less judgment than devo-

18 *

A A

tion to my Lord's honor and profit, and good affection to us. His argument my Lord heard most attentively, and accepted most kindly of many right hearty thanks, assuring him that, at his return — which should be within two days — from the Court, he would resolve. The occasion was very fitly ministered by my Lord himself, by advertising Spencer that the Queen had signed at two of the clock, and had given him a hundred pounds in lands, simple fee, and 30*l.* in parks, which, for her quietness' sake, and in respect of his friend, he was content to accept without any further contention. And. so I wish you as myself,

Your entire loving brother,
ANTHONY BACON.

No. VI.

ESSEX TO * * *.

(Orig. at Lambeth Palace, 657, 90.)

MY LORD, —

By the advancement of Sir Thomas Egerton to the place of Lord-Keeper (in which choice I think my country very happy), there is void the office of Master of the Rolls. I do, both for private and public respects, wish Mr. F. B. to it before all men, and should think much done for her Majesty's service if he were so placed as his virtues might be active, which now lie as it were buried. What success I have had in commending him to her

Majesty your Lordship knows. I would not the second time hurt him with my care and kindness. But I will commend unto your Lordship his cause; not as his alone, or as mine — his friend, but as a public cause, wherein your Lordship shall have honor to the world, satisfaction to see worthy fruit of your own work, and exceeding thankfulness from us both. And so I rest,

Your Lordship's cousin and friend,

E.

ESSEX TO SIR JOHN FORTESCUE.

(Orig. at Lambeth Palace, 657, 90.)

COUSIN, —

I do commend unto you both present actions and absent friends, — I mean those that are absent from me, so as I can neither defend them from wrong nor help to that right their virtue deserves. And, because an occasion offers itself before the rest, I will commend unto you one above the rest. The place is the Mastership of the Rolls; the man, Mr. Francis Bacon, a kind and worthy friend to us both. If your labors in it prevail, I will owe it you as a particular debt, though you may challenge it as a debt of the state.

And so, wishing you all happiness, I rest,

Your cousin and friend,

E.

Cousin, — I pray you remember my good Dr. Browne. I shall challenge you for a great unkindness if his suit succeed ill.

No. VII.

EXTRACTS FROM THE COUNCIL REGISTER, APRIL 25, 1614.

(Orig. in Privy Council Office.)

Present : —

Lord Chancellor.

Earl of Pembroke.

Lord Wotton.

Mr. Secretary Winwood.

Sir Julius Cæsar.

Sir Thomas Lake.

A LETTER TO SIR FRANCIS BACON, KNIGHT, HIS MAJES-
TY'S ATTORNEY-GENERAL.

We send you here enclosed the Petition of one Richard
Arrowsmith, his Majesty's servant, wherein he complain-
eth unto us, that in February last a number of people
gathered together in the night and, in disguised apparel,
did riotously pull up and overthrow a hedge and ditch
which he had caused to be made about a copse called
Newland, for preservation of his Majesty's game in that
part of the forest of Windsor; and do pray and require
you (if upon further information you shall find the
offence to deserve it) to send for such and so many of
the offenders as you shall think fit, and to proceed
against them in the Star Chamber, the next term, in
the behalf of his Majesty, according as is accustomed in
cases of like nature. And so, &c.

COUNCIL REGISTER, OCT. 19, 1614.

(Orig. in Privy Council Office.)

Ut supra with the Lord Archbishop.

A LETTER TO SIR FRANCIS BACON, KNIGHT, HIS MAJESTY'S ATTORNEY-GENERAL.

Whereas his Majesty hath taken notice of a great resort of gentlemen of quality and livelihood, together with their wives and families, unto the city of London, and other principal cities and towns of this realm, with a purpose (as it appeareth) to settle their habitation there, for saving of charges and other private respects. His Majesty, considering of his great wisdom how prejudicial these courses may prove to the general government of the kingdom, when the country shall be deprived of the assistance and presence of so many gentlemen, who for the most part bear office or authority in the counties where they dwell, besides the great decay of hospitality and other inconveniences that will ensue thereupon, is therefore pleased that a Proclamation shall be published, enjoining and commanding all such persons aforementioned to repair unto their several dwellings in the country, before the last of November next, there to abide and continue as heretofore they have usually done, which we require you to draw accordingly and to make ready for his Majesty's signature with as much convenient expedition as you may. And so, &c.

(Orig. in Privy Council Office.)

At Whitehall, on Tuesday the 20th of February, 1615.

Present : —

The Lord Archbishop of Canterbury.

Lord Treasurer.	Lord Bishop of Winchester.
Lord Privy Seal.	Lord Knollis.
Duke of Lennox.	Mr. Secretary Winwood.
Lord Chamberlain.	Mr. Secretary Lake.
Earl of Mar.	Mr. Chancellor of the Ex-
Earl of Dunfermline.	chequer.

Master of the Rolls.

Upon a difference depending at the Board between the Dutch Congregation of the town of Colchester and one William Goodwin and others of that town, as will appear by petitions offered to the Board by both parties. Forasmuch as the matter consisting of many parties will require a full and deliberate hearing for the better settling of the trade of Bay and Say making, in that place. Their Lordships have this day ordered that his Majesty's Attorney-General, calling all parties before him, do hear and examine the differences and allegations on both sides, and thereupon to make report of his opinion thereof, and what course he thinketh fit to be observed therein, in writing, by Thursday next in the afternoon, that such further order may thereupon be taken as shall be expedient.

(Orig. in Privy Council Office.)

APr. VII. 4.

At the Court at Whitehall, on Wednesday in the afternoon, the 5th of April, 1615 : —

Present : —

Lord Archbishop of Canterbury.

Lord Chancellor.	Mr. Secretary Winwood.
Lord Treasurer.	Mr. Chancellor of the Exchequer.
Duke of Lennox.	
Lord Chamberlain.	Lord Chief Justice.
Lord Fenton.	Mr. Chancellor of the Duchy.
Lord Knollis.	Sir Thomas Lake.

William Martin, Recorder of the city of Exeter, being heretofore sent for by order from their Lordships, and this day called unto the Board, and charged by his Majesty's Attorney-General to have lately written a History of England, wherein were many passages so unaptly inserted as might justly have drawn some heavy and severe censure upon him for the same. On his humble submission and hearty repentance and acknowledgment of his fault, their Lordships were pleased to become mediators unto his Majesty for his grace and favor to be extended towards him, which being happily obtained, he is freely dismissed from all further attendance ; being first enjoined by their Lordships to manifest hereafter in some short declaration in writing (as he hath already done by words) the true sense and understanding he hath of his offence, together with his repentance for the same. And it is further ordered by their Lordships that the bond which he sealed to his Majesty's use for his appearance at the Board should be cancelled and delivered unto him.

No. VIII.

REPORT BY THE BARONS OF THE EXCHEQUER, THE SOLICITOR
GENERAL (SIR FRANCIS BACON), AND THE RECORDER
OF LONDON, TO THE PRIVY COUNCIL.

(Orig. in State Paper Office.)

MAY IT PLEASE YOUR LORDSHIPS, —

We have received your honorable letters bearing date
the 25th day of this instant month of June, and enclosed
in the same a note of a suit which has been of late presented to his Majesty and by him referred to your Lordships' consideration : the substance of which suit is to
have a warrant directed to some officer to demand and
collect fines upon actions of debt and other finable actions
to be sued in all other Courts of England (other than
the Courts held at Westminster), concerning which your
Lordships require us to certify you our opinions in all
points at our speediest opportunity. We have therefore,
according to your honorable directions, considered of the
suit. And do find it a matter of so great importance as
we must humbly pray leave to have time to confer with
the rest of the Judges, that upon our joint conference
your Lordships may have the more full satisfaction both
for law and conveniency. Humbly taking our leaves,
this 28th of June, 1608.

                Your Lordships' to command.